YOUNG
EXPLORER'S
ADVENTURE
GUIDE
VOLUME 5

DREAMING ROBOT PRESS

Publisher's Cataloging-in-Publication data

Names: Weaver, Sean, 1968- , editor. | Weaver, Corie, 1970- editor.
Title: Young explorer's adventure guide , volume 5 / edited by Sean and Corie Weaver.
Description: Las Vegas, NM: Dreaming Robot Press, 2018.
Identifiers: ISBN 978-1-940924-42-7 (pbk.) | 978-1-940924-43-4 ebook | LCCN 2018908966
Subjects: LCSH Short stories. | Science Fiction. | Children's stories, American. | BISAC JUVENILE FICTION /
Science Fiction | JUVENILE FICTION / Short Stories
Classification: LCC PZ7 .T9332 Yo 2018 | DDC [Fic]–dc23

Contents

Acknowledgements

Thanks to our families for putting up with all the madness, our authors for sharing our vision, and our friends for helping spread the word. We'd also ask for a round of applause for our editorial team of Amanda Coffin and Sue Currin and this year's cover illustrator, Jose Garcia (Garciartist)

Together we're creating a better universe.

Permissions

"Asmodeus Flight" originally published in Ghost in the Cogs, 2015, reprinted by permission of the author.

"Mr. Pock Pock!" originally published by Shelia Crosby, 2016, reprinted by permission of the author.

Introduction

by Bethany Brookshire

Some adults have more in common with kids than others.
There are the adults who try to act like they're still kids. I'm not
talking about them. There are the adults who try to impress kids
by acting as though they "get" kids in some adult way.
I'm not talking about them either.
The adults who get kids the most are writers of stories. It's not
because they act like kids. (Though maybe they do; I don't
judge.) It's not because they've studied about child minds or
how kids grow and develop. (Though maybe they have.) It's not
because they're smarter or wiser. (Though maybe they are.) No.
It's because writers — especially writers of stories — have something in common with kids.
Writers are dreamers. They dream of the future. They dream of
connections between people and things. They dream of ideas.
They dream of things that will never exist. Even writers who
write adult history books dream. They dream about the past,
that's all.
Kids are dreamers too. The world could be so much more
amazing than it is. Why can't there be air balloon pirates? Or
giant, feathered, intelligent *T. rexes*? Kids are who they want to
be, and where they want to be, in their dreams. In worlds where
they are heroes. In their dreams, they write their own stories.
They save themselves.

We've all been kids. We've all dreamed. But as most adults grow older, their dreams shrink. Dreams of planets and moons and galaxies become dreams of jobs, family, and a beach vacation. They are important dreams, just as important as the big ones. But they are smaller.

Writers' dreams, though, never shrank. Their dreams stayed big. And these writers have written down those dreams for us. Dreams that kids (and a few adults) will recognize.

The writers in this book have something else in common with kids. They know how kids feel. These characters aren't mini-adults. They get angry. They get scared. They feel hopeful. Their characters make all the good, brave choices that kids make. And they make some of the bad choices kids make, too.

This book is full of new, exciting worlds, filled with people you want to meet. They are smart. They figure things out. They save themselves, and maybe save civilization on the way. Just like us.

Every one of the writers in this collection of stories is a wonderful dreamer. In this book, they have shown us their dreams. They dream of Earth. They dream of space. They dream of robots and old car races. They dream of kids who save themselves. Some of these dreams are so wonderful that I wish they had their own, full-length books. I hope they will someday. I want to spend more time in these worlds. I want to read more of these dreams.

I think you will, too.

Join these writers. Visit worlds populated with half cats and giant stick-insect engineers. Where jokes are deadly serious, and doing as you're told can get you killed. If you're lucky you might see a space dragon or two.

Some of these stories are about success. Some are about fear. Some are about failure. All are like lighthouses at the edges of the galaxy. They shine to remind us that when we dream of the stars, we aren't alone. We have these stories, and these writers.

And these writers dream, too.

These worlds are ready to be shared, and their characters waiting to be met. So take this book to a comfortable spot. Settle in. Fasten your seatbelt. And make sure to bring a flashlight. Trust me. It will help you hang on to your dreams.

Bethany Brookshire has a B.S. in biology and a B.A. in philosophy from The College of William and Mary, and a Ph.D. in physiology and pharmacology from Wake Forest University School of Medicine. She is the guest editor of The Open Laboratory Anthology of Science Blogging, 2009, and the winner of the Society for Neuroscience Next Generation Award and the Three Quarks Daily Science Writing Award, among others. She blogs at Eureka! Lab and at Scicurious. You can follow her on Twitter as @scicurious.

"The future belongs to those who
believe in the beauty of their dreams."
~ Eleanor Roosevelt

Machine Language

by Sherry D. Ramsey

Sherry D. Ramsey is a writer, editor, publisher, creativity addict and self-confessed Internet geek. She writes for all ages, and she loves mysteries and magic as much as she loves spaceships and aliens–so much that she often smooshes them together in interesting ways. Sherry lives in Nova Scotia with her husband, children, and dogs, where she consumes far more coffee and chocolate than is likely good for her. You can visit her online at www. sherrydramsey.com; keep up with her much more pithy musings and catch glimpses of her life on Twitter and Instagram @sdramsey.

Yuka pushed the joystick control forward with her right hand, sending the remote rover probe scuttling down the side of a grassy hill. With her left hand, she zoomed the rover's camera out for a better view of the entire valley. The mechanical fingers of her prosthetic left arm responded slower than she would have liked, so the camera panned out in jerky starts and stops. She glanced down at the pale green "skin" covering the hand and sighed. She wouldn't even care so much that it didn't look like a real hand if only it worked better.

The rover's camera revealed yet another deep, thickly-forested valley waiting at the bottom of the hill. Trees like overgrown funguses stretched tall, spindly fingers toward the low-hanging cloud cover. Yuka squinted at the screen. The vegetation changed from one valley to the next, and these trees were different again, sprouting lacy, white, leaf-like growths along their trunks and branches. At the very top, they brightened to orange and wove together in a dense canopy like a mushroom cap. She took her hand from the joystick and made a quick note on her tablet.

"Something interesting?"

Yuka jumped at the voice so close behind her, and her prosthetic hand jerked on the camera control. The joystick spun, and the image on the screen darted to one side, blurring. It refocused on some tall, bluish grass to the left of the rover.

"Not really, ma'am. Just comparing the trees from the last valley."

"I don't see trees on your screen." Subchief Caterzina Sano's voice was accusing as she bent over to peer at Yuka's screen.

"I just—" Yuka bit off the explanation. Sano wouldn't want to hear it. "I'll readjust the camera, ma'am."

"Just get the rover down into the valley and take your readings," Sano said. "Don't waste time. We can't afford it."

She turned and strode off before Yuka could say anything else. Yuka ground her teeth. She knew there was no time to waste in exploring this planet, but she was doing her best.

At thirteen years old, it wasn't like she'd been trained for this sort of thing. She sighed, flexed her mechanized fingers a few times, and maneuvered the camera around to the front again. She set the rover rolling and bumping down the oddly-colored hill.

The bumping didn't bother Yuka, because she couldn't feel it. She sat at a console aboard the *UECS Strelka*, the colony ship limping toward this planet they'd named Sulis. She wasn't supposed to be doing this job. She wasn't even supposed to be awake. And she certainly wasn't supposed to have lost her left arm in a near-catastrophic accident. One that left the *Strelka* off-course, heavily damaged, and missing more than half of the crew and colonists who'd been in coldsleep on the decks below. But there was no time to worry about *supposed to*. There was only *the way things are now*. That meant figuring out if they could survive on this planet they had managed to find, and what part of it offered them the best chance.

"She sure doesn't like us," Arten Ikanez said from the console a few feet away. He was a few years older than Yuka, a skinny boy with shoulder-length dark brown hair and an always-worried face. "Do you think it's these?" He pointed to his legs. From the knees down, Arten had green-skinned prosthetic legs and feet, like Yuka's arm. They dangled from the chair seat, falling just a couple of inches short of the floor, and he waggled them comically. In spite of everything, he and Yuka were some of the lucky ones. They'd survived the accident and suffered injuries the ship's medical systems could actually deal with. Many more had died in the collision with the asteroid, or been too badly injured to survive long once their coldsleep pods shut down and they awoke.

A few, like Subchief Caterzina Sano, hadn't been injured at all. But there weren't many Fulls, like her, on the ship now. Almost everyone had needed something repaired or replaced after the accident. Yuka had woken from coldsleep to find her left arm completely replaced, her parents gone, and the *Strelka* in a critical situation. There hadn't been much time to feel sad yet.

"I don't think she likes anybody, even the other Fulls," Yuka said in a low voice. "If we settle on this planet, I want a habitat as far away from hers as I can get."

If they didn't settle on this planet...but Yuka wouldn't think about that. Everyone knew most of their fuel had vented in the accident.

Sulis wasn't the most welcoming place, but it was the only planet they'd had the fuel to reach. A rocky world with a sharp axial tilt that meant extreme seasons and wild weather for much of the planet. In the temperate areas, high mountain crags stretched up to the limits of the breathable atmosphere, creating deep valleys and lowlands between them—biomes almost completely separated from each other. Although plants and other creatures had developed here, their isolation had created a wide diversity in the strange types of life that called the planet home. So far, they'd found no evidence of highly evolved, intelligent life on Sulis, which was a good thing for the hopeful colonists.

The remote rovers could move faster than the lumbering, damaged colony ship, so they'd been sent ahead to explore the planet. Yuka and a handful of others operated them, discovering what they could about their chances of survival on the surface. They'd learned that the air, although thin, was breathable in the valleys, and the water would be drinkable with treatment. Now they had to find out what else already lived here, if they'd be able to grow plants in the soil, and what other dangers might face them on the surface.

So Yuka rolled her rover around, exploring and gathering samples of plants, earth, and water to analyze. Until the rover's screen showed something that was absolutely, definitely, not a tree.

⟨▣⟩

Yuka's first thought was that it was another *Strelka* rover, although she knew they were spread far and wide across the habitable areas of the planet, exploring. She was surprised to see another one but then even more surprised. It was not a rover. It stood much taller than the squat *Strelka* rovers—probably almost five feet. Six insect-like legs sprouted from a square base, allowing it to walk smoothly across the rough terrain. Its tall, angular body rose from the dark metallic base, and an arm fitted with interchangeable tools hung down on each side. It wasn't at all humanoid-shaped, but an array of sensors and lights near the top looked almost like a face.

It moved toward a small pink lizard-like creature perched on a rock.

Yuka gasped and Arten turned from his screen. "What?"
She shook her head. "Nothing," she managed, keeping her
voice casual. She didn't want anyone else to see this until she
knew what it was. Maybe it was another robot explorer from
the *Strelka*, and she didn't want to look like an idiot for not
knowing that. She used her prosthetic hand to turn the rover's
camera straight toward the other robot and zoom in as far as
it could. Up close, it looked even more alien. Its surface shimmered with tiny, interlocking hexagon shapes.

Yuka almost told Arten then, but the pink lizard moved, and
the strange robot veered off to follow. It turned away from
Yuka's rover and scuttled smoothly into the cluster of trees at
the base of the hill. It didn't return.

"Hey, you want to get something to eat once the shift is over?"
Arten asked, breaking into her concentration. "It must be
almost dinner time; my stomach's rumbling."

Considering their reduced rations, everyone's stomach rumbled
a lot of the time, but Yuka didn't say that. She realized she'd
been staring at the trees for far too long and nodded to Arten.
"Sure, that'd be great."

She pushed the joystick, turning her rover to travel away from
where the other robot had vanished. She set the rover's sights
on a small pond about half a kilometer from its current position and sent it trundling in that direction. She'd collect some
water samples before the shift was over, so Subchief Caterzina
Sano couldn't accuse her of doing nothing, and then she'd put
the rover into sleep and secure mode for the night while its
tiny internal lab analyzed the samples.

And hope that when she came back to work in the morning,
the strange robot would be long gone and never bother her
rover again.

When their shift was over, Yuka and Arten shut down their
consoles and followed the long, dim, echoing corridor to the

cafeteria. If the voyage had gone according to plan, these corridors would have bustled—half the crew and colonists on board would be awake while the other half slept. Then the teams would have switched places halfway through the journey. Now there were not even enough of them, with everyone who was left awake, to fill the hallways. With so many of their food supplies destroyed in the accident, Yuka supposed that was just as well. Their power reserves were also low, so the corridor lights stayed dim on the couple of undamaged decks still in use.

As they walked—slowly, to accommodate Arten's slightly unsteady gait on his green-skinned legs, Yuka asked casually, "Are all of our rovers exactly the same? Would I recognize another one if mine saw it?"

"There shouldn't be two in the same location," Arten said. "But I think they're all alike. Except for the couple of submarine ones Gyllis and Malkan operate in the oceans."

Yuka nodded, her chest heavy with disappointment. "That's what I thought."

"Why?"

"Oh, no reason," she lied. "Just curious. I wonder what all the animals down there think of these new mechanical creatures running around."

"The good thing is, I don't think they think," Arten said with a grin. "So that leaves room for us."

Yuka was glad to reach their destination. The cafeteria was a beacon of light and sound. Even though food was rationed, everyone felt better after eating something, so at mealtimes conversation and laughter flowed in better supply than the food. The legacy of the accident was everywhere, though—artificial limbs like Yuka's and Arten's in a rainbow of colors. The med units had been forced to synthesize replacement skin and limbs from materials that were never intended for that purpose, so the survivors sported shades from green to blue to pale yellow and grey. No-one tried to hide their prosthetic parts, since almost everyone who'd survived had needed something replaced. Many colonists had mechanized hands, arms, legs and feet. Yuka's bunk mate Gyllis had sky-blue skin on the entire left side of her face and a glassy-looking left eye with a pinprick of red electronic glow at its center. Trawley sported a bald head the color of a sunflower where the skin of his scalp had been burned away.

Yuka and Arten picked up trays and collected bowls of pale, watery-looking soup and a handful of reconstituted bread nuggets. The soup smelled better than it looked, and Yuka's stomach rumbled as she filled a glass with water. Not exactly fresh—it had been recycled lots of times already. But it was still cool and drinkable. They found seats at a table with Gyllis, who scooted her chair aside to make room for Yuka.

Across the room, a voice rose in anger. Yuka spotted Subchief Caterzina Sano. She sat at a table with some other Fulls, none of whom looked very happy. The Fulls tended to keep to themselves, although Yuka knew one of the boys, Natil. Natil worked on the ship's computer systems, helping restore them as much as possible after the accident, and he'd helped her fix a problem with her rover's programming. He caught her eye and grimaced, looking like he'd rather be sitting at her table instead. He looked miserable. Yuka wasn't sure why the Fulls didn't mingle much with the rest of them; she wondered if they thought themselves better, since they were still whole, still entirely flesh-and-blood humans. But Natil didn't look like he thought that. He looked like a trapped animal.

Yuka realized everyone at her table was staring at her. "What?" Gyllis grinned and waved a hand in front of Yuka's face. "I said, did you find anything interesting today? Where's your brain? Out in space or down on Sulis?" she joked.

"Very funny." Yuka rolled her eyes and took a bite of the soft bread nugget, to allow herself time to answer. "I left the rover analyzing some water samples," she said, reminding herself it was not a lie. She was just leaving out the part about the robot she'd seen—or thought she'd seen. "The valley I was in looked pretty nice. The trees—"

Across the cafeteria, a hand slapped loudly down on a tabletop. "—have to make a decision soon!" Subchief Sano's angry voice filled the room.

"Calm down, Caterzina." Another of the Fulls, a man named Dr. Howsie, spoke in a loud but oddly calming voice. Dr. Howsie was a biologist. He often came around the rover stations asking for the latest reports on plants and animals so he could study them. "We need to learn more. We still have time—"

"Not much," Sano ground out, and even though her voice was lower now, such a hush had fallen over the cafeteria that everyone must have heard it.

Yuka felt as if something stirred and sloshed the soup in her stomach. What if the robot she'd seen meant they couldn't land on Sulis? What if something or someone else already lived there and wouldn't welcome them?

Or what if the robot could give them information about the planet, information that could help them decide what to do? *Maybe I didn't even see it,* Yuka told herself. *I won't say anything until I'm sure.*

A little voice inside her head told her there might not be time to be sure, but she pushed it away and ate her soup.

Yuka did not have to return to her console until the morning; even in their desperate circumstances, people needed time to eat and sleep to continue doing their jobs. But as she lay awake in her bunk, thinking about the strange robot, sleep seemed far away. When Gyllis' slow, even breathing in the other bunk signaled she was asleep, Yuka slipped out of bed and into her clothes. With the lights in the corridor dimmed even further for the ship's artificial night, she could barely see, but she knew the way to the rover control bay.

The bay lay in quiet darkness, standby lights blinking on and off randomly in the gloom like sleepy but watchful eyes. The rovers didn't run at night; there weren't enough operators to form a night shift. While the colonists slept, the rovers recharged their power sources, analyzed samples, and ran reports. Yuka had the bay to herself. She wondered if she could find the strange robot again without prying eyes peering over her shoulder.

The pads of her right-hand fingers on the touchscreen made barely-heard soft thuds as she brought the console to life. Yuka had to concentrate to press lightly with the green-skinned prosthetic fingers on her left hand as well, to keep them from making a much louder noise.

The screen glowed to life, showing the eerie nighttime view of the rover's surroundings, the lake water lapping purplish and dark nearby. It was night on that part of the planet right now, too, so the rover's cameras brought the landscape to life with its thermal imaging. The dark water was cool, but the grasses and trees glowed slightly warmer, their outlines flickering dull yellow on Yuka's screen as she turned the rover. She'd send it back to the trees where she'd seen—*maybe* seen—the robot. Because the robot might know a lot about the planet. If it was real, maybe it could help them.

But when she turned the rover, she didn't have to send it anywhere. The robot stood right there, balanced on its spidery legs. It had come looking for her. Well, no, not for *her.* But for her rover.

Yuka realized she had gasped and covered her mouth with her right hand, thinking. The robot was mostly a dark shape, cool in the thermal imaging, but glowing warmer here and there where its internal systems produced heat.

She waited for it to do something, but it just sat there. Yuka blew out a long breath. *All right,* she thought. *It's real, and this is my chance. I need to communicate with it somehow.*

Well, she'd had brief training about what to do if the rover encountered any intelligent life-form. Unlikely, since they hadn't detected any signs of civilization on the planet, but possible. With a few keystrokes, Yuka opened the rover's communications manual in a small window on her screen. It was capable of communicating in various ways; sending machine language code, displaying basic pictograms and full language databases on its own screen, and even playing text-to-speech sounds through a tiny speaker. She slowly typed a message for the rover to speak, the fingers of her left hand awkward on the touchscreen. She sent it as a databurst too.

<*Are you from the* Strelka?>

The robot didn't respond in any language Yuka understood, although a string of symbols appeared, glowing blue on part of its dark front surface that hadn't even looked like a screen. It also sent a rush of data at the rover, which received it but did not produce any kind of translation for Yuka.

Hunching over the console, Yuka scanned through the manual. Finally she found:

Rover 1491 Exploration Units are capable of quickly learning and teaching unfamiliar languages through Fredkin gates, statistical analysis, science-based platforming, and lexical chunking.

Yuka frowned. That sounded encouraging, although she didn't understand some of the terms. She kept reading.

By executing the subroutine Language_A36 and allowing the Rover 1491 time to interact with the foreign language user, any language can be deciphered and communication established.

That sounded a bit too easy, but Yuka didn't know what else to try. Scrolling through the commands on her screen, she found *Language_A36* and set it to run. The rover sent out a burst of data as unreadable to her as the one the robot had transmitted. She held her breath, wondering how the robot would respond. Answer? Leave? Produce a weird weapon from somewhere and blow her rover to bits?

But after a moment, the robot sent another stream of data to the rover. The word *Analyzing* displayed briefly on her screen before the rover sent the robot another data burst.

Yuka sat back in her chair and let go the breath she'd been holding. It would take her months or years to learn to communicate with an alien or an artificial intelligence like the robot, but the rover's computer could do it much faster.

Overnight? said the voice of doubt in the back of Yuka's mind.

Maybe, Yuka answered, watching the unreadable data bounce back and forth between the two machines. After a moment, she got up. Maybe now, she could get some sleep.

After breakfast the next morning, Subchief Caterzina Sano stopped all the rover techs on their way into the control bay. They crowded in a knot in the doorway while she stood with folded arms.

"We must find the most habitable places on the planet, and we must find them soon," she said. Her grim face looked older than it had the day before. "Our supplies are running low, and so is our fuel. We have to conserve enough to get everyone down to the surface on the shuttles when we leave the ship for the last time. And we're getting closer to the planet all the time. We're down to days now."

No one answered, but everyone nodded. They'd heard all this before, and Yuka thought everyone understood the situation. But Sano seemed unable to stop reminding them. Arten caught Yuka's eye and rolled his own, making sure Sano couldn't see him, and Yuka smothered a smile.

"If several valleys seem equally welcoming, we may divide into two or more landing teams, to increase our chances of finding the best spot to settle," she continued. "It's extremely important to get all your data collected and analyzed so we can make final decisions."

Yuka frowned. No-one had ever mentioned splitting up before. There were so few of them left from the original numbers on the ship–dividing them on the planet didn't make sense. Others in the group seemed about to say something, but the look in Sano's eyes stopped them. She turned and left them to get to work. People whispered and grumbled, but Yuka tuned them out. She'd worry about it later. She had to see what had happened with the rover and the robot.

Yuka brought her rover console to life and pushed the camera control to point straight down at the ground when the screen powered on. She didn't want anyone looking over her shoulder and seeing anything to make them ask questions. She'd spend a couple of minutes looking at the data from last night and then send the rover about its usual business.

Her report screen showed page after page of communications data between the rover and the robot. She scrolled through them quickly. The first pages were pure gibberish. Strings of numbers, unrecognizable symbols, and then...scientific formulas? The symbols and numbers changed to pictograms, and finally, an alphabet appeared. The formulas came again. Yuka felt butterflies of excitement in her stomach. Had the machines found common ground and begun to communicate with each other?

She glanced around, but everyone was busy with their rovers. She opened the communications screen and, after flexing her mechanized fingers to lubricate the joints, typed in a data message to send to the robot.

<Hello. What can you tell me about this planet?>

The robot returned a data string, which appeared on Yuka's screen as gibberish, but then her rover offered a translation.

<Controller acknowledged. Pass code?>

Pass code? Yuka had no pass code to use for a robot that hadn't even come from the *Strelka!* She thought for a moment.

<No pass code> she sent. *<My name is Yuka. Who are you?>*

<No Controller named Yuka. Not authorized to access data.>
Yuka pressed her lips together. She'd managed to set up communications with an alien robot, and it wouldn't talk to her
without a pass code? This was ridiculous. But maybe if it
wouldn't give her information about the planet, it could tell
her other things.

So what is a Controller? she wondered. But maybe she shouldn't
let the robot know she didn't know that. She typed and sent,
<Are the Controllers on the planet?>
<Controllers follow Scouts.>
Hmm. Like the *Strelka* had sent the rovers ahead? Well, maybe
that was something. The Controllers might not be here yet.
<Are you a Scout?>
<Scout 34957. Pass code?>
Yuka sighed, but she felt like she was getting somewhere. This
robot seemed to be an advance information-gatherer, like the
rovers. But if the Controllers were coming to this planet— she
gulped. When? Might as well ask.
<When will the Controllers arrive?>
<Controllers follow Scouts.>
So maybe it didn't know. Okay, how long had the robot been
here? The *Strelka* rovers had been there for five days. But how
could she get a meaningful answer about that from the robot?
A day or a year would probably mean something completely
different to the robot compared to her Earth-based sense of time.
Yuka considered what she already knew about this planet.
The planet's tilt and rotation speed combined to give it a "day"
that was longer than Earth's—about 28 hours. That's how long
it took between one sunrise and the next on Sulis. On the
Strelka, they'd started lengthening the day and night cycles so
the colonists could begin to adjust.
*<Scout 34957, have you observed the length of time from sunrise to
sunrise on the planet?>*
<Yes. Pass code?>

Yuka bit back a yelp of frustration. She didn't know how the robot decided what information it would give her and what it considered secret. Pressing her lips together, she awkwardly typed, <*The time from sunrise to sunrise is 28 hours. How many hours has Scout 34957 been on the planet?*> She held her breath, waiting for a reply.

She heard Subchief Sano's voice out in the corridor. She'd have to clear her screens and look busy with normal exploration in a minute. Yuka still didn't feel ready to share the news of the robot's existence with anyone.

Finally the reply came back. A real answer.

<*1,185,520 hours*>

Yuka stared at the huge number. She quickly tapped it into the calculator on her screen and did the math. 1,185,520 divided by 28 gave her 42,340 days on the planet. To give the number meaning, even though the days were longer here, she divided it again, by 365, the number of days in an Earth year. Sano's voice came again, closer this time. Yuka had just enough time to see the answer before she closed the calculator and her other screens.

116. The robot had been here more than 116 Earth years, waiting for its Controllers to arrive.

As Yuka switched to her normal routine, her thoughts raced faster than the rover. The robot's makers weren't coming after all this time, which was probably good. But imagine if the colonists could access over a hundred years' worth of planetary data! They wouldn't even need the rovers any more, and they'd be ready to plan for settling the planet in the very best place. Yuka needed that data. But how was she going to get it?

Yuka went to her bunk early that night, caught a few hours of sleep, and slipped out to return to the deserted rover control bay again. She decided she'd have to tell someone else about the robot tomorrow—it was too important to keep to herself.

But she wanted one more try at getting the information herself. She was about to step into the rover bay when she heard it—a low sob. Yuka whirled to peer down the dim corridor, but it was deserted. She was about to dismiss it as her overtired imagination when the sound came again. On quiet feet, she made her way down the hall. In an empty medical bay, she found the source.

It was Natil. He sat on the floor, his back against the wall and his knees drawn up to his chest. A surgical kit lay open on the floor beside him, although the instruments were all in place. He didn't notice Yuka staring at him.

"Natil?" She kept her voice barely more than a whisper, but still he started.

"Yuka!" His eyes went to the surgical kit and then back to her. He covered his face with his hands, and another sob escaped.

Yuka lowered herself to sit beside him. "What are you doing here?"

His voice was muffled. "I could ask you the same thing."

She half-smiled. "True. We could agree to keep each other's secrets, though."

He drew a deep breath and blew it out in a long sigh. "I envy you, you know."

"Me?" Yuka was surprised. "What's so great about me?"

Natil reached over and tapped her mechanical arm. "This."

Yuka stared at her prosthetic. "It doesn't work so great. It's only...only a substitute for a <u>real</u> arm. You're still a Full."

He sighed. "Which means I'm stuck with Sano and the other Fulls, when I'd rather be with you and Arten and Gyllis."

She switched her focus to him and his tear-reddened eyes. "You're welcome with us any time. Don't you know that?"

He shook his head. "It's not that easy. Sano says the Fulls have to stick together. She makes us stay. That's why she wants two camps on the planet. One for the Fulls and one for everyone else."

Yuka blinked, taking this in. "I knew she didn't like us—but I don't understand why. Does she think we're that much of a drain on resources, that we won't be able to keep up?"

But Natil was shaking his head. "Just the opposite." He tapped Yuka's arm again. "Don't you realize the strength you have there? That your hand is capable of so much more than a flesh hand? That Arten could cover terrain with his feet that would wear me out? That Gyllis can see things with that eye—things a Full couldn't match without special equipment? No, Sano doesn't see you as weak. She's *afraid* of you. All of you."

Yuka twisted her body to face Natil, to argue with him. She bumped the surgical kit on the floor and realized with sudden horror what it meant. She slowly picked it up, holding it out to him. "Natil? What were you—what were you going to do with this?"

He swallowed and gave her a weak smile. "I thought, if I wasn't a Full any longer...and Gyllis' eye is really pretty cool..."

Yuka's eyes went wide, and she shook her head. "No! You mustn't! You wouldn't really do that to yourself—"

Natil sighed. "No. I couldn't do it. Which means I'm stuck with Sano." He brushed a hand across his still-wet eyes. "That's why I was crying."

If only we could access the robot's data, Yuka thought. *We'd have the answer to the very best spot to settle on the planet, and everyone could to go there together. I can't tell Sano about the robot now. She'll use it to help only the Fulls.*

She looked at Natil. Natil, who worked with computers.

Yuka held out a hand to him. "Come with me," she said. "We've got work to do."

⟞🚀⟝

An hour later, Natil sat back in the chair Yuka had pulled up for him at her rover station. He shook his head. "I can't do it," he said. "I can't crack a pass code in an alien language, even after all the communications work the rover did. That *you* did," he added. "We'd have to know more about these Controllers, their culture, about the robot's programming–I don't even know where to start."

Yuka blinked back tears. She'd been so sure Natil would be the answer. "All right. Let's find out what we can." Her left hand was getting better at typing, and she quickly sent <*Scout, what do the Controllers look like?*>

She wasn't sure the scout robot would have an answer for that, but in a moment, an image appeared on her screen. She didn't know what she'd been expecting–some kind of weird, blobby alien, maybe–but the Controller was not like that.

"Another robot!" Natil breathed.

The Controller had only four legs, unlike the scout robot's six, but they were jointed like the robot's. The Controller also had four arms, with sockets at the ends that looked like they could adapt to various shapes and purposes. The lower body was sleek and streamlined, perfectly suited to support the robot's limbs. But it was the upper part of the Controller that made Yuka gasp.

The upper part of the Controller had a head, and a face.

Not a human head and face–definitely an alien species, because the shape of the head and the placement of the eyes and mouth were just *wrong*...and there was no recognizable nose... but the Controllers were part machine and part flesh. At the base of the neck the blue-green skin melded with the sleek metal gradually and seamlessly, so it was hard to tell where the two parts joined. She thought of the little ridge of skin, always a bit tender, where her prosthetic arm attached to her shoulder. Had the Controllers once replaced limbs and other body parts that way, too, and eventually become something that was neither creature nor machine, but a perfect blend of both?

"Not a robot. It's a cyborg," Natil said, correcting himself when he saw what she saw. "But–how long did you say the scout robot has been here?"

"At least 116 years," Yuka said. "I guess the Controllers could live that long if they're mostly machines, but I still have a feeling they're not coming. So the scout is never going to get to share its data with them."

"Wait. Wait, wait," Natil said, holding his palms up. "*You're* a cyborg, what if—"

"I'm a cyborg?" Yuka stared at him.

He shrugged. "Well, sure. A cyborg is an organism with enhanced abilities, or repairs made with artificial parts or technology, right?" He looked pointedly at her arm.

Yuka held up her left hand, flexing the green fingers. "I guess so. I never thought of it that way."

"So if you could show the scout that you're *like* a Controller—"

"Or even convince it that I'm just a different kind of Controller," Yuka said, catching Natil's enthusiasm, "it might give me the data even if I don't have a pass code."

Natil grinned. "I think it's worth a try."

Yuka thought for a minute. "Could you get that surgical kit you had earlier?"

Natil looked momentarily confused, then nodded and left the rover bay. Yuka sent a message to the scout.

<Scout, this is Yuka. I am like your Controllers, but a different kind. I have no pass code, but need your data. Will you assist?>

There was no answer right away. Was the robot scout "thinking" about it? What would its programming allow? Natil came back with the surgical kit in his hand and a worried look on his face.

"What are you—"

"Don't worry." Yuka took the kit and opened it, selecting a laser scalpel. Carefully, she sliced a long opening down the green covering on her left forearm. She saw Natil grimace and shook her head slightly. "It doesn't hurt. I feel a little tingling that lets me know the skin has been damaged, but that's it." She peeled back the skin to expose the inner workings of the arm—metal bones, thin wires, electronic circuits, and microprocessors. She crossed the arm over her chest, resting her left hand against her right shoulder.

"Take a picture of me," she told Natil. "Get the arm, and my face." He took the picture quickly and loaded the file into the rover control console. Yuka sent the image to the robot scout.

<*This is me, Yuka,*> she typed. <*I am like the Controllers. I do not think your Controllers are coming—you have been here a long, long time. More than 42,000 sunrises. But I am here, with my people. I would like to work with you. May I have the planet data?*>

No answer. They waited.

"What's taking it so long?" Yuka folded the green skin back, covering the inner workings of her arm. "I know it has to translate the language and make sense of what I said, but it was getting pretty fast at that."

"I guess it has to go through its programming to find if it has instructions for this situation," Natil said. "I don't know what level of artificial intelligence the scout has—if it can think for itself or apply reason to a problem. If it's only limited-memory AI, and they didn't code in any protocols for—"

The robot scout's message interrupted him, appearing on Yuka's screen.

<*Welcome, Controller Yuka,*> it read. <*I also would like to work with you. Preparing planetary data for export.*>

"You did it!" Natil grinned.

"*We* did it," Yuka said. "And with this, we're all going down to the planet together. We can find the very best place to settle. Even Sano won't be able to argue with that."

She looked at her screen, where the rover showed her the robot scout, balanced on its spindly but strong legs. Behind it, blue grasses waved in the breeze, and purple water lapped at the shoreline. It was a strange planet, inhabited by many strange things, including this robot.

But it was about to become home.

Dark Skies Over Deadwood

by Dana M. Evans

Dana Evans has been many things: doctor, professor, author, and lifelong geek. When she's not writing she can be found haunting her local comic book shops, wandering a renaissance fair or cosplaying at conventions. She spends a lot of time visiting the 1800s with her steampunk group and would love to steam her way through the sky. A history buff, she's spent time exploring places as diverse as the standing stones of Wales, Salem Massachusetts and old west towns like Deadwood and Tombstone. She lives in Ohio with her supremely lazy cat, Kanda.

The dawn air bordered on cold as it slid over the *Minerva's* wooden deck. Aurelia tightened her aviator's scarf and settled her goggles over her eyes to keep the chilly sting out. Her boots thumped unevenly—heavier on the right side thanks to her spring-driven prosthetic leg—as she crossed to the captain of the best airship in the country. Aurelia's mother stared out at the horizon, piloting her ship below the clouds.

"Are we almost to Deadwood?" Aurelia asked as the ship's sapphire-hued air bladder rustled in the wind.

Her mother chuckled and pointed off the starboard forward railing. "Just follow the crow. We'll be there before noon."

"I can't wait to see Whirlwind Horse." Aurelia loved the old Lakota merchant. Whirlwind Horse made coming to Deadwood worth it. Her mother's airship had two major routes:

from Pittsburgh to the west taking coal and steel and returning with the various ores dragged out of the ground. The other route took some of the gold, silver, and steel to Italy. Aurelia loved Italy and couldn't understand why her grandparents had ever left. While she wasn't on the ground often—usually in the coldest of months—she did like the home they shared with her grandmother out in the country outside of Pittsburgh.

Compared to Rome or even Pittsburgh, Deadwood seemed rough and unruly. Having to deal with airship pirates was all the rough and unruly Aurelia needed in her life. Her right leg twinged painfully at the thought of pirates, and she reached down to rub it, feeling only metal beneath her fingertips. It seemed strange that a missing limb could hurt so often and so badly, darn those air rats. Her mother could legally hunt pirates, and the *Minerva* often did.

"Why aren't we there yet?" Aurelia whined, typical of most twelve-year-olds wanting to be there already. Her mother ignored it. "Will we be here long?"

"Long enough for you to get into trouble." Her mother laughed.

Aurelia made a face at her then tromped out to the railing, running her fingers over the polished wood. She loved watching the land sail by. When a pirate attack took her leg, Aurelia's mother feared she'd never want to sail again, but there was no place Aurelia would rather be. Pirates would learn to fear her.

⟨🚀⟩

Aurelia refused to give up her ship-board trousers and boots when she headed into town—corsets and layers of underskirts were designed by the devil. Her stump ached from the stress of clumping down from the airship docking piers at the top of the hill near Mount Moriah Cemetery. Whirlwind Horse's mercantile and dry goods sat closer to the bottom of the steep hill not too far from the Bullock Hotel. Her phlogiston gun thumped against her hip as she walked.

Ground-side noise made Aurelia want to cover her ears. People were everywhere, their voices loud enough to be heard almost a deck-length away. Sounds rumbled out of the saloons even though it was barely past noon. Several of the taller buildings had their second stories shuttered. Aurelia wasn't supposed to know what went on in those roosts for the soiled doves, but she did. She dodged cowboys who'd come for entertainment, miners on their day off, women out shopping for their households, and kids running about everywhere.

Aurelia strolled past the No. 10 Saloon, resisting the urge to peek inside. Everyone knew Wild Bill Hickok had been killed there. She couldn't help being curious. If her mother caught her trying to get inside a saloon, she'd be skinned and made into part of the *Minerva*'s air bladders. At the end of the next block, she turned the corner.

Whirlwind Horse's store was big, one of the best in all of Deadwood, if you asked Aurelia. Her grandma said if Tecumseh hadn't avoided being executed all those years ago and hadn't banded the Natives together, things would have been different and worse, at least for them. Now they found a way to share the land with the European colonists. Tecumesh's success made Aurelia very happy because she hated to think of anything bad happening to old Whirlwind Horse.

When she walked up to the front door, a Lakota boy sat outside on the wooden sidewalk. He was about her age and looked angry enough for two people. He scowled at her as if her mere presence offended him. It could, she knew, between her being a girl in pants and the fact the alliance between the Natives and the Europeans was uneasy.

"Is Whirlwind Horse working today?" she asked, determined to be as bright as he was gray.

"Grandfather's in."

She didn't know Whirlwind Horse had grandchildren. "I'm Aurelia Marchetti."

His glare lessened. "From the *Minerva*? Grandfather is expecting you." He stood and opened the door for her. "I'm John Spotted Crow."

"Nice to meet you."

John followed her in. "Tunkashila," he called, catching Whirlwind Horse's attention. "Someone from the Airship *Minerva* is here." His eye slid to her. "Looks kinda young though."

Aurelia gave him the hairy eye.

"Aurelia!" Whirlwind Horse boomed, throwing his arms wide. She ran to him and let him envelop her. He smelled of tobacco and his thick, graying braid tickled her neck. "And Kangi, she's the same age as you. How are you, my girl?" Whirlwind Horse let her go with a pat on her shoulder.

"Fine. Mom and the crew will be along with some goods for you later. She's let me loose."

"Wakan Tanka, save us. If anyone should have been named Whirlwind, it's you." He smiled, and his grandson snorted.

"What are you laughing at?" she demanded.

John turned with a flip of his glossy, raven braid. "Didn't laugh." He banged his way back out.

"Doesn't talk much, does he?"

"You'll have to forgive his ill manners. My daughter and her husband were killed in a fire several weeks ago while Kangi and I were out. I was teaching him some of the ways of the wicasa wakan, a holy man, just as my grandfather taught me." His voice cracked as tears sprang to his eyes. A few coursed down his wrinkled cheeks.

"I'm so sorry." Aurelia hugged him again. He rubbed her shoulders.

"Thank you, dear." Whirlwind Horse took a step back, wiping his eyes. "Kangi misses his parents and the plains. Maybe you could give him a friendly ear. It's not been easy on him moving here."

Aurelia tracked Kangi's path, unsure of that. She moved around so much she didn't feel particularly attached to any one place, except the *Minerva*, but she did know how it felt to lose a parent. "I can try."

She could practically feel Whirlwind Horse's mood lightening. "Pilomaya," he said. Thank you, one of the few words in Lakota she knew. "And did you come just to visit, Aurelia, or was there something I can help you with?"

"Looking for a gift for Mom's birthday, but it can wait."

"I'll set some things aside she might like."

"Thanks." She thumped her way outside to find John. He was right where he'd been when she met him. Aurelia decided against sitting next to him. It wasn't very ladylike to squat on the sidewalk like a toad. More importantly, her prosthetic leg made getting off the ground tricky sometimes. She settled on leaning against a free hitching post.

He eyed her warily. "Yeah?"

"Why does your grandfather call you Kangi?" It might seem a strange question, but it was bugging her. She liked to learn and knowing another word in a different language could only be a good thing.

"It's my name. Your people call me John Spotted Crow." He waved a hand at her. "But in Lakota Kangi Gleska means Spotted Crow."

"Mmm, which word means crow? I only know the few words your grandfather taught me."

Tension fled his shoulders, loosening them, as if it somehow meant something that his grandfather trusted her and so should he. "Kangi means crow."

"Would you rather I call you Kangi?"

He lifted a shoulder, letting it fall. "If you want. Do they call you Aurelia?"

She nodded. "They told my grandparents we'd do better with more English names, people being weird about foreign-sounding stuff and all, but we took to the air. No one cares much about that stuff on airships."

Kangi smiled faintly. "I know how you feel. Back home, we don't use the English names." He tugged his long braid. "I don't mind being called Spotted Crow, but I prefer Kangi."

"Then I'll call you Kangi."

"Grandfather sent you to talk to me, didn't he?"

"I would have anyhow. I don't get to see a lot of kids my age. I'm sorry about your parents though. I lost my dad two years ago, so I know the hurt."

Kangi squeezed his dark eyes shut tight. "Thanks. I still can't believe they're gone."

"It's terrible."

They didn't say anything for a few minutes and then Kangi asked, "Want to go do something?"

"Whatcha got in mind?" She bounced on her heels.

He opened his hands. "Sadly, nothing."

"Ever been on an airship?" When Kangi shook his head, Aurelia asked, "Want to see the *Minerva*?"

Kangi glanced over his shoulder at his grandfather's store then sprang to his feet. "Tunkashila, may I go to Aurelia's ship?" he bellowed.

Whirlwind Horse poked his head out. "Fine. Take the day off. You deserve it. Have fun. And you." He pointed at Aurelia. "Don't fill my grandson's head with ideas of high-flying adventures."

She chuckled. "Why else take him? Plenty of fun to be had in the air."

Whirlwind Horse sighed and retreated inside.

"I guess there are airship pirates around here," Kangi said.

"Anywhere they're pulling gold and silver out of the ground you get thieves. Wish I could take you for a flight. Anyone named Spotted Crow should be in the air."

He smirked at her and started up the walkway. They didn't get more than a few steps when a Chinese boy blasted around the corner, stumbling to a stop when he saw them.

"Hey, Kangi! Oh, Aurelia! You're back!"

"Hi, Ling." Aurelia threw her arms wide and hugged him.

"I guess you know Ling Xue," Kangi said dryly.

"Mom deals with his uncle. Ling, we were just about to go to the *Minerva*."

"Can I come with you?" Ling asked in his soft accented voice.

"I was coming to see if Kangi had the afternoon free."

"I do."

"Sure. Mom would love to see you."

"Kangi, do you have your pony?" Ling asked.

He nodded. "Why?"

Ling gestured to Aurelia. "Didn't you notice?"

"He just met me."

"Do you mean her limp?"

Aurelia hiked up her pant leg to show off her shiny metal prosthetic leg. "Lost it to airship pirates."

Kangi's eyes widened. "Terrifying." He darted down the alley and came back with a small mud-brown mare. He held the mare steady. "Can you ride? Wind is pretty mild."

Aurelia wrinkled her nose. "I'm not very good."

"I'll help."

Kangi helped her up then swung up behind her. He nudged his horse into action. As Wind lurched forward, Aurelia buried her fingers in the pony's wiry brown mane. Kangi kept Wind to a walk so Ling could keep up, chattering excitably about everything Aurelia had missed since the last time she'd been in Deadwood.

Kangi murmured in her ear. "You ride like a sack of flour."

She reached back and pinched his lean belly. He yelped then laughed, offering up no apologies. Boys, they were all annoying sometimes. They reached the top of the hill quickly enough, and Kangi hitched Wind to one of the many posts near the docking piers.

Aurelia waved them on, leading the way up the ladder to the *Minerva*. The *Minerva's* belly was opened as workers emptied her hold. They'd fill it back up with different goods. Aurelia ignored them as she had little to do with those goings-on. When she climbed on deck with her companions, she quickly spotted her mother leaning over the side, watching the procedure.

"Mom!"

Her mother straightened, turning her way. "You're back early. Oh, Ling, nice to see you. Who else have you brought with you?"

"This is Kangi, Whirlwind Horse's grandson. Kangi, this is my mom, Captain Osanna Marchetti."

"Nice to meet you, ma'am."

"Same here." She smiled at Kangi. "Aurelia, you're giving a tour, I suppose."

"I am. Whirlwind Horse said we can't steal his grandson away." Aurelia reached over, thumping Kangi's shoulder. "I might disagree."

Her mother snorted. "Get to know the boy before you recruit him. For all you know he might be afraid of heights." She nodded with her chin toward Kangi who stared over the edge of the railing, his skin several shades lighter now.

"We're not even in the air yet." Aurelia clamped a hand on his arm, pulling him away from the rail.

"This might be high enough," he muttered. "Not sure man was meant to soar like a bird."

"Wrong!" she replied cheerily.

Kangi relaxed some once she took him on the tour. Ling joined in, having been on board several times. Kangi's eyes went back to normal human size once they were below deck. How disappointing, she thought. Truly, someone named Crow should soar. Neither Ling nor Kangi could be pried away from the engines. Aurelia liked them, too, but her strength lay more with navigation than tinkering with engines.

Kangi seemed unimpressed with her quarters and couldn't be lured up into the rigging with Ling and her, not for anything. Finally, her mother shooed them off ship to go find trouble elsewhere. Kangi unhitched Wind but had his gaze on the *Minerva*.

"Part of me would like to take a ride, but the rest of me is sure it'll be terrifying," Kangi said then turned to her. "I'm amazed how you can climb like a squirrel with your prosthetic leg."

"I do my best to not let it slow me down," she replied, puffing up proudly.

"You've succeeded." Kangi smiled. "So what should we do next? Your mother clearly has had enough of our company."

"Mom is always too busy when we first land. We can come back another day if you want. At some point I have to go back to your grandfather's store and buy Mom's birthday gift."

"We can go back now if you want. There's not much to do here unless you're a gambler." Kangi sighed. "If we were home, I could take you to do so many things on the plains."

Aurelia didn't miss Ling's cocked eyebrow and surmised there wasn't much to do on the plains either. "That would have been fun," she said diplomatically.

"We could play mahjong today or tomorrow. I'm teaching Kangi how to play." Ling said brightly.

"He's taught me too. It's pretty fun. I could show you poker. Mom doesn't know I know. I've watched the air men playing. We don't have to gamble though." She shrugged. "Or we can use penny candy."

"We can get that at Grandfather's store."

"Sounds like we have our trouble to get into." Aurelia grinned. Being around friends her age was going to be so much fun.

Aurelia sauntered down a back street with Kangi and Ling, having spent the last two days with them playing mahjong and poker and exploring the city. Ling led them into Mount Moriah Cemetery so they could visit Wild Bill Hickok's grave. Another of Ling's friends had gone with them then, enamored with the sharpshooter until he heard some of Aurelia's stories about airship pirates. All three boys decided *she* was even more interesting than some old gambler. Aurelia floated as high as the *Minerva* on their admiration.

Glancing around at the alleyway, she asked, "Why are we coming here?"

"I have a letter to deliver for my uncle." Ling waved the creamy envelope bearing Chinese characters. He had tried to show her a little bit of their calligraphy, but she had no aptitude for it.

A scream echoed in the tight alleyway, sending Aurelia's heart into her throat. She'd heard men in pain before, and she knew she heard it now. A door burst open, and a man stumbled out, blood streaming from his neck. He fell in the street, and three other men raced out of the door. They jerked to a stop, seeing Aurelia and her friends.

"Run!" Kangi cried.

They wheeled around, fleeing toward the mouth of the back street. The main street had more people. They might not be entirely safe there but safer than down a blind alley. Aurelia heard the men thundering behind them as she struggled to keep up to the boys. Her prosthetic leg was great, but she had never run long distances on it. An airship wasn't that big. The hard thumping sent blossoms of sparking pain racing up from her stump, and she could feel the leather straps straining as the limb threatened to twist off center.

Kangi and Ling dropped back enough so they could each grab a hand, pulling her along. Aurelia knew they meant well, but they could easily yank her faster than her prosthesis could keep up.

"Don't shoot them!" one of the men cried out behind them. "Do you know how much someone would pay for kids like them in certain place? We'll take them to Renteger."

Aurelia didn't want to know about those certain places, and she was losing the foot race.

"In here." Ling kicked a door open, its lock barely putting up a fight. "It's the Green Door. Places to hide."

The Green Door was an infamous brothel. Aurelia knew it had not only places to hide but bouncers to deal with the men behind them. If rumor had it right, they could run from the top floor here all the way down the block through interconnecting corridors linking building to building and come out in a more respectable establishment. These corridors were a way to hide from the police.

Kangi pulled her after him, up the back stairs. Ling trailed them, practically kicking her boots off her feet. He screamed suddenly. She and Kangi whipped around to see one of the men dragging Ling back toward the door.

"No!" Kangi tried to force past her.

At the same time, two burly men jogged down the stairs hollering, "What are you kids doing in here?"

One of their pursuers took a shot, ripping the wooden stair rail up. The two doormen yelped, flattening against the wall. The men disappeared out the door with a struggling Ling. Kangi and Aurelia tried to follow, but the bouncers took hold of them.

"Are you crazy kids? You'll get yourselves shot."

"They don't want to kill us!" Aurelia shouted. She wormed free, but by the time she reached the street, the men were gone.

Next to her, Kangi shook with fear or rage—or both, she decided. "I can't lose someone else!"

Behind them, the doormen slammed the door. They'd be of no help.

"We need to get Sheriff Bullock," Kangi said.

"And then we need to get to the *Minerva*." Aurelia rubbed her thigh. "I know Renteger. He's the captain of a pirate airship, the *Raptor*. I bet they'll be taking wind fast now. They have to know the sheriff will round up a posse and come after them."

"Bullock doesn't have airships," Kangi protested, running for the main street.

Aurelia ran after him, her thigh muscles cramping. "Maybe not, but I *do*."

He glanced over his shoulder then hustled her into the nearest store. "Will your mother help?"

"Of course. She likes Ling, and she isn't going to let them sell him into slavery somewhere."

"Stay here. I'll be right back as soon as I tell the sheriff."

Aurelia wanted to protest, but she listened to her leg and to reason. She suspected if she took her limb off now she'd see blisters on her stump. She nodded and Kangi raced off, almost flying like his namesake. Impatience and fear ate her up as she waited. Aurelia took shelter in the store, looking out the window. She didn't think the men would be back, but she didn't want to chance loitering about in the street.

To her surprise, Kangi rode back up on Wind. She limped out as he slithered off the mare. Kangi boosted her up and swung into place behind her. He urged Wind into a gallop, making Aurelia cling tightly as the ride punished her spine.

"The sheriff wanted to talk to me too long about the dead man and the people who took Ling. I had to make a run for it if we want your mother to get to the skies. I'll talk to him later once we get Ling back." Kangi's voice sounded tight and stressed in her ear. "I should have talked to the Chinese mayor too."

Aurelia knew the Chinese had their own separate city within a city, but she didn't know if they had their own separate lawmen. "Bullock will probably do that," she reassured him even though she knew it might not be true.

Kangi grunted, urging Wind even faster. When they reached the docks, he tied Wind to the post. Aurelia didn't wait for him to start climbing the ladder to the *Minerva*. She prayed her mother would be on board, supervising whatever needed doing and not somewhere in town, something she probably should have thought of sooner.

Luckily her mother was watching Dodson and his men replace a piece of decking. She widened her eyes seeing them.

"What's wrong?"

"We saw a man die in front of us, and those men tried to kidnap us!" Aurelia cried.

"They got Ling!"

"Oh my god." Her mother swept Aurelia up in a hug.

"We got the lawmen after them," Kangi added.

"And they're taking Ling to Renteger to sell him. We can't let that happen, Mom!"

Letting Aurelia go, her mother stalked over and slapped a hand to the ship's control panel setting off the general call-to-arms siren. The head-shredding noise would be heard all through the city. Her mother looked to Aurelia. "Standard pirate protocol."

Aurelia nodded, grabbing Kangi's hand. She dragged him deeper into the ship to the weapons locker. Selecting two phlogiston guns, Aurelia handed one to Kangi. He eyed it, obviously unfamiliar with the weapon. She tapped a control toggle on its side. "If you push this down, it'll stun whoever you hit. Up, and you can kill them. You have several shots on stun, fewer on the kill setting. You'll probably need another weapon. The adults always want us to hang back, but you need to protect yourself. Hard to know what pirates will do. Can you shoot at all?"

He narrowed his eyes. "I'm Lakota. We're natural warriors," he huffed.

Knowing he was worried about Ling, Aurelia didn't comment about him getting defensive.

"But I've only shot rifles, not this," Kangi admitted more contritely.

"Point and shoot, only no kickback like with a rifle." Aurelia helped herself to a pistol as well.

Kangi found a long slender staff. He swished it and smiled, nodding to himself.

"That's not a weapon. The rigger monkeys use it to untangle ropes if necessary," Aurelia said.

Kangi shrugged. "It'll do."

"All right then. Come on." She inclined her head toward the door. He slipped out and she followed.

By the time they returned to the deck, airship men were boiling over the railing. Excitement slipped deep into Aurelia's skin. Fear, too, of course, but she couldn't deny the rush of chasing down pirates. The battles were terrifying, but the chase thrilled her. Aurelia wanted to be the best fighter pilot. One day, she felt confident she would be.

"How will your mother even know where to find Renteger?" Kangi asked, his voice low. "He won't be here at the port."

"No, they'll be at some hidden docking port. The pirates are pretty tricky about that," Aurelia said, nudging Kangi toward the pilot house. "Mom will want us to stay here. It'll be safer." Aurelia felt the ship lurch slightly.

Kangi grabbed for her hand. "What was that?"

"We're casting off."

"Wakan Tanka!" The color drained from his face. "I didn't think about that."

Belatedly she remembered Kangi had been uneasy with the idea of flight. "You want to save Ling, right?"

He swallowed hard, giving a brief nod.

"It'll be all right." Aurelia knew she couldn't actually promise that. They were potentially flying into a firefight. Anything could happen, and almost all of it bad. Kangi probably understood, so she let the lie stand.

Kangi licked his lips. "We need to save him."

Aurelia gripped the butt of her phlogiston gun. "We will."

Kangi gasped as the ship began to rise. Aurelia edged out to the rail. There was no immediate danger, not until they actually found the *Raptor*. She sent up a little prayer that the men would have Ling on the pirate ship. For all she knew Renteger could have other ways out of town. She shook her head, refusing to allow herself to think that way. If that was the case, the sheriff and his men would be Ling's only hope, and she had no idea if Bullock was any good. She had to trust he was.

"Oh! This is amazing." Kangi leaned on the rail, staring down even as he trembled.

She covered his hand with hers. "Isn't it?"

"What if I fall over in the fight?"

"Better pray you transfigure into your namesake because it's a long way down."

"I'll stay by the wall like you said." Kangi inched back.

Aurelia beckoned for him to come back. "It's safe for now."

Reluctantly he rejoined her. They watched the land go by as the *Minerva* circled. The tension in Aurelia ebbed some, but fear they would somehow miss the *Raptor* or that Renteger had left by wagon grew.

Kangi jumped when a new alarm sounded.

"They've sighted the *Raptor*," Aurelia said, twisting and turning, trying to see where it was. The pilot house blocked part of her view, but the red air bladder glided into sight. Her heart revved up in time with the *Minerva*'s engines.

She reached for Kangi to pull him back to the pilot house wall, but he was already in motion. He was smart enough to know he didn't belong at the rail when the firefight started. He winced, half-ducking when the phlogiston cannons roared, making the decking sway and buck.

"Steady now," she said. Aurelia didn't blame him for being afraid. It wouldn't take much to end it all. She unholstered her phlogiston pistol. It would be her primary weapon. A stunned prisoner could be bartered with, and she was young. Her mother didn't want her to seriously hurt anyone unless there was no choice. Aurelia didn't want that either.

"What if we lose?" Kangi gripped his staff tightly.

She shook her head violently. "Don't even think it." She stared at the *Raptor.* "We'd be prisoners waiting to be sold or dead."

"I'm not going to let that happen," Kangi growled. "I've already lost too much."

"I understand," she replied grimly.

Not entering the battle was one of hardest things Aurelia had ever done. Kangi appeared torn between wanting to leap into the fray or staying right where he was. It would come to them soon enough, she knew from past battles. The screams were the worst part, echoing into her heart as she prayed they didn't come from her own people.

The blue-white crackling spray of a phlogiston pistol stabbed the pilot house just in front of her and Kangi. He said something in Lakota that she suspected was a swear word. She added her own under her breath in Italian.

"Aurelia," Kangi hissed, pointing behind her with the stick.

She whipped around, bringing her gun up. She stunned a pirate without hesitation, spotting the second man a little too late to get her pistol around. Kangi swatted that man hard with his stick, a huge, nearly manic grin spreading across his face. He swung the stick again, knocking the man down.

"Counted coup!" he proclaimed, proud of himself.

"So that's what that means. You whack someone with a stick?" Aurelia lifted a hank of rope from the side of the pilot housing.

"Not quite. It's considered braver to touch an enemy than to kill him."

"Excellent. Here." She passed him the rope, not entirely seeing

the wisdom in that philosophy. "Tie them up. I'll stand guard."
Kangi obeyed. As he did so, Aurelia heard the grappling hooks
deploy. Kangi made a strange sound as the ship lurched. Judging by the motion, they were hauling the *Raptor* in, not the
other way around. Aurelia allowed herself a smile.

"We're going to board them, Kangi. It's almost over."

"Good," he muttered, finishing up his knots.

"Time to surrender, Renteger!" her mother cried, leaping the
rail with three of her men.

The wind snatched away the response but Aurelia's gut
clenched hearing more gun fire. More men leapt to the other
ship, Kangi looked to her for clues as to what they do next.

"We wait," she said.

"For what?"

The all clear alarm shrilled.

"For that. Come on." Aurelia climbed onto the railing, preparing to jump to the *Raptor*.

Kangi grabbed the rail, gazing down first then over to the other ship. "We're jumping? Are you insane?"

Aurelia jumped. He'd either come or not. With a strangled
cry, Kangi jumped. His boots skittered on the bloody decking,
nearly toppling him. Aurelia caught his arm, steadying him.
She inclined her head to the open passageway her mother and
her men were dragging another man through. Aurelia assumed
that must be Captain Renteger.

She and Kangi hurried down the ladder into the hold, her
prosthetic leg jarring as she went. Aurelia couldn't contain a
gasp when she saw not just Ling chained up in the hold but a
half dozen more boys and girls, all Chinese or Native.

Her mother threw Renteger to the ground in front of his cap-
tives. "Where were you taking them?"

"Like I'd tell you," he snarled. "What does anyone care?
They're just Red and Yellow."

Her mother booted him in the jaw, surprising Aurelia, who wasn't used to that level of violence from her. Renteger's eyes rolled up, and he crumpled like wet paper. Her mother turned to her men. "Let's get these kids out of here."

Aurelia and Kangi sprang forward to free Ling. He flung his arms around her, pulling Aurelia tight to his sweat-soured body.

"You're all right!" he cried.

"Me? We were worried sick about you." She kissed his cheek.

Ling, noodle-legged, let Kangi help him to the deck. A couple of planks had been laid down between the ships, much to Kangi's obvious relief. Aurelia took that easy way over, too, her leg telling her it had had enough excitement for one day. One by one they chivvied the kidnapped children across to the *Minerva*. Most of Renteger's men remained on the *Raptor* trussed up in their own hold with Marchetti's men watching over them.

They tied up the *Raptor* to the *Minerva*, and her powerful engines slowly carted them both back toward Deadwood's docking port. At the rail next to her Ling looked out, an expression of peace on his face. Kangi clung to the rail with a death grip. They said little, and that allowed Aurelia to hear a hissing noise.

She glanced up, scowled then bellowed, "We have a slow leak, Captain. Must have taken some shrapnel."

"Go seal it."

Aurelia ran and got some patch. Kangi's jaw dropped when she pulled herself up on the railing and caught hold of the rigging rope ladder. Aurelia ascended toward the bladder.

"Are you insane?" Kangi roared.

"There's a hole in the bladder," Ling said placidly. "Would you prefer we crash?"

"We could crash?" Kangi bolted from the rail to the wall of the pilot house as if it could protect him.

"Not if I do my job right," Aurelia called down. With practiced hands, it didn't take her long to seal the hole. She leaned back and watched the ground moving below her. The ropes she clung to slowly twisted in the wind, giving her a thrill before she climbed back down to the deck.

"You can open your eyes now, Kangi. She's back," Ling said dryly.

Aurelia clapped Kangi on the back. "That was fun. Next time join me."

Whatever he muttered in Lakota was lost on her, but the tone wasn't. She shouldn't tease him. "Scarier things await," she promised, and he shot her a quizzical look. "Explaining all this to Sheriff Bullock."

Kangi shuddered.

Explaining everything to the sheriff had unexpected consequences that led to Aurelia having to wear a corset and gown and stupid velvet shoes studded with jet beads. The town threw the crew of the *Minerva*, plus Kangi, a hero's party. The food was fine and the band made good music, but it didn't make her like a corset any better. She had just finished two busy days helping her mother and the crew strip the spoils from the *Raptor*, and Aurelia had to wonder how fast the judge would be summoned to Deadwood to deal with Renteger. It wasn't her concern any more.

Her mother patted Aurelia's hand. "Smile, daughter. Sometimes it's fun to dress up." She inclined her head to Kangi and Ling, who sat next to her. Whirlwind Horse sat beside his grandson. "We might turn them into airship men yet."

Aurelia laughed. "Maybe Ling."

"Kangi is the only crow afraid of flying," Ling said, and Kangi punched his shoulder.

"We might have to change his name. Afraid of Clouds." Aurelia smiled at him, and he wrinkled his nose.

"I'm fine with clouds. It's the drop that gets me." Kangi shuddered. "Maybe I'll get used to it."

"I'm not sure I want to see you in the sky," Whirlwind Horse said. "Stay on the ground and dance with a pretty girl."

Kangi turned redder, but he stood and held out a hand to Aurelia.

"I want the next dance," Ling piped up.

"It's yours," she promised then leaned in closer to Kangi. "I'm a terrible dancer."

"I don't even know what I'm doing," he admitted.

"Perfect. Let's show them how heroes do it."

"I can see tomorrow's headlines. 'Two heroes maimed on the dance hall floor.'" Kangi frowned but led her out onto the floor.

They danced far worse than they fought bad guys, but of the two, Aurelia would rather be good at the latter. She didn't need to ask a fortune-teller to explain that she, Kangi, and Ling had many adventures still waiting for them. Aurelia looked forward to every one of them.

The Ground Shifted

by anne m. gibson

anne m. gibson is a principal ux designer and general troublemaker just close enough to Valley Forge, Pennsylvania to think a wander through a revolutionary battlefield is not noteworthy. In addition to designing websites, she writes about websites (or much weirder things), plays competitive pinball, and watches the terriers destroy things.

Rosetta piloted her support pod through the front gate and parked it as close to the front porch as she could. She glanced around, but the neighborhood was quiet. Sure that no one was watching, she pulled up the message from the university on her tablet again.

We are honored to inform you of your admission to Left University, North American Coalition, Earth.

Rosetta had not applied to the university. She hadn't completed any college applications at all. She was only a seventh year student—she didn't even know what she wanted to study yet! *It has to be Uncle,* she thought. Every time she read the message, her chest tightened.

Rosetta slid the tablet back into her pocket, then carefully removed the safety straps in her pod and climbed out. She took a deep breath, her right hand steadying her against the body of the pod. The shiny black plastic of the hoverpod that allowed Rosetta to navigate her school and her town made her feel stable. She wished, as she did every day, that her uncle allowed the hoverpod in the house—or even an old-fashioned wheelchair! But Uncle said not using a pod would make her "stronger."

Muscle strength wasn't Rosetta's problem. Severe dizziness, nausea, and a condition the doctors called "vertigo" were her problems. She had problems with her vision, problems with her eyes and ears. Rosetta's doctors called it "a life-altering ideopathic condition."

Rosetta called it "being Rosetta."

People told her she didn't see the world the way they did. To Rosetta's eyes, every surface was a roiling, swirly mess of tiny balls bouncing around. Nothing was stable, especially her balance. The air sparkled around her, filled with tiny balls of light. The floor rolled and danced like an angry sea. If she didn't hold onto something, Rosetta fell. Her olive complexion hid the bruises she was constantly accumulating, but her thin frame did little to protect her bony arms and legs from breaking.

Rosetta was tired of falling down, tired of nausea, tired of sickness. She was tired of nothing behaving the way people told her it did. She was tired of squinting and headaches and doctors' visits. Rosetta was tired.

She stood at the base of the porch stairs, one foot in the flower garden, only a meter from the front door. Rosetta looked up at the house—she'd never called it home—and sighed. It was an ancient Victorian home, almost three hundred years old. It was supposed to be a twin, with her parents in the left half and her uncle in the right half. All the other houses on the street were twins.

But the left half, which had belonged to Rosetta's parents, was gone. Rosetta's parents had illegally performed a dangerous physics experiment, and the whole house had blown up. Uncle regularly reminded Rosetta that he was the one who had swooped in to save her life.

Uncle was Mama's brother. Uncle was a professor of particle physics. He had a doctorate in applied nuclear dynamics. Nothing mattered to Uncle except being nominated for a Nobel prize.

Rosetta grabbed for the wrought-iron railing, which seemed to dodge out of reach, then climbed the steps almost easily with the support of the rail. At the top, she lunged for the arm of a wooden rocking chair Uncle said gave the house "personality" (as if the missing half of the building didn't) and used that to steady herself enough to reach the wall. One arm rested against the wall, the other opened the door, and she was inside.

With her hand on the living room wall and the door firmly closed, Rosetta followed the wall to the door to the second floor stairs, intending to go up to her room. When the door detected her, it slid open automatically.

Half a cat stared up at Rosetta from its seat on the third step from the bottom. Rosetta gasped and let go of the wall. The hardwood shifted under her feet and she fell, almost striking her head on a lamp table. Nausea and pain gripped her tighter than fear. She crawled to the wall and leaned against it, the vertigo subsiding.

The orange tabby walked down the steps and sat at Rosetta's feet. After a moment, it rubbed its right cheek against her ankle. It didn't have a left cheek, or a left anything else for that matter. It looked as if someone had cleaved the cat in half with a blade, then covered the flat half with fur.

Rosetta yanked her feet away from the animal and pulled out her tablet. "There's a half a cat in the house," she texted her uncle.

"Don't make up stories," Uncle texted back.

Rosetta sighed. She switched to a universal channel and texted her Aunt Emma, on the moon base. Auntie always listened to Rosetta. "Do you know anything about cats? There's a half a cat in the house."

Auntie wrote back. "Orange tabby? That's the house's security system. I wonder what kicked that on."

"You know about this?" Rosetta replied. "It's a half a cat."

"Well, technically it's a holographic presentation of half a cat. The house's AI sends her in when there's something it can't do and needs the inhabitants to take over." Auntie replied. "I wonder if the ventilation system is clogged again."

"WHY IS IT ONLY HALF A CAT?" Rosetta stabbed into the keyboard.

"You've only got a half a house, so she's only half a cat," Auntie replied.

The cat walked away gracefully. Her half-tail whisked through the air. She bounded up onto the sofa cushion and curled up, rolled onto her back, and stretched out in the sunny spot for a nap.

Rosetta shrugged and headed upstairs. She followed the railing and the wall to the attic stairs, then finally up to her tiny loft bedroom. She closed the door firmly to protect her room from errant half-cats. Exhausted, she collapsed onto the bed's broken-down mattress and took a nap.

When Rosetta woke, she found the half-cat asleep next to her on the bed. Tentatively, she reached out and stroked her soft neck. The cat felt solid enough. She purred like a real cat. Rosetta waved her hand where the left half of the cat's face should have been. It was clearly nonexistent.

"I think I'll call you Molly," Rosetta said. The half-cat purred.

Rosetta went downstairs and used the food generator to make dinner—chicken, corn, and potatoes. She shooed the cat away from the leftover chicken, then wondered if holographs ate. She used her tablet's universal network to research holographs and artificial intelligences and cats. After she cleaned up the dishes, Rosetta returned to her room, finished her studying, and worked on a programming project.

She kept an eye on the bedroom window overlooking the road,

as she did every night, waiting to see if Uncle was coming home from the lab. If she was awake when he arrived, he'd leave her alone.

When he hadn't arrived by 1:30, she decided he probably was staying at the lab and went to bed.

The click of her bedroom door slowly opening woke Rosetta up. She kept her eyes closed and moved not a muscle.

Uncle shook her shoulder roughly. "Get up," he demanded.

Rosetta pulled herself up to sitting against the wall. She pulled the blankets close around her legs. "What do you want?"

"Answers," he slurred. Alcohol and cigarettes infused the air around him. "Which way is the spin?"

"I don't know," Rosetta replied. "I tell you every night I don't know."

"Answer me! Which way is the spin?"

"I don't know what you're talking about!"

"It's a simple question! Is the universe left-handed or right-handed?"

As a professor, Uncle was expected to publish papers about particle physics on a regular basis, and he was overdue on his deadlines. For some reason, Uncle believed that Rosetta could answer his research questions. This wasn't the first paper he'd harassed her about, and Rosetta doubted it would be the last. She didn't know why *she* was supposed to be able to answer. Lying had gotten her a spanking as a child.

Uncle leaned in close to her face. The wine on his breath made her eyes tear up. "You can't walk. You can't think. You can't answer the only question you've ever been asked. You're a failure," he whispered viciously. Rosetta ignored him. She stared at the wall behind his head and ignored his ravings until he was too tired to continue.

When he rose to leave, she blurted out, "I got an acceptance letter to Left University."

He stared at her for a long time. "You'll go, and you'll study physics like your mother," he growled.

"What if I won't?" she asked, barely able to breathe around the fear in her chest.

He stared at her again, then walked out, slamming the door behind.

"I'm not going, you abusive bastard," Rosetta muttered, then immediately regretted her words. So many girls had it so much worse than she did. And was it his fault she couldn't answer his questions? No, it was hers. She didn't know why, but it was hers.

Rosetta cried herself back to sleep.

Saturday morning Rosetta rose late. Uncle's room was empty. There was no sign of the half-cat. She showered, dressed, and put her long black hair in a bun. By the time she was done it was well past noon.

Rosetta ate cereal for breakfast, keeping an eye out for the half-cat. She remembered reading that once the application was triggered, it would act like a normal cat until it found an opportunity to communicate its message. Didn't cats like milk? But the cat didn't appear, so Rosetta messaged her friends on her tablet while she ate.

After cleaning up her dishes, she decided to go back to her programming project. She slid her tablet into a pocket and began walking around the house's walls to return to her room.

When Rosetta reached the basement door, Molly walked out of the wall and stood in her path. Rosetta blinked.

"Excuse me, kitty," she said and tried to step around. Molly shifted to block her way. "Come on, move," Rosetta said, nudging at the half-cat.

"Mrrarow," Molly answered, and batted at Rosetta's foot, claws extended.

"Well! Okay then!" Rosetta snapped. She looked around. There was nowhere to turn around that wouldn't force her to let go of the wall. "I'm not going to crawl around you, cat."

The cat hissed in agreement.

"What do you want me to do? Go downstairs into Uncle's lab? I'm not allowed. I don't even have the code."

"Mrrrawwwrrrrowwwww!" The cat glared at her with its one angry eye, batted at Rosetta's foot, and stared at the basement door. It hissed open. Well, that made sense, since the cat was the house, Rosetta supposed.

"I'm not doing it, cat! Now move!" She tried to step over the sizable mound of fur, and this time Molly wrapped her paws around Rosetta's ankle and bit down, hard. That was an unexpected software feature.

"Ow! Fine. Fine! I'll go downstairs!" She kicked her foot free of the tabby and pulled the door open. Rosetta stomped down the steps.

The lights rose automatically. A computer worktable the length of the back wall glowed under bundles of equipment and flasks of strange liquids. On the other walls, hundreds of data cubes about particle physics lined the shelves. The middle of the room was filled with more equipment and notes and garbage. The basement smelled of acrid chemicals, stale coffee, and a hint of rotten bananas.

Something hummed very low, a sound more felt than heard. It bothered Rosetta, but now that she had come down she was curious. What was so important that she was never allowed down here?

Molly stretched herself across the steps and glared at Rosetta, making it clear the stairs were closed. Whatever the cat wanted, it had something to do with Rosetta exploring Uncle's lab.

Rosetta began walking along the edges of the room. When she reached the door in the far wall, Rosetta paused. At first, it looked like all the other automated sliding doors in the house. The humming was louder from behind the door.

Molly jumped down from the stairs and stood at Rosetta's feet.

"Half-cat," Rosetta asked, "why would there be a door here? That should be the basement of Mama and Papa's house. Why would they connect the two houses?"

Molly's only response was to wind herself around Rosetta's legs, a move that was both comforting and disorienting.

"Do you suppose there's a brick wall behind it, like in the cartoons?" Her curiosity nagged at her like an itch. "I bet you could open it up," she said, "and I could just peek."

Molly looked up at her with one half-open eye and a half-smirk. "But if we open it, do I really want to see what's inside?" Rosetta asked. "I'm in enough trouble as it is." She shook her head.

The cat wandered off. Rosetta felt relieved. She continued her walk until she reached the mess on the back wall. Rosetta picked her way very carefully through the collection of equipment and mounds of paperwork.

I shouldn't be down here, she thought over and over until she was sure the thought itself would drive her mad. The vertigo was hard enough to handle without her internal battles. She took a deep breath of relief when she finally put her hand on the polished, glowing counter.

Halfway down the length of the computer worktable, Rosetta paused in front of an odd device about half the size of the cat. It was rounded and smooth, blue, scraped up, and vaguely egg-shaped. The device had no visible external knobs, screens, or features. It was surrounded by various hand tools, a circular saw, and even a gas blowtorch. Scorch marks on the counter indicated her uncle had tried to melt it. Rosetta should have passed by it without even a moment's notice, but something about the chipped blue paint stirred up a memory.

"This looks familiar. I think this was in Mama and Papa's house," Rosetta said. She looked at Molly, who was perched on the wooden steps again. The semi-feline was cleaning her only front paw with half a tongue, paying Rosetta no mind. "You could at least pretend to be interested," Rosetta replied. She received a disgusted look for her troubles.

Rosetta leaned down in front of the device to get a better look. "I wonder what it does," she said.

A green light shot out of the egg, danced across Rosetta's face, and locked on to her right eye. "Identity confirmed. Hello, Rosetta Walker."

Rosetta jumped back a full foot, lost her balance, saw the world swirl around her, and fell to the dirty concrete floor. She managed to avoid hitting her head, but her elbow took a beating. "Ugh." She brushed particles of dirt off her hands, trying to get her bearings. She fought against the swiftly tilting ground and rose again. "What is this? Tobacco? It stinks like old cabbage down here."

The mechanical voice said nothing further, but the egg cracked around its middle and swung open on an invisible hinge.

Rosetta reached in and pulled out an old tablet, the kind her parents would have used.

The screen lit up. Words streaked across the surface while a voice read the message aloud. "Critical message for Rosetta Walker. Begin?"

I should take this upstairs, Rosetta thought. She shook her head. She could take the tablet, but there was no way to carry the bulky case up three flights of stairs and keep her balance. Besides, Uncle was sure to notice it was missing. She didn't want to think of how he might react. *Maybe I should text Auntie,* she thought, but what would she say? "I broke into Uncle's lab and took something for me?" Rosetta shook her head again.

She looked around the basement. She listened carefully for Uncle's car but heard only the neighbor's yapping terrier. The half-cat napped on the stair. Dust motes danced in the light around the bare bulbs in the ceiling.

"Yes," she said.

"Neural network activated," the tablet replied. The space

around Rosetta morphed.

Rosetta was no longer holding the tablet in the basement. She was sitting on a picnic blanket in a park she'd visited with her parents before the accident. The cool autumn air carried the smell of fallen leaves from the babbling creek at the bottom of the hill to Rosetta's nose. Under her palms, thick grass poked through the thin woven blanket. It seemed to be late afternoon in this place, though at home it was only mid-morning.

Her mother sat next to her, her hand brushing against Rosetta's. "Hello, darling," she said. In this—Holograph? Recording? Did it matter?—Mama hadn't aged. Rosetta was shocked at just how young her mother looked now that she was a teen herself.

Mama spoke, and part of Rosetta knew that the tablet and its network were responsible for the voice, but her heart said otherwise. A well of tears long thought exhausted overflowed and trickled down Rosetta's cheeks.

"I'm so glad you're still here, at home," Mama said. "Molly's programming has determined that you are old enough now to know what's been done to you, and to reverse it. We spent hours on the application. We're so glad it worked!"

"How do I explain this disaster?" Mama looked across the park, deep in thought it seemed. She sighed.

"Your father and I worked at Left University with my brother, your Uncle Al. Together we studied how subatomic particles, little tiny pieces of the world we live in, could become visible to human beings. Our work was based on some of the alien microbes from Proxima Centauri B when it was colonized. This discovery would be groundbreaking work, possibly good enough for a Nobel."

Rosetta watched Mama stare into the sunset. The woman's words caught in her throat. Mama pinched the bridge of her nose, but it didn't stop the tears from leaking out around her fingers. Rosetta squeezed her hand, not sure whether she could, or should, hug the phantasm before her.

"There was a medical experiment, a very dangerous experiment, that we designed. If it worked correctly, it would temporarily let a person see particles that are normally too small for the human eye. We wanted to see the building blocks of the universe directly."

"We pitched the experiment to the University, but it was so dangerous they wouldn't allow us to run it. They were right, of course, but we were so eager, and so stupid..." The words caught in Mama's throat, but after a moment, she continued.

"Uncle Al volunteered to be our test subject, and we decided we'd try it anyway, here in the basement of our house." Rosetta tilted her head. The tablet didn't realize she was in Uncle's house. That meant Uncle must have taken the tablet out of her house. But how? The house blew up, didn't it?

Mama smiled with tears in her eyes, and brushed a stray hair away from her daughter's cheek. Twilight began to obscure the finer features of Mama's face, but her eyes shone with pride. Then they turned to anger, and she faced into the sunset once again.

"Your uncle volunteered—insisted—he would receive the treatment. It involved a lot of radiation, so he could be the only one in the room at the time. The experimental device we designed would complete the procedure, and we would stay upstairs where it was safe."

"Maybe fear got the best of him. Maybe this was his original intention. I don't know. I strapped Al into the seat myself while your father activated the program. We went upstairs, and I started to make a cup of tea, when suddenly we heard you crying in the basement. When we reached the device we found you sitting where your uncle should have been instead. You, our darling wonder, our delight! You were never meant to be involved. I dropped you off at the neighbor's house myself!" Mama's hands clenched into fists.

Rosetta suddenly remembered a walk home with Uncle. She remembered a sticky grape lollypop he'd given her as he led her to the basement. He promised her a brand new purple bunny toy if she would sit quietly in the strange chair in the basement for just a few minutes. Then there was a flash, and a horrible smell, and nothing.

"Oh, my baby. You stopped walking. You stopped talking. You're currently in the hospital, and I'm writing this by your bedside. We designed and programmed a reversal process, but you're far too small and injured for us to risk using it on you right now, and your father and I won't live long enough to see it through. The radiation we absorbed from the device when we entered the basement is eating away at us every moment. It's been two weeks since the accident and, if we're lucky, we'll live another six weeks."

Mama sighed and shook her head. "Your uncle wants to see if the experiment worked. He wants to use you to see the subatomic structure of everything around you to explore that universe. Your safety lies in his greed. You are now his greatest hope of discovery. He won't dare to let you out of his sight as long as he thinks he can get a Nobel out of it."

Mama held up the tablet that Rosetta had discovered in the basement. "We created this tablet archive for you, and coded it to your brain waves so you can learn what we know. Read it carefully. The tablet contains everything we know. It is your birthright, and once you've read it, no one can take it from you."

"We love you. We have always loved you."

The darkness obscured all but the faintest outlines of their surroundings. Rosetta launched herself at the fading image of her mother. For one blissful moment, Rosetta's mother held her tight.

When the transmission ended, Rosetta found herself hugging Molly. The cat bit Rosetta's ear, then launched herself off of the girl's shoulder and stalked away haughtily.

Rosetta laughed, cried, then dried her eyes with the hem of her tee-shirt. She felt...was it smarter? More knowledgeable? Achingly lonely.

"Message for Rosetta Walker, one of 48," the tablet in her hand said. "Begin?"

Rosetta did not hesitate. "Yes!"

Each of the "messages" contained a voyage into the past. Her mother or father explained something important about her heritage, her family, or the science that brought them together. One contained Mama's chicken dumpling recipe, which no one else in the family had been able to recreate. Another told her the story of her first pet, a turtle named Chicken. Yet another transported Rosetta to a park bench outside an ice cream shop, where her father told her the worst physics-based jokes and puns that he'd ever heard; he'd kept a collection in the lab. Some of the messages were only a few seconds; others were almost ten minutes long.

The messages weren't like classroom lessons. Instead of memorizing their contents, Rosetta absorbed them through the neural network connection, so she soon understood complex subjects as if she'd always known them. What she knew now, she'd never forget.

She did hope maybe some of the worst puns in her father's collection would fade a little over time.

Many of the four dozen messages discussed the accident. Mama explained that Uncle was planning to conceal her house using cloaking technology he "borrowed" from the government. Rosetta's father didn't approve of the cover-up, but her mother was afraid Rosetta would be sent into foster care if the truth of the matter came out.

"Maybe it's for the best," her father said, "since you'll have to use the device in our basement to reverse the damage."

"Maybe he'll change his mind," Rosetta's mother added. "Maybe everything will be okay, and you'll be able to do everything everyone else does. Maybe you'll be happy the way you are."

I mean, living with Uncle sucks, but what choice do I have? Rosetta thought. *And I'm different from everyone else, but I'm still me, I still have friends. Auntie always suggested I do the best with what I have. But if I had a choice?* Rosetta shook her head.

The second-to-last message was different from all the others. She found herself back at the park with both of her parents at her side. They were very gaunt and their skin discolored. Her mother had lost almost all her hair, and her father had a funny cough. *This must be close to when they died,* Rosetta thought. She was suddenly horrified. *Uncle did this. He killed them. He isn't a good person.*

They each took one of her hands.

"Rosetta, it's time for you to make a very dangerous decision. The last message contains the instructions for using the sub-atomic microvision device. If it works, it will restore your vision and repair the damage done to your brain," Mama said.

Papa continued. "But you absolutely must understand that using the device is extremely risky. If you're interrupted or distracted in any way, you could be injured further. You could go blind. You could experience more brain damage. You could end up like us, poisoned by the radiation. You could die."

"You don't have to do this," Papa said. "You could hide the tablet from your uncle and stay the way you are. If you're happy, if you're healthy, that's what we urge you to do." Mama nodded in agreement. Both of her parents squeezed her hands.

"This is the last gift we can give you," Mama said. "It's the gift of last resort, a dangerous, deadly gift. A gift that may end your life instead of restarting it. We are dying proof that there are no guarantees."

"Rosetta, we love you very much," Papa said. "Please don't use the device unless you have to. We'll meet you again in the next world, we promise, and we hope you'll be full of years of love and laughter on that day. We love you, little Rose."

Rosetta threw herself into her parents' arms one last time as the message faded away.

"Message for Rosetta Walker, 48 of 48," the tablet announced. "Begin?"

"I have to do it," she said, but her hands shook, belying her words. "I can't do it," she replied.

Rosetta had never really thought about dying before. Her crazy vision made everything she did exhausting, but it hadn't really been a threat to her life. This device had killed her parents. It wasn't even remotely safe. She felt as if she were holding two hand grenades and being given the choice to pull one of the pins. "I can't do it," Rosetta repeated.

Her uncle's drunken face shoved its way into her mind, demanding answers of her. He was already trying to force her down a path of his choosing. If he figured out she knew she was seeing elementary particles, she would become nothing more than a rat in his lab. He probably would get his Nobel prize.

And what would Rosetta get? The knowledge that her uncle killed her parents, and she could do nothing about it, because she couldn't even cross a sidewalk without her support pod.

But she had her support pod. She was able to do anything anyone else could do, as long as she had support. She had her friends and her family on the moon. Surely when she showed Auntie the messages she'd be able to do *something*. She could still be Rosetta and still get out from under Uncle's thumb.

And even if she did run the procedure, Rosetta realized, she'd never be "normal." She'd seen things no other human had seen. She knew more about physics than any of the kids at school, maybe even more than the teachers. She didn't have to change.

"No," she gasped, suddenly realizing she'd been holding her breath. *He did this to me. It doesn't have to define me. I'll still be me no matter what.*

"Cancel message?" the tablet asked.

"I have to do it. I have to know," she said to the tablet. "Play message," she demanded.

"Neural network activated," the machine replied. In less than a second, Rosetta knew what she needed to do.

A car rumbled overhead into the driveway next to the house. *It must be Uncle.*

Molly shot down from her perch on the stairs and raced to the odd basement door. It opened, and the half-cat disappeared inside.

Rosetta traced her way around the room until she reached the door and stepped through onto an invisible floor. Invisible dust filled her nostrils. The humming rattled her teeth, but Rosetta didn't hesitate.

She guessed correctly at the location of a light switch on a transparent wall, but the light, source unknown, illuminated a large amount of nothing visible. Rosetta snarled at the inconvenience. She followed a wall she couldn't see until she tripped over a cord she couldn't see. Rosetta gave the cord a yank, then another, until it popped out of the wall. She fell backward. A huge machine materialized as it rattled and vibrated to a halt.

"Mrrow." Molly wrapped herself around Rosetta's ankles once again. The cat's left half coalesced into place.

The room Rosetta stood in was a basement now. Thick dust obscured the floorboards. Long-neglected lights flickered in the ceiling. A few of Rosetta's toys still rested on the stair treads. It was if, after the accident, Uncle had set up the cloaking projector and then left again.

In the center of the room, a chair connected to a console, and an incredibly scary-looking robotic arm sat waiting.

"What the hell?" Uncle slammed his way through the first floor of the house.

Rosetta half-tripped, half-crawled across the open floor to the chair. Dust particles danced so wildly in the air she could barely see her way. Nausea gripped her so fiercely she was sure she was going to be sick, but fear—of her uncle, of the device—kept her moving. She grabbed the chair arm and hauled herself up into its seat, then connected the tablet to the device. "Activate process Rosetta Two," she commanded.

"Beginning phase one," the tablet announced. The room suddenly stank of hot roses and wet cat. The robot arm swung forward, so close to Rosetta's eyes face that she almost screamed. A stasis field formed around her. She couldn't blink or move her arms; she could barely breathe. Rosetta's mind flooded with memories of her childhood encounter with the device, and she panicked. Had the stasis field not held her in place, she surely would have dived from the chair and been exposed to toxic radiation.

A bright laser burned into both of her eyes from the robotic arm. It hurt worse than any pain Rosetta could imagine. When it stopped, her eyelids snapped shut. The floor jolted beneath her in a not-unfamiliar way. She opened her eyes when the feeling finally passed.

The whole universe had changed.

The cement floor was a smooth, solid surface, not a roiling mass of tiny spinning balls. The walls, the ceiling, even the chair, were impassible, the way they had always been described. "I... I've been seeing things all wrong this whole time," Rosetta said. She was baffled. "Mama was right! I've been seeing particles this whole time."

Rosetta looked around in wonder. "Everything's so solid. Why, it doesn't move at all!" She tapped her hand against the console, expecting to see the tiny balls bounce around the edges of her palm. "So that's what opaque means."

"Well, if I knew this is what everyone else saw, I probably could have answered all those doctors' questions," Rosetta grumbled in the general direction of the cat. Then she did a double-take. "Molly, you're beautiful!" Rosetta exclaimed.

"Phase one complete. Beginning phase two," the tablet announced.

Uncle's thick shoes pounded down the stairs. As the second

phase of the process began, she heard Uncle's expletive-filled tirade come to a sudden stop. *He must have seen the case,* she thought. *He knows.*

"Rosetta? Rosetta, I can explain everything," Uncle called, in the first imploring tone of voice he had ever used.

She urged the machine to run faster.

"Rosetta, come out here, I mean it!" Uncle demanded. When she did not reply a second time, he crossed the basement of the right house and keyed open the doorway to the left. Rosetta saw his eyes widen when he recognized the machine was running.

When he stepped forward, Molly launched herself off the floor and clawed her way up his chest. The whole cat used all her faculties to attack the man's face. They both howled in anger. *She's been saving that up,* Rosetta thought. *That's been a long time coming.* Uncle flung the holographic cat off his chest.

The device beeped. "Process complete," it announced. The stasis field released.

The floor stopped tumbling inside Rosetta's head. The world righted itself on its axis, shook out its skirts, and stood tall. All that had been done was now undone.

Uncle grabbed Rosetta by the right wrist and dragged her off the chair, pulling her up onto her feet. "You broken, worthless, horrible girl. You broke into my chest! You stole my secrets! Give me back those secrets!"

"You want a secret, Uncle? The universe is left-handed," she said. Her left hook smashed into the weak point of his jaw so hard she felt the joint shatter. "And so am I." He staggered to his knees.

"All this time, I thought it was an accident, but it was you! You killed my parents! You took away the life I was supposed to have! Well, you wanted me to be strong without my chair, here you go." She wrenched her right wrist out of his grip, then slammed it into his nose.

Rosetta shook out both hands. She strode across the center of the basement, surefooted and angry. She stormed up the steps and out to the front yard.

When she reached the front walk, Rosetta stopped and stared at her support pod. She had never considered the possibility of a cure, the possibility that she might not need her pod. She felt the ground shift beneath her, but not in the way it always had. Now what shifted was how people would see her, and how she saw herself.

When the shift was over, she was still Rosetta. She had changed, but at the core, she was still the same person she had been yesterday.

She turned and looked at her whole house, both halves of a twin she hadn't seen since she was a child. It was everything she remembered. Tears momentarily clouded her eyes. She wished Mama and Papa could see it.

Molly stared down from Rosetta's attic window, a complete cat. She raised her nose as if there were a question to be answered.

"Keep him in the basement," Rosetta called. "I'll be back with the police."

Rosetta squared her shoulders, walked through the gate, and headed toward the police station a few blocks over. She pulled her tablet out of her pocket and vidcalled her aunt. "Auntie? We need to talk. Well, for one thing, I have a whole cat and a whole house again," she began.

Thunderbolt Trail

by Harold R. Thompson

In addition to writing short science fiction and fantasy for both adults and young adults, Harold R. Thompson is the author of the *Empire and Honor* series of historical adventure novels, which includes *Dudley's Fusiliers*, *Guns of Sevastopol* and *Sword of the Mogul*. His latest novel, *The End of the Tether*, is a dramatization of the siege of Yorktown during the American Revolution. Thompson lives in Nova Scotia and, when not writing or spending time with his family, works for Parks Canada.

The transport truck was bullet shaped, white and sky-blue and chrome, but as an object of pure wonder it was nothing compared to what emerged from its rear cargo doors: Dad's car, a 1976 Toyota Celica GT two-door hard top, painted a gleaming metallic green with silver rocker panel stripes and steel wheels, no worse for wear after its long journey.

"Only American cars can race," said a tall man dressed in a black coat. His mouth had a sour twist, and his skin was pale to the point of sickly. I knew he must be the racer they called the Undertaker. "You should know better, Cam."

I didn't like the way he spoke to my father, and my face flushed in anger and humiliation. Maybe I took it a little hard, but I was still hypersensitive to every little perceived slight or failure.

"And you brought a kid?" the Undertaker added, giving me

nothing more than a flick of his eyes. "Isn't that a little irresponsible? He's your co-driver?"

"He's my navigator," Dad said. "He's twelve. He can handle it."

Dad's words should have given me strength, but I just shrank a bit more into myself. I wanted to say something, but I couldn't find the words. All I could think was that maybe this was a mistake after all. About eighteen months had passed since the death of my mother, and I had no confidence. I was always looking over my shoulder, waiting for the next bad thing to happen.

Dad believed in me. For my birthday that spring, he'd bought me a new map book, a brand new hard copy of the *Road Atlas of the United States*.

"Andy," he'd said, "what do you say you come with me this year?"

I knew Mom would never have approved. She'd have said I was too young to understand the issues and the consequences, but I thought I did and had always wanted to go.

Now, facing the dreaded Undertaker, I was sure I'd just let my father down by my very presence. We were about to be turned away. I gazed around at our surroundings, trying to take it all in before we had to head back home-the row of other electric trucks, the green meadows and distant forest that made this remote farm, just west of Bar Harbor, Maine, the perfect place to plan a secret subversion that I so desperately wanted to be a part of, to prove that I could be useful.

The Undertaker gave me his best stink look.

"It doesn't matter if he can handle it or not," he said, still not talking to me. "The rules say only American cars."

"This isn't about rules," said Dad. "It's about freedom."

Something about the way Dad said that gave me a little boost. At that moment, another car rolled up, going slowly, its engine a low rumble. It was a 1972 Dodge Challenger, painted a sparkling blue. I knew my cars.

The Dodge stopped. The driver's door opened and the driver got out, a woman who seemed a little older than Mom would have been. Her hair was a halo of orange frizz, and she wore blue jeans, a denim shirt and a pink neckerchief.

"Sign him up, Undertaker," she said.

The Undertaker glared at her.

"We agreed only American cars!"

The woman put her hands on her hips.

"It doesn't matter, and we need as many racers as we can get. Gasoline automobiles built this country, they were its lifeblood for over a century, and we're tired of being treated like criminals because we have an enthusiasm. Yes, even Toyota drivers. This is about freedom, like Cam says, so sign him up!"

The Undertaker sighed.

"You're the boss," he said, and he reached into a black briefcase thing he had dangling from one shoulder. From it he took a way-finder, a tiny tablet computer that contained information about all of the checkpoints and fuel dumps.

"Thanks, Misty," Dad said to the woman.

The Undertaker turned on his heels and I watched his receding back, a bit stunned that we'd made it in after all.

"Is that the guy you beat last time?" I asked Dad.

Dad smiled. "Yes."

"He's one of the bad guys," I said.

Dad placed one warm hand on my back.

"Things aren't always what they seem," he said. "He can take things too seriously sometimes, but he's one of us."

I'd watched Dad rebuild that Celica for over a year, turning a rusted hulk he'd found in a field into a shining, roaring piece of the past come to life. The project gave him, and me, something to think about after losing Mom. I wasn't so nervous when I was in the garage, just sitting there as my father worked, usually poring over one of my maps, my latest obsession, wondering about all the places we could go when that car was finally ready.

Dad had talked as he worked, telling me story after story.

"They called him the Thunderbolt," he said. "He was the first person after the ban to make the run across the country. Did the same run for five years in a row and never got caught. He was a legend, identified only by the golden lightning bolt on his helmet."

I loved that story in the same way that I loved old cars. The story was a legend, something bigger than the mean and rule-bound society that had created the ban, the total prohibition of gasoline and any vehicle that used it. The ban had started in Europe in the early '20s and then had spread to North America. By then most people were driving electrics, and the auto-car was poised to take over, so there was little public protest. Vintage cars were still permitted under the new law, but only if their internal guts were replaced by electric conversions.

To put an electric motor in a Mustang or a Corvette or a Charger or a Camaro, even less in a Ferrari or a Lamborghini or a Jaguar, made no sense to me.

"The race is named for Thunderbolt," Dad's story continued. "The Thunderbolt Trail. It goes from a secret location on the east coast to another secret location on the west coast. It's a celebration of these old cars, but also a protest. When there were millions of gasoline automobiles, they created a massive environmental problem, but we think that banning them outright was an overreaction. We haven't banned steam engines or wood fires, and that's because there's not enough of them to have any real impact anymore. The same is true for gasoline cars."

Mom had thought the ban was wrong, too, but also that the race was silly and too dangerous. Anyone caught by the TRD, the Traffic Regulatory Division (or Tread), would receive a hefty fine and would lose their car. The car would then be destroyed. Not put in a museum, but destroyed.

I'd always thought that was horrible, downright evil, and that the unjust ban needed to be opposed. I thought Dad was a hero for doing so, like a storybook pirate—the good kind—or Robin Hood.

"Whatever happened to Thunderbolt?" I asked.

"No one knows," Dad had said. "Some say he's still out there." And he'd winked.

I stood close to Dad as all of the drive teams gathered in the farmyard. Everyone there had smuggled their cars to this place in the transport trucks. There were forty-six teams. Many of the drivers wore funny costumes, and some of the cars were based on famous Hollywood vehicles. One team in white coveralls was driving a Dodge Challenger like Misty's, though older and painted white.

"Ever see the old movie *Vanishing Point?*" one of the drivers had asked me as I admired the car. I shook my head, and the man shrugged, adding, "This is just like the car in that movie."

There were also two men in a rainbow-striped Corvette dressed as superheroes in pink capes. A pair of cowgirls drove a dark red Chevy Camaro. The Undertaker wore a black top hat and drove a black 2024 Ford Mustang with an eight-hundred horse-power V8 that dwarfed our Celica's modified one-fifty horse-power in-line four-cylinder. The power of that engine made me a little upset.

"This race isn't just about speed," my father said reassuringly. "It's about the route you pick and how you avoid obstacles. That makes your job really important. You have your maps?"

I nodded.

"We're doing this old school," Dad said, grinning. He'd insist-ed that GPS was not as good as a paper map in the hands of a good navigator, that it got things wrong, and that the TRD could use it to track us if they knew where to look.

Dad had also given me full control over deciding our route, but suddenly I was terrified that I'd screw the whole thing up. I stood there, the adults towering around me, and held my new map book in tight fingers. A teenage girl appeared with a tray of tiny glasses of water. She was handing them out to everyone, and when I took mine I saw that my hand was shaking.

Misty stood on a wooden box in the middle of the gathering and raised her glass in a toast.

"To internal combustion," she said, "power and speed."

That gave me shivers, and I raised my glass with the others. I really was a part of this. I had to just give up that fear if I could, or just push through it.

We sipped our water.

"Come on," said Dad.

We ran to the car, jumped in, fastened our safety belts and donned our disruptor hoods. The hoods were made of mesh and were designed to prevent TRD drones from being able to identify our faces. Most of the drivers didn't bother with them, but my dad insisted. I didn't mind, because it made me feel like an outlaw.

I opened my map book. I'd already plotted a course.

"Head out and turn left," I said, annoyed at the quaver in my voice.

The cars were leaving the farm one by one. As they passed the laser beam set up at the farm exit, their start time was recorded. The best time would win.

The car ahead of us exited the farm, its tires spitting gravel as it too turned left, the driver gunning the engine. Then it was our turn.

We passed the laser and were in the race.

My heart was pounding the entire way from Bar Harbor to

Interstate 95. All the cars were packed together in a clump, tearing up the snaky tangle of secondary roads. We were going faster than I'd ever seen Dad drive before. Most vehicles on the highways were automated, and there was no longer a posted speed limit, so there was no longer any such thing as speeding. I was still a little scared, but that first part of the ride was a real thrill. I felt the nervousness start to subside.

After a while the cars started to disappear, one by one, as the navigators chose their own routes to the first checkpoint. I'd decided to stick to the main highways, and Dad didn't object, didn't second-guess me at all. We tore straight down old 95. Beyond Saratoga Springs, we came to Interstate 90, where Dad zipped from lane to lane, passing one funny little pastel auto-car after another. I caught a few glimpses of passengers gaping from windows, and some held up their phones and took pictures. I waved. I was part of something special.

"Maybe the Tread won't see us?" I said.

Dad shrugged. "Sometimes we fool them and they don't."

Our first checkpoint turned out to be an underground parking garage just outside Syracuse. I counted fifteen cars already there when we arrived, and that made me a little agitated. One was the Undertaker's; he glared from his window as he pulled away.

The fuel dump was really a gas pump hidden behind a concrete wall. Dad filled the Celica's little tank.

"Good job getting us here," he said as he jumped back in the car.

"In sixteenth place," I groused.

"We're doing fine, Andy. That puts us in the top third."

I realized this was true.

"So where to now?" Dad said.

I checked the way-finder. "The next checkpoint's in Ohio. I guess we should just stay on the Ninety."

"You're the navigator," Dad said.

West of Cleveland, the interstate was filled with racers. There was Misty's blue Challenger, two older model Mustangs, and a red and white 1973 Dodge Charger.

That was when the TRD finally took notice.

I spotted a pair of eye-drones to the right of the highway, keeping pace with our little green Celica. Looking behind us, I saw even more, a cloud of about a dozen quadcopters closing in, flying low.

"Drones, Dad!"

For some reason I wasn't afraid. We were barrelling along so fast and had come so far, I was riding on a kind of high, a peak of excitement, a sense of confidence I hadn't felt in a long time. And I trusted my father.

"Watch this," said Dad.

He depressed the accelerator. The drones fell far behind.

"Yeah, Dad!" I cheered.

A car roared by on our left, a black Mustang. The Undertaker. I think my mouth fell open in dismay, but Dad seemed unperturbed.

"The fact that he had to pass us," he said, "means that he was behind us. That means you must have picked a better route than he did!"

I felt satisfaction at that and, for the first time since the whole adventure had begun, I started to actually believe in myself.

But the Undertaker was still in front of us.

After a while, Dad eased off the gas, and I saw the speedometer drop to eighty miles an hour from about one hundred and twenty. I was about to shout out, to tell Dad to keep going, but one look through the windshield stopped me.

"There's something ahead," I said.

"Sharp eyes," said Dad.

The thing grew larger, wide and white across the road. Around us, all of the autocars on the road were pulling over and stopping; their passengers had no control. It was the TRD. People were getting out of their autocars and just staring.

"Inflatable barricade," Dad said, and I finally understood what I was seeing, a massive white balloon stretching across and overlapping the sides of the highway. The TRD was trying to stop the race. They could have put up a hard barrier, concrete or steel, or they could have laid down caltrops or spiked chains to puncture the racers' tires, but all that would have been unsafe, and the TRD was concerned with public safety. So instead they'd blocked the road with a massive air pillow.

Dad pulled to the side of the road while I buried my nose in the map, looking for an alternative route. I was starting to panic. There was nothing, no exits nearby. Our only hope was to turn around and go back, maybe dip south.

Misty's Challenger roared past. I saw Misty in the driver's seat, giving us a thumbs up. She was driving straight for the barricade.

"She won't make it," Dad said.

I just watched, not comprehending. Most of the racers were slowing down like us, but Misty charged ahead at full speed. When her car struck the barricade, it seemed to disappear, buried in the white folds. I heard a great tearing and booming, and the entire barricade suddenly shrank in upon itself. The huge balloon may have been tough enough to stop a little electric, but not a 1972 Dodge Challenger with a modified V8.

Dad eased the Celica forward. The barricade has deflated and lay in shreds across the pavement. Dad took it easy, driving slowly as we crossed the mess. Misty's car had stopped, and was tangled in bits of composite fabric, lying on its side. Misty was sitting on it.

She gave me another thumbs up.

"Sacrifice," I said, at last seeing what she'd done.

Dad floored it on the open road beyond.

After that, I decided to stay off the main roads. I had fun choosing the route west, buoyed by our escape.

Dad kept driving as night fell. I watched news clips on my phone, trying to find out what was going on and discovering that several other racers, those on different routes, had been caught in inflatable barricades.

"Too bad," Dad said, "but at least media have noticed us."

After that my eyes became heavy, and I slept.

In the morning, I woke to see my father grinning at me. He still seemed fresh. He'd been driving for a full day now, relying on energy drinks and snacks, but he seemed to be doing fine.

I took a peanut butter sandwich from our cooler and had it for breakfast.

The next checkpoint was a farm just outside Little River, Kansas, and there the way-finder revealed the finish line: a botanical garden just south of Fort Bragg, California. Dad drove at a steady eighty-five miles an hour. The narrow roads through Utah and Nevada took us past wide-open dusty spaces and snow-capped peaks then through the dark majesty of Tahoe National Forest. Labels and lines from my map book came to life around me.

For a while we needed to return to the interstate, even though I didn't want to, but there was no other way through. I spied a few more drones, but the TRD didn't show itself in force.

"They're planning something," Dad said.

This gave me a sudden burst of nerves. We'd come this close. Only a few more hours!

We reached California, and as we roared through the little towns, I noticed people on the side of the road. They'd come out to see us. Some waved and shouted.

"There's only one route to the finish line," I told Dad, and that was worrisome. The route was a narrow paved road through Jackson State Forest. When we reached it, the remaining racers seemed to appear from nowhere, and suddenly it was like those first moments in Maine, with everyone driving in a great seething column. I saw who was still with us, the cowgirls and the rainbow superheroes, and there was the white Challenger, but it was the Undertaker's Mustang in the lead.

Dad stayed over to the right of the road and, though he was keeping pace, he wasn't trying to pass. I knew this wasn't good enough.

"He's going to win!" I said.

Dad shook his head. "We're all too close, and it's not safe. Just hang on."

I peered ahead, my nerves on fire again. I think I saw the barricade before my father did. It was another massive white inflatable, but in front, there were dark lines across the pavement. The TRD was using spikes after all.

All of the drivers must have seen it, but no one slowed.

I looked at my map. There had to be a way out of this. Then I saw it: a little dotted line, connecting to another, branching off from this route. A dirt side road. I knew we hadn't passed it yet. I wasn't sure where it went, but it was our only chance.

"Take the next right, Dad!" I shouted. "Right up there!"

"I see it," Dad said.

Because we were already on the shoulder, we didn't have to cross in front of anyone. Dad took a hard right, and we were roaring through choking dust.

The rest of the cars continued toward the TRD obstacle.

I followed the dotted lines in my map book. There were a bunch of side roads here. We took another left, and my heart leapt into my mouth. This road linked up with the main route.

We hit asphalt and found that we'd bypassed the barricade.

Cheers rose up from all sides, making my hair stand on end. The road was now lined with people, some cheering and others protesting. I saw a sign that said "No Dirty Engines" and another that said "From Sea to Shining Sea."

My map showed a green square ahead. The botanical gardens and the finish line.

Dad pulled the Celica into the garden gate. A crowd of people were following on foot. There was no way to keep this location secret now.

Dad came to a stop in the parking lot. There were race officials waiting there to meet us. One was Misty.

"I flew the rest of the way last night," she said after rushing to the window. Dad pushed open his door and got out. Misty threw her arms around him. "We haven't checked your time yet, but there's no doubt that you're the winner. You won!"

I was out on the pavement and jumping up and down as the people cheered, even though I saw the drones overhead, just hovering. I pulled off my disruptor hood. I was just a kid, after all. I waved to the crowd.

We'd won, thanks to my map reading and a bit of luck. I knew then that I could do anything. I imagined my mother's presence, smiling down on me, her pride greater than her concern.

The Undertaker pulled into the lot, and the crowd parted. We turned to face him. There was a huge dent in the right front fender of the Mustang.

The Undertaker got out. He stared at Dad for a few seconds, wearing that sour frown.

"I have reinforced tires to avoid punctures," the Undertaker said. "I was the only one to get through the barricade, but it took me a few attempts."

He held out his hand. Dad shook it. They looked each other in the eye.

I knew then that Dad had been right. The Undertaker was one of us.

"We have to go," the Undertaker added. "The TRD are right behind me."

Dad pointed to the Celica. I turned and looked, and I think I cried out in astonishment.

Both rear tires were flat. Somehow I hadn't noticed.

"Hit something on that dirt road," Dad said. "There were probably caltrops across its entrance. No reinforced tires here. We're stuck."

Everyone had gone, fled, the Undertaker included. Dad and I leaned against the car and waited.

"That was quite a ride, wasn't it?" Dad said. He was calm as always, but I couldn't speak. All my triumph of a few minutes ago was gone. I felt like somehow I'd failed, that the route I'd picked had been flawed. I'd let Dad down after all. And now I could hear Mom's voice telling us how dumb this race was, and now look what had happened, and I felt like I'd let her down too.

Tears started to pour down my cheeks. I couldn't help it.

I felt Dad's hand on my back.

"You did it, Andy," he murmured. "You played your part, and it was a success. Now I'm going to play my part. I won't let you down."

I didn't know what he meant. Drones were everywhere, and a blue transport truck with TRD markings had entered the parking lot, lining up with the Toyota. A TRD official in a blue uniform got out and approached. He was an older man with white eyebrows.

"Follow your car inside, please," he said.

There was a heaviness in my stomach, and my limbs were like lead, but Dad kept his hand on my back and guided me forward as the Celica was hoisted into the back of the truck. Other TRD officials were there, and they started busying themselves around the car. Taking it apart, I thought. Destroying it already.

I felt the transport begin to move.

"Well, now," the older TRD man said. "You think this is how you gain sympathy for your cause? Through this dangerous and irresponsible race?"

Dad just smiled.

"Maybe," he said. "I think we piqued public interest. Maybe they'll start to see that it isn't really about cars, that it's much bigger than that. And I'm happy to say that we won the race."

The TRD man chuckled. "Yes, and I'm here to give you your prize."

He went to a shelf and took down a helmet. He held the helmet under his arm. On the front of the helmet was a golden lightning bolt.

I stared. Sparks were exploding in my head. Things weren't what they'd seemed.

With his other hand, the man opened the front door of the Celica.

I looked at the car. The TRD men hadn't started to take it apart. They'd changed the flat tires.

I started to laugh. Mom was smiling again. Dad winked.

"In you go!" said Thunderbolt.

We pulled on our safety belts. Dad revved the engine. The back of the transport truck opened and I saw that we were back in the state forest. The road stretched away into the tunnel of massive trees. My heart was soaring.

Dad backed out, spun the car, and hit the gas.

A Meal for Dragons

by L.G. Keltner

L.G. Keltner fell in love with reading and decided she wanted to be a science fiction writer at age six. She holds a bachelor's degree in writing from Drake University. Her short stories have appeared in several anthologies, including the *2018 Young Explorer's Adventure Guide*. She also writes novels and hopes to see them published someday. L.G. lives in Iowa with her husband and three children. When not writing, she enjoys amateur astronomy and playing trivia games.

My name is Ryssa, and I've got a story to tell. It has spaceships and dragons in it, if that helps. It sounds impossible, but if there's one thing I've learned, it's that fantastical stories lurk around every corner, and some of them are true.

I spent the first eleven years of my life living on *Mother Ship 3*. It's one of seven ships that departed Earth centuries ago. They all set out in their own directions with the goal of finding suitable planets and setting up colonies on them. Each ship went from planet to planet, dropping off colonists before continuing onward.

Until one standard Earth year ago, I'd never left *Mother Ship 3*, and neither had my parents.

When I was little, my friends and I wove stories about what might have happened to Earth since we'd left it. Sometimes we decided it exploded. Sometimes our sun swelled and burned it to a crisp. My dad said an environmental disaster made it impossible to live there anymore, though he didn't know much about it. Details fade, he said. People forget things, and stories change. Those stories are all I have of Earth. They're all any of us have.

Teachers told us tales of the men and women who first set off in our fine ship and some of the planets we'd colonized along the way. Those tales sounded like grand, sweeping adventures to my young ears. The best part, though, was that they were real, and since my family was chosen to be part of the next colonization wave, I found joy in imagining the adventures awaiting us.

I spent a lot of time imagining what Earth was like and wondering how it felt to walk on any planet. During my long walks down familiar hallways, I pretended they were passages taking me to distant lands. There was so much to explore, after all, even on our own ship. Compared to outer space, *Mother Ship 3* is tiny, but for the millions of people living on it, it's enormous. In my years living there, I only ever saw a small portion of it.

I wanted to see all of it, but there were rules about where I could and could not go. Of the parts I did see, some were shiny and lit up as if brand new. The science section had to be kept in perfect working order, as did the bridge where the captain and navigation officer worked. Other sections were dingy, with peeling paint and faulty wiring. These sections were often considered hazardous, but people still lived there. People could go there, but most chose not to. I wasn't allowed to go there alone.

There was one place on the ship that would always be off limits to me and most of the others I knew.

We all talked about the living quarters where the richest people on the ship lived. Tales of golden tile floors and beautiful fountains filled with colorful animals fueled my imagination. I wanted to see all these things, and I didn't understand why we weren't allowed to go there and have a look.

I was seven when I asked my mom about it, and she gave me the same look she always did when she didn't want to answer. She sat beside me on our narrow gray sofa and folded her hands in her lap. "People want to feel safe, and sometimes they feel safest when they can control who comes into the places where they live."

Maybe that made sense to my mother, but it confused me. "Why?"

She grew visibly more uncomfortable. "They might be worried that someone will try to steal from them, or maybe hurt them."

"I won't do that!" I cried.

"I know that, sweetheart." Mom patted my hand. "A lot of people fear things that seem different from them. I don't feel that way, but I'm an explorer. It would be silly for an explorer to feel that way, now wouldn't it?"

My mom had applied to be in the next batch of colonists when she turned sixteen. My father too.

I nodded. "That wouldn't make any sense."

"Exactly." Mom ran her hand through her short dark hair and sighed. "Maybe we'll never see some of the fancier parts of this ship, but we do have one thing to be excited about."

I leaned toward her, eager to hear what she had to say. "What's that?"

"You remember the planet I told you about? Prosperos?"

There was no way I could have forgotten. The planet Prosperos was discovered by long-range scans a few years before I was born. Some of my earliest memories involved stories of this new and unknown world.

"We're going to explore it and make sure it's safe before the other colonists get sent down," Mom told me.

"That sounds dangerous," I said thoughtfully. I didn't know what to think about that.

"Yes, but it's part of our job. Someone needs to do it." Then she leaned close and whispered, like she was letting me in on a big secret. "That also means that we get to see this new world before everyone else. Isn't that exciting?"

A big grin spread across my face. "Yes!"

I had a lot of ideas about what our first few months on Prosperos would be like, but none of them came close to reality. Instead of trekking through uncharted forests alongside our parents, my siblings and I spent most of our time in our family dwelling. As the oldest, it often fell to me to keep the others in line while Mom and Dad got to do far more exciting things. I didn't feel like much of an explorer most days.

When we finally got our chance at an adventure, it started with me making a terrible decision. I knew telling my little sister Maree she could roller-skate indoors wasn't a good idea, but she wore me down with her begging and tugging at my leg.

"Fine!" I yelled. "You can skate for ten minutes. Mom will be back soon, so you have to be out of those skates before she gets here." Mom went to tow in a supply pod that had been dropped that morning, and she'd already been out for an hour. My plan seemed simple. Let her skate and get bored with it like she always did, then distract her with coloring books. I didn't account for her obsession with the seed room and the amount of damage such a little girl on wheels could do.

When Maree careened into the room and plowed into Mom's stack of seed containers, my heart jumped into my throat. The tops popped off three of them, sending their contents high into the air. The sound of them hitting the floor mimicked that of a moderate rain storm. They bounced and rolled into all corners of the room.

"Maree!" I cried as I surveyed the damage.

She'd come to a stop, her little hands gripping the edge of Mom's workstation. Her eyes were wide, her mouth open in an

O. Then tears sprang to her eyes, her face crumpling.

Normally I'd be more worried about making my sister cry, but I knew exactly how angry our parents would be when they found out about this. Being part of the first wave to settle on this new world was a big deal. We had to help get everything ready for the people who would follow us. It was a big responsibility.

So, there I was. Maree was crying, seeds were everywhere, and Mom could get back at any time.

Solution: desperately try to re-sort thousands of seeds in the hope that Mom's trip out would take *way* longer than expected.

That was tricky enough, but I still had to keep an eye on Maree in the process.

"Maree, don't play with that!" I called over my shoulder as she reached for one of Mom's trowels.

"I'm bored!" Maree stuck out her lower lip in a dramatic pout. I should have been grateful her tears dried up so quickly, but I felt annoyed she'd ignored the toys I gathered for her and went instead for something she wasn't supposed to have.

Ugh!

"Jacob, get in here!" I shouted.

A loud groan was followed by the sound of heavy footsteps. My younger brother trudged into the room and stopped beside me. "What do you want?"

"Have you changed your mind about helping me sort these seeds?" I asked.

"Nope."

This didn't surprise me. He'd happily help our parents, but he enjoyed tormenting me. "Then tell Maree a story to keep her entertained. You can do that, can't you?"

The grin that spread across his face should have warned me what was coming. Instead I was too preoccupied to give it any thought.

"Did you know the sun is going to disappear today? In the middle of the day." His voice dripped with amusement.

"Where is the sun going?" Maree asked.

Jacob leaned close. "A giant space dragon is eating it," he whispered menacingly.

Her brown eyes grew wide. "We need the sun!"

"The dragon needs to eat," he said with a shrug. "Don't worry, though. He'll probably choke on it and puke it back up."

"Ew!" Maree leaned closer. "Then what?"

"Well, let's hope he doesn't puke on us, because that would be nasty. Then he'll realize he's still hungry and come looking for something else to eat. I've heard he enjoys annoying little sisters."

She gasped.

I whipped around and jabbed a finger at Jacob's chest. "Don't scare her. It's just an eclipse. How happy do you think Mom and Dad will be if she can't sleep tonight?"

He grinned. "Be honest, Ryssa. You want me to stop because my story was scaring you too."

I snorted. "No. I want you to stop because you're gross, and your voice is irritating."

He stuck his tongue out at me.

I turned back to my impossible task. I must have sorted hundreds of seeds back into their containers, but the state of the room made it appear as though I'd done nothing at all. I felt defeated.

Jacob kept talking about the dragon in a hushed tone. "His scales protect him from guns and lasers, so he can't be killed. Nothing can stop him from eating his fill of anyone and anything that gets in his way. Maybe he'll decide eating the sun isn't enough and turn around to take a bite out of the planet."

Maree clapped her hand over her mouth to stifle another gasp. "The dragon! Mom and Dad are out there! When is the dragon coming?"

"Soon," Jacob said menacingly, curling his fingers to look like claws. He snarled. "It's already on its way here."

"Jacob!" I was tempted to lob a handful of seeds at him, but that would've only made my life harder. "Stop scaring her!" I turned to Maree. "There's just going to be an eclipse. It'll last about half an hour. That's it. The sun will come back. I promise."

I've heard about solar eclipses that happened on Earth. Those were caused by Earth's moon. This eclipse was going to be caused by *Mother Ship 3*. Dad told me it needed to park above us to do some important scans.

At that moment, I didn't care about *Mother Ship 3* or anything other than getting through an afternoon filled with seeds. It was getting beyond frustrating that I was dealing with all the sorting by myself while Jacob was only trying to make things worse. When Jacob launched back into his story of flying terror and sharp teeth, I reached my breaking point.

I stopped my work and looked him in the eye. "If you don't stop terrorizing our sister and help me sort these seeds now, I'll tell Dad you were the one who ate his stash of cookies."

Cookies are rare since they aren't a high-priority item. *Mother Ship 3* could only send a few small luxuries. Desserts, delicious as they might be, are not vital to our mission. Those that do get sent down are prized, and when they disappear unexpectedly, it is bad for morale. That's what Dad said when he confronted all us kids about it later.

Jacob glared at me, and for a moment, I thought he might be stubborn about it just to bug me. Then his shoulders slumped, and he stooped down to scoop up a handful of seeds. He made a great show of plonking them down on the work bench but started sorting without another word.

I smiled to myself, relishing my small victory. I still didn't think we stood a chance of finishing the cleanup in time, but I figured Mom would be less likely to give us a mountain of extra chores if only a small spill remained as opposed to a massive one.

I don't know how much time passed before I looked up from my work again. I only remember not seeing Maree in the corner. "Where'd she go?"

Jacob looked up from his task. "I think she went to get a juice pack."

That made me feel better. She was probably sitting at the kitchen table, drinking her juice, and she'd come back when she was finished.

I took a pile of large purple seeds that smelled like sweaty feet and dumped it into its bin. Mom had it labeled with a super-long name I had no idea how to say. Scientists like to use big, long names for everything.

Another ten minutes elapsed before I started to worry. Maree really should have been done with her drink by then, and I started thinking about all the different ways she could have gotten herself into trouble.

"I'll be right back. Keep working," I said to Jacob.

He grumbled but didn't argue.

I hurried across our little dwelling and skidded into the kitchen. The table was empty.

It's okay, I thought. *Maybe she finished her juice and needed to go to the bathroom.*

Our bathroom was tiny, just big enough for a toilet, sink, and a narrow shower. Maree wasn't there.

Then I ran to the bedroom I shared with my siblings. My single bed sat in one corner of the room, and the bunk bed Jacob and Maree used sat across from it. Toys were scattered across our green rug. Maree would play there for hours, pretending her dolls and dinosaurs were engaged in an epic battle.

She wasn't there either.

My stomach began to turn. Where else could she be? I quickly searched the remaining rooms and hoped she'd jump out, laughing about how she'd managed to scare me.

No such luck.

That's when I remembered her fear and curiosity in response to Jacob's story about the space dragon. I bolted for the door, knowing both these feelings could lead people to do stupid things.

The front door was closed. I opened it and stepped out into the early afternoon. A few small clouds dotted the soft violet sky, the sun still shining at full strength.

"Maree!" I called. "Maree, are you out here?"

I didn't expect a reply, and I didn't get one. I scrutinized the area. Our yard had a row of giant blue ferns with leaves almost as big as me, as well as squat little bushes with yellow flowers that glowed at night. There were plenty of places she could be hiding, but I doubted she was. If she was worried about Mom and Dad, she would've already made it farther than that. I just wished I knew which way she might've gone.

I tried shouting for her one more time. "Maree! Get back here now, and you won't get in trouble!"

Jacob poked his head outside a few seconds later. At least my yelling got someone's attention. "What is it?" he asked.

I whirled around to face him. My fear quickly turned to fury. "Maree's gone, and it's your fault!"

His mouth dropped open in disbelief. "What? How is it my fault?"

"You scared her with that ridiculous story about space dragons, that's why! Now she probably thinks Mom and Dad are in danger and went to find them." I couldn't think of any other reason she would have suddenly left alone. She knew better than that.

The color drained from Jacob's face as he let the door close behind him. "How was I supposed to know? At worst I thought she might go hide under the bed. Did you check there?"

I nodded.

He looked helpless, his eyes wide as he gazed off into the distance. "How are we going to figure out which way she went?"

That was a good question. We had an idea of what she wanted to do, but she was also five. Would she even know which direction she needed to go to find either of our parents? I doubted it.

"Hopefully she left some fresh footprints," I said. "Either way, we need to hurry. Let's grab some stuff and go."

Jacob and I raided the supply shed that stood beside our home. My thoughts were full of terrible images as we gathered what we might need, and I felt a little sick. The animals on Prosperos tended to be big and weren't used to humans yet. All kinds of predators lived out there, and I shuddered as I thought about little Maree encountering one of them.

I dug out a flat black disc I recognized as a camouflage unit. It was supposed to project a hologram around the person using it, making them blend in with their surroundings. I tried to start it, only to realize the battery was dead. With a sigh, I tossed the useless device back into the drawer. In the end, I settled on grabbing a handful of little balls that would flash in multiple colors when activated. During one trip outside our little abode, I saw Dad use them to distract a group of little orange animals long enough to get to a piece of equipment he needed.

Jacob approached me with a couple of super-bright flashlights and a can of stinky spray. We weren't supposed to get any on our bare skin, but spraying it in a predator's face was supposed to drive them away. This was all we had access to, so we needed to make the best of it.

"Okay," I said. "We'd better get going if we want to catch her."

Jacob hesitated for a second. "What about Dad? Or Mom? Shouldn't we call them?"

I'd already considered this. We had a com unit in the kitchen.

We were supposed to use it to call in situations like this one, but I couldn't do it. They'd have told us to wait for them to come back, and that would've wasted valuable time. However, not letting them know at all would've been irresponsible. "We'll send them a message and let them know what's happening. Then we'll go. We can't afford to wait until they get back to us."

I was being reckless, but I didn't care. Maree needed our help.

The message we sent was brief.

Maree wandered off. We went to look for her. Sorry.

When we stepped outside again, I glanced at the sun. It was a bad idea, of course. Looking directly at a star for too long can burn your eyes so bad you go blind. The fraction of a second I did look told me that the eclipse hadn't started yet. It was weird, knowing that this massive ship was somewhere up there, but we couldn't see it.

I looked back down at the ground, trying to ignore the little spots swimming in my vision. As they cleared, I noticed little footprints pressed into the red dirt. They led away from the door. "Here," I said, pointing.

Jacob nodded as we set out to follow them. We walked through an invisible fence designed to let only humans in or out of our yard. The farther we walked, the closer together various plants grew. Soon the vegetation was so thick we could barely see Maree's footprints. We moved slowly, gently pushing thin yellow grasses and bluish-purple leaves aside with our toes so we could follow her trail.

After several minutes of walking, Jacob grabbed my arm. "What's that?" he asked. He pointed to three round purple things. I bent over for a closer look and immediately smelled them. They were the seeds that reeked of smelly feet. That same odor still coated my hands.

"Maree must have had some seeds stuck to her clothes or something," I said.

We walked and walked, picking our way through bushes filled

with buzzing creatures with bright red wings and weaving past trees at least two hundred feet tall. She must have been moving fast to have gone as far as she had, and I worried about whether we'd be able to catch up with her.

Jacob's face was pinched with worry, and I would have bet he was thinking the same thing. "We can't be too far away from her," I told him, hoping to reassure us both.

When the tracks led us to a dense patch of giant ferns, I paused. They grew so near to one another I didn't know how we were going to make it through them. Except we had to.

Once we started to push our way through the ferns, the sharp edges of the leaves jabbing at us from every direction, Maree's footprints disappeared. At first, I thought the ground was harder there, but it didn't feel that way beneath my feet. Then I assumed shadows were making it harder to see her path.

I pushed onward, though it felt hopeless. If we couldn't see which way she'd gone, how would we ever find her?

"Look!" Jacob shouted, barging in front of me to tap at something with his foot.

A line of the purple seeds.

"She's always been the messy one," I said, this time grateful for Maree's untidy tendencies.

We kept going that way, though it wasn't easy. We stopped several times and used our flashlights to find the next grouping of seeds. We were so consumed with looking for Maree's trail that I forgot entirely about the eclipse. It became apparent something was changing when the scattered seeds got harder to see. Then it got harder to see anything else.

I looked up at the small patch of sky visible above me. The last of the sunlight was fading fast.

"*Mother Ship 3*," I whispered.

The sun had been almost directly above us the last time I looked. It was gone then, a thin halo of shimmering light surrounding the hull of the ship we once called home. Stars hovered in the sky around it, and my breath caught in my throat. For a moment, I almost forgot the reason we were out there. Then the wind howled around us, and the whole world seemed to sway as the ferns came alive.

Jacob cast me a look I could barely see in the darkness, but it was enough to get us both moving again. He forged on ahead of me as we continued onward.

Another gust of wind, much stronger than the others, sent the ferns crashing into each other. Thousands of ferns colliding caused an eerie sound to ring in my ears. I lost sight of Jacob as the colossal blue leaves swallowed him whole.

"Jacob!" I barely heard my own voice as the wind swirled around me.

Don't panic, I told myself. *He's not far away. I'll find him soon, and we'll find Maree before anything bad happens to her. All of us are going to be fine.*

My heart raced as I pushed forward. I didn't waste my energy on screaming. Jacob wouldn't be able to hear me no matter how loudly I shouted, and there might be frightened animals nearby with better hearing that could use my voice to locate me. I didn't want to take that risk.

I kept walking, shoving the heavy plants to the side as I went. Beads of sweat burst out of my skin, running down my face and arms.

How did Maree push her way through this? Did she make it out again? Or is she lost in here? Then I thought of the lack of footprints we'd wondered about earlier. *Or maybe she crawled through.*

The trunks of these ferns were quite far apart. They had to be if the plants had a chance of growing to full size. A little girl like Maree might've had some luck getting through that way.

I'm bigger than Maree, but I might be able to do that too.

I dropped to my knees and held my flashlight out in front of me. I sighed in relief when the beam spread out wide, highlighting dirt and dozens of blue trunks. I crawled. It was often a tight squeeze, my shoulders scraping painfully against the ferns, but it was much faster to move that way.

Something soon caught my eye. I swung the light around to get a better look. Feet. Those were definitely feet clad in brown shoes. Jacob!

He wasn't moving anymore. I was grateful for that at first, because I was going to catch him more easily. Then, as I neared his position, worry began gnawing at the pit of my stomach. *Why did he stop? Is he waiting for me to find him, or is he in trouble?*

When I was close enough, I reached out and wrapped my fingers around his ankle. He jumped at the touch. Then he started kicking at me with his other foot.

I let go when pain flared in my hand. "Jacob, it's me!" My voice still didn't sound all that loud compared to everything else, but he was also aiming his light downward to see what grabbed him.

He dropped to his knees, the joy of seeing me again clear on his face. "There you are!"

We stayed there a moment to catch our breath. Now that I'd stopped moving, I was noticing things. Little cuts covered my arms, face, and legs. Only a few of them were deep enough to bleed, but all of them burned from the sweat that kept coming. I knew I'd look terrible once daylight returned. Jacob didn't look any better.

"Come on," I said, close enough to his ear for him to understand me. "Let's get out of here."

We crawled on until the fern forest thinned out again. It couldn't have been all that long, but it felt like forever. I allowed myself a little smile once we were able to walk normally again. Another couple of minutes passed before we reached a wide clearing we'd never seen before. The clearing was filled with thick, wiry blades of grass that would appear purple with bright red tips in full view of the sun, but in the muted light, they looked like mangled, shadowy claws. Maree stood in the middle of them, her head barely hovering above it all.

The wind had calmed, gusting just enough to ruffle my tangled hair. I regretted not tying it back before we left. "Maree!"

She turned in our direction.

Jacob and I hurtled through the gnarled grass to get to her. My legs ached, and the rough grasses scraped against my irritated skin, but seeing Maree gave me the strength to keep going.

When I reached her, I grabbed her shoulders. The happiness I felt in seeing her again gave way to anger. "Why? Why did you come out here? Do you know how dangerous that was?"

She stuck her lower lip out in a pout. It had been cut at some point during her journey; dried blood crusted the corner of her mouth. "The dragon ate it," she said, pointing up at the sun.

The sight was amazing, and to someone who didn't understand what it was, potentially terrifying. I leaned in close to look her in the eye. "There's no such thing as space dragons, okay? They don't exist. *Mother Ship 3* is in front of the sun right now. That's why we can't see it."

"But Jacob told me about the dragon!" Maree looked back at me with stubborn eyes as if daring me to prove dragons weren't real.

I looked up at our brother, who had a pained look on his face. He felt terrible, and I didn't have the heart to yell at him just then. He crouched so he could talk to her. "Maree, it was a story. I wanted to tell you a fun, scary story. I never meant for you to come out here like this."

Her dirt-caked face fell, revealing her distress. She really wanted to believe there were dragons.

Jacob shook his head. "If you thought a dragon was out here, why did you leave? Did you think our parents were in danger? They can take care of themselves."

Maree opened her mouth to reply, but a mighty shriek cut her off. All three of us turned in time to see a monstrously large *thing* swoop into view. Its wings had to be bigger than me, and its body was covered in pebbly, grayish skin. Tufts of feathers sprung from the back of its stubby, thick neck and ran down the ridge of its back, all the way to the tip of its tail. Six long, powerful legs sprouted from its body, the toes of each armed with long, curling claws. It screamed again, the sound rattling my bones as it soared closer. The creature began to fly in circles around us, steadily dropping lower and lower as it did.

"It's a dragon!" Maree declared, her voice filled with awe.

I couldn't speak. I couldn't move. All I could do was stare as this unknown animal hovered above us. It passed in front of the eclipsed sun, the faint aura of light highlighting the edges of its wings.

Then I came back to my senses. As beautiful as the sight was, it was also deadly. I snatched the predator spray from Jacob's pocket, aiming it high over my head. My other hand was poised to hurl the flashing orbs I'd brought along as a distraction. I didn't know if either would be enough to stop it from attacking us, but I had to try.

Jacob moved to shield Maree, but she wiggled out of his grasp. "Here, dragon! I have something for you!" she shouted.

With a few flaps of its enormous wings, it swooped closer. It was too dark to see much of its face, but long teeth glinted faintly within a gaping hole that must have been its mouth. I was getting ready to use the repellent when Maree dipped her hands into her pants pockets and brought out a bunch of the purple seeds. "Here!" she called as she tossed them high into the air.

They didn't fly high enough to reach the creature, but they must have gotten close enough for it to get a good whiff of them. The large dragon-like thing reared its head back and let out a great snort.

Then it sneezed. Droplets of saliva showered down around us, landing on our upturned faces. If I wasn't still worried about our safety, I would've been grossed out.

The great beast gracefully turned and flew away. Several tense moments passed before I began to believe we were safe. At last, I sighed and wiped the spit from my cheeks. "Maree, why did you throw seeds at it?"

"It was hungry," she said simply. "I thought the seeds might taste better than the sun."

I blinked, stunned by her logic. "You came out here to feed a space dragon?" I asked.

She nodded. "We need the sun. I wanted to get it back."

I grinned, feeling more than a little impressed. My younger sister did something dangerous, but her idea was also kind of smart. "You still shouldn't have come out here by yourself, but I do like your thinking, kiddo." I laughed when Maree curled her lip at being called "kiddo."

Jacob nudged my shoulder. "Come on. We can talk more about this later. I want to go home before anything else with big teeth tries to attack us."

We'd only been walking for a few minutes when the sky brightened again. The sun's return eased our passage home.

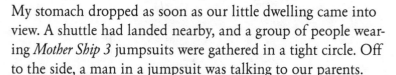

My stomach dropped as soon as our little dwelling came into view. A shuttle had landed nearby, and a group of people wearing *Mother Ship 3* jumpsuits were gathered in a tight circle. Off to the side, a man in a jumpsuit was talking to our parents.

It was a search party. They'd called people in to come looking for us.

When they finally saw us, Mom and Dad rushed over and scooped us up into a big hug. There were tears of joy. Then the relief vanished, and I braced myself for what I knew was coming. Maybe the sharp teeth of a space dragon would've been preferable to angry parents.

Dad frowned at me, his eyebrows arched in disapproval. "What were you thinking?" he demanded.

I opened my mouth to speak, but I couldn't find the words. Maree had no such problem. She giggled, her entire face alight with her accomplishment. "Daddy! I fed the dragon!"

His expression turned to one of confusion and concern. He looked from me to Jacob for an explanation. We were about to get into a ton of trouble, of that I had no doubt. But hey, at least Maree saw her dragon. It would make a great story to tell.

Rockets, Robots, and Bears

by Damien Mckeating

Damien was born and a short time after that he developed a love of fantasy and the supernatural. A childhood spent reading and writing led him inextricably to study film and screenwriting at university. He worked for a time as a radio copywriter but left it all behind to work in special needs education. He's most recently had stories published in *Writer's Magazine* (Dec 2017) and in the *Irish Imbas Celtic Mythology Collection 2017*. He writes daily and is currently the oldest he has ever been.

The snowmobile slowed and came to a stop. Amy climbed down off the driver's seat and knelt down by the engine.

"The battery is dead," she said. Her stomach felt hot and angry. It was her fault. She had taken them out too far, and now they couldn't get home. They didn't have far to go, and on the snowmobile it would have been easy, but walking it would be hard. She looked up at the sky. It would be dark soon, and the clouds were heavy with more snow. A storm was coming.

"Bear," Thomas said as he climbed off the passenger seat. He was eleven, three years younger than Amy, and had been born with Down's syndrome. That meant a lot of things, but for Thomas it meant it took him longer to learn things and he had trouble talking, although Amy could always understand him.

"There are no bears," she said.

"Bear," Thomas said and pointed to the forest of pine trees nearby.

Amy sighed. He had been obsessed with bears for months.

"There are no bears!" She knew she shouldn't shout at him. Really she was angry with herself. "Sorry," she said when she saw him sulking.

If they followed the edge of the forest they would get back to the town but not before the storm got them. Amy opened up the snowmobile's seat and took out the emergency pack. She took out a flare and fired it up. It *whooshed* into life. She dropped it onto the snow and a trail of colourful smoke curled away into the sky.

"Someone will find us," she said. "We'll build a shelter like Mum taught us, okay?" She'd get told off for taking her brother so far and letting the battery run out, but it was better than being outside in a storm.

Her history teacher said that long ago the world was different, that the island they lived on hadn't been covered in snow. Then the Big Change had come, and now the island was frozen for most of the year. Amy wished it could be warmer.

"Let's get up to the trees," Amy said. "We'll light a fire and keep the bears away."

"Pfff!" Thomas waved his hands around, miming the flames of a fire.

"Yeah. Fire," Amy agreed.

She slung the emergency pack onto her shoulder, and they trudged through the snow towards the trees. Amy pulled her hood up over her head and kept her snow goggles on. She knew Thomas wouldn't tease her, but she was embarrassed and wanted to hide. How could she have been so stupid?

She screamed as a hole opened up under her feet. She dropped down through the snow and disappeared into a dark pit. She hit the ground, and it knocked the scream out of her. She rolled and heard Thomas fall after her. They lay in a heap together and stared up at the hole above them.

"Are you okay?" she asked.

"Kay," Thomas replied.

Her legs ached and she was shaking, but Amy didn't think she was hurt. The fall hadn't been far, but it was too high for them to climb back out. She took a torch from the pack and shined it around the cave.

No, she corrected herself. Not a cave. It was man-made. The walls and floors were covered in dirty and broken tiles. The walls around them were collapsed, but ahead of them were two metal staircases. They led down into a dark and wide open space, and when Amy shined the torch around, she could see walls of broken glass and doorways with crumbling signs over them.

"It's a shopping arcade," she said. "I've seen pictures of them." Years ago everything anyone had ever needed would have been here, just waiting for them to come and get it. "It must have been lost under the snows for years."

"Gone," Thomas replied.

"Or maybe not," she said. "Maybe there's something we can use to climb out. We should have a look."

They crept to the staircases, and Thomas held her hand. "These were called escalators," she said as they went down the metal steps.

"Sclator," Thomas whispered.

It was quiet. The world down here had been forgotten. All that were left now were rubbish and bad smells. Amy wrinkled her nose. It smelled like a wet dog.

"Bear," Thomas pointed.

Amy was about to tell him to be quiet when she saw what he was pointing at. There were scratch marks on the tiles, deep scratch marks made by something big. What if it was a bear?

Amy held Thomas' hand and led them farther into the dead shopping arcade. They went past an old hardware store and a collapsed toy shop. She jumped as they walked past a shop window filled with mannequins. They looked like broken people, some missing arms, legs, or heads, and she imagined them chasing after her.

"We should go back," Amy said, suddenly afraid. They should just check the hardware store and leave.

A crunching noise came out of the darkness ahead of them. Thomas clutched her hand. Amy felt her heart jump and beat faster. Something was coming towards them. The noise got louder, crushing the broken glass and tiles as it went.

"Here," Amy whispered and pulled Thomas after her.

They crept into the shop with the broken mannequins. Amy turned off her torch and bit her lip to keep from crying. She had never been so scared. She and Thomas crouched between the mannequins, and she tried not to imagine them starting to move.

The crunching sound got louder until it was right in front of them. A robot on rubber tracks rolled to a stop in front of the shop. It was bulky and square, with two long, telescopic, tentacle-like arms that waved around its body.

Amy felt her mouth hang open. It was a robot from the old world! She had never seen anything like it. She couldn't believe it was still working. She heard Thomas gasp and knew he was thinking the same thing.

The robot's head turned from side to side, and Amy could see the glow of its eyes. It looked straight at them.

"Come out, now." Its voice was like a bad radio signal.

It must be able to see in the dark, Amy thought as she and Thomas walked out. They stood in front of the robot, and its head moved to look them up and down.

"Clothing not recognised," it said. "Hardware unaccounted for," the pincers on the end of a tentacle arm grabbed for Amy's torch.

"Hey!" she shouted and pulled the torch away.

"Shoplifters!" the robot declared, and a red light on its head began to flash. "Shoplifters!"

"What? No!" Amy started to protest, but the robot grabbed them. One arm wrapped around her and one around Thomas. It picked them both up and carried them away. "Where are you taking us?" Amy struggled.

"The authorities have been informed. You will be held for further questioning."

It took them deeper into the shopping arcade. Amy tried to keep track of where they were going, but the robot moved quickly through the darkness. Thomas started to cry, and Amy had to fight not to cry too.

"It'll be okay," she told him.

The robot rolled over a broken door and took them down a narrow corridor. It turned through another doorway and into a small room where it dropped Amy and Thomas on the floor.

"The authorities are on their way," it said. "You will be detained here until they arrive."

It pulled the door shut as it left. Amy heard it rolling away. She ran up to the door and tried the handle but it was locked. They were trapped.

She dropped down onto the floor and blinked back tears. "I'm sorry," she said. "This is my fault."

Thomas sat with her and hugged her. "Shhh," he said.

Amy wiped her nose on her sleeve. "They'll see the flare and come looking for us," she said. "They'll find us." She said it to make Thomas feel better. She didn't think they would find them. If it snowed again, their tracks would be lost. The shopping arcade had been lost for years, buried underground since the Big Change. They might never be found.

Amy turned the torch on and flashed it around the room. It was dirty and small and except for an old chair was completely empty.

What were they going to do?

Amy frowned as she thought. The robot must be an old security guard. The years had fried its circuits. When no "authorities" turned up she didn't trust it to let them go. It would just leave them here to starve.

She opened up the emergency pack and went through what they had: a small toolkit, food and water for two days, a folding shovel, first aid kit, a roll of tape, tissues, and two more flares.

"We have to escape," Amy decided.

"Robot," Thomas complained.

"Yeah, he's a bit broken." Amy paused as she said it. The robot was broken; almost everything in the arcade was broken, and that might include the room they were in.

She ran to the door and started to pull at it. Thomas joined her and together they rattled the door in its frame. It was loose but they didn't have the strength to break it.

She searched the room again, but there was only the chair. Thomas sat in it and laughed as the legs on it wobbled.

"Quick, off," Amy said. She took a screwdriver from the toolkit and removed one of the legs. She took it to the door and managed to wedge it into a small gap.

"Push," she told Thomas.

Together they used the chair leg as a lever. They pushed with all of their strength, and with a sudden *crack* the door splintered and came off its hinges. It dropped to the floor with a bang, and Amy almost went with it.

They gathered up their pack and went out into the dark corridor. They knew the robot could see them in the dark, so they might as well use the torch. Amy searched the shops and signs but didn't see anything she could recognise.

"Where are we?" she whispered.

Thomas pulled on her arm and dragged her over to a tall metal stand. There was a map on it of the whole shopping arcade.

"Dere," Thomas pointed to a big arrow on the map that said "You Are Here."

They searched for the nearest escalators and found them not far from where they were.

"That must be where we fell in," Amy said. "It's not far. We can get there easy."

Something growled in the darkness. They both went cold. Amy felt her insides shrink, as if she might disappear into herself. They crouched down on the floor, hiding by the map, and Amy turned off the torch.

"Bear," Thomas said.

"Quiet," Amy whispered.

They could hear it moving. It growled deep in its throat like it was complaining. Its claws scratched over the tiles and they heard rubbish being crushed under its paws.

Amy held her breath and hugged Thomas tight.

The bear moved with slow steps. It sounded like it was the other side of the map. It grunted out a breath and sniffed at the air.

Amy closed her eyes.

It moved again, its steps going away from them.

Amy dared to risk taking a peek and saw the shadow of the bear, huge and black, walking away from them. It was going the same way they needed to. It walked a little farther, its head rolling from side to side as it padded away, and then it lay down with a grunt.

Amy stared at it. She tried to breathe slowly. She tried to stop her hands from shaking. She had to pretend to be calm, even if she wasn't, so Thomas wouldn't be scared. But she wasn't calm. She was terrified.

They were going to have to sneak past the bear.

No, they couldn't do that. Amy sat with her back against the map and stared into the darkness. She might be able to, but

Thomas wasn't as quick or as quiet as she was. And she wasn't going to leave him behind. But if they waited here, then either the bear or the robot would find them.

The robot... Amy wondered if the robot and the bear had ever met each other. Would the robot try to arrest the bear? If that happened, then it might be enough of a distraction for them to escape. But what would they do once they got to the escalators and the hole? They still wouldn't be able to climb up. She had the flares to signal for help, but she wasn't sure she could throw one up through the hole. Then she remembered the hardware store...

"I've got a plan," she whispered after a while. "We need to wait for the robot to come back."

She couldn't be certain he would come back, but if he was a guard, then he might have a route that he patrolled. They sat together, holding onto each other and staring into the darkness. It felt like forever. They had no idea what time it was, but they knew the storm was coming, and once it did they would never be rescued.

Moving slowly, Amy opened her pack and took out one of the flares. She clutched it tightly, ready to move as she heard...

The crunch of the robot's tracks.

It was nearby. She heard the bear grunt, but it didn't move. Maybe the bear had been clever enough to stay off the robot's route? Well Amy was about to change that.

Thomas pulled at her arm as the crunching of the robot's tracks got nearer. It was going to pass right by them.

"Ready," Amy said.

She stood up and swallowed her fear. She was going to pretend she knew what she was doing.

In one smooth movement she ripped the cap off the flare and threw it as hard as she could towards the bear.

It roared as she ducked down behind the map. The robot raced past them, its tracks bouncing over the rough ground.

"Stop!" its static filled voice shouted at the bear.

"Run," Amy hissed.

She grabbed Thomas by the hand and they ran. Staying close to the shops, their knees bent, heads down, they ran for their lives.

The flare lit up the arcade in stuttering shadows. The huge bear, its fur sticking out in spiky clumps, rose up onto its legs to roar at the robot. It was huge, a terrifying beast. The poor robot didn't stand a chance.

"Shoplifter!" the robot whined, and its red light flashed.

Amy pulled Thomas along. He was clumsier than her, and his balance had never been good, but she made him run. Her stomach twisted and clenched as she heard the bear grab and crush the robot.

Don't see us, she pleaded silently. *Please, don't see us.*

They stumbled through the arcade, tripping and sliding over the rubbish until Amy saw the hardware store. She turned towards it and hoped it had everything she needed for the last part of her plan.

With no idea where she needed to look, Amy risked turning on the torch. She scanned the aisles of the shop, the beam of torchlight bouncing around from shelf to shelf. Pots, pans, shovels, rakes, tubes, pipes—all sat broken, rusted, and dusty.

"Here!" Amy smiled as she found the cleaning section. She grabbed a bottle of white vinegar and a tub of baking soda.

They ran back to the escalators, and as they climbed up, Amy realised she couldn't hear the bear and robot fighting anymore. She hoped the bear had been arrested.

She dropped to the floor underneath the hole. The sky above them was dark, and snow had begun to fall. Amy tipped open the emergency pack and emptied out a bottle of water. She half filled it with the white vinegar, the smell stinging her nose.

Thomas watched her with open-mouthed curiosity.

"We need to get the flare out of the hole," she said. "So we'll make a rocket." She ripped open the packet of baking soda and hoped it would be okay. It had been in a sealed plastic tub, so she had to trust it was fine. She tipped some onto a tissue and rolled it up. "Okay, hold this." She passed the bottle to Thomas. With shaking hands, she taped a flare to the side of the rocket. Out of the first aid kit she took three finger splints, like lollipop sticks, and stuck them to the rocket to make a tripod.

"Ready?" she said to Thomas.

He nodded.

Amy took a deep breath. She had to be fast now.

She dropped the baking soda in the tissue into the bottle, lit the flare, and blocked the bottle's hole with a bandage. She turned it upside down and stood it up using the lollipop stick tripod.

Inside the bottle, the soda and vinegar began to fizz.

Amy and Thomas backed away from the rocket.

The pressure inside built up as the vinegar and soda bubbled.

Amy closed her eyes.

And the rocket exploded.

It flew up, flying out of the hole and taking the flare with it.

Thomas laughed and pointed, and Amy laughed with him.

"They'll find us," she smiled.

A growl made them turn. The bear was coming towards them, charging towards the escalators as it grumbled and roared.

"Amy! Thomas!" a woman's face appeared over the hole.

"Mum!" Amy shouted.

"Hold on."

"Bear!" Thomas shouted.

"What?" their mum shouted back.

"Get Thomas," Amy told them.

She turned to face the bear and started waving the torch

around. "Here!" she shouted. "Look!" She flashed the torch in
its face as she walked down the escalators. The bear roared and
turned towards her.

It was so fast. Amy knew she couldn't outrun it. But she didn't
plan to.

She glanced over her shoulder and saw a rope drop through.
Thomas grabbed hold of it as Amy climbed onto the escalator.
The bear charged up the steps and she jumped.

For a heartbeat she hung over nothing and thought she was
going to fall to the ground. She'd lie there, her legs broken,
and wait for the bear to eat her. But she hit the other escalator,
slipped and dropped the torch but didn't fall.

Above her she saw Thomas rising up as the rope pulled him
out of the hole.

"Send it back down!" Amy shouted.

The bear lunged for her. Amy didn't know if bears could jump,
but this one tried. It was big enough to stretch from one escalator to the other. Its claws reached out and tore into the plastic
and metal.

Amy screamed and ran back up. The bear roared and scrambled behind her, tearing apart the stairs as it tried to reach her.

The rope dropped back through the hole.

The bear came after her.

"Now!" Amy yelled.

She jumped and grabbed the rope with both hands.

She soared up, her legs dangling in the air.

The bear stretched and swung for her.

Its claws shaved the bottom of her boots.

And Amy came up into the world. Her mum pulled her clear.
Thomas was already with their dad. A whole search party was
gathered around them.

"It's a bear!" someone shouted. "An actual bear. I thought they
were all dead."

To Amy it felt like everyone took a turn hugging her and kissing her on the head. People were crying, and she cried too. Everyone was so happy about finding them that no one even told her off (yet). And they were all excited about what they might find in the shopping arcade—if they managed to scare the bear away.

The snow came faster and they started home. Amy found herself sitting next to Thomas. He raised his hands and roared. "Bear!"

"Yeah," Amy agreed with a smile. "Bear."

Where Home Is a Journey

by Jeannie Warner

> Jeannie Warner spent her formative years in Colorado, Canada, and Southern California, and is not afraid to abandon even the most luxurious domestic environs for an opportunity to travel almost anywhere. She has a useless degree in musicology, a checkered career in computer security, and aspirations of world domination.
>
> Jeannie's writing credits include previous *Young Explorers' Adventure Guide* stories, public service warnings on the topics of IT Security, an unpublished body of Victorian fiction, a great many topical blogs and poems of dubious quality and content, as well as publications in *Tightbeam Speculative Fiction* magazine, short stories on Amazon, as well as a collection of snarky notes to a former upstairs neighbor. She currently lives in Northern California.

Jeannie enjoys hockey, fencing, making music, dancing, and believes strongly that yes is more fun than no. Feel free to buy her a dark and stormy whenever you see her.

It was second night watch on the bridge, and Ollie was sitting cross-legged in the navigation chair with open news feeds. She had an elbow propped on one knee and her chin in her hands, reading the various reports coming across the interstellar wave.

She was the only one currently on the bridge of the *New London*, which gave her a pleasant sense of being in charge. Even if it was only on a pre-set course. Usually Captain Dodger wanted two crew members to be on watch, but he had come to trust Ollie.

A scratching at the door indicated another of the crew was still awake. Ollie swung the chair around to look as Mouse entered. Mouse was one of the smaller youths who made up the crew of the FAGN ship, *New London*. Ollie was certain that she and Mouse were of an age, although no one kept track of exact birthdays anymore, with space travel making calendars obsolete.

If he stood upright and stretched as he far as he could, Mouse might reach three and a half feet, but he was missing his legs below the knee—an accident when he was a baby on a mining ship. Mouse also never grew up properly with regular planetary gravity, so his bones were bowed and warped, with his muscles pulling them out of line over the years. His title—he was recently promoted by Dodger—was Chief Engineer, and it was written proudly across the chest of his grey coveralls in permanent marker. "Ollie, got a sec?"

"Sure. What's up?" She swiveled her chair to study the boy. "You look uneasy."

He shifted foot to foot. "Reckon so. I got this bad feeling."

When someone like Mouse got a bad feeling, you paid attention. In space, when things went wrong, they could go terribly bad in a hurry. "What about?" Ollie unfolded and picked up the ship's log to write down his words.

"Well, it's another leak, ainnit?" Mouse wrung his hands as he talked, a nervous habit. "We got into the suits in time again, and Mattie checked our blood sat after. No harm done. This time. But these leaks, they keep happening."

Ollie felt a sour pit in her stomach. "They do keep happening. Ever since..." She didn't want to talk about the man who sabotaged their ship. Not when it had been, in her mind, her fault for trusting someone she shouldn't have.   "Yeah."

Mouse let it go there, to Ollie's relief. "But I just keep getting this bad feeling. It wakes me up at night, and I lie there listening to creaks. I started dreaming about how I's the ship, and I's leaking all my bad parts into my good parts. And then there's the ghosts."

Ollie didn't quite understand about the ghosts, but she wasn't entirely sure she was ready to know the inside of Mouse's brain. She chose a more practical question. "What do you want to do about it? We don't have enough credits for a proper dry dock and a full check. Even if we could find a non-Federated station willing to do it."

Mouse slid down in the hatch and started picking nervously at the seams of his trousers. "I know." They all knew the state of the ship's budget until they found someplace to sell their cargo. But he didn't move.

The girl sighed. "Come on. I ain't Dodger. You can talk to me."

"I think we need a new ship."

That got all of Ollie's attention, and she sat straight up. "What? You think it's that bad?"

"I'm terrified," Mouse whispered. "I spend every waking hour going over every single hose, every connection, every inch of every electrical wire. I keep finding little things. But how soon until I miss something? I dream that it's all gonna blow, and it'll be my fault. And I'll have killed everyone. I wake up sick, Ollie. Every time."

Mouse couldn't even look at her as he talked, not until the end when he said her name and finally met her eyes. The kid looked bad, and Ollie could see shadows and hollows she hadn't noticed before. "But we can't afford a new ship yet. I mean, maybe when we find someone to buy all our data and charts."

"I know," Mouse said. "But my dreams say if we stay here, we're gonna die. And I don't wanna kill everyone because I missed something. I can't go on like this."

Ollie was the officer of the watch, which meant problems were her responsibility. "Okay. I'll talk to the captain."

Mouse's smile was weak but genuine. "Thanks, Ollie. I'm gonna go play with the Verniers some more. In a vac suit."

"Be safe," Ollie nodded. She turned around to hit a button marked *Captain* with a small gold crown painted beside it and spoke into the mic. "Captain Dodger, this is the bridge. Can you come up?"

Mouse got up, waved his thanks with a weak smile, and headed back to Engineering. In a few minutes, Captain Dodger appeared at the same doorway.

Dodger was one of the tallest of the crew, although he also lacked the inches of someone planet born and raised. Like most kids in space, his hair and eyes were dark, his skin pallid with a dusky hue. He was dressed in his long underwear under his oversized captain's coat, which was draped around his shoulders. He yawned as he looked around to all the screens, evaluating the peaceful scene and green lights in a moment. "S'up?"

"Captain." Ollie saluted, because she knew he liked it when she did. "We have a situation."

Dodger looked more alert. "What kind?"

The girl considered all the ways to approach the matter and decided to be straight up without mentioning the dream. "Mouse thinks the ship has gone off. Past what he can rig and what we can afford to fix."

Dodger snatched the duty log up and started brushing his fingers over recent entries from the different stations and on-duty crewmen. "He don't say that here."

"No. But he recorded each time he's made a fix. Look at the numbers. You know how many times we've all had to hustle into vac suits." Ollie gestured to the slender locker where the lock wasn't even on the vacuum suit door anymore, it was used so often.

"Yeah. But that don't mean we need a new ship." Dodger

reached out to stroke the console with fond fingertips. "This is my ship. This is our home."

Ollie sighed, "Yeah. And we all love it, Captain. You know we do. But what if Mouse is right? What if it's going to poison us in our sleep, and we don't wake up? We just drift on in space until we freeze to death? You're always bragging how much Mouse saved us in credits for repairs over the last couple years. It doesn't make sense to ignore him when he says he's sure the ship is on its last thrusters."

Dodger didn't like the idea of his ship being broken. But he thought on it, tapping his fingers on his hips, and came to an unhappy conclusion. "Ain't gonna ignore him," he said at last.

Ollie nodded. "Maybe we don't even find a new ship right off. We could sign on somewhere and keep an eye out. Wait for your word on the right opportunity. We still have those star charts and data chips we salvaged last month. That'll go far."

Thinking about money always cheered Dodger up. "Well, I don't like it. But maybe if I sent my sister on the *Indian Princess* a wave, she might know of something."

Ollie started hitting the buttons for the communications system. "That's a great idea. Didn't she make Captain?"

Dodger twirled around once on the second chair. "Maybe." Ollie judged by his smile that he was pleased and proud of his older sister.

"Got the *Princess*," Ollie confirmed as a light went green. She bent to speak into the microphone. "*Indian Princess*, this is the *New London*. Captain Arty Dodger to speak with Captain Callie Dodger. Do you copy?"

A hissing sound accompanied the reply. "Copy that, *New London*. Artemis Dodger, what are you up to?" It was Callie herself who appeared on the screen in front of them, grinning.

"The usual," Dodger said, winking back. "Bummer about your promotion."

Callie laughed, "Yeah, yeah. I knew it'd eat at you that I got mine first. That's why I sent the message."

Ollie watched the two, smiling. It made her happy, like she was part of an extended family.

"Well, here's the thing, Callie. The *London's* got herself too beat up. I have a mess of data chips to sell, and we need a safe harbor for a while. Maybe, and it's painin' me ta say it, we need honest employment while I look for a new ship." Dodger laid it all out directly. "You hear anything, could maybe suggest some ideas?"

Callie's pursed her lips, and Ollie watched as she typed on her console. "Let me check. I did hear something about a waystation hiring folks like crazy. Ex-FAGNs, ex-miners, ex-cruisers, they're not fussy. Reckon you could sell the *London* at pretty good salvage rates there too."

Dodger waved Ollie off, and the girl headed out. She poked her head into Engineering and gave Mouse a thumbs up, then whistled her way to the galley to see about making tea for everyone on duty.

Two shifts later, Dodger called for a meeting in the cargo bay. Everyone lined up in their cleanest overalls, standing up as straight as they could manage given the way their bones were twisted. Growing up in lower gravities did that—muscles pulled the bones out of shape. Out in space protein was scarce, gravity was rare, and accidents twisted the body; you grow how you grow, and the children of the stars were no two alike. Muscles were all that mattered when you were moving around heavy cargo. *Muscles and brains*, Ollie thought with pride.

"Attention!" Ollie called, and Dodger looked pleased as everyone stiffened on command.

Dodger inspected the crew. "Short question. Are Engineering and Maintenance agreed the *London's* on her way out?" This time the nods were unanimously slower, more dejected.

"Bad's bad, Cap'n," Bongo offered up a shrug. "I've been sleepin' in my vac suit. And that ain't rest."

There was a stir of agreement again. Everyone had.

"Well, I talked to my sister Callie. Seems there's a waystation that's in need of hands. Reckon we could go see if they'll take us all at once. Maybe find a buyer for our data, salvage the *London*, and keep an eye out for a new ship." Dodger didn't look happy about it.

Ollie asked questions for all. "What's the traffic there like? Do you think we could get a good price for the star charts we're carrying?"

"Callie thinks so," Dodger says. "Says there's a lot of mining and science ships logging through that station. Between selling our data and scrapping the *London*, we should have enough to buy ourselves a decent ship. Or at least, a decent salvage we could fix into a good ship. There's abandoned ships galore, what with FAGN over."

The Federal Association for Generational Navy program used to be something creative to do with all the children born in space whose parents either couldn't (because they were dead) or wouldn't (because sometimes it happened) take responsibility. The program had imploded a while back, but some of the ships were still flying.

"Wouldn't mind flyin' on an XM-319," Mattie said. "We could carry a lot of salvage in one of those holds."

"Something like that," Dodger agreed with the older girl. "So. Everyone pack up what you don't care to leave behind. We're docking at the station in four hours." And that was that.

Mattie and Ollie had been sharing a room for a couple years. The walls of their berth were plain white fiberglass with grey banded reinforcements. There was a single light panel overhead, which flickered until you hit your fist against the wall above the switch. A slab bed wide enough for two small people stuck out from the wall.

"I'm thinkin' we should take blankets," Mattie said. "We don't know what kinda berth we'll be gettin'."

Ollie sat on the bed and sighed. Her pile of possessions was much smaller than Mattie's, and easily tucked into the pockets of her coveralls. By nature, she preferred reading to collecting trinkets. "Probably. I've gotten used to this being home."

Mattie stopped packing and smiled at the smaller girl. Ollie was planet-born, and something of an oddity on the crew with her white-blond hair, blue eyes, and pale skin. Mattie ruffled the girl's hair. "It'll always be home. But the big-H Home travels with you. Home's your people and your happy place."

That cheered Ollie. "I like that." She continued packing with a lighter heart.

Four hours later, the *New London* docked at Efrafa Waystation. The crew gathered at the bottom of the gangplank to marvel at the air. "It's so warm here!" Bongo looked around in surprise. "Can't believe they heat landing pad air. This place must be rich!"

"Rich is good," Ollie said. "We need someone to buy our booty."

"*New London*, proceed to decontamination stations!" The loudspeaker nearby blared abruptly, startling everyone. Tiny jumped but didn't quite upset Mouse's cart. (Here on a station with full gravity, Tiny pulled his legless bunkmate around on a small red wagon.)

"Decom. Well, reckon that's a good idea for a station," Dodger nodded, determined to be agreeable. He strode to the door with the blinking lights.

Ollie patted the pockets where the data chips were protected and sealed before starting after him. The rest of the crew fell in line.

Decom proved to be a simple enough process; ultra-violet light bathed them all, followed with a warm air and powder burst that the speaker said was a general antibiotic. The crew scrubbed up in the basins along the wall, then filed into a waiting room on the other side. This room, too, was warm with full gravity, and the chairs were identical blue plastic.

Mouse, Ollie noticed, looked nervously around him with each sound and whoosh of air. She hoped his dreams would be better with the change.

The door in front of them opened, and a large man entered the room. He was followed by a short, robotic assistant that had a visual screen at Ollie's eye level. Dodger instinctively rose to his feet, but the newcomer was taller by more than a head.

The man had dark hair and eyes and the uniform of a Federation officer. A major, Ollie mused to herself. The stranger's face and expression were pleasant. Ollie couldn't read his feelings behind his eyes. "Hello, *New London*. Who's in charge here?"

"That'd be me," Dodger tried for another inch of height by standing up very tall with squared shoulders. "Cap'n Arty Dodger. You got my signal then?" He held out a hand, and the major took it.

"We did. And we understand your position." Their clasp was brief, with only a wince on Dodger's face indicating how hard the man gripped. "I notice by your designation that *London* was a FAGN ship? Well, don't worry. Personally, I think closing that program down was a lot of political arm-waving. Cause of the month, that sort of thing." He turned to address the rest of the crew. "I'm Major Wharton."

Nailed it, thought Ollie.

"We're a working station, so if you want to stay, you'll all have to sign on under my command here and be assigned duties. No one lazes around on the Efrafa."

"Moon to moon?" Ollie asked quickly, suspicious of the easy terms.

"Certainly, at-will hiring can be arranged," the Major nodded, his gaze lingering on the girl's pale hair and face. "We have a lot of activity on this station, so if you'll indicate your areas of specialty, we'll find you each the right job to fill it. First though, everyone does a tour on maintenance and engineering to learn the station."

Dodger didn't like that part. "Everyone? Even a captain?"

The Major's gaze returned to Dodger, and he looked the stripling over with interest. "Well, that depends. Did you pass Federation rank examinations and get the official designation?"

A slow flush of color darkened Dodger's cheeks, but his gaze was steady. "My exam was...delayed by the program collapsing."

A faint smile touched the Major's lips. "Ah. Well, perhaps you'll accept my sponsorship. You are excused from duty rotation to refresh your materials and study for the examination as soon as possible."

The prospect and offer cheered Dodger in an instant, and he bowed his head. "That'll do nicely. Thanks, Major." He turned to beam a smile at the rest of us. "Well, get on then! I'll be in contact when I've got me some papers and a line on a new ship. Meanwhile, dismissed!"

Dodger followed the major out of the room, while the robot light chirped green. "Follow me, please." The robot led the crew through a warren of hallways and passages, following always a red line labeled at intersections as Engineering. It was at the center of Efrafa's wheel-like structure, the whole waystation in turn floating in orbit above a mining planet. Ollie liked the way the corridors were labeled, and noted the directions and colors for berths (blue) and the canteen (green) as well.

Engineering was a huge section of the station. The ceilings stretched overhead more than two stories up, with stations all around the curving walls and walkways accessing well-lit and blinking panels. Across from the entrance were doors showing where the engine room itself was, along with warnings on the nuclear core entrance about danger and alarms.

As the robot wheeled around, describing each duty station, the newcomers were the subject of a lot of looks. Ollie noticed that many of the waystation's workers were not much older than her own crew, and many of them clearly twisted of limb in the way of most FAGN-raised children. Some, she thought to herself, didn't look happy at all.

Must be hard if they always run full gravity, Ollie thought. *That aches when you're not used to it.* She cast a quick look toward Mouse and Tiny, who both looked like they were already struggling a little. "You okay?" Ollie whispered as she fell back a little.

"Just gotta settle in!" Tiny put on a brave face. Mouse shrugged and hunched a little on his cart. Ollie took the handle from Tiny, taking her turn at pulling Mouse about.

An engineering chief walked up to the *London's* crew. "Welcome! Wharton told me I had some new faces to expect. That's good. That's very good, indeed." He looked at the youths bunched around Mouse's wagon. The chief was clearly planet-born with straight arms and legs, standing over six feet tall.

"*New Londoners*, reporting for duty assignment." Ollie spoke for the lot of them, lifting her chin to look him in the eye.

If the Chief was surprised that the group deferred to Ollie, he didn't show it. "Excellent. We'll have you on the rotation starting this very shift. Who is—? Ah." He spotted the writing across Mouse's chest, hand-lettered decorations of rank. "You're chief engineer. What's your name?"

"Mouse," the smaller boy muttered but held out a hand.

The chief smiled and bent to take it. Ollie noticed that his shake was gentler than Major Wharton's. "Chief Mouse. I like it. Well, I've got your assignments all lined up." He straightened and looked around. "Ottsie! Tan! Shattenkirk! Come on over and pick up your new shift partners." He looked back to Mouse. "We share and share alike down here. Everyone works. Everyone is on the duty lottery. No exceptions."

At his word, a few coverall-dressed crew youths and one older woman detached themselves from their stations to approach. The crew were separated off into their learner stations.

Ollie was pleased to find that her previous study of the *New London's* engines, systems, and processes served her well. Her assigned mentor, whose coverall tag read Joker, seemed delighted with Ollie. "You, delightful girl, are saving me from reactor scrubbing! Best news ever!" She attached a small box to Ollie's belt, tapped it twice. "There you go. All set. Clean away and make sure you get all the tanks flushed!" The box beeped slowly, intermittently, with a tiny green light.

Ollie was a thorough sort of learner. Before she started, she wanted to read the maintenance logs on this station servicing Efrafa's nuclear generators, comparing them the *New London's* fuel-based engines. There were a lot more schematics for a much larger system.

She asked Joker for more drawings of the reactor and venting systems, but the woman just showed her where the tanks were, gave her something that smelled like solvent, and a hand-held machine to buff metal. Joker didn't seem to care about duties and rotations and paperwork. "Just scrub everything you see! Pull those levers twice! It's in the manual. You have five hours. I'm out." And she rushed off through an airlock door, leaving Ollie alone with schematics, schedules, and supplies.

Two hours later, the box attached to Ollie was beeping yellow, and far more frequently. Ollie looked down at it, somewhat annoyed, and pulled it off her belt to look at the unit closely. "Geiger counter," she read the label aloud, then paused. She flipped hurriedly back through previous documents on radiation and exposure, then checked the box again. "Oh, this isn't good."

Radiation poisoning is nothing to mess around with. Ollie went and banged on the door, which Joker must have locked behind her. She kept at it though, kicking and swearing as Bongo and Dodger did when they were fighting with heavy loads. At last the door opened, and Mattie looked quizzical. "Hey, how come you're all alone in here?"

"She locked me in!" Ollie was angry and showed her beeping Geiger counter.

"That ain't right." Mattie frowned heavily. She looked down to her electronic clipboard. "Not sure where she went. But those numbers don't look good."

Ollie shut the opening to the reactor area, and snatched at the clipboard. "I wanna check something." She delved into the duty roster. "This is odd," she said after a few minutes.

"What is?"

"There's no follow-up on the roster for Joker after she was supposed to do this shift on reactor flush."

Mattie came over to peer over her shoulder. "Maybe that's the final trip around Engineering? Does she go to another department?"

The girls were silent as they looked over the previous week. Then the one after. No Joker. "I'm checking another person on reactor flush duty!" Ollie declared, looking things up. No one, it appeared, ever had any duty after their tour on reactor flush and cleaning. But they did show up on medical records. Ollie's skin crawled, and she felt sick.

Mattie returned after about five minutes, dragging a medical kit robot behind her. Ollie couldn't tell it from the first robot who signed them in.

It was beeping. "WARNING. You are tampering with my programmed schedule. WARNING."

"Oh, we're going to tamper with more than that," Mattie said. Lickity-split with a screwdriver, a pair of small tweezers, and a little bit of humming, she had the faceplate hanging off by its wires as she went to work on the brain inside. "Aha! Got it. Now ask."

Ollie cleared her throat. "What is the duty rotation after flushing the reactor in Engineering?"

There was a faint beep. "Sick bay."

The girls exchanged glances. Ollie went on with her question-

ing. "How long does the average assignment to sick bay last?"
"Two days."

Another pause, before Ollie prodded it with another question.
"Where after that?"

"Usually the compactor. But occasionally recycling for compost."

Both girls gasped. "That's it? Does flushing the reactor always kill people?"

"No," the robot said. "The radiation kills people."

Mattie spoke up, the screwdriver clenched tight in her hand.
"Do you record all the questions that are asked of you?"

"Yes, I do," the robot said. "My function is—"

Ollie never heard the function. The moment the robot said yes, Mattie traded her screwdriver for wire snips and started hacking at the wires. She went on until all the lights were out. Silently, the two girls shoved the robot's chassis into a closet.

Ollie's stomach sank into her boots. When she spoke again, it was a whisper. "So. They want new kids in because there's a shift that kills folk regular-like."

"I noticed they were all real friendly to me on duty," said Mattie. "I didn't want to think it was creepy. I wanted it to be nice."

Ollie said, "We gotta get out of here. But I'll tell you for nothing, this is gonna be a hard sell to Dodger."

Mattie rummaged through the robot's medical pack and pulled out an antibiotic applicator and punched Ollie in the arm with the shot. "Well, that's why you're acting First Mate. You get around him best."

Ollie blinked a little as she rubbed the injection site. "Ow! I am?"

"Dodger said so the other night, while you was on duty," Mattie smiled a little at last. "Said we's to mind you when he was asleep and you was on the bridge."

The unexpected promotion left Ollie feeling proud, if unsteady.

"I see. Well then. Here's our options." She started. "We can't tell anyone in Engineering we're leaving, or they'll try to stop us. They could get violent. How about you guys go grab the vac suits off the *New London* and head for the salvage deckyard? Maybe there's something there we can do for a quick trade. And here." She held out the data chips. "In case you need leverage."

"Yes'm!" Mattie saluted sloppily, and it gave Ollie heart. "I'll see if Mouse or Blink can access another one of those robots on the way out and cancel our record of being here."

Ollie nodded. "I'll grab Dodger and meet you at the salvage. Get Tiny and Mouse and the others. Tell them about the death shift. Get whatever will get a new ship up and moving for the cost of the *London* in parts."

Ollie darted out in search of Dodger. With only a few polite questions, she found a door at the end of officers' row, and knocked on it.

Dodger looked surprised when he opened the door. "S'up?"

Ollie saluted smartly. "I need to talk to you."

The dark-eyed boy stared at her for a long minute, then sighed. "Come in. I'm not gonna like this, am I?"

"Depends. Wanna leave right now?" Ollie decided it was best not to beat around the bush.

Dodger frowned. "No. No, I don't." He pulled her inside his room and closed the door. He crossed his arms and set his chin at a stubborn angle. "I started the exam study. They're gonna get me that Federation approval of rank. Equivalencies of experience an' all that. The major said I's a genius from just the prelims; it shouldn't take longer than a month to watch the training, take the tests."

Ollie sighed, stuffing her hands deep into her pockets. "Well, is that certification test worth trading for me?"

The question caught Dodger off guard. "What are you on about?"

"The nuclear power for this station. You know, all that gravity, heat, and light we've been admiring? Well, seems anyone new gets tapped to do the dirty work. And by dirty, I mean they flush the reactor and die of radiation poisoning."

Dodger protested. "Maybe a single dose won't kill—"

"Yes, it will, Dodge," Ollie stopped him there and tapped him on the chest with her fingertip. "It's both stats from the schedule and a matter of meds. Once a month, a kid disappears off the roster for good. Always to sick bay, then spaced. I got a bad dose today, and I left early. Had to shoot up on antibiotics, and I'll need a doc later."

Dodger scrubbed his face with his hands and ran his fingers through his hair. "This bites hard, Ollie. It bites me real hard."

"I know." Greatly daring, Ollie reached out to take one of his hands to hold. "Did the major sign something promising you the test and protection? You got it in writing?"

"Yeah," Dodger nodded, and his hand was chilly in hers. "Course I did. A deal's a deal. Iron-clad."

The girl took a deep breath and moistened her lips. "Well, what if...what if we lot went down and found a ship. We still need to find a buyer for the chips. You stay here and get that rank and paperwork. We go get me a proper doctoring somewhere else."

"No way," Dodger shook his head hard. "I ain't gonna abandon my crew."

"You ain't doing anything like that, Captain Dodger," Ollie squeezed his hand firmly. "You're going to get all official and registered and real in the eyes of the Feds, and then we're going to pick you back up here in a month even if we have to break you outta jail. I'll even send Callie a wave and see if she and the *Indian Princess* can join us for backup in case you have some problems convincing them to honor the leaving part of your contract."

Dodger's fingers tightened a little around Ollie's at last. "I reckon she'd come to see me get the stripes, sure enough." He stared at Ollie a long moment, then cracked a smile. "You sure come a long way from the scared waif we picked up back when."

"Well, I had a good example to learn from how to be brave."
Ollie let go of his hand, and saluted again. "You gave me a
home, Cap'n Dodger. I'll keep it together for you while you're
busy."

The boy nodded at that. "You got a plan?"

Ollie tilted her head toward the door behind her. "The others
are already on their way to comb over the salvage yard to see
what we can get flying."

Dodger nodded, then turns to dig into his small carrysack for
credits. "Then you take these. It's all I got, and some from the
little bit we had left in the *London's* inventory. Buy whatever
you need to get us into the air."

Credits were a welcome surprise, and Ollie's spirits lifted. "Well, if
we have to rename a broken ship, what should we call it?"

Dodger shrugged. "You call it the *Newer London*, 'course.
And remind them what I said. When I'm not there, you're in
charge." He clapped her on the shoulder. "You all get a good
price for those data chips, mind!"

"Yes sir. Of course," Ollie whispered. She saluted one more
time, then turned to head off to the salvage deck yards with
hope in her heart.

A yellow line took Ollie through the waystation to the flight
deck for decommissioned ships. Junk and parts spilled out
of plastic crates everywhere, and she picked her way carefully
through and around the maze of pieces. Mouse rolled up on
his tiny wagon, pushing himself along. "Ollie! Come see. It
ain't pretty, but I think it'll fly. That way." He indicated a dark
bulk off to the side near the mouth of the deck.

The ship he indicated was not anything like the clean lines of
the *New London*, and it was small. Ollie stared up the ramp,
calculating mass and fuel needs in her head. "I don't know this
model," she admitted. "Can't read the number designation.
What's it used for?"

"P6-4807c." Mouse looked pleased. "It's a courier. Or it was.

Tiny's on board now seeing if it's spaceworthy." He paused, then looked up at her soberly. "Mattie told us what you found out, what you got dosed with. That ain't right."

Ollie grimaced. "I should have known no-questions-asked was too good to be true. Need a hand getting your wagon up the ramp?"

"Thanks," Mouse said, shifting to pick up a couple of small scrap items beside him. "Ready!"

The girl pulled her chief engineer up the ramp into the small hold of the ship. She could hear the others calling to one another, checking systems. "Is Mattie on board?"

"She's seeing if she can sweet-talk someone out of some fuel," Mouse said. "And by sweet-talk, I mean she had a few credits, a data chip, and a knife so I wasn't gonna ask. Not when she has that look in her eye."

The crew set about checking systems for electrical responses and spaceworthiness. Ollie went to the bridge and was checking the navigation computer when she felt someone was watching, and she turned slowly.

They were all standing there, heads poking around the doorway. Mattie was with them, and she was the first to speak. "Got us some fuel. Enough to get to Rumicon, where we can try to sell the rest of the stuff. Where's Dodger? He coming?"

Ollie took a deep breath and stood up. She faced the group, feeling very small and scared. "Dodger ain't coming. He's made a deal to get himself that captaincy official-like. He'll have his papers. Grown-up papers."

"What does he need them for?" Bongo sounded angry, but Ollie could tell by the hint of quaver in his tone that he was nervous.

Mattie saved Ollie from answering by turning to the boy. "Look, fool, if Dodger gets his papers, then he's an official. He'll have graduated FAGN and gone legit as a captain. We wouldn't have to be so nervous all the time. We could stop hiding and doing odd jobs and accept real Federation jobs with cargo and licenses and make real money."

Bongo protested. "But he's our captain!" There was a bit more arguing among the crew at that, with Bongo and Tiny raising their voices.

"Hey!" Mouse drew himself up to his full height on the wagon, balancing on his knee stubs. "Everyone, stop. Dodger is our captain, sure. What are our captain's orders, Ollie?"

Ollie straightened her shoulders and tried for a calm tone in spite of the way her knees were shaking. "Captain Dodger said I was First Mate. And I am in command for the next month. We're to try to find a ship and sell our cargo, then come back and pick him up." She looked around at each face, making eye contact. "Maybe it'll be a rescue, we'll see. We do our jobs like normal. And we find us a *Newer London*. You think we can do that?"

There was silence, and Ollie held her breath. Then Mattie straightened and saluted her. "Aye aye, Miz Ollie. If Dodger said it, I'm good. We find a ship, we come get him, we go legit. And go find you a real doctor, who won't throw you back into a reactor."

The others chorused their agreements: "Aye."

"Legit, huh?"

"That'll be new."

"Radiation'd only help you look purtier, Mouse."

With Mattie's snappy salute, the rest fell into line and the muttering stopped. Ollie's smile broke through. "Well, I reckon we better get off this waystation before someone notices, eh?"

"Yes ma'am!"

And just like that, Ollie was in command. She took the main seat at the controls, wrapping her fingers around them. "Let's go find us a new home." And with a low hum, the ship took off. As one, the crew all turned to go about the business of flying their mission.

Ollie was scared, but proud. Her first command was underway.

The Last Laugh

by William B. Wolfe

If it's unbelievable, William Wolfe probably believes in it—and writes about it. From ghosts to extraterrestrials, psychic cats, fairy folk, and black-eyed kids, nothing is too weird to guest star in his stories and books. "Too weird," he believes, is just about the right amount of weird. He grew up near the weirdly named community of Monkey's Eyebrow, Kentucky, reading every science fiction and fantasy book he could lay hands on and eventually becoming a journalist, where he learned that the truth is often more unbelievable than fiction. He lives in Louisville, Kentucky, with his weird family and their weirder cat, Mr. Bitey. He's the author of *Twain's Treasure*, book one of *The Phantom Files* series.

Despite her happy-sounding name, Rayann Gladberry was a sour old prune. She was particularly pruney the day she almost killed Danny Williams.

It's not that my sixth-grade teacher couldn't smile. Whenever there was criticism to dish out or punishment to inflict, Ms. Gladberry's lips twisted into a creepy, crooked, counterfeit of happiness—something an undertaker might fashion on a dead man's face using stiff wires and thick layers of makeup.

Even worse, Ms. Gladberry's dreadful smile seemed to spread to more of my classmates each day, and I was terrified that it might infect me. That's why I kept my face blank. Better never to smile at all than to wear one of those gruesome grins.

These were my rules for survival at Hays Middle School: Keep your head down, your mouth shut, and your expressions unreadable. Don't raise your hand. Don't attract attention. Never, ever argue with Ms. Gladberry.

And I never did. Not until it was a matter of life and death.

The teacher had been scowling all day, ever since her meeting with Ms. Sykes, the principal, that morning. As Ms. Gladberry strode between rows of seats, her black skirt brushing against the tile floor and the heels of her tightly laced ankle boots click-clacking with each step, her Discipline Wand flicked up and down in her grip, as if seeking out a target.

We were all afraid of the Wand. One touch on low setting could send a charging junkyard dog howling away. The highest setting usually sent a victim into convulsions. Repeated use was like seating the victim in an electric chair. These torture sessions were known as "Corrections."

Mrs. Gladberry paused at my desk, stiff and cold as a marble statue, her eyes drilling into me as if burrowing to my soul. "Clarisse Burnett," she said, "according to the Rules of Citizenship, what are the three keys to a contented life?"

I pretended to think about the answer, but I had memorized all 50 rules long ago. I never wanted to feel "the kiss of the Wand," as Ms. Gladberry threatened when feeling poetic. "The three keys to a contented life are service, obedience, and loyalty to the Authorities," I answered.

Ms. Gladberry frowned at my answer—probably because it was right. She turned to the desk across from me and glared at Danny Williams, a dark-haired boy with soft features and kind eyes who had often been the target of her cruelty.

"Mr. Williams, fill in the missing word in this sentence from the Rules: 'A sound mind is a *what?* mind.'"

Danny's posture went rigid, and fear filled his wide eyes. This was not going to be good.

Danny wasn't stupid, but when Ms. Gladberry confronted

him, he panicked. And when he panicked, he couldn't think straight.

"A sound mind," Danny started, is a..." He hesitated. The Wand moved closer, and Ms. Gladberry's hand twitched.

I tried to mentally beam the answer to Danny: *A sober mind. Say it, Danny. Sober!* The confusion on Danny's face only increased.

"A sound mind," Danny started again, his voice rising, "is an ... alert mind?"

Ms. Gladberry smiled her creepy smile, and the Wand flipped forward, tickling Danny's neck. His body jerked left and right as if he were a puppet and Ms. Gladberry was yanking his strings. A small whimper escaped his clenched teeth, and there were scattered gasps around the classroom. A few students reflected Ms. Gladberry's grin, but no one laughed. No one ever laughed, unless they wanted a Correction that would make Danny's look like a mama's goodnight kiss.

"Try again," Ms. Gladberry barked, and I winced. Usually, she supplied the answer after a single stroke of the Wand. Now she was just being cruel. Or crueler.

"I don't know," Danny said, a pleading note to his voice.

"Then perhaps you should study harder," Ms. Gladberry said, twisting a knob on the Wand to increase its voltage. "Answer the question."

Danny shook, whether from the effects of the shock or fear, I couldn't tell. His eyes fixed on the Wand, and he spoke in a trembling voice. "A sound mind is...is... a resolute mind?"

The Wand flicked to Danny's ear and *popped* as it discharged. Danny jerked, then froze. Blood trickled from his mouth, a sign that he had bitten his tongue during the convulsion. His head slumped to his chest, and he mumbled incoherently.

I wanted to cry. Danny wasn't a close friend, but he was a friend. We walked together after school some days, and sometimes he looked my way and smiled—a real smile that made me happy. But as much as I hated what was happening, I couldn't say anything, or Ms. Gladberry might turn her Wand on me.

The teacher twisted the power setting to its highest setting. "Once again, and I hope no more Corrections are necessary," she said.

I couldn't believe it. Danny was only semi-conscious, and there was no way he could guess the answer. She was going to Wand him *again!*

My heart pounded, and I longed to close my eyes and hold my hands over my ears so that I wouldn't see or hear what I knew was seconds away. A third zap from the Wand might send Danny to his grave. And no one would do anything about it because teachers were considered Authorities. No one could challenge them—except a higher Authority.

A feeling stronger than fear and horror gripped me: *anger.* I was not going to let Ms. Gladberry get away with this. I leapt from my seat, leaned over Danny and put a hand to his throat, checking his pulse.

"Miss Burnett, return to your seat," Ms. Gladberry barked.

I ignored her and put my ear closed to Danny's mouth. "Are you okay? Say something!"

Danny mumbled just loudly enough for me to hear. "What the *joke* is she trying to do? Kill me?"

I froze. The J-word was the worst word you could say. If Ms. Gladberry heard, it would go on his Permanent Record, like a criminal record. He would have a cloud hanging over him for the rest of his life.

Ms. Gladberry waved her Wand at me. "Miss Burnett, do as I said," she said, danger in her voice.

"But Ms. Gladberry, the Nineteenth Rule requires us to 'Render aid to any citizen in distress.' Danny is bleeding. I have to make sure that he's going to be okay."

At first there was shock in her face—disbelief that a student had argued with her. The look of surprise quickly faded and was replaced by cold hatred. I had just made a dangerous enemy. But Ms. Gladberry couldn't argue with the Rules in front of the class. "Just make it quick," she growled.

I took Danny's face between my palms and waited until his eyes focused on my face.

"Danny, this is Clarisse. You are in Ms. Gladberry's class, and you've had a Correction. You'll be okay, but you must answer her question. If you pay close attention, I know that you'll remember it, right?"

Danny nodded, but I kept hands on his flushed and sweaty cheeks. "You're SO cold. BRRR!" I said, squeezing his face *hard* on the second and fourth words. Danny's eyes opened wide, and he gave a slight nod.

"The boy is fine. Sit down, Miss Burnett," the teacher said.

I slipped back into my seat, praying that Danny had gotten my secret message. Ms. Gladberry repeated her question, wagging the Wand inches from Danny's face.

Danny didn't wait for her to strike again. "A sound mind is a *sober* mind," he said.

Ms. Gladberry's face fell in disappointment. "That is right. At last," she said. "Isn't it amazing how the Discipline Wand can help a student focus?"

Then the teacher turned to me, all glower and glare.

"As for you, Miss Burnett, you would be wise to avoid quoting the Rules of Citizenship to your instructor in the future, or I might be tempted to reinforce your learning with a Correction."

"Yes ma'am," I said, as politely as I could. "I meant no disrespect." But I could tell that I was in her crosshairs now.

This was not funny. Not funny at all.

After school, Danny walked next to me as we made our way through the busy city toward our homes.

Thank you for . . . today," he said. "You were very brave."

I shrugged. "Things were going too far."

Danny looked all around before opening his mouth again. We were alone in a crowd, surrounded by busy people too engrossed in their own concerns to pay attention to a couple of 12-year-olds. But even so, he spoke in a whisper. "Things have already gone too far. Not just in class, but everywhere."

I shrugged again. He was right. The Rules of Citizenship were supposed to help people live together peacefully. But for years, the Council of Authorities had been making the Rules more and more restrictive. What had once been a prohibition against "cruel humor" had been expanded to include all types of humor. The J-word could send someone to jail. Laughter could cost you your life—especially if you laughed at the wrong person. Three years ago, Mr. Freeman, the janitor, had laughed when our mayor had misspelled "potatoes" while administering a school spelling bee. Hooded men dragged the janitor from his home that night, and he was never seen again.

Nobody liked it, but what could we do?

As if to answer, Danny motioned me into an empty alley and handed me a folded note. "What's that?" I asked, wondering if he was going to ask me to be his girlfriend or something lame like that.

"It's called a knock-knock," Danny said. "Read it."

I unfolded the paper and saw four lines:

Knock, knock!

Who's there?

Needle.

Needle who?

Needle little help getting in the door.

I stared at Danny. "I don't get it."

"Read it out loud," he instructed.

It wasn't till I got to "Needle little help" that I understood. It was double-meaning word play—risky, but not officially banned by the Rules.

I groaned, and Danny handed me another slip.

Knock, Knock!

Who's there?

Ketchup.

Ketchup who?

Ketchup with me and I'll tell you!

This time, I groaned right away, and a tiny smile curled my lips. It was stupid, but so stupid that it was fun.

"One more," I pleaded. Danny looked at me hard, as if trying to decide whether to trust me with something important.

"Knock, knock." he said.

After a few seconds, I realized that I was supposed to fill in the next line.

"Who's there?" I said.

"Joe King," Danny replied.

"Joe King who?"

"Joe King around can be dangerous, but it can also change the world."

I felt the blood drain from my face. "What are you talking about?"

"I'm talking about the J-word: jokes! These are knock-knock jokes."

I stepped back. "No! They're word play! The Rules say we can't tell . . . J-words."

"The Rules say that a teacher can Wand her students to death. I swear, Clarisse, one more touch of that shock stick, and I would not be standing here now," Danny said. "The Rules also say that it's okay to drag a man out of his house, torture, and kill him if he laughs at an Authority. The Rules must be changed—or abolished. We have to fight back."

My heart pounded and my head swam. Get rid of the Rules? I hated the Rules and the world that had produced them. But they were as much a part of life as eating and sleeping. The idea that we could make them go away was terrifying, but also the most exciting thought that had ever entered my head.

Whispered words escaped me before I could clamp my mouth shut. "How could we do that?"

"If you want to know, come with me," Danny answered.

Struck silent by fear—or was it excitement?—I could only nod and follow Danny out onto the street. He led me into an old industrial part of town, stopping at 451 Far Heights Road. The building there had been abandoned for years, judging from the fading graffiti on its brick walls and grass growing through the meandering cracks that ran across its empty parking lot.

"This place gives me the creeps," I said.

That's only on the outside," Danny said. "Inside—well, let me just say that knock-knocks are just the fringe of a new world you're going to discover. That is, if you can get past the entrance exam."

"Entrance exam? What's that?" I grumbled.

Danny smiled. "It's the exam you have to pass to enter. You'll do fine. I believe in you."

He hurried me around to the back of the building, where we faced a rusty, windowless metal door. Danny stepped up and pushed an intercom button next to a speaker grill.

"Knock, knock," he said.

After a moment, a girl's voice replied over the scratchy speaker. "Who's there?"

"Robin."

"Robin who?"

"Robin YOU! Hand over all your money."

There was a momentary chuckle before the speaker clicked off and the door opened. A blonde girl beamed with joy—until she saw me. Then her smile turned upside down, and her nose wrinkled, as if I'd sprayed her with skunk juice.

"Who's that?" she asked.

"A friend. She saved my life today," Danny said.

"Is she funny?"

"Well, that's what we're about to find out," Danny said. He stepped inside, closing the door in my face.

I punched the intercom button. "What's the big idea?"

"I said there would be an exam," Danny said through the speaker. "This is it. Now, be funny."

"Are you kidding me?" I snapped. "I saved your life, and this is my thank-you?"

There was no reply.

"I'm serious. Let me in, or I'm going home."

No reply.

"This isn't fair! I've never even heard a J-word before today. Now I have to write one?

Still no answer.

I wound my hands into fists and beat at the door. I wasn't sure, but I thought I heard the girl laughing from inside.

It looked like I would have to play the game their way. Fine. I would show them—especially that blonde hyena. I thought of all the names I knew till I found a name that might have a double meaning.

I pushed the intercom button. "Knock, knock."

The response was immediate. "Who's there?"

"Doris."

"Doris who?"

"Doris locked. Now open it and let me in right now!"

Seconds later, I faced my nemesis, a sheepish grin on her face. "Is it true that you never heard a knock-knock before today?"

I nodded, keeping my lips tight and my eyes wary.

"Not bad," she said, giving me a respectful head bob. "I'm Phyllis."

"My name is—" I said, before Phyllis cut me off.

"No real names," she said. "We only use stage names here—names that we borrow from the great comedians. Makes it harder to trace us back to our families."

"I don't know any great comedians," I said.

"I do," Phyllis said. "So from now on, or until you decide to change it, your name here is Carol. The boy you came here with is Robin."

She thrust out a hand, and I shook it nervously. What kind of madhouse had I walked into? "Where's Dan—I mean Robin?" I asked.

"He had to check in with the leader of our little tribe. Let me show you around."

I didn't recognize any of the other kids we passed. They were all about my age but must have gone to different schools.

"Our job here," Phyllis said, "is to preserve and spread all of the greatest forms of humor of the past—or at least those jokes and sketches that we've been able to find in our comedy underground."

"Why haven't I heard about this before?" I asked, and Phyllis rapped her knuckles on my head. "Uh, what part of 'underground' confused you?"

My face burned, but Phyllis gave me a friendly punch in the shoulder. "Just kidding. Lighten up and look around."

Just ahead stood a boy with a big, black, phony mustache attached to his upper lip and a cigar pinched between his thumb and index finger. He waved the cigar around as he spoke in an odd, accented voice.

"One morning I shot an elephant in my pajamas. How he got into my pajamas I'll never know," he said. I must have smiled, because his eyes locked onto mine as he continued his patter. "The secret of life is honesty and fair dealing. If you can fake that, you've got it made." The absurdity almost made me chuckle. Almost.

"That's Julius," Phyllis said. "He's practicing his Groucho jokes."

I didn't know what a Groucho was, but I knew what the J-word meant—and the dangers of saying it. My face must have gone white, because Phyllis gave me a hug. "It's OK. You're safe here. We can say the J-word—and any other word. But let's move on."

Next came two girls and a boy, eye-poking, fake slapping, and nyuk-nyuk-nyuk laughing at one another. "Those are the Stooges," Phyllis said. "Low-brow humor, but timeless."

"Hi, Ellen," Phyllis said, as we walked past a girl with short, blonde hair and a big grin. "Tell me one."

"My grandmother started walking five miles a day when she was 60," the girl said. "She's 97 now, and we don't know where the heck she is."

I *laughed.* Out loud! I was almost surprised when no one came around the corner to zap me with a Wand.

Next came another boy, wearing an ill-fitting suit and tugging at his necktie, his eyes bulging nearly out of their sockets.

"I came from a real tough neighborhood," he said, "Why, every time I shut the window, I hurt a burglar's fingers. I tell you, I don't get no respect."

"That's Rod. His specialty is one-liners," Phyllis explained.

We stopped next to a short girl with long, dark hair sitting on the floor before a camera that appeared to have exploded. Dozens of springs, screws, electronic circuit boards, memory chips, and a lens as big around and half as long as her arm were strewn about.

"Gilda, this is Carol," Phyllis said.

Gilda looked up and flashed a smile bright enough to take pictures by. "I heard Robin talking about you when he came in. Says you saved his life."

"He exaggerates," I replied, but it felt good know he had said so. "Are you a comedian, too, Gilda?"

"We all are. But we have other jobs too," Gilda said. "I'm the camera girl."

"Don't be modest, Gilda. No one else here is," Phyllis said, then added, "Gilda is a photography genius. Someday, people are going to see her videos around the world."

A tall, spindly boy passing behind Gilda noogied the crown of her head.

"That's what everyone says," he said. "But her work's not going anywhere without me."

"That rude interruption is Carlin, our tech master and online expert," Gilda said. "As much I hate to admit it, he's right. He's our key to notoriety."

"I'm sorry," I said, "but I don't understand any of this. Who are you guys, really? What's with the secret headquarters and the entrance test and the subterfuge? Is the goal just to make some videos?"

"The goal," said someone behind me, "is revolution."

I turned to find a girl with piercing green eyes, high, arched brows, and long, curly, fox-red hair. I spoke with caution. "What kind of revolution?"

"A very serious one—but also hilarious," she said, deadpan, but with a twinkle in her eyes. "And you need to be a part of it."

⟨⟩

I was soon in a meeting room, sitting at a round table with Danny/Robin and the green-eyed girl, who had introduced herself as "Lucy, the master of ceremonies at this comedy club."

"You must have lots of questions," Lucy said, "and I promise that I'll answer them all. But first, I have one for you."

I gave her a go-ahead nod, and she leaned in toward me, placing her hands flat on the table. "Carol, why don't the Authorities allow us to laugh and tell jokes?"

I recalled the Rule in a heartbeat.

"Jokes are a cruel insult to human dignity. Laughter is an attack on the weak, wounded, and helpless."

Lucy frowned. "That's what the Rules say. But you've heard our comedians here telling jokes. You told one yourself to gain entrance to the building. Were they cruel? Would laughter have been an attack on anyone?"

"No," I admitted. "It was all fun. It made me happy."

"Then why is it forbidden to laugh? Why is it a crime to tell a joke?"

"Maybe," I said, "some people don't like to be laughed at."

Lucy leaned back in her chair. "People don't like to be dragged away from their families in the middle of the night by masked men. People don't like to be tortured by shock sticks. And those things aren't illegal."

"Then why?"

"Because humor and laughter are subversive," Lucy said. "That means they can cause trouble for the people who rule us. They undermine power without openly challenging it. They give power to the powerless. That's why tyrants like the Authorities have always feared humor and ridicule. That's why the Authorities won't rest until the last laugh has been silenced. And that's why we refuse to let that happen."

A chill swept over me. To talk this way was treason. If the Authorities knew, we would all go to prison—or worse. Even me, just for being here. My face must have said everything I was thinking, because Lucy leaned back in her chair and smiled.

"You're afraid? You should be. But so should the Authorities. They have bullets. We have laughter. They have guards, guns, informants, and prisons. We have irony, sarcasm, satire, and parody—and a huge collection of joke books. We're more than an even match, I'd say."

My hands trembled. My mouth felt desert dry. I wasn't sure how I had gotten myself mixed up with these crazy kids, but I wanted no part of them.

I stood up, knees wobbly. "Good luck and all that, but this is not for me."

Danny's eyes flashed. "You said you wanted to fight back! I thought you wanted in."

"I never said I wanted to die for a hopeless cause," I said. "As of this second, I'm out."

"I'm afraid that's not possible," Lucy said. "You were in the moment you stood up to your teacher. Ms. Gladberry was ready to kill Robin just for the fun of it. What do you think she'll do to the girl who defied her?"

I knew, with sudden dread certainty, that Lucy was right. It wouldn't be long before I would feel the kiss of the Wand, and it would be a deadly romance. "Then I'm doomed," I said, my voice a whisper.

"No, you're not!" Danny said. "We have a plan. But we need you to be a part of it."

"Why me?"

Lucy spoke. "Robin tells me that you are the student audio-video technician for your class."

I nodded. "Every student has to participate in one classroom activity. Mine is to manage input to SchoolCam, the school district's remote-learning program. It's easy. Whenever Ms. Gladberry thinks she has an especially clever lesson, I fire up the video camera and record her submission. She's never been chosen, but her dream is to be seen on video everywhere."

Lucy laughed and clapped her hands. "Delightful," she said. "If you help us, we can make her dream come true—and get Ms. Gladberry out of your hair forever. Are you with us?"

"One hundred percent," I said. As if I had any choice.

"Good," Lucy said. "Because we've got some work to do tonight if we're going to turn the table on the very unfunny Ms. Gladberry."

I took my seat in class the next day exhausted, exhilarated, and terrified. It had been a long night and an early morning, sneaking out of home after bedtime, slipping into the school to get things ready in the classroom, and returning home just barely before my morning get-ready-for-school wake-up.

The classroom's closed-circuit video was rigged, and everything was ready for the comedy sketch of a lifetime. At least, that's what Danny and I hoped and prayed. Because if it fell apart, our lifetimes might be extremely short.

When Danny came in, he passed by Ms. Gladberry's desk and stumbled over a paper-filled trash can. He caught the can before it could tip over and grinned as other students rolled their eyes at his clumsiness.

Ms. Gladberry entered the classroom and gave me the stink eye. I could see that Lucy had had been right. I would be the object of her wrath for as long as she remained a teacher. Sooner or later, she would find an excuse to give me a Correction, and I probably wouldn't walk away from it.

"Quiet," Ms. Gladberry said, even though no one was talking. "This is a serious class for serious students. I'll put up with no foolishness today, or you will bear the consequences. Is that clear to all?"

"Yes, ma'am," we all answered back, Danny and I perhaps the loudest. But my mind was shouting something else at the teacher: *Just shut up and sit down.*

As if in answer to my call, Ms. Gladberry marched to her desk and plopped into her well-padded chair. A loud, prolonged *ppppfffffffffftttttttt* rolled out of the seat, where the Stooges had inserted what they called a "whoopie cushion" into the padding.

Ms. Gladberry's eyes went wide and her face went white as gasps, chittering, and even a few quickly extinguished yelps of laughter sounded around the classroom. "That wasn't me!" the teacher insisted, jumping up from the chair and pounding on the cushion to expose its guilt. But the Stooges had used a one-time-only device, so no one believed her.

A moment later, a white cloud started rising from the trash can Danny had almost knocked over. "Smoke! Fire!" students screamed. In fact, it was just the vapors releasing from a cotton-wrapped block of dry ice—frozen carbon dioxide—that had been hidden under the papers, waiting for Danny's "stumble" to knock it into a pan of warm water.

Just as Lucille had predicted, Ms. Gladberry stomped franticly into the can, extinguishing the "fire" as the papers soaked up the water. But when she tried to pull her boot out, it refused to comply—most likely because of the quick-setting glue released when the teacher's stomping had crushed the plastic packets containing it.

Ms. Gladberry hopped on her free boot and shook the one in the can in a vain effort to free herself. Snickers broke out around the classroom at the sight of our fearsome educator bouncing about like a dancing bear. Even I couldn't keep a straight face.

"You barn of braying asses!" Ms. Gladberry screeched. "The next laugh I hear will be the last laugh—the last breath—for the child responsible." She punched a key-code into the locked drawer at her desk where she kept the Wand, then screamed as a dozen gray mice—courtesy of Gilda's lock-hacking skills—streamed out, some to the top of her desk, some to the floor, and some up the ramp of her outstretched arm.

Our teacher had always seemed fearless, but when confronted by the scampering rodents, she dissolved into terror.

"Help me, please!" Ms. Gladberry wailed. No one moved. She slapped at her shirt, where the fleeing mice had burrowed, and at her legs, where some of the terrified mice had climbed. By this time, everyone in the class, even Danny and I, were caught up in laughter no law could stop. Finally, after thrashing about enough to shake off the mice, her anger overcame her fear, and the teacher reached into the drawer, grasped the Wand, and headed straight for me. I made no effort to wipe the grin from my face.

"You did this, didn't you?" she bellowed. "I'll kill you and anyone else who defies me!"

"No, Ms. Gladberry," I pleaded. "That's against the Rules."

"Rules," the teacher said, "are meant to be broken." She thrust the shock stick against my neck, turned its voltage to full blast, and squeezed the trigger.

A terrible scream filled the classroom. Not my scream, but Ms. Gladberry's. The Wand had delivered its charge not through its tip, but back to the holder—thanks to Julius, who turned out to be as good with electronics as he was with his cigar and fake mustache. The teacher fell to the floor in spasms, her legs kicking so hard that the trash can crumpled around her foot to form a sort of metal boot.

When the convulsions ended, Ms. Gladberry pushed the Wand aside and crawled on hands and knees to her desk. There, she pulled herself upright, glaring at me with a hatred that sent shivers down my spine.

Arms outstretched, she zombie-walked forward, her can-boot clanking ridiculously with each step. I could have run, but I needed this scene to play out. "I don't need the Wand to deal with you, my pretty," she said when she finally reached my desk. "I'll strangle you with my bare hands."

As if on cue, the classroom door opened, and a bald and burly security guard swept in, pulling Ms. Gladberry aside and hand-cuffing her hands behind her back.

"Stop! What are you doing? I'm the victim here. Those students tried to kill me! Arrest *them*," Ms. Gladberry wailed as she was being dragged from the room. As her screeches faded, in came Ms. Sykes.

"Can anyone *please* tell me what is going on in this classroom?" she asked.

Students looked blankly at the principal and shook their heads. "Something's wrong with Ms. Gladberry," Danny finally offered, his comment not exactly helpful. "She's been acting really weird for a while now, kind of paranoid, and today she just flipped."

Everyone nodded. It was as good an explanation as any, and no one else wanted to meet the principal's stare.

"And I suppose no one knows how this whole fiasco wound up being recorded on the classroom video broadcast?"

I raised my hand. "She told me she had a special lesson planned for today and she wanted to submit it to SchoolCam."

Ms. Sykes sighed. "And would you know how this video was streamed live throughout the district?"

I gave my best shocked-and-surprised look. "That shouldn't happen! It's supposed to be stored for review and editing."

"Yes, I am aware of that," Ms. Sykes said. "What I want to know is why that didn't happen."

I shook my head. "Can't imagine. Honestly, I wouldn't even know how to do that." Which was true. Carlin was behind that the network hacking.

Ms. Sykes nodded. I figured that she was ready to dump the blame for everything onto Ms. Gladberry and avoid a long investigation that could only focus more attention on her school. "Crazed Teacher Escorted from School after Mishap" made a much better headline than "Hays Middle School under Investigation by Authorities."

"Children, we'll find a substitute to fill in for Ms. Gladberry this afternoon" the principal said. *"And for the rest of forever,"* I added in my thoughts.

⟞⊡⟝

"I tell ya, I don't get no respect," Rod said, raising his slice of pepperoni pizza and wrapping a long, string of melty mozzarella around his tongue. "You had to go and start the fun without me."

"No one could be there except for Carol and Robin. But you helped as much as anybody," Lucy said, mid-bite of her sausage and mushroom. "Your glue-in-the-trash-can idea was brilliant. Everyone did his or her job and did it well. That's why we're kicking off this revolution with a pizza party!"

I nearly choked on an anchovy. "Revolution? What revolution?"

"The revolution you planted, Carol," said Danny/Robin. *(I had to get used to his stage name.)* "We're getting reports that our video has spread nationwide. No matter how fast the Authorities shut down one web site, another anonymous site pops up. It's everywhere—and people can't stop laughing."

"WHAT? I thought this was only going out to the district," I said.

"Oh, right. I connected it to an internet feed. I forgot to mention that," Carlin said with a wink.

I moaned. "You guys said this was just to get rid of Ms. Gladberry."

"It was," Lucy said. "And to give everyone a good laugh. The laugh is mightier than the sword, you know. If we get enough people laughing at the Authorities, they will have to change. It's hard to have absolute power when people see your leaders as clowns."

"And what about us?" I asked. "We're on the video too."

"Not really," Gilda said. "Just you and Ms. Gladberry. I added a motion tracker to the camera. It was zoomed in on the teacher the whole time. It's funnier that way."

"I'm hearing rumors that other 'reality' videos are popping up around the country already," Phyllis said. "I think we've started something."

"Why didn't anyone tell me all of this?" I said, angry despite our success.

"We didn't want you to worry," Lucy said. "You were the most important part of the operation."

"Just because I knew how to set up the class cam?"

"No, silly. We have half a dozen people who could do that. You had that one, amazing, indispensable talent that makes a master comedian."

I raised my eyebrows.

"You knew how to drive your teacher crazy, absolutely berserk, mad enough to flip her wig and try to kill you. And you played her like a fiddle."

"Really? That was me?" I asked. "Am I really *that* annoying?"

Robin gave me a smile. "Just ask any of your friends."

Everyone clapped, and then Lucy started laughing, joined by Robin, Gilda, Carlin, Rod, Phyllis, and everyone. Even the Stooges joined in with a series of high-pitched *whoop, whoop, whoop, whoops.*

Me? I started laughing, too, louder and harder than I could have imagined possible. Laughing until I grabbed my sides, gasped, doubled over, and rolled on the floor. I was still laughing when everyone else had run out of breath.

It seemed what they said was true. The last laugh was the best!

Yawn Us to Sleep and Devour Our Dreams
by David Turnbull

David Turnbull is a member of the Clockhouse London group of genre writers. He writes mainly short fiction and has had numerous short stories published in magazines and anthologies, as well as having stories read at live events such as Liars League London, Solstice Shorts and Virtual Futures. He was born in Scotland, but now lives in London. He can be found at www.tumsh.co.uk.

Lillian told herself that she definitely wasn't a deserter. A deserter would leave for good. That wasn't her plan. She wasn't running away. She was going to go back. She just needed a break. A little while to be her old self. A normal twelve-year-old instead of a resistance fighter.

Just an hour or so to spend in the company of her family. It wasn't much to ask, was it? Sure, she'd be punished, confined to camp, given latrine-cleaning duties for at least a month. But she didn't care.

Head down, she hurried through the eerie stillness of the familiar downtown streets. She could hear the other members of her patrol calling out to each other as they scavenged for supplies of tinned food. She wondered how long it would be before they noticed that her voice was missing. She passed a wall onto which red graffiti had been sprayed in the early days of the invasion. It read:

Yawn us to sleep and devour our dreams,
But we shall fight back with flashlight beams

She wondered who had come up with the rhyme and whether or not the Yawning Men could even read.

Across the street one of them was watching her from a department store window. He was skulking amongst the mannequins, wan and gaunt, delicate tresses of his snow-white hair draping the bone-thin angles of his shoulders, his pink eyes coldly tracing her every step.

Lillian pulled down the bill of her red baseball cap and avoided looking at him. She didn't run. She didn't have to worry about being pursued. Yawning Men never ventured into the open during daylight hours.

Six months ago, their hazily shimmering ship had emerged through a rip in the sky. At first it appeared on and off in random sequences. It was dismissed as some sort of fakery. No one believed its ever-bleeding colors, fluctuating shape and constantly altering size were truly there.

The general consensus was that it was being imagined as some sort of mass hallucination. No one realized the threat it posed until it was too late. By the time more ships sliced through the skies above other towns and cities across the globe, a slow, lethargic invasion had already commenced.

From what the grown-ups had been able to piece together, the Yawning Men were a race of marauding parasitical entities. They moved relentlessly between dimensions, systematically feeding on the populations of the worlds they encountered.

Lillian knew the Yawning Man in the store wanted to paralyze her with his hypnotic stare and contaminate her with the contagion of his yawn. He wanted to lull her into a deep and unshakable sleep. His aim was to have her sit down right there on the pavement and close her eyes.

Angry now, she deliberately crossed the street and came level with him. Her heart was pounding, her knuckles clenched to trembling fists. But she wanted to show him she wasn't afraid. He was yawning, his ghostly face pressed against the glass, thin jaw stretched as wide as physically possible. The urge to yawn with him was starting to burn inside her. Lillian checked that her chunky rubber flashlight was still hanging from her belt in the holster she had cut from an old sport sock. If she felt herself weakening, she'd grab the torch and shine the yellow beam right into the dreadful pink swirl of his eyes. It would send him retreating into the shadows of the store.

Keep on walking, she told herself. *Don't look back.*

The remainder of the street stretched out before her. Like Beauty's castle in that old fairy tale, it was littered with hundreds of sleeping citizens—seated hunched over on the sidewalk, curled up on their sides in doorways, arms wrapped around streetlamps, heads lolling to the side.

And in the road too—buses full of slumbering passengers, tourists sprawled out in the back seats of taxis, car drivers slumped over steering wheels. All of them sleeping the enchanted sleep induced by the Yawning Men, waiting for their innermost dreams to be feasted upon when the sun sank low in the sky once more.

Dangling down from the ceiling in the hallway of her parent's house were a dozen or more assorted wind chimes that she'd hung there with the aid of a stepladder. Back in the early stages of the invasion, they were her alarm system. Being too short to set them off, she passed easily back and forth under them. But Yawning Men were impossibly tall. If a Yawning Man had ever tried to come in through the front door, he would have been bound to set off a cacophony of harmonious clangs to alert her.

Lillian entered the front room. The members of her family were seated exactly where she had left them almost four months ago. Mom and Dad on the sofa, her brother Rick on one of the two armchairs.

She pushed the red baseball cap onto her forehead and, in the fussy manner that had previously become her ritual, checked their pulses to make sure that none of them had died in their deep, deep sleep, tutting to herself all the while about the state they'd gotten into while she'd been away.

Her mother's head had slumped onto her father's shoulder. Her father's head was leaning in the opposite direction. She straightened them up and wedged a cushion between their heads to stop them falling in on each other again.

Her brother had slid down into the armchair and was all crumpled in on himself. She pushed one of the dining chairs behind the armchair and climbed up on it so she could reach over and twist her hands into his sweatshirt in order to haul him upright. It had taken her a while to figure out how to do this properly, but now that she had the knack, it was relatively easy.

Her father started to snore, so she pinched his nostrils to stop him. Her mother's mouth had fallen wide. It gave a hollow little click when she pushed it shut. She noticed drool gleaming on her brother's chin and dabbed it dry with a tissue.

Lillian wasn't sure which one of them had been infected first, but Dad was her prime suspect. It would have been on the train home from work. A Yawning Man would have sat down in the same carriage as him, all gangly and awkward. He'd have caught someone in his pink stare and yawned, long and wide and noisily. After a moment that person would have yawned right back. And then someone else would have seen that person yawning and yawned in turn, because once the infection started to spread no one could stop it. And the yawn would have proliferated through the carriage like the plague that it was, passing from person to person, while the Yawning Man just sat there, spindly arms folded, a smug, self-satisfied grin on his narrow lips.

And Dad would have come home, drowsy eyelids drooping

down, constantly yawning and stretching. Mom would have
started yawning. Rick would have started yawning. And soon
they'd all have drifted off into the deep, catatonic sleep that
still imprisoned them. Mom and Dad on the sofa. Rick in the
armchair. Just where she had found them when she came home
from netball practice—just where they remained till now.

Lillian tried to grab their attention.

"It's my birthday in ten days' time. You all better wake up
before that. I'm expecting a cake with thirteen candles and lots
of presents."

It felt like ages since she had given up on trying to awaken
them. She shook them. Nothing. She poked each of them hard
with her finger. Nothing. She shouted right into their faces.
Nothing.

The more frustrated she became the more her anger boiled
inside her.

She took Mom's favorite vase from the bookshelf and held
it precariously in front of her. "Look," she said. "I have your
Aunt Jayne's precious vase. What if I drop it? What if it smash-
es to pieces?"

Mom went right on sleeping.

She brought Dad's toolbox from under the kitchen sink.

"I'm touching your tools. I've got your claw hammer."

She put it down and swapped it for a pair of pliers.

"I've got these scissor thingies. What if I cut off my finger?"

When not even a flicker of an eyelid came back in response,
she marched upstairs and fetched Rick's precious Xbox.

"Look what I found," she said. "What if I break it?"

Rick just carried on sleeping.

"What if I drop it?"

Nothing.

"I'm fed up looking after you guys!" she yelled, her face blush-
ing a fiery red. "You should think yourselves lucky I came back

to see you at all. I've got work to do, you know. I'm in the
army now. Yes, that's right, Dad, your little princess is in the
army. What do you think about that?"

Nothing—not the slightest reaction.

She didn't mean to fall asleep.

She'd prepared a family meal of tinned ham she'd sliced in the
kitchen, laid it out on plates with some crackers, set the plates
on their laps, sat down in the other armchair, stared at the
blank TV screen, pretended they were eating together, watching
their favorite show.

She talked breathlessly for hours, telling them all about training camp and the scavenging missions she went on with the
other members of her patrol, all of whom were teenagers like
her. She told them all about Euan Hoo. But not about the
secret crush she had on him. And about how they all made a
big joke about his name.

Euan Hoo else?

You get it?

You and who else?

She told them about Abdul, the moody one, and about Marty,
who was the only one in the patrol who was younger than her
and who kept making her laugh by calling her Big Sis. She told
them about Jomoke, their patrol leader who was fearless and
feisty.

She kept saying that she had to go soon and that the patrol
would be looking for her. But it felt so nice to be with them
all again, even if they couldn't talk back and just went right
on sleeping. So she gave herself another ten minutes, and then
another, and then another.

And she must have dozed off.

Now it was dark. She could tell by the depth of the darkness
that filled the room that it was late. Far too late to risk going
back into the streets. The Yawning Men would be on the prowl

now. If the patrol had been searching for her, Jomoke would probably have called it off by now and ordered them back to camp for their own safety.

Lillian was buzzing with pent-up energy. Even before the invasion, it hadn't been unusual for her to wake up buzzing. She could feel the blood crashing in her skull. About a year ago, long before the Yawning Men's strange craft had appeared in the sky, Mom and Dad had taken her to see specialist, who'd suggested she might have something called ADS. Attention Deficit Syndrome. There had been talk of some sort of medication, but Mom wouldn't agree.

Rick started calling her a weirdo.

That was why she fitted in so well with the resistance. They were a weird bunch. Half of the adults had insomnia, and the other half had sleep apnea. A lot of the kids had ADS or similar conditions. The theory was that sleep disorders and stuff like that make you virtually immune to the yawn.

Jomoke called them the army of freaks.

This time, though, it wasn't just the usual adrenalin rush in her veins that made her eyes snap open. It was the strange, queasy feeling that came over her. She couldn't quite put her finger on it—an odd tensing of her muscles, a tingling in her nerves.

Then it hit her.

A Yawning Man was nearby.

Careful not to move too quickly, she reached down and slipped her torch from its sport-sock holster. Narrowing her eyes to accustom them to the darkness, she scanned the corners of the room, her finger hovering over the on-switch of the torch. When she was sure that it was safe, she crouched low as she tiptoed across the room to the window.

Stepping to one side of the open curtains, she peered through a little gap.

A Yawning Man was coming along the street in a ghostly, juddering motion, wispy, white hair trailing out behind him, pale skin reflecting the glow of the moon and making him seem almost luminous.

She knew exactly where he was heading.

Her neighbor, Mr. Choudhary, was seated fast asleep in the road, his back resting against the front wheel of his blue Mazda, legs splayed wide, leather briefcase resting on his lap. When she'd first seen him like that, she'd had the notion to try and drag him up his garden path and into the shelter of his porch. But he proved far too heavy, so she'd had no choice other than to prop him up and leave him there.

Now the Yawning Man was hungrily honing in on him. As the hideous creature drew nearer, she could see how gruesome he truly looked. Impossibly skinny, sunken, almost skeletal features, porcine eyes, thin slashes like scars for nostrils. His round mouth was curved to a perfect O, standing ever ready to stretch to an exaggerated yawn.

And worst of all, now that she had time to study one of them more closely, the loose hanging item that she had always taken to be a pale robe of some sort appeared to be hideous, leathery folds of the creature's own albino flesh.

She bit her lip to stop herself from crying out, her hand gripping tightly around the circumference of the torch, index finger resting against the on-button, ready to press down and send out a protective beam.

The Yawning Man drew level with Mr. Choudhary. He looked down, his long neck dipping vulture-like between narrow shoulders, white hair hanging like pale drapes. He raised his right hand, and the long, arachnid finger curled into a claw. The slash of his nostril flared.

Lillian knew what was going to happen next.

Before she had become fully aware of the nocturnal nature of the Yawning Men, she had ventured out of the house one evening at sunset. Walking cautiously through streets full of slumbering souls, her hope had been to try and find someone else who was still awake.

She had hidden herself behind a garden hedge when she caught sight of the juddering approach of a Yawning Man. At the side of the road, a postal delivery truck was parked. The driver was hanging half way out the rolled-down window, his arm dangling limply down the side of the door, deep in a yawn-induced sleep.

Lillian saw the Yawning Man curve his long fingers around the postman's head and hold them there for a good while before lifting his hand away. When he did, a swirling miasma of streaks and colors rose up as if emerging straight out the poor man's head. The Yawning Man leaned forward and sucked all of this into his mouth through the wide yaw of his anemic lips. And Lillian knew without the shadow of a doubt that it was devouring the essence of postman's sleep-induced dreams.

Now the same thing was about to happen to her neighbor.

She simply could not drag her eyes away. The Yawning Man reached for Mr. Choudhary's head, and his long, bleached fingers slid through thick black hair to curve around the skull. Just as she had witnessed on the previous occasion, the Yawning Man remained in that position for what seemed like an endlessly frozen moment of time.

Then he pulled his arm back, and all of Mr. Choudhary's dreams came flooding out in a kaleidoscopic palette of jagged shapes that seemed to weep into each other and then separate like bright starbursts, only to meld again. And in amongst all of this, there were shapes that looked like faces.

Faces that Lillian recognized. Mrs. Choudhary was in there, as were Amala and Riza, the Choudharys' twin daughters who were a year younger than Lillian and whom she had known almost all her life. Mr. Choudhary had been dreaming of his family, themselves asleep inside his house, so near, yet so very far away from him.

The Yawning Man pushed his long and narrow head into the vortex of the dream and sucked it all in through the exaggerated O of his mouth, stealing away everything that poor Mr. Choudhary had been clinging to in his endless slumber.

The Yawning Man seemed to tremble with delight. He raised his head to the night sky. Lillian cocked her own head to see what he was looking at. And there it was, the Yawning Man's shimmering dream ship, bleeding psychedelic color, intermittently sending out vast, arachnid tentacles only for them to contract and distort.

Lillian's hands began to tremble so much that the torch slipped from her grip. It clattered noisily onto the wooden floor. The Yawning Man's head whipped round, white hair fanning around it, pink eyes honing in on the window. Lillian ducked down below the ledge and pulled her knees tightly against her chest.

She heard the feet of the Yawning Man come shuffling through the gravel on the driveway. There came a dull thump, and she knew that his pale face was pressed up against the glass. She bit down on her lip to stop herself crying out and tasted the tang of blood in her mouth. The torch lay tantalizingly close to her. But if she reached out to grab it, the Yawning Man might see her arm.

She waited, terrified that at any minute she would be showered in shattered crystals of glass. She watched the luminous face of her wristwatch and followed the second hand as it ticked down a full five minutes before she heard the shuffling of the Yawning Man's ponderous departure through the gravel. She let another five minutes drag by before she allowed herself to start sobbing with relief.

Lillian was exhausted by the time she arrived at the supermarket. All the way there, dazzled by the morning sun, she had leapt over sleeping bodies, dodged in between them, wound and wove around them. Every time she ran past a shop window with a Yawning Man lurking there, she had spitefully shone her torch in his eyes and sent him scurrying away.

The supermarket had been where she'd last seen Jomoke and the other members of the scavenging patrol. It was supposed to be their rendezvous before heading back to the camp.

She found the note on the supermarket counter. This was the procedure that had been drummed into them. If one of your patrol goes missing, do not assume the worst. Leave a note in case they show up later.

The note was written in Marty's chicken-scratch scrawl.

Hey, Big Sis,

What's up? Where you been? We have to go before it gets dark. But if you find my note, stay here. We'll come back. I'll make sure.

Marty

XXX

Lillian felt a lump come to her throat when she read the words. She blinked back the tears that welled up in her eyes and wondered if it would be best to wait for them inside or out.

She decided that first she would try to see if there was anything she could scavenge up for breakfast. The shelves were mostly empty now, but maybe there was a box of unopened cornflakes or something. One thing was for sure, she wasn't going to eat inside the store. The place was starting to stink from all the defrosted meat that was rotting inside the redundant chill cabinets.

As she turned the corner into the next aisle, she ran into something that took her completely by surprise. A tomato ketchup bottle was smashed against the floor tiles, its contents splattered like the bloody evidence of some gruesome murder. It was still wet, and the tangy smell of tomatoes was strong. It hadn't congealed or even gone tacky.

This had happened recently.

She saw red footprints leading away from the mess of ketchup. Her heart tipped a somersault in her chest. Maybe someone else was awake. Someone who had maybe been hiding out in the city for weeks on end and knew nothing about the resistance.

"Hello?" she called out.

What if they were already gone?

The city was huge—so many streets and alleyways—so many districts and suburbs. How would she ever find them again?

"Hello?" she called again.

At first there was no reply.

Then from the back of the store came the sound of someone moving around in the stock room. Clicking on the torch, she passed between the plastic curtains. Tall shelves towered on either side. Washing powder and bottles of bleach to the left, toilet tissue and dog food to the right.

"Where are you?" she called out.

A noise came from the far end of the shelving.

She had only taken two steps when the torch blinked out, leaving her in total darkness. She slapped her free hand against the rubber side of the torch. The bulb flickered, went out, and then flickered on again. The batteries were failing.

Not wanting to take the chance that they might fail again and leave her vulnerable in the darkness, she broke into a trot and ran to the end of the shelving. A Yawning Man stepped out in front of her, pale and ghostlike, his robe of flesh rippling sickeningly around him.

The creature fixed her with his pink eyes and began to yawn. Lillian swung the beam of her torch straight into his face, and he ducked back behind the shelving. She started to run and found her way back into the shop, which was blocked by two more Yawning Men who had appeared suddenly in front of the plastic curtain. When she turned back the other way, the first Yawning Man had been joined by an equally ghostly companion.

Four of them!

She was surrounded. She'd walked into a trap. The smashed ketchup bottle and footprints had clearly been intended to lure her into the back of the store. The Yawning Men began to close in on her, yawning endlessly. She flashed the beam of the torch at the two in front of her and then swung around and flashed it at the two behind.

The torch blinked out. She slapped it hard. This time the bulb did not respond. She could hear them yawning in the darkness, passing the yawn from one to the next and trying to pass it on to her. She slapped the torch again. Still it would not work. She felt a yawn forming deep in her throat. She tried to swallow it back down. She heard the Yawning Men come shuffling closer to her. The first let out a loud yawn, followed immediately by the second, then the third, then the fourth.

With four of them joining forces, the urge to yawn became irresistible. Whatever immunity her ADS gave her was waning. The yawn inside her was desperate to be released. She felt that if she didn't let it go, it would burst right out of her chest.

The quartet of Yawning Men yawned in melodious unison. It was like a creepy lullaby. Lillian felt her mouth stretch wide. She sucked in a huge, involuntary lungful of air, and the burgeoning yawn was at last liberated.

No! she heard own voice screaming inside her head. *Fight it.*

But even as she thought the words, another yawn was already escaping from her mouth. Her fingers went slack. The torch fell from her hand and rolled away across the warehouse floor. Lillian felt herself swaying precariously from side to side as her eyelids grew heavy.

She yawned again. It felt so satisfying. She slumped onto her knees.

She was so very sleepy. Wouldn't it be nice to lie down and just let sleep take her? *Just for a little while,* she promised herself. *I'll wake up soon enough.*

She was vaguely conscious of something long and spidery clamping itself around her skull. A dream was weaving itself into her head. She was playing a game Monopoly with the family. Rick had just started to shake the dice. Mom had accumulated three red hotels. Dad had rows of green houses.

Just go with the dream, she told herself, *it's a far better place to be.*

For what seemed like an endless moment, the game of Monopoly played on. Then she was somewhere else entirely. Somewhere that shimmered and blinked in odd hues and shades of everchanging color.

The Yawning Men's ship.

In her dream she had somehow been transported to their ship. All around her, on the walls and the ceiling and the floors were raised, gelatinous polyps. And inside them she could see the kaleidoscope swirl of people's stolen dreams.

She knew that soon her own dream would be sealed inside one of those polyps. Looking closer, she could see spidery, sinuous veins creeping out from the polyps in all directions. The ship seemed to pulse and throb, as if it were drawing energy from the dreams. Greedily devouring them.

It's alive, thought Lillian. *It's not a ship at all. It's a living entity. It's like the Queen in her nest. And the Yawning Men are like soldier ants, endlessly foraging for food to feed her insatiable appetite.*

A sharp and sudden white light snapped her awake again. So bright she thought she was right in the middle of an explosion. She found herself back inside the warehouse and sat bolt upright, blinking her eyes.

Around her the Yawning Men began to howl in terror, the heels of their long-fingered hands pressed tightly against the sunken sockets of their pink eyes, bumping into each other as they tried desperately to escape the searing lights that seemed to be coming at them from more than one direction.

One after the other they seemed to break up and dissolve before her eyes, multiplying into billions of tiny, shimmering particles, and they rose toward the ceiling of the warehouse before escaping through an air vent.

"Are you all right, Lil?" asked a voice to Lillian's left.

Lillian blushed, recognizing Euan Hoo's voice and struggling unsteadily to her feet. "Y-yes."

Someone grabbed her tightly by the wrist, and she found herself being hauled back through the plastic curtains and straight through the store to the front exit. Only when she was outside in the sunlight was she able to get a proper look at the person who had dragged her along so roughly.

It was Jomoke. Her long black hair was braided into dreadlocks. She wore a faded tee-shirt with a picture of Jay Z on the front, a red tartan skirt, and a pair of scuffed hiking boots with yellow laces.

"You were dead lucky," she said. "If we hadn't come back when we did..."

"Hey, sis!" A small red-haired boy emerged through the supermarket doorway, dusting off his battered leather jacket. A second boy emerged behind him, a good deal taller, the hood of his black sweatshirt pulled up over his head.

"Hey, Marty. Hey, Abdul," said Lillian.

"You can't just act like nothing happened," said Jomoke. "Where did you go? We thought something really bad had happened to you."

"I went home to check on my parents and my brother," admitted Lillian. "I kind of fell asleep. By the time I woke up, it was too dark to try and find you guys."

"I knew you'd be okay," said Marty, grinning at her. "I told them you'd be okay. I said we should come back in the morning. That's how come I left the note."

Jomoke scowled at him, as if to say *stop letting her off the hook.*

"What kind of light was that you used back there?" asked Lillian, desperate to try and change the subject. "How come it's so bright?"

"Halogen bulbs," said Euan. "A lot more powerful than standard flashlight bulbs."

"You saw what happened to the Yawning Men," said Jomoke. "They don't like halogen. No one is sure yet if it actually kills them or if it just sends them back to where they came from. But those bulbs are going to be standard issue from now on."

Lillian bowed her head.

"I don't suppose *I'll* be getting to use one for a good while."

"Why?" asked Marty.

"Well, I kind of went AWOL, didn't I?" said Lillian. "I'm probably going to be confined to barracks, cleaning out the latrines."

"They may not notice," said Abdul sullenly from under his hood. "Something happened."

Lillian felt her heart skip. She didn't like the sound of that.

"Nothing bad." Euan smiled at her and made her blush all over again.

"One of the sleepers might be waking up," said Marty.

"It's a big might," cautioned Jomoke. "You know the hospital ward where they have dozens of sleepers all lined up in beds?"

Lilian nodded. "The ones they experiment on to see if they can be woken."

Jomoke nodded back.

"They've started experimenting with smells."

"Really noxious, gut-churning smells," interrupted Marty, screwing up his nose.

"Yesterday they wafted this smell under a sleeper's nose..."

"And he coughed and opened his eyes," said Marty.

"It might only have been some sort of reflex." Abdul still had his hood pulled up over his head.

"But he might be on the verge of waking up," said Marty, fidgeting hyperactively from foot to foot.

"Anyway," said Jomoke, "the camp is going crazy, and the grown-ups are calling all sorts of meetings. We reported your disappearance to the commander, but I'm not sure if she took all that much notice."

Lillian felt some relief wash over her.

"I found out something too."

She told them what she had learned about the Yawning Men's ship and how it probably wasn't a ship at all but a living entity. She even told them her theory about it being like a Queen and her soldier ants.

Marty whistled though his teeth. "The commander is sure going to take notice of you now!"

"This is big," agreed Jomoke. "This is really big. We'd better get you back to camp as soon as we can." She began to walk rapidly along the street, beckoning them to follow.

They all fell in behind her, single file. Lillian was in the middle. They passed a gas station where a Yawning Man stood staring at them from the booth. Abdul zapped him with his halogen bulb, and he spiraled away into nothing.

Lillian didn't know if it was her ADS kicking in, but she felt wildly elated and overly excited. Ideas were racing through her head. For the first time in months it seemed possible to her that the Yawning Men could actually be defeated, and it felt so good to be back with her patrol.

Maybe she was cut out to be a soldier after all?

They passed the graffiti she'd seen the previous day. The words started repeating over and over inside her head, till eventually they matched the rhythm of the steady pace Jomoke had set for them.

Yawn us to sleep and devour our dreams,
But we shall fight back with flashlight beams
It felt to Lillian like a marching song.

The Great Airship Ride of Patrick Gearhart
by Roan Clay

Roan Clay lives in Alberta, Canada, has always loved to read. He began writing while he was in middle school, and since then, he has written a fantasy novel and many poems and short stories. Adventure and tales of the imagination have always fascinated him.

The *Hannah Beth* was a first-class airship, and when Patrick first saw her, moored at the aerial dock, he could not take his eyes off her. When he and his parents went aboard, he could not go near the edges of the gondola because the great height made him dizzy. Now he sat and dangled his legs between the rails over miles of sky, feeling like a king between the winds.

At last he stood up, calling to his mother, "I'm going to look around."

"All right, Pat. Make sure you stay out of the crew's way!"

He ran his hand along the brass rails that separated him from the clouds, then spread his arms, and he was flying, the wind pushing up on his wings, a master of the sky.

Crewmen walked by on all sides. He remembered what he had promised his mother, and he did not speak to them. Engineers and ordinary crewmen, he stared at their serious faces, the differences in their uniforms. Don't speak to us, don't interrupt us, let us do our jobs, their faces said.

When he got to the back of the gondola he stared at the engines, hanging like ominous twins out of the rear of the huge envelope above him.

Pat spoke reverently into the wind, "Beardmore Hurricane diesels." One of the crew stopped and looked at him. "You interested in engines, boy?"

"I like the airship."

The man was tall in a thick uniform, with the fur all around the high collar, an officer's cap on his head. He came and leaned on the rail beside Patrick. "See the rudder? Those black lines beside it, they turn it left or right. They're connected to the controls up in the pilot house."

The man kept talking, pointing out things Patrick had never noticed.

Patrick looked at the man's uniform, the three silver bars and small silver airship on his sleeve. "Are you the captain?" the boy asked.

"No, I'm one of the mates. I run the ship if there's nobody else."

Patrick took his courage in both hands and said, "Do you mind if I come and take a look at the pilot house? I won't touch anything, and I'll leave when you tell me to."

The man bit his lower lip, then he looked at Patrick, nodded and smiled. "Yes. I think I can bring an especially interested guest on a tour. You are especially interested, aren't you?"

"Oh, yes!"

The officer brought out a set of huge alligator-toothed keys and inserted two of them into a large door marked "Crew Only." He motioned for Patrick to follow him. At the top of the stairs there was another door, and the man opened this one and let the boy into a room bathed in sunshine.

There were seven large panes of glass, bulging out from the rest of the gondola like the airship's nose. A circle of brass gleamed in the center of the floor. In this circle there was a big wheel, a series of levers, and a smaller wheel, facing sideways. A man

stood operating the levers and wheels with tiny motions, looking back and forth between the clouds outside and a panel of
instruments beside him.

"This is Hawkins, Pilot's Mate. He's standing in the pilot's
ring. Nobody can ever step inside that ring unless they actually
have steering duty, or the pilot calls on them. Even the captain
can't, unless the general alarm is sounding."

"Why would the general alarm sound?"

"It never has. Only if there's a serious problem with the gas
pressure, or the electrical systems, or the ballast. There are other, little alarms, but the general alarm is the big one."

At last the pilot adjusted the sideways wheel back just a fraction, and there was a metallic clattering in the floor.

"That's the power level. He just eased it back." The door
clicked open on the other end of the pilot house, and the
captain came in. Patrick remembered seeing him, talking with
important-looking guests and ignoring him and his parents
and the rest of the second-class passengers. The bearded man
in gold braid stared at him now.

"What's the meaning of this, Gable? Why is a child in my pilot
house?"

"Sir, the young man expressed a real interest in the working of
the ship and asked some intelligent questions, so I told him
it would be all right if he did not touch anything." The man
spoke fast before the Captain could interrupt.

"Gable, you will take it outside and tell it to stay there. I did
not think I needed to say this, but there will be no one—*no
one*—but qualified crew in any official section. Now will do
nicely, Mr. Gable."

"Yes, sir."

The response was immediate and respectful. Patrick and
Forward Mate Gable went back down the stairs. When they
were outside, Gable shrugged and smiled. "I'm sorry, Patrick. I
thought it would be all right."

"Thank you anyway! I had a wonderful time!"

Gable moved to tousle Patrick's hair, then stopped himself and offered his hand to shake instead. "And what is your last name, Patrick?"

"Gearhart. And what is your first name?"

Officer Gable laughed. "Theodore. Call me Ted. It's been a very great pleasure meeting you, Mr. Gearhart." Ted Gable turned to go, stopped and said, "Wait here."

Patrick stood in the middle of the clouds, his mind spinning. Soon Ted came back with a book, thin and heavy, with a maroon cover and a white title—*An Airshipman's Basic Manual.*

"We might not be able to talk again, but this will tell you more than I can. Good luck to you, Patrick." He gave a salute, turned, and walked away.

Their long vacation had begun in Vancouver, British Columbia, and they had traced down the Rocky Mountains, then crossed to the Alleghenies and New York, and now they were over the Atlantic. There had been nothing but clouds and fog over the ocean, but now it was clear as a sapphire—good light for reading.

He read through meals, games out on the deck, murder mysteries, and other activities in the huge lounge. While the others had laughed, eaten, and drunk, his mind had been exploring the ship, performing maintenance on the cloth bladders full of helium, fuel tanks, and ballast tanks that collected water from the burning fuel.

All these people went about their lives without a thought for what made the trip happen. The ship could be destroyed, the passengers killed in hundreds of ways. The pilot could steer them on a deadly course, and they could spiral down to be crushed on the surface of the sea. Every crewman kept them all from dying every day, and the passengers ignored them. All they ever saw was Patrick Gearhart, his head down, reading.

"Patrick, do you want to come and play with us?"

She had asked him before, and some of the others laughed at her for inviting him. She was a year younger than him, and three inches shorter, a big-eyed girl with black braids and freckles. She looked like she was always surprised. He glanced up from his book. "No, thank you. I'm all right."

She came closer, craning her neck to look at the words. Her friends called her, and she waved them off and lifted the corner of the book gently. "Is it about the ship?"

"Yes."

"Is it interesting?"

He took a moment to finish the paragraph. "Very. I didn't think I'd be able to understand it, but it explains everything really well."

She sat down on the bench with him. "So, you can steer the ship now?"

"I haven't had the training. But I think I understand *how* to pilot her."

"Her?"

"Yes, any kind of a ship is called 'her.'"

At the beginning of the voyage, he had played games with the girl and her friends. He remembered how patiently she had explained the rules to him, when the others would push him around or scream at him for not understanding. He flipped back to the beginning and showed her some of the diagrams. "See? It labels all the ship parts, tells you how they connect, everything. It says how to fly it, how to fix things, even how the uniforms work."

"Really?" She pointed at a small woman. "So, what's her job?"

He gave her a quick look, head to toe. "Beret and two stripes. She's a midshipman—an officer-in-training. She sleeps in the middle section and reports to one of the mates for her duties."

"What's she going to do now, can you guess?"

"Well, she's heading to the forward telegraph—see that big brass thing? If we hear two dings, that means she's telling the pilot everything's all right down below. Two dings for all's-well, and two groups of three dings means something's very wrong."

"Like what?"

"Like a hostage situation, or a medical emergency. Something like that."

The midshipman unlocked the console with a silver key, and there were two dings.

"Wow! You know things like that, just because you've read this book! Can I borrow it?"

"It's not mine."

That night Patrick and the girl, Kara, read the book together. The party broke up at 10:30, and they went to their cabins. Patrick slept soundly, and he did not hear the wind howling into a gale. He did not feel the ship being tossed back and forth. His parents sat up and held onto their chairs in fear while he dreamed.

In the morning, all the deck chairs were tied to the walls or stowed away, and everything was wet. His parents went into the lounge.

"Patrick, hurry! Get in out of the wind!"

He followed his parents into the lounge, sat in a corner, and took his book out while his parents played cards.

Soon Kara came in and motioned him to follow her, and they went to the door. She pointed. "It's about time for the ringing of that telegraph! What do you think it'll be this time?"

"Two bells, the same as always. If the storm did any damage, they fixed it by now."

They watched as the midshipman came down toward the forward end of the gondola. She unlocked the telegraph, and there were three dings, and then three more.

A bank of cloud blew away, and they saw the other ship.

It hung like a whale off the starboard bow. They had seen many other airships, all well-lighted transports and cruise vessels. This one's dark envelope was curved and soft, full of patches. The gondola was a huge, open boat full of people, and it hung down from the envelope in a black mesh of rope. There were no signals, no voices. Only guns.

And there was one big gun in the front of the gondola, pointed right at them.

Forward Mate Gable said, "Excuse me, but there has been a slight incident, and the captain has asked that you all return to your cabins until it is dealt with."

The people in the lounge began to trail out and meet the ones coming out of the dining room. His mother glanced around to make sure he was there.

"Come along, son. Don't hold the others up."

Kara was beside him, and together they took the passage to their rooms. They were at the back of the line, so they were still in the hallway when the great crash came.

They fell against each other, hit the wall, rolled across the floor and pulled themselves upright with the brass rail. The air was full of black smoke.

The explosion had been loud. It must have been close.

"Did it get the envelope? Is it going to burn?" she asked.

He shook his head. "Helium doesn't burn—hydrogen does. Come on, let's keep going to our rooms."

They walked until the smoke was clear, and they were outside again, back where they had started. They must have gotten turned around. They stopped and stared.

The big gun was smoking, and the crew was loading it again. Their engines made a high-pitched whine, like two furious bees. The crew of the *Hannah Beth* was busy running back and forth, the officers giving orders. They all carried weapons.

"Where did they hit?" he asked, craning his neck around to see.

"Somewhere up above," she said.

He looked up. "That would mean the pilot house. It makes sense."

The girl nodded, a light of interest in her eyes. "Yes, that means the ship would have no pilot now! Means we're helpless! You should go there!"

"Kara, I've read a book, but I've never even been inside the pilot's circle!"

"But what if you're the only one?"

She darted out into the confusion, and he called for her to come back. Then he ran after her.

They could almost count the hairs on the pirates' heads. A pile of deck chairs had broken loose, and they climbed over it. The crew was busy taking up shooting positions along the rail, not noticing the two children running toward the rear of the gondola.

"Kara, we need to get back to our parents! Imagine how worried they are!"

She went around the corner and turned to him. "What do you think those pirates will do to our parents?"

"We still need the keys..." He slapped the door to the stairs leading to the pilot house, and it swung open by itself.

A huge section of the stairs was missing.

There was a volley of gunshots from outside. Kara's eyes were even bigger. "Patrick, give me a boost! I'll find something to help you climb up!"

He made a cup with his hands. The buttons on her coat scraped his face as he lifted her, and she crawled onto the stairs above. He heard her rummaging around, then a red emergency ladder came down, and he climbed it, and they went through the pilot house door.

She was right. It was empty. There was a big, jagged hole across three of the huge windows, right in front of the pilot's circle, and part of the floor was missing. But the circle was unbroken.

"You know how to steer it, Patrick! You go ahead!"

The air was icy, with the wind blowing in. "Yes. But first—" He went to the closet where the spare coats were kept and brought two out. They were too big and covered with insignia but very warm. They belted them on and pulled on the gloves they found in the pockets, and Patrick pulled a pilot's cap down over his ears and stepped inside the pilot's circle.

There was a blast of guns down below, and some of the bullets shattered the glass in front of him. Without thinking, he pulled the ship hard to port.

There were yells from below as people lurched off their feet. He reached for the altitude control, and the ship rode smoothly upward, away from the pirates.

Just then the floor shook with a loud boom. Without looking, he knew the rest of the stairs were gone.

He stabilized their course, just as the book had said. "The mirror is missing on your side. Could you take a look?"

"Okay." She leaned over. "I think I see it. It's in the clouds, off down below us. We should be safe for a while."

"I wonder what happened to the pilot," he said. "I wonder what happened to Ted."

"Who's Ted?"

"Forward Mate Gable. My friend, the one who gave me the book. He might have been standing here when the shot came."

"But he might be all right too!"

"Yes—yes, that's right!" He felt himself relaxing, and the levers felt more natural in his hands.

She watched him in his gauntlets and his cap and greatcoat, and smiled. "Patrick—you're a pilot, Patrick!"

He smiled over his shoulder at her. "And you're a pilot's mate, Kara! What's your last name?"

"Hamilton."

"Pilot's Mate Hamilton, why don't you go put on a cap too? You might have to take over for me."

"What? Me?"

"Well, if I'm indisposed or something."

She went and did it, and they stood together in the pilot house, the masters of the airship, riders on the winds.

Soon there were sounds of people shouting back and forth. Patrick and Kara recognized their names, and they shouted back, but no one could hear them. Then the ship's telephone rang, and Pilot's Mate Kara Hamilton went and answered it.

"Yes, pilot house!"

The voice on the other end was so loud, Patrick could hear it. "This is the captain speaking! Who is flying this ship?"

She smiled. "Right now, it's Pilot's Mate Patrick Gearhart!"

There was silence on the other end, then the captain spoke again, as if he found the words painful. "And—is—everything all right up there?"

"So far, yes!"

"Call him 'sir,'" Patrick said, and Kara straightened up.

"I'm sorry—yes sir!"

There were a few grumbled words, and the captain hung up the phone.

Patrick was laughing. "He could hear how young you are, and there was nothing he could do about it!" They were still calling down below, and he recognized his father's voice, full of fear. "You'd better get on the phone again. Ask for the below watch, and tell them we're safe up in the pilot house. Then our parents can stop worrying."

He was steering the ship up over a mighty castle of clouds. The pirates' airship appeared through them.

At first he did not know what the dim shape was. Then there

was a flash of cannon, and then they heard the boom, and the cannonball hummed past them.

He and Kara both screamed, and there was screaming from down below. He pointed the ship down toward the clouds. The pirates would need time to reload. The *Hannah Beth* had to be far away by then.

"Sound the all-decks alarm!" he ordered, "That silver knob on the wall behind me, pull it twice!"

She did, and a loud hooting filled the air five times.

This was crazy. There should have been an actual pilot here. Suddenly, all these lives depended on him. They stood staring painfully through the clouds all around.

The black ship would not be standing still. He worked the *Hannah Beth* into a turn in the middle of the cloud, and angled her down.

The phone rang on the wall. Kara answered and then shouted, "Pull up! Pull up! We're nearly at the water!"

His knees bent as the deck moved up under him, and suddenly the clouds were gone, and he saw the ocean below, the mountains and valleys of the waves, almost touching them. He was covered in sweat.

"We've got two more ships on our tail!" Kara shouted, "I think they're faster than us! Better increase speed!"

He moved the wheel forward until he could hear the engines moan through the ship. They bounced up and down across the layers of hot and cold air, skimming like a stone across a pond. The phone rang, and Kara answered it and yelled above the howl of the wind, "They say decrease speed! The engines are near the red line! Close to exploding!"

He turned the wheel back again. He thought he could feel the hot breath of the pirates on the back of his neck.

There was a rattling at the door, and Kara went and opened it, bending to help a man who was crawling through.

"Ted!" Patrick cried, then turned back to his work as the wind blew them suddenly to one side, and Ted and Kara had to support themselves against the wall.

"Gearhart, the captain's not too happy about this!"

Patrick did not turn this time. "I'm sorry about that, Ted! How do you feel about it?"

The man laughed. "It may not matter! We're not fast enough to stay away from them for long!"

Patrick's face was numb, and his fingers were getting stiff on the wheel. "Will you take over, Ted?"

Kara said, "Patrick, he's hurt!"

There was a distant boom but no sign of the cannonball. A long miss. He looked back at Ted Gable and saw the bloodstain running down his arm.

"Is anybody else coming up here, Ted?"

"They're all pretty busy. I'll take over—the wound's not too bad. You've done enough."

Patrick shook his head. "No. You're still bleeding."

"I'll take over, Patrick." He stepped toward him.

"Stop." Patrick's voice was hard. "I'm in the pilot's circle. You're unfit to fly—look, you can't even stand on your feet. Officer Gable, sit down and rest. Kara, see what you can do for him."

Gable nodded, stumbled to the bench against the wall and sat down, wrapping the coat tightly around him. The cold wind was strong against their faces.

Patrick did not mind for himself. It helped him stay awake.

He saw one of the pirate airships in the corner of his eye, and he pulled the *Hannah Beth* over. But there was a dark ship on the other side as well.

Now he saw the other ships, dotted through the clouds around them.

"There were rumors of a pirate fleet," Ted said weakly, "but we didn't know for sure."

"Now we do," Patrick said, and he pulled them up higher.

"What do they want?" Kara said.

Gable's voice was weak. "The ship is full of rich passengers. They all have money and jewelry. There might be ransom too."

"Is that why they were only shooting at the pilot house?"

"Yes. This room will be their main target."

Patrick thought for a moment. "How long can we go on full power without an engine exploding?"

"Not too long."

The cabin was silent except for the howl of the wind. His heart seemed to stop beating as he came within range of the pirates' guns, and he saw the faces of the people standing around the big cannons, and red flashes bloomed from the muzzles. He pushed the wheel forward all the way, bringing them up fast, and the broken window screamed in the wind. The hull vibrated as a shot hit the *Hannah Beth's* keel.

Ted got up and went to the phone, calling down below.

"Is everyone all right?" Patrick asked.

"Yes, but they can see clouds through the floor. Minor injuries."

"I see land!" Kara shouted, and she went and leaned far out through the window, keeping away from the sharp edges. "Where are we?"

"It should be France," Ted said, "But the way we've been drifting, it could be England or Belgium. The pirates should give up soon. They don't like to be over land, where the police can get them."

"No, they're still with us!" Kara pointed. "They took a while to catch up, but they're with us!"

Patrick's teeth clenched, and he edged the ship faster. Of all the five hundred ways of ruining an airship, he had flirted with at least a hundred of them. All that, to be boarded by pirates within sight of land.

"They're closing in," Kara shouted, "readying their guns!"

They had no weapons to defend themselves with, but there was something...

"Is hydrogen cheaper than helium?"

Ted said, "Yes, it is. You can make hydrogen out of water if you have to. Why?"

"Well, pirates usually don't have a lot of extra money, do they? I mean, they have to fill their airships with whatever they can get cheap. Where are they right now?"

"On either side of us."

"Good. Make a call to evacuate the envelope, and let me know when they're about to fire."

"How can I tell that?"

"When they step away from the gun!" Ted yelled, beginning to understand. He got up and made the call while Kara kept watch.

"Looks like they're priming the guns to fire," she said.

They waited. The silence was deadly. They were perfectly still, like bugs in amber.

"NOW!"

He brought the ship down so fast they seemed to lift up off the floor. The grass lunged at them, and he pulled up, and there was a great explosion behind them.

When she got her balance back, Kara looked out the side window. "One of them exploded! It's all lit up!"

He gritted his teeth and kept flying away from the falling wreckage and the other pirate ships.

The phone rang.

"The shot went through our envelope, but nobody was hurt! We'll need to make repairs, though. Land soon, Patrick!"

They skimmed over the fields, hitting fences, cattle and horses running, shocked by the great beast that blew from one field to another until he shut off the engines, and the ship slowly came to rest on the brow of a large hill.

Eventually, they brought a ladder and let them out. Patrick walked away from the ship, and the world was solid again, and he collapsed on the warm grass and fell fast asleep.

That night Kara told the story, and the rest of the passengers listened, camped out on the fragrant lawn.

Patrick did not know. He lay in a warm blanket by a fire in the farmer's house, and his dreams were long and wonderful and full of grass and flying.

Abby's Run

by Mike Barretta

Mike Barretta is a retired U.S. Naval aviator who currently works for a defense contractor as a pilot. He holds a Master's degree in Strategic Planning and International Negotiation from the Naval Post-Graduate School and a Master's in English from the University of West Florida. His wife, Mary, to whom he has been married to for 23 years, is living proof that he is not such a bad guy once you get to know him. His stories have appeared in *Baen's Universe*, *Redstone, New Scientist, Orson Scott Card's Intergalactic Medicine Show* and various anthologies.

"It's beautiful, isn't it?" asked Mark. He made another adjustment to the Google Mars image. Mars, a blurry gold, orange, and green pastel smear, sharpened to razor focus. Icons identified the planetary features. He switched to a clean view of the planet without the identifying tags. On the dark side of the terminator, the break between light and day, the city lights of Mars stretched along the shoreline of a future sea. "It's pretty, isn't it?

"It's pretty," said Abby. She stared for a moment and then turned away, uninterested. Once, she loved looking at Mars because she did it with her mother. Alone, they would traverse the surface of the faraway world. Her mother would name the forests, prairies, and vast, ice-swept tundra that girdled the planet at the upper and lower latitudes. Things so far away were patient and undemanding.

Her father touched her shoulder and she stiffened.

"I'm sorry, Abby." He pulled back.

Normally, her father touching her did not make her tighten up, but things were different now that it was just him and her brother. Her mom understood her, because they were the same. Her brother and father were like each other, and though they were patient and kind, they did not really understand.

She stepped away from the telescope feed and sat down in her chair.

"I don't want to go," said Jackson. "I have friends here."

"You'll have friends there," said his father.

"I don't want some stupid, dust-ball planet. It's poison. I don't want my bones to get brittle. I don't want dust vacuumed out of my lungs. I don't want to be mutated," said Jackson.

"You're not going to get mutated," said Mark. "Abby, you would like to go, wouldn't you? To see Mom's plants?"

She nodded. She really didn't, but she knew what her father wanted her to say. She wanted to stay home, sit in her chair, and read.

"Well, I'm not going," said Jackson.

"Okay, just go to bed," said Mark. "We'll talk tomorrow."

"She never talks," said Jackson. "It's like she doesn't care."

"She does."

"Then she should say so." He turned to his sister. "Say so! Say so! Say you care!"

"Enough, Jackson."

Jackson left, stomping his anger and frustration into the floor, making a spectacle that she could not understand. She didn't even understand her own rages.

"He doesn't mean it, Abby. He is just angry and frustrated."

She knew all about angry and frustrated. Mom held them all together. She was the sun, and they just orbited around her. She didn't know how to do what her mom did. How did her mother keep two noisy, needy men from flinging off into space and leaving her alone?

"Abby, I'm going to go to bed. Can you turn the lights out for me?"

She nodded. No one ever put her to bed. Jackson had to be told; otherwise, he would play games all night long. She was terribly reasonable about such things.

With the living room to herself, she opened the last of her mother's hardbound journals. It was like peering into the diary of a mad scientist or a Victorian explorer. All of her mother's ideas started here in these journals. Her mother was a botanical engineer and designed gardens for other worlds. She loved plants, and the backyard garden, a flowered refuge of custom plant designs, testified to her abilities.

Abby was a careful reader, never turning the pages until she had read and understood all the words on the previous ones. It was hard work. She reached the last pages of the last journal and saw that not only had her mother designed gardens for Mars; she had also designed the gardeners. She called them Aranyani, after the Hindu goddess of the forest and the animals that lived there.

Maybe she would want to go to Mars to meet the Aranyani. The thought thrilled and frightened her at the same time.

Seifert, her companion cat, entered the room and leapt from the floor to her lap with casual, feline grace. The cat settled; she stroked him and he purred just as if he were real. The gentle rumbling soothed her.

Abby hated Phobos. She thought the three-month transit to Mars was terrible, but this moon—a relentlessly ugly, underground, pressurized city, teaming with people and warmed with body heat—was a horror. If any place fit her definition of hell, this was it. It was too loud, chaotic, and dirty. Clumps of debris and trash kicked up by the myriad people floated forever before settling in the low gravity. Sweaty people pressed, jostled, and pushed. She was on the edge of panic.

She wanted to sit down and cover her ears with her hands and squeeze her eyes tight and scream, but that would just delay their departure. Fortunes were made here, and no one could spare the time for a screaming little girl. Knowing that she would be here, she'd prepared by reading. Through her discomfort, she sorted the place into patterns. It calmed her a bit. She held her father's hand and when overwhelmed, saturated with stimulation, she shut her eyes to the chaos and let herself be led.

The rumbling and booming of the launched drop capsules reverberated through the spray-coated walls of the terminal. She jumped every time the moon shuddered. Phobos station manufactured the drop capsules on-site with industrial fabricators, filled them with cargo and passengers, and dropped them to the landing fields outside the Martian colonies.

The ozone smell of hot metal laced the air. They waited, sitting on uncomfortable pressed-plastic seats. Their names were called, and her father presented ID and ticket vouchers. No exchanged pleasantries or courtesies involved. No one had the time. The loadmaster strapped them into the cramped capsule with her father in the center seat directly in front of the display. She sat to his left and her brother to his right. The loadmaster snugged their harnesses. Elasticized net secured their few authorized belongings, including the cat, to the inner hull of the capsule.

The cat yowled loudly, in the manner of cats. The only reason she could take him to Mars was that he was categorized as an essential medical device.

"Seifert is fine," said her father. "He is just being a cat. Enough, Seifert."

The cat quieted.

"Too much like a cat," said Jackson, "if you ask me."

"He isn't really a cat," said Abby.

She was grateful for that. She had read up on cats and decided that the robotic one was better. Cats could be unpredictable, and if there was anything that she loved more in the world than predictability, she had not discovered it yet.

"In about 45 minutes you are going to be on the surface of Mars," said the loadmaster. "The process is completely automated, so there is nothing for you to do but remain strapped in. The display is just so you have something to look at, and it provides a basic communication function. Just speak, and we will hear you. We can see you through the display's camera, so no funny business. Remain strapped in until the recovery team secures your capsule and comes inside to get you. Everyone good?"

"Got it," said Jackson.

"Okay," said Mark.

"When I seal the capsule, you're going to hear a lot of banging and odd mechanical noises and such. That is just us loading you. Nothing to be alarmed over. The most important part is to stay seated. The only way you can get hurt is if you get out of the seat."

"Are you okay, sweetie?"

Abby locked eyes for a moment with loadmaster but didn't respond.

"She doesn't speak much," said Jackson.

"Okay, then." The loadmaster looked at her father. "I am going to close you up—safe drop!"

The loadmaster backed out, picked up a flexible sheet of metal and smoothed it over the door flange. Electro-adhesives sealed the door space tight. Air hissed as the capsule pressurized.

The capsule lurched, and she reached over to grab her father's hand.

Seifert struggled against the webbing and curled into an ungraceful ball. The cat was bigger than before, doubling in size from domestic housecat size to bobcat size. Its chassis had been upgraded to titanium ceramic with sealed bearings at the joints and a new high-endurance battery. Mars did not cater to robot animals, medically necessary or otherwise. The cat had to last.

The exterior cameras fed the display panel. Their capsule bounced over rollers on the conveyor and passed through an airlock into sunlight. Junk, waiting for salvage, littered the surface of Phobos.

"Launch in ten seconds," said launch control. The monitor screen counter decremented... and then...

Not much. A fog of crystals enveloped the capsule, a gentle push, and they were rising above the surface of Phobos toward Mars.

"Launch is nominal. You are tracking well. You should feel some minor kicks as the engines fine-tune your descent. Ground has your beacon, and we have passed control to them."

"That was easy," said Jackson. "I'm going to Mars to get mutated."

"You're not going to get mutated," said his father.

⋖▦▸

The capsule engines fired and fired again. The capsule wobbled about its axis. She had not read about wobbling.

"Mr. Demerly, this is recovery control. Your capsule experienced an engine misfire, and we are correcting your trajectory. There might be a slight delay on your recovery. Nothing to worry over. We don't want to alarm you."

That was wrong, thought Abby. Even she knew that just saying those things would cause worry and alarm.

The engine rumbled again, and the monitor bloomed orange and white. The capsule vibrated as they hit atmosphere. Something was wrong. She felt it. She knew it. She had read everything she could find on the descent process, including the technical manuals. She probably knew the sequence better than the ones who pushed the buttons.

"Hey, you, recovery guys. Are we okay? We're shaking pretty bad," said her father.

The monitor showed a swirling glow of reentry plasma. The speaker screeched white noise. The straps bit into her shoulders. Mars shook in the monitor, and it felt like they were rising.

"We skipped," said Abby. "We skipped." One in a million. She had read about it. Too shallow an angle, and instead of falling into atmosphere and slowing down, the capsule skips like a stone across the water.

Engines fired again, a long sustained thrust, then the bottom fell out, and it felt like they were riding an out-of-control elevator. The capsule spun about its longitudinal axis. Her head throbbed with pressure. Her vision reddened; blood pooled in her head and feet. Red-out, she concluded. The monitor blanked as the exterior camera burned off. White noise hissed, and the rumblings of atmospheric plasma flow filled the cabin. At least they were falling towards something now rather than skipping off Mars to float forever in the dark. She lost consciousness, and it wasn't as bad as she thought.

She woke still strapped into her seat. Her shoulders hurt from where the straps had bit into them when the capsule hit the ground. Her father was slumped, held upright only by the harness. His seat had collapsed, sliding under the instrument panel with his legs taking up all the impact forces. His legs bent oddly below the knees, broken. Her father's eyes were dilated, and he looked unalarmed. That was wrong. His mandatory Mars-rated medical implant must have kicked in, manufacturing pain blockers. Jackson was still in his seat, blinking stupidly, his face set in a grimace, his left shoulder slumped where his collarbone had broken. Deflated airbags draped the cabin. Sunlight and cold air seeped in through a peeled-back section of the hull. It was a cold morning on Mars. Her father stirred.

"Abby, are you okay?" asked her father.

"Yes sir," she said.

"Jackson are you okay?"

"No, my shoulder is funny. I'm mutated already."

"Okay, just sit still for now."

Seifert squirmed and broke free from the wall webbing and padded around them to take his place next to her. The cat rubbed his face and body on her legs.

"Best thing we can do is wait for them to find us," said her father.

"We skipped," said Abby.

"What does that mean?"

"No one is coming. We skipped away and are too far." She knew this because she knew most everything about Mars. The orbital infrastructure around Mars concentrated upon the inhabited side of the planet and not the wild side.

"They're coming."

Her father tried to move and gasped in pain. He slumped back down. "We have to wait for them to find us."

Abby unstrapped and took a soft case down from the wall that held some of their clothes. She opened it up and stuffed the clothes into the cracked hull to keep out the cold air. She knew they couldn't wait. If they were to get help, they would have to get it themselves.

She knew everything about the planet, all the townships, out-posts, remote sensing stations. The only person in the universe who could know more was her mother. She took the crash tool from the wall bracket and used the pry bar end to lever the flight instrument panel from the console. As she thought, it was self-contained, powered from its own battery and just clipped in place. She disconnected the wire harness and reboot-ed the panel. It opened to a welcome screen. If she was lucky, it would have GPS, and she could figure out where they were. She switched off the electro-adhesives and pushed open the door panel. It peeled back and she poked her head outside to see if she could get some bearings. The Emergency Position Indicating Radio Beacon would be outside the door. If it had not self-activated, she could turn it on.

"What do you see, Abby?" asked her father.

They'd landed in a forest. Martian trees, three times taller than the largest trees to grow on Earth, soared above her. These trees grew only on the wild side of mars. Immense central trunks of the Redwood-Banyan splice met in graceful arching buttresses. Rays of weak light penetrated the needled canopy, spotlighting the ground. Carpets of flowering ground cover, sprays of fern, and metallic-colored grasses filled the space between the colossal trees. The capsule's massive red and white parachute hung torn far above in the tangled branches. That was how they survived, she guessed. The trees had snagged the streaming parachute. Molten stubs of antennas marred the capsule's burned hull. The emergency beacon was destroyed, and an overhead satellite could not see them through the forest canopy. The instrument panel booted and displayed their GPS position. She knew where she was; she just couldn't tell anybody.

Something moved in a cluster of ferns. She ducked back in, letting the door panel adhere into position. Her brother was in pain with his broken shoulder, but he would be fine. Her father's pants had ridden up, and she saw his calves and ankles. They were gray. The veins and arteries in his legs were kinked off like a garden hose. She touched them. His legs were cold, and she couldn't find a pulse.

"Dad. I have to straighten your legs."

"Don't. Abby, the pain blockers are fading. Help is coming. They will do it."

"I have to." She positioned herself for leverage.

"Abby, don't. They're coming. The pain killers are wearing off."

She moved his left leg, uncrossing it from the right, and he screamed. She set it back down.

"Stop, Abby, stop! You're hurting him," said Jackson.

"Abby, please, let me breathe first."

If she didn't straighten his legs out, he would lose them.

She straightened his left leg. Her father bit down on a scream and passed out from pain. She straightened the other and stuffed clothing under his legs to support them.

"You killed him, Abby, you killed him."

Her father moaned, but he did not wake.

"Jackson, I have to go."

"Dad said stay. Help is coming"

"They're not. They can't." Mars was much smaller than earth but still big enough to get lost in.

"Dad is wrong. I have to get help," said Abby.

She dressed in the cold weather gear, clipping the titanium crash tool and one of the survival kits to her belt.

"Abby, please don't go. I need you," said Jackson.

She touched her father's legs and felt their returning warmth. He would be okay for a while.

She opened the door and climbed out, holding the detached instrument panel. Seifert followed.

Jackson watched her with a mix of fear and anger.

"Abby don't," said Jackson.

She sealed the capsule shut against Jackson's angry protests. The capsule's batteries should keep them warm for two or three days. She looked around the forest and shivered. Even on the warmest days, Mars barely reached 50 degrees.

Seifert poked his nose into the leaf litter, testing the new Martian smells. He turned his head, alert for movement. The wildside forest was a biological proving ground where engineers prototyped Martian creatures, including predators. She might have need for teeth and claws.

She held up the panel. It displayed a map of Mars and showed her position. Her destination was a research station a bit over 25 kilometers away.

"Seifert, this way." She walked and the cat followed.

The underbrush was sparse and the path was clear. Short wiry grass left no mark of her passing. She walked beneath the cathedral-like arches of an immense tree. The primary trunk was at least twenty meters across. Twelve meters up, the bark hung in ragged strips. Something big had marked its territory. Brush rustled and she caught movement from the corner of her eye and froze.

Long-legged, rabbit-faced creatures stepped daintily out of the bush. Like deer, only larger and more slender, they stood three meters tall. The broad-chested male, sporting a crown of twisted antlers, led a harem of antlerless females. The animals dipped their heads to the grass and nibbled one at a time as if choreographed. The male's floppy ears shot up, and it let out a quiet chuff. All of them came to the alert covering a sector. The muscles in their legs quivered.

They bolted as if on cue, taking immense leaps from a standing start that took them from her sight. She backed into some bushes and hid.

A pack of other creatures, the famed predator rats, burst into view. The animals were not the largest predators on Mars, but they were the most successful. The leopard-spotted rats paused and sniffed. They diverged significantly from their humble Earthbound ancestors. They were powerfully built, slender-waisted like cheetahs, and broad-chested. Scaly whip-tails swished the cold air. These were forest variants, slightly smaller and more muscular than the ones that lived on the open savannahs, but still incredibly dangerous. Razor-sharp incisors overhung their lips. She sat still. If there was anything she was good at, it was sitting still. The rats sniffed the air and sprang off in a coordinated pack to follow the rabbit-faced deer.

When she was sure they were gone, she said, "Let's go, Seifert."

A distance away, she heard a raucous shrieking. Seifert's fur bristled, and its ears pinned back. The rats had caught something.

She selected a course through the forest and walked as swiftly and as silently as she could. She needed to be careful. To run was to be heard, was to be seen, was to be caught, and maybe...eaten. She heard the skittering chirps and cries of various creatures but could not identify them. It was one thing to read about Mars and its creatures but quite another to experience them.

The rising sun and her exertions warmed her. Seifert stopped. She paused and listened. She didn't hear anything.

"Seifert, is there anything here?"

The cat cocked his head, and she looked where he was looking. She saw it.

The Aranyani, the forest guardian from her mother's sketchbook, floated. All the creatures on Mars were derivatives of something from Earth except the Aranyani. Her mother had created a strange design and then smuggled it to Mars. The Aranyani did not appear on any register of Martian life.

The creature clung to a tree branch supported by twin bladders that looked like glass Christmas tree balls. Two solar wings captured the light. The remainder of its limbs dangled beneath the body. Two eyestalks extended laterally from its body. Three eye bulbs twitched independently at the end of each stalk. It had a cord wrapped around its body from which various tools dangled. The creature released the branch and floated higher, stretching long arms to grip branches to direct its flight. It reached an open expanse with no branches, exhaled hard through its siphon, and jetted to the next tree. It was gone. She was sure it had not gone far.

By her estimate, she had walked approximately halfway to the research station. The sky was darkening, but it was too soon for sunset by her reckoning. Rain storms were rare on Mars, but dust storms were not uncommon, and the thickening atmosphere made them just as dangerous as dust storms on Earth. A big storm smothered machines, roads, townships, and even entire forests. She could smell the ozone and the crackle of electricity. She needed shelter. The wind picked up, and the air turned a hazy pink. The wild-side forest was large so there was little chance of the storm burying it. She was another story. She wrapped her face and shielded her eyes. Tree trunks creaked and swayed in the wind. Dust abraded her skin. She crouched in the lee of the wind between uplifted roots. The forest groaned, and branches cracked free and fell to the ground. Eerie ball lightning gathered and flowed down the tree trunks in luminous cascades.

A thick branch plummeted from above and covered her. Spiny seedpods hit the ground like grenades, and a nest of small furry creatures boiled out of the hollow branch and fled into the surrounding brush. The whole forest was in motion, and the violence of it all filled Abby's head. She could not see farther than the length of her outstretched hand. She closed her eyes, pulled her hoodie tight with its drawstring to protect her face, and wrapped her arms around Seifert. He purred loudly, and she focused on the comforting noise. The storm grew stronger, and she clamped her hands over her ears to fend it off. Despite the warmth of the cat, she shivered and wanted nothing more than to be back home on Earth. She had a chair and books to read. "I want to go home, Seifert," she said. She held him tight. She did not know when, but sometime, in the midst of the storm, she fell asleep.

"Is Abby okay?" asked Jackson.

"Yes, she is fine," said Mark.

"How do you know?"

"Jackson, I don't know. How could I know?" He tried to move, and a lance of pain ran up his broken legs.

"Ahhh," he grimaced. "She is okay, Jackson. She has to be."

"Dad...I'm worried."

"I'm worried too."

"Will Abby get help?"

"Yes."

"How do you know?"

"I just do."

He knew because she was like her mother, beautiful, fiercely intelligent, and infuriatingly difficult. He'd met his wife in college, and slowly, he won her over with patience and respect, giving her the space she needed and enduring her long periods of silence.

At the end of their final undergraduate semester, he saw her, wrapped in cool fog, unfocused and soft. Blades of morning light slanted through the tall oaks, and he thought she was the most beautiful woman he had ever seen. She smiled at him and joined him for coffee. As they walked, their hands accidentally intertwined, and he knew that he was in love with this strange and brilliant woman.

"Because she is her mother's daughter."

She woke to find herself covered in brush. Her jacket's outer shell was blasted with gritty sand and wet with dew. The instrument panel that had ridden out the storm tucked into her jacket still worked. Seifert looked like he had gone through the washing machine's rinse cycle. After the storm's passage, the temperature had dropped, and the forest was hushed with fog. It would not take long for the sun to burn it off. Fat-bodied lizards emerged from their hiding places and licked the leaves. She pulled herself clear. The branches had a spongy bark, and the needles were soft. Seifert leaped ahead, moving from branch to branch, his head traversing slowly, scanning for threats. She heard a plaintive mewling and saw the Aranyani.

The Aranyani lay pinned to the ground, speared by a broken branch through one of its floatation bladders. The creature spotted her and extended its eyestalks. The three eyes twitched, pupils expanding and contracting as the creature took her measure. "I won't hurt you," she said. "Seifert, stay here." The cat sat down. She approached cautiously.

The creature took its knife from its cord and held it up at her. The knife did not look like metal or stone but rather like a piece of plastic. It did look sharp, though. She set the instrument panel down and walked toward it empty-handed. From her mother's journals, she knew it was far stronger than she was. She touched the hand that held the knife and pushed gently.

"It's okay. I won't hurt you." The creature lowered its knife. She moved slowly and unclipped the crash tool from her belt. She gripped the impaling branch and sawed with the tool's serrated edge. The creature watched, whistling in pain.

"I'm sorry," she said.

The branch came free and she tossed it away. She gently lifted the limp folds of the bladder clear of the branch. Free, the creature rose up towering over her and skittered away towards clear ground, dragging its pierced bladder. It folded its limbs under its body and settled down.

The Aranyani could walk on land, but it was a flying creature. A pierced bladder was practically a death sentence. No matter how smart the Aranyani was, predator rats or some other carnivore would find it.

She approached the creature again.

"Be still. I can help more," she said.

The Aranyani whistled a tune up and down the register, and she wondered if her mother had given them language. She worked through the folds of its damaged bladder and found the first puncture. "This will hurt," she said. With needle and thread from the survival kit, she stitched the puncture wounds closed. The Aranyani watched her and trembled but did not move. With a small bottle, she sprayed both puncture wounds with a sterile liquid bandage.

The Aranyani reached out with a hand that had six spade-tipped fingers arranged like flower petals. Each finger was tipped with a small sharp claw. Its hands played across her clothes and touched her face and hair. Seifert pinned his ears back and hissed.

"It's okay, Seifert."

The Aranyani reached out and touched the cat.

In the distance, a pack of predator rats yipped.

"I have to go," she said. "My brother and father need help. You should climb." She pointed up.

The creature understood and rose up on its six limbs and scuttle-walked to the tree. It sank its claws into the soft bark and pulled itself up until it reached a branch safely out of reach of the rats. There it perched, unfurling its stained-glass solar wings to soak up the weak sunlight. Its damaged bladder hung limply, but she could see that it was starting to fill.

She gathered her supplies back up and consulted the instrument panel. She marked her position and then charted her course to the research station. She estimated the station was still a few hours away.

She left the Aranyani behind.

The sun warmed her enough that she could unzip her jacket. The solar reflectors made a bright spot in the sky as they captured and concentrated solar energy on Mars. The reflectors were the least of the engineering efforts that made Mars habitable. At the heart of the planet, a black hole, and a companion white hole, both man-made, orbited through the core, increasing gravity. The black hole sucked in gigatons of Mars' core, and the white hole spewed it out. The liquefied core spun, generating a magnetosphere that protected the planet from solar radiation.

Seifert ranged ahead of her just out of sight, scouting the

ground and returning. The cat vanished in the brush, and she caught up to him. Seifert froze in place. Ahead, a megatherium, a massive, two-legged beast, pulled branches with its long prehensile tongue. Powerful arms snapped the branches free. The animal worked it jaws side to side, crunching loudly on the various pinecones and nuts that needed its digestive system to erode the tough outer shells. The creature gave her a sideways glance and returned to its feeding. The megatherium was the largest creature on Mars, and if its size could not deter predators, then its long, scything claws would.

She detoured around the animal and checked her instrument panel. By her reckoning, the research station should be close. The forest thinned and opened into a glade of bright green knee-high grass, portions of which had been churned by a herd of grazing animals. Metallic light glinted, and she knew that it was the research station's solar array. The ground crunched beneath her feet, and she looked down and saw bones. Broken skeletons stretched out around her. Bird-like creatures flushed from the grass ahead of her, and she knew she was too far away to be the cause. A predator rat, five meters ahead, lifted its sleek head and fixed its gaze upon her.

Another and another of the pack hunters lifted their heads. Their ears flattened, and they crouch-walked towards her, stalking, not quite sure what she was. The alpha rat charged her with the speed of a cheetah. Seifert was faster, intercepting the leaping rat midair and bowling it over, latching onto the rat's body with his ceramic claws. The other rats startled at the sudden turn and lost focus on her. Nothing ever attacked them.

She broke into a run to the station, hoping someone was there. Behind her, Seifert tangled with the rats. The others had recovered from their shock and joined the fight. She didn't think the rats could destroy Seifert, but they certainly could hurt him.

The cold, thin air burned her lungs to exhaustion. The tethered crash tool beat against her legs. She hit the research station door at full speed and leaned on the lever handle lock. Locked. She turned to see the rats ganged up on Seifert, snapping and clawing at the machine-cat. The alpha rat grabbed Seifert by the scruff of his neck and shook. Seifert went limp, his systems overwhelmed with violence, and the rat tossed him away.

The rats turned to her.

She unclipped the crash tool, jammed its blunt end between the reinforced doorframe and steel door. She pried as hard as she could. The door wouldn't budge. She spun to face the closing rats, lifting the crash tool like a bat. The rats stalked closer, low to the ground, the blades of their shoulders shifting in time with each cautious step. Low, menacing growls rumbled deep in their throats. They snapped at one another, eager for the first bite.

A shadow fell across her, and the rats shifted their gaze to the sky above her head. She expected something far worse than hungry rats the size of leopards.

Three Aranyani hovered above the roof of the station, wings spread, floatation bladders expanded to their full measure, eye booms extended. The creatures held long, thin, spear-like weapons and shorter hollow tubes. They drifted over her towards her attackers, and the rats backed down, ears flat and tails tucked. Together, they broke into a run away from the Aranyani.

Seifert rebooted, rose from the grass, and the rats leapt over him in their enthusiasm to escape. The Aranyani were much more than just gardeners, she thought. They ruled the forest. Seifert came to her and rubbed his face against her leg. She scratched his head. Tufts of fur had been pulled out, and his left ear was torn a bit, but otherwise, the cat appeared undamaged from the fight.

Her Aranyani, the one with the bandage, drifted to her and

reached out towards the crash tool. She handed it over. The creature gently moved her aside and slipped the tool's prying end into the door gap. The creature braced itself with its remaining limbs and pulled. The doorframe deformed, and the bolt broke free, springing the door open.

For such delicate looking creatures, the Aranyani were incredibly strong. No wonder the rats did not wish to tangle with them. Her friend held out the tool to her, and she pushed it back.

"You take it. It's yours." The titanium tool was light enough that the Aranyani could fly with it.

The creature whistled, stepped clear, and fully inflated its bladders. It pushed off gently and rose into the sky, unfurling its wings and tilting them to sail the breeze. It drifted over the others, and they followed.

She went inside and turned on the station's power.

Mark shivered with cold and pain. His medical implant could no longer make painkillers. Jackson had made a nest for himself with clothes they had brought to Mars. The drop ship's battery had exhausted itself. They had propped the door open to let in fresh air, and one night they had heard something big and terrible outside. Claws slipped under the door. The door peeled and buckled, but whatever it was, it lost interest and went away.

Abby was gone, and perhaps tomorrow or maybe the next day, he would tell Jackson that he would need to go out and try. His heart was broken with grief. Mars was a wild world and no place for his daughter. She was lost in it, and he could not protect her. They should have stayed home.

Through the hull of the capsule, he heard the wind, like the storm that had passed the day before. It rose in pitch and then faded away abruptly. The door pulled away, and bright Mars light flooded the cabin. He blinked in the blinding light, half expecting terrible claws to reach in and pull him out.

"Daddy," said Abby, "I brought help."

His daughter scrambled into the cabin, mindful of his legs. She leaned into him, and he wrapped his arms around her. Instead of recoiling, she hugged him back.

Another person appeared in the doorway. "Mr. Demerly, we're your recovery team. We are going to have you and your family out of here in a few minutes." The man crowded in. "Your daughter told us what happened. She is a remarkable young woman."

"Just like her mother," said Mark.

Jackson opened his eyes.

"Abby, it's you," he said.

"It's me," said Abby.

Juliet Silver and the Orb of Fortunes
by Wendy Nikel

Wendy Nikel is a speculative fiction author with a degree in elementary education, a fondness for road trips, and a terrible habit of forgetting where she's left her cup of tea. Her short fiction has been published by *Fantastic Stories of the Imagination*, *Daily Science Fiction*, *Nature: Futures*, and elsewhere. Her time travel novellas, *The Continuum* and *The Grandmother Paradox* were published by World Weaver Press in 2018. For more info, visit wendynikel.com.

A bronze hook shot from the side of the *Realm of Impossibility*, whistled through the nighttime air, and caught upon the docking edge of the skybarge *Nocturne*. The clanking of the winch was muffled by waves of lively, tinkling music wafting from inside the sparkling barge.

As the airship drew alongside through effervescent clouds, Juliet Silver stood at the *Realm*'s helm, gauging its approach and running her fingers over the silk ribbons on her gown. She'd never worn anything so elegant, unless her delicate chain-mail armor counted. Perhaps that was why she felt such uncertainty about their plans for the evening: the gown she'd commissioned was perfectly suited for the chancellor's starlit gala aboard the skybarge, but it was not, however, well-suited for fighting in.

Juliet smoothed the skirt, which fell like layers of petals around her, and her hand brushed the hilt of the knife con-

cealed in its folds. She hoped she wouldn't need to use it.
Her first mate, Geofferies, had offered to serve as her escort
on this mission, though he looked even less at ease in his
sky-black suit and top hat than she was in her elaborate gown.
She took his offered arm and, with the other, slipped the final
piece of her disguise—a delicate silver mask, inlaid with diamonds and star-studded rivets—into place.

"Keep to your posts," she called to her crew. "We may need to
make a hasty retreat."

Clouds sharp with ice crystals shrouded the barge, and high-al-
titude dragon-bugs darted about, lured in by the sugary scent
of lemonbean cookies and aromatic tea. From the ground,
the barge with its billowing silk tents probably looked like a
strange, luminous cloud. Only those with the proper invitation
could gain entrance.

The proper invitation... or the proper disguise.

At the outer flap, a man with glimmering tattoos and a black
mask that curved downward like a crow's beak held out a
gloved hand, blocking their way.

Instinctively, Juliet's fingers twitched for her sword, but—quickly recalling the role she played this evening—she raised her
palm instead, brandishing the magistrate's mark upon it.

The guard grunted his approval, not even bothering to lean in
and double-check that the mark was, indeed, the same that was
painted upon the hands of the elite at their invitation's acceptance. Obtaining the exact design of this party's mark had cost
Juliet a pretty penny; she hoped it'd be worth it.

Juliet ducked into the tent flap, and when she straightened
up, her breath caught in her throat. Pale, luminous balloons
lined the upper reaches of the tent, with strands of streamers
glittering down from them. Plates of hors d'oeuvres bobbed
along the tent's outermost walls, propelled through the air by
contraptions of sparkling gears and propellers leaving glittery
bubbles in their wake.

In the center of the room, an enormous glass cylinder emitted strands of music resembling an entire orchestra. Wires and strands of light within it flickered and danced in rhythm with the tune. The magistrate's guests circled around it in perfect synchronization, imitating the inner workings of the machine itself. "This is first waltz," Geofferies muttered in Juliet's ear. "The next will be a quadrillette. We shall make our way to the magistrate's side so that when the music begins again, you'll have an opportunity to take a turn around the floor with him."

Juliet nodded, grateful that she had someone so knowledgeable about social graces to assist her. Goodness knows a former teashop girl like herself wouldn't have known which dance would follow. How Geofferies—a grizzled old airship sailor who regularly scorned the use of eating utensils—had learned such things was a matter of great curiosity, but Juliet would never ask. She knew, with her own unassuming history, that the choices one made were far more important than the situation into which one was born.

Geofferies twirled her across the floor, making it easy for her to follow his lead, even with her limited dancing experience. She could only hope, when the time came to swap partners, that the magistrate would be as skilled. They circled around, closer and closer to the thin, harsh-looking man, dressed starkly in red as was customary for the host of such an affair. His partner, a woman with a sandy complexion and short, lavender hair, wore a close-fitting gown of black and a pure-white mask. Finally, the waltz ended and the quadrillette began. As the guests broke into groups of four couples, Juliet found herself facing the magistrate. If he was curious about her identity, he did not show it, but instead bowed stiffly and offered his arm. *One turn*, Geofferies mouthed.

Juliet nodded. One turn around the floor was all the time she had to confront the man who'd been evading her for the past three months.

"It's a lovely party, Magistrate Phillips," she said as the dance began, careful to pronounce each letter in the manner of the upper class, just as she'd been taught years ago by Madame Chari, the owner of the tea shop where she'd once worked. "Might I ask you a question, sir? One that's been troubling me for some time?"

"You may," he said, bobbing his head on his unnaturally long neck.

"Tell me, sir, why you have ordered the blockade on Portmouth harbor?"

The magistrate did not skip a beat, but behind the scarlet-dyed peacock feathers that made up his mask, his eyes flashed. "You're that pirate who's been pestering me."

"Indeed," Juliet said, tipping her head with a smile. "And since you would not deign to meet with me as a pirate, I thought to meet you as an equal instead."

A rude and nasally noise came from behind his mask. "My equal you will never be, pirate-girl."

"The only difference between our wealth is that I collect mine in full daylight," Juliet retorted, unable to hold her tongue. "I've heard how the guards at the blockade will look the other way for certain captains with heavy pockets, and I suspect at least a portion of the coin that changes hands eventually makes its way into yours."

Before the magistrate could respond, a cry rose from the other end of the tent, followed by a crescendo of shrieks. The music-maker, unlike any human orchestra, played undeterred through it all, even as the dancers bumped to a halt around the floor, running haphazardly together like clashing gears.

"Magistrate Phillips!" a voice called out.

"Someone stop him!"

Near the outer edge of now-frozen dancers, a figure in a purple cape slipped through the crowd. He gave one glance backward, his features obscured by a skull-faced mask, and disappeared into the night.

The magistrate's gaze met Juliet's, and she pulled away. Suspicion clouded his eyes.

One of the guards in his crow's-beak mask rushed up, panting. "Madame Sanchez has been robbed."

"What a curious coincidence." The magistrate crossed his arms and turned up his lips in a sneer. "How odd, indeed, that a crime is committed on my skybarge the very moment my attention has been diverted by a *pirate*."

"You know this had nothing to do with me." Juliet's fingers twitched toward her concealed knife.

"Do I?"

"No need to be hasty," Geofferies said, stepping in and stilling her arm. "The lady has done *nothing* wrong."

His meaning was clear: the magistrate would love a reason to arrest her—had probably been looking for one for quite some time. She'd gained some notoriety in her time at the helm of the *Realm of Impossibility*, yet those she plundered all had their own reasons for not wanting to involve the authorities. Being an airship pilot was a sticky job, and there were few who could keep their hands entirely clean.

"He's right," Juliet said. "We had nothing to do with this. We don't even know what was taken."

"It was a moonstone, sir," the guard said, leaning in.

"A moonstone?" The magistrate frowned, obviously just as unfamiliar with the name as Juliet was.

"Yes, sir. That's what she called it. She was wearing it earlier—a perfectly spherical stone with a surface like glass and with eerie wisps of movement within it. It has to be the most hypnotic thing I've ever seen."

Juliet caught Geofferies' eye. Madame Sanchez' moonstone sounded curiously like a mysterious object that they had picked up a few months earlier aboard the *Realm*, and which they'd taken to simply calling "the orb." They'd kept it locked in a safe until they could uncover what it was, but each lead thus far had turned up empty. Could it be that here, among the opulence of the magistrate's fete, they'd stumbled upon another one of these rare gems?

"I'd like to speak with the victim," Juliet said.

"Certainly not," Magistrate Phillips said. "She'll be taking a balloon down to the surface immediately."

"Then let us pursue the thief. We'll bring the moonstone back here and, in exchange for our services, you'll agree to lift the blockade."

"Or," the magistrate said with a gleam in his eye, "I hold your first mate here under suspicion of conspiring to steal Madame Sanchez' moonstone and using it as leverage against me. You may not be aware of this, but your dance partner here has quite the history, plenty for me to detain him as a suspect."

Juliet ground her teeth as the guards moved in to take hold of Geofferies. He, in turn, simply squared his shoulders and raised his chin. If only she had her sword. But, no. That would do no good in getting the blockade lifted.

"If I return the stone to Madame Sanchez and bring the true thief to you, you'll have to release him," Juliet said. The matter of the blockade, it seemed, would have to wait.

The magistrate narrowed his eyes, and that was all the acknowledgement that Juliet needed. She turned to Geofferies, who in turn nodded, his lips forming the words, "Go on, then."

Shooting the magistrate a final scowl, Juliet turned on her heel and strode from the tent before he could change his mind.

Fortunately, Juliet's crew had seen the thief clearly, taking off toward the north in a sleek, black cloudcruiser.

"An expensive little thing it was," Sofia, the ship's tinkerer said. "It's perhaps no common thief we're dealing with here."

"Do you think you could track it?" Juliet asked.

Sofia had recently invented a contraption that could map the shifting of the air. In addition to accurately gauging the currents that would most efficiently drive their own ship, they could also detect where obstructions had disturbed or blocked the air's flow, thus pinpointing the paths of other airships. "We'll soon find out how well it works," Sofia said with a smile.

The contraption hung from a platform beside the ship's wheel, and Sofia stood with her head hunched over it, winding the mechanism on its side. When the air currents appeared beneath the glass as bright white tendrils of smoke, one path stood out against the others — a narrow silver sliver that cut through the thicker currents in a line slightly askew from the rest.

"There. That must be them," she said, pointing to the line. "They're heading north; follow that path."

Pursuing the ever-shifting lines of Sofia's contraption took some concentration, but the *Realm of Impossibility* was one of the quickest airships in the skies, and the tinkerer and captain worked well together. Choosing the fastest courses through the airstreams, they caught up to the sleek, black cloudcruiser high above the peaks of the Frostblade Mountains. It blended into the night sky so perfectly that had they not known precisely where to find it, they might have easily overlooked it.

"Pull alongside," Juliet told Second Officer Jameson, handing over the wheel. Then she turned to Sofia, "I want you to take our orb from the safe and wrap it in an oil rag in your toolbelt; I have a feeling we may want it close at hand."

Juliet passed her crew on the decks throwing heavy chains over the edge of the ship and snagging the cloudcruiser's lines. Slowly, they reeled in the smaller ship, until the distance between the two was narrow enough for Juliet to leap.

The door to the bridge stood ajar, and Juliet crept in, her sword drawn and ready.

The thief sat with his back to her, seemingly unaware of her presence aboard the ship or the *Realm's* iron grip upon it. His purple cape lay draped over the edge of a crate with two masks beside it: one, the skull-faced one and another a mask of pure white.

Juliet shifted from one foot to the other, just enough to peer over the thief's shoulder at whatever had so enthralled him that he hadn't noticed her rather grand entrance.

Submerged in a bowl of water upon the table was Madame Sanchez' moonstone. The water refracted oddly around it, forming strange and mesmerizing ripples that snagged on Juliet's mind, reeling in her consciousness like a winch. She gripped the hilt of her sword and let its cold metal dig into her palms, the sensation of the physical world drawing her from the stone's strange grasp.

As she watched, the thief pulled a large gold coin from his suit and dropped it into the water. It sank slowly, as though time itself had been altered, and the moment it touched the moonstone, a tiny *clink* reverberated off it and not one, but *two* gold coins settled on the bottom of the bowl.

Juliet drew in her breath, and at that moment, the thief's trance-like state was broken. He spun around in his seat, and Juliet realized that it wasn't a man at all, but a woman—the same woman who'd been dancing with the magistrate at the gala. The fabric of the slim, black dress had been pulled back and gathered behind her, no doubt to be hidden beneath the purple cloak as she'd made her escape from the skybarge, and her dark hair was wound tightly against the nape of her neck. The lavender wig she'd been wearing at the gala tumbled from her lap.

"Who are you?" the woman asked, seemingly more irritated than surprised. "I thought Phillips was going to send his usual man out to pick it up tomorrow."

"His usual man couldn't make it," Juliet said, casually sheathing her sword, "and the magistrate was concerned that you'd drawn too much attention to yourself at the gala this evening.

He wanted to ensure that prize was delivered safely, so he sent me to intercept you."

"And you are?" The woman's eyes narrowed.

"I'm Juliet Silver." A smile spread across her face at the look of surprise her declaration elicited.

"The pirate?"

"You know as well as I do that the magistrate doesn't always keep to his side of the law."

The woman grunted in agreement and turned to the table to retrieve the moonstone. "You can tell Phillips that I already took my cut," she said, pocketing the two gold coins and offering the gem to Juliet. "I suppose now we know how a pathetic orphan girl who once sold flowers on a street corner became one of the wealthiest women in the city, don't we?"

It took Juliet a moment to realize that she was talking about Madame Sanchez. She turned the stone over in her hand before tucking it into her pocket. "Yes, I suppose we do."

"You wouldn't believe it, the way she carries on about her charities for the *less fortunate* that she used to be worse off than half those dirty ne'er-do-wells." The woman laughed, the sound unpleasantly harsh to Juliet's ears.

"I'll be sure to relay your amusement," Juliet said, stepping to the door, "when I deliver this to the magistrate."

"No need, Miss Silver." When the door swung fully open, there stood the magistrate himself with two of his crow-beaked guards flanking him, their pistols drawn. Juliet peered over his shoulder to where an entire troop of his men held the *Realm*'s crew hostage, the magistrate's own ship tethered to the *Realm*'s stern. "As you can see, I've arrived just in time to retrieve the item myself. The stone, please."

Juliet glared at him and reached for the stone but refused to give it up so easily. "Why send us after the ship at all, if you'd been the one to arrange its theft?"

"Was I to admit that to my guests?" The magistrate laughed.

"I had to at least pretend as though I wanted the stone found. Truthfully, I never suspected you'd overtake Chhaya's cloud-cruiser before my own ship did. Now hand it over, and we'll forget that this has happened."

Juliet hesitated, the stone still in hand.

From behind her, the thief called Chhaya laughed. "It seems to me you've met your match, Phillips."

"I'll deal with you later," he snarled at her. "Now, Miss Silver. Give me the stone. I'll even allow you access to Portmouth Harbor. That is what you wanted, isn't it?"

It was a slimy deal, the harbor access for her silence. And what about Madame Sanchez? Was she to believe her moonstone lost forever while Magistrate Phillips fed his own greed? But the magistrate stood between Juliet and her ship, and she and her crew were outnumbered and outgunned. If only there were some way to ensure that the stone was returned to its proper owner...

Over the magistrate's shoulder, Juliet's eye met Sofia's. The tinkerer, standing on the aft deck of the *Realm*, touched her toolbelt, and Juliet had an idea.

"My *greatest* concern," Juliet said, projecting her voice across the gap between the two ships and never taking her eye from Sofia, "no matter *what* happens, is that Madame Sanchez is reunited with her moonstone. It truly is a *one-of-a-kind* treasure."

The magistrate snorted at the sentiment. "I'm afraid that's not part of the deal."

"Then the deal is off." With a defiant smile, Juliet flung the moonstone away. It sailed upward through the air, over the ship's railing, and then arched downward toward the far-off icy peaks of the Frostblade Mountains.

"No!" the magistrate screamed. "You! To the ship! Arrest her! Arrest them all!"

The outburst sent the crew of the *Realm* reaching for their swords, and in the chaos that followed the magistrate's conflicting orders, Juliet's crew quickly backed the magistrate's guards off their airship and severed the *Realm* from its tether.

The unfortunate—though not unexpected—consequence of this was that Juliet, with her sword now drawn, was quickly cut off from her own ship by a mob of the magistrate's men.

"Go!" she yelled to Second Officer Jameson. The guards overtook her and knocked her sword from her hand. Her crew looked on as they bound her arms behind her, obviously bewildered that she would give up the fight so easily.

"Go on, then!" she shouted again. "And listen to Sofia! She knows what to do!"

The jail cell into which Juliet was thrown was cold and damp, as expected. What was not altogether expected, however, was the company of her cell mate.

"This is all your fault, you know," Chhaya said. She paced the tiny room, kicking at Juliet's boots each time she passed the bunk bed where the airship captain sat. "If you'd just given him what he wanted, he'd have had no reason to turn us in. Now who will believe our word against his? I never should have taken your word that you were working for him."

Juliet leaned back against the concrete wall. "You're right."

Chhaya looked up, surprised. "I am?"

"Of course. You ought to have known that I'd never work for such a scoundrel."

"Some of us can't afford to be so noble," Chhaya said bitterly as she sat beside her on the lumpy mattress. "Some of us must take the jobs that are offered to us... particularly when they're offered by someone as powerful as the magistrate. I've heard of how the *Realm*'s former captain took you under his wing, how he taught you all you know and left you the ship in his will. Not all of us are so lucky to have such benefactors. Some of us have had to learn to survive on our own, without anyone else willing to lend us a hand."

"Sounds like a harsh life."

Chhaya scoffed. "You obviously have no idea."

Juliet studied the woman. Her expensive clothing and ship had told one story, but the scars and calluses on her hands told another.

"You could work for me," Juliet suggested.

Chhaya rolled her eyes. "Yes, I'm sure you'll be running many profitable ventures from here in this cell."

"Oh, I don't intend to remain here long. In fact, I think I hear someone in the corridor now." Juliet stood and peered out the small, barred window of the cell's door. Looking back at her were Sofia's golden eyes.

"Hurry," the tinkerer said to the stout jailkeeper who'd rushed up beside her with a large ring of keys. She turned back to Juliet. "It's good to see you again, Captain. We'll have you out in a jiffy."

"You're letting her go free?" Chhaya exclaimed, jumping up from the bunk.

"Madame Sanchez wrote an official testimony," the jailer said as the lock unlatched and the door swung open. "Her moonstone has been returned safely, and therefore, she is dropping all charges against Miss Silver and Mr. Geofferies."

"You'll need to release Chhaya as well," Juliet said.

The jailer stuttered. "I... I've only been told to release you and your crewman."

"Yes, well, Chhaya is part of the *Realm*'s crew now, too," Juliet said. "That is, if she'll accept the position. Why don't you go release Geofferies while we sort out the details?"

As soon as the jailer ducked out into the corridor, Chhaya looked to the other two women. "Returned safely? How can that be? You threw that orb overboard! It's bound to be lost among the peaks of the Frostblade Mountains forever."

"Yes, well," Sofia said, raising one shoulder. "Perhaps someday we may mount an expedition to find it. The mountains are known to be cruel, but thanks to my air tracking device, I do have a decent idea of where it might be. But let's just suffice it to say that Madame Sanchez's orb of fortune was not quite the *one-of-a-kind* treasure everyone had suspected."

"You had one?" Chhaya looked to Juliet for confirmation. "And you just *gave* it to the old bird? Don't you know what a treasure like that is worth?"

"Yes, well," Juliet said, nodding toward the hallway where Geofferies had just appeared, "there are some things more valuable than all the world's fortunes."

"You don't even know how she acquired it."

"Nor does it matter. What matters is that she will undoubtedly do far more noble things with it than Magistrate Phillips would have done. Now, what do you say, Chhaya? Will you join us?"

A week later, the *Realm of Impossibility* landed on a long stretch of open land just south of Portmouth harbor. The harbor itself was still closed to all but the magistrate's men, but it was no longer a concern for Juliet or her crew. When Sofia had returned the moonstone, she'd told Madame Sanchez why their crew had been at the magistrate's gala in the first place, and the wealthy socialite had immediately bought up the properties adjacent to the Portmouth Children's Home and cleared an open field upon it, perfect for the children to play upon in the summertime and large enough for an airship to land in.

The children rushed out at the sight of the familiar ship, and Chhaya, who was standing at the helm with Juliet, stared out at their vibrant faces in awe.

"This is why you'd been petitioning the magistrate? Why you were so upset about the closed harbor?" she asked. "For these... children?"

"Many of them have had to learn to survive on their own, without anyone willing to lend them a hand." Juliet linked her arm in her crewmate's. "But that's where we come in. Now, come help me unload these parcels; the children will all be eager to meet their newest benefactress."

Sisters and Other Life-Forms

by Rachel Delaney Craft

Rachel Delaney Craft lives in sunny Colorado, where she writes speculative fiction for children and teens. Her work has appeared in the children's magazines *Cricket* and *Ask*, the YA fiction podcast *Cast of Wonders*, and the Colorado Book Award-winning anthology *FOUND*. She spends her free time doing yoga, gardening, and walking her Jack Russell terrier. She spends her non-free time working as an engineer at an aerospace company and daydreaming about writing full-time. You can read more about her at racheldelaneycraft.com or follow her on Twitter @RDCwrites.

"It's not your fault. It's not your fault."

I kept telling myself this as I waited for the cryotube's cooler to pump down. Its rhythmic wheezing echoed the same reply: *Yes, it is. Yes, it is.*

As the temperature dial crept downward, I glanced at the face in the rapidly frosting glass.

"She shouldn't have even been on the ship," I muttered. This was *my* pilot's test, *my* first solo orbit. If Mom and Dad hadn't insisted Sera come along "just in case," none of this would have happened. I wouldn't have crash-landed on an uncharted moon. I wouldn't have lost all communication with the rest of the galaxy, not to mention all access to my nav files. And I wouldn't be freezing my big sister in a cryotube.

The tube's blue light blinked: chill complete.

Now that Sera was safely frozen, I looked around the shuttle. Most of it had survived the crash, except the first-aid module— also my fault. I should have made sure it was securely locked before takeoff. Its cover had come open when the asteroid hit, sending its contents flying—including the laser suture, which had shattered against the shuttle wall. The gash in Sera's thigh was too deep for simple gauze, with blood spurting in torrents from her femoral artery. She had lost consciousness quickly, and without the laser suture to close her wound, my only option was to freeze her until we reached a medi-base.

"Bixby," I said, "what's your report?"

Bixby, my D-class organo-robotic two-seater shuttlecraft, made a series of beeps and blips as his computers processed the request. I had upgraded most of his parts over the years, but he was still older than my grandparents, and he was a slow thinker.

"Life support systems at seventeen percent," he replied. "Navigation files offline. Radar and lidar offline. Communication systems offline."

I walked around the pilot's chair to examine the dashboard, where most of Bixby's computer system was housed. "This all looks intact. So why is everything offline?"

Bixby thought for a moment. "Energy deficiency. Solar panels at twelve percent capacity. I have only enough power for essential functions."

I nodded. "Essential functions" meant he could talk to me, and he could filter the air inside the shuttle so I could breathe in this moon's oxygen-deficient atmosphere. He didn't have enough juice to get us off the ground, let alone fly us back home to Silar Three. He didn't even have enough to keep Sera's cryotube cold.

I went to the rear of the shuttle, where Bixby's backup solar panels were locked in padded, shockproof compartments.

"Aha." The compartments were intact. I opened one after another, pulling out two, four, six, eight solar panels. There were ten backups total, enough to power Bixby's slowest cruise speed and all life support systems. Enough to get us out of here.

"Oh." I opened the last compartment, and my heart sank. It was empty. Then I remembered: on my last practice mission, two of Bixby's panels had shorted. I'd replaced them and then forgotten to restock the emergency compartment.

I knew exactly what Sera would say if she wasn't in cryostasis. *This is why Mom and Dad wanted me to come with you.*

Grinding my teeth, I glanced back at Sera's cryotube. At least I didn't have to listen to her now. That would only stress me out further, and we'd be too busy arguing to get any repairs done.

A pang of guilt jabbed my rib cage. *Really?* said Sera's voice in my mind. *You're not even sorry you killed me?*

"You're not dead," I muttered. At least, not yet.

"Okay, Bix." I glanced out the windshield at the clump of megacacti where we'd landed. "Find a place to sun yourself. I'll get suited up."

With a creak of metallic joints, Bixby stood and started lumbering across the desert. They don't call D-classes "dinosaurs" just because they're ancient, but also because they move like stegosauruses on land. Bixby was built for flying, not walking, and the sand would wreak havoc on his terrapads. But his compromised solar panels needed all the sun they could get.

Bixby emerged from the cactus grove and knelt on his forward thrusters, while I zipped up my exosuit and pulled the oxygenated plexibubble over my head. It smelled like mothballs. Grimacing, I buckled on my tool belt, opened the door, and stepped outside.

Holy cosmos, this moon was hot. I closed the door quickly, hoping to keep Bixby's interior—and Sera's cryotube—as cool as possible. As I clambered onto Bixby's back, he leaned forward and back, calculating the optimal angle for his solar panels.

Not that it mattered, I thought as I surveyed the damage. Bixby's body was built of a toughened, self-healing polymer, but the solar cells on his back were more fragile. After we crashed, Bixby had skidded across the sand through the megacacti, and their spiny arms had crushed or scraped off most of his solar panels. Many of the remaining ones weren't functioning; they should have been emitting a faint green glow as they charged in the sunlight, but they were dark. A few flickered weakly, the light spreading like veins across their microcrystalline silicon surfaces, then disappearing.

With only a few cells still operational, it would take a week to accumulate enough power for a trip back to Silar Three. And we didn't have a week—we only had as much time as the cryotube could stay cold. It could last indefinitely while drawing power from Bixby, if he had any. Without a power source, its internal battery would last five days, tops—less than that on this face-meltingly hot moon.

"How does it look?" Bixby asked.

I shook my head. "Not good."

I climbed down, landing in a cloud of sand, then trudged back inside. Already Bixby's interior had increased in temperature—three degrees, by my suit's temp sensor. I groaned. I needed to get the backup solar panels installed, and soon, or Sera would melt.

I paused beside Sera's cryotube. Its blue light blinked insistently, telling me it was running on battery power—or maybe telling me I was being a bad sister. I should have been crying, or sniffling at the very least, replaying fond memories in my head. I should have been whispering to the cryotube, saying things like "I love you" and "Can you forgive me?"

But when I peered into the frosty glass over Sera's face, all I could think about was the way her hand-me-down suits squeezed my stomach until my eyes bugged out. Or how she always called me "Max-*ine*" even though she knew I hated my full name, whether or not I'd been named after our first ancestor to colonize Mars. Or my fifth-grade science fair, which I won with my robotic root implant that made plants grow 2.7 times faster. The judges had swarmed around my poster, taking photos and shaking my hand until it was numb, while I stood there wearing my shiny blue ribbon and a pathetic grin. I'd stayed up all night preparing to answer questions like "Did you observe any increase in pollen production?" and "What's the tensile strength of the implant alloy?"

But all they said was, "You're Seramina Tut's sister, right? Wow, you've got some brains in that family!"

That was all anyone cared about: brains. Sera was a natural researcher. She studied things. She could memorize page-long equations and multiply six-digit numbers in her head. I was more of mechanic, a tinkerer, good with my hands—that's why I was the youngest person on Silar Three to take the pilot's test. My parents liked to say we complemented each other, though I didn't agree. Most of the time, I was just annoyed with Sera for getting all the attention.

I hefted the first solar panel. The panels were over two feet wide, and heavy. I would have to take them up one by one; I couldn't risk dropping any. By the time I got the panel onto Bixby's back, I was hunched over and panting, fogging up my plexibubble.

Stand up straight, Maxine. That's what Sera would have said.

"Max," I muttered, my mind wandering to the science fair. To my voice, drowned out by all the stupid judges. "I'm *Max* Tut."

While I installed the new panel on Bixby's back, I took a look around. The ground on this moon was mostly sand, of a deep red color—probably rich in iron. Clumps of megacacti as tall as buildings dotted the landscape. The faint outline of mountains broke the horizon in the distance. I squinted against the sun, looking for signs of life: birds nesting on the cacti, sandworms burrowing in the ground. I didn't see any. But it was unlikely this moon had developed plant life without some kind of animals to go with it.

A series of beeps and whines told me Bixby was running his usual scans with his terrapads.

"Terrain is silica-based," he said. "Small quantities of water detected. Plant and animal life likely."

I grunted as I locked the panel's connector into Bixby's socket. "Let's hope that animal life doesn't come sniffing around while I'm working on you."

Bixby was a science vessel; he had zero weapons and only basic shielding capabilities, which were useless now, anyway. If the animals on this moon were as big as the cacti, they could do some serious damage to Bixby. Then it wouldn't matter if I got the solar panels working.

"This terrain does not match any in my database," Bixby said, stating the obvious. "It is closest to the volcanic beaches of the Hawaiian Islands on Earth One. Are we on Earth One?"

"Of course not," I snapped, pulling a screwdriver from my belt. Silar Three's solar system wasn't even in the same galaxy as Earth One. "This place is uncharted. It must have come out of a wormhole or something."

Bixby whirred thoughtfully. "My records show a temporal distortion approximately one minute before the asteroid struck me. That would be consistent with a wormhole."

I began screwing the panel down. "The asteroid probably came through it too. But the moon got pulled into Silar Three's orbit. The asteroid didn't."

If anyone on Silar Three knew we were here, they could easily launch a shuttle—a fully charged, fast-moving one—to retrieve us. But I had no way to contact them, and it could be days or weeks before their sensors noticed the new moon, especially with the wormhole's magnetic interference.

"Since this moon is uncharted," Bixby said, "would you like me to run additional scans?"

"No. Save your energy." The panel glowed green, and I climbed down.

I walked past Sera's cryotube to retrieve the next solar panel. *This is amazing.* That's what she would have said if she was awake. *Can you believe it? We discovered a new moon!*

"Whatever," I said, lifting the panel carefully.

Come on, Maxine. Don't you know how rare wormholes are? And the odds of an entire moon coming through, right before our eyes—

I groaned. "Please be quiet."

"Captain Max?" said Bixby. "Is that an order to cease communications?"

"Huh? Oh. No, I was just...talking to myself." Stuck on this moon less than an hour, and I was already losing my marbles. Sera was right; this should have been the best day of my life. This discovery would make headlines. Years of research—and many pilot missions—would follow, to explore and study the moon. And who knew what secrets it might hold? The juice from its cacti might cure a disease on Silar Three. We could build habitation pods from iron extracted from the sand. The moon might even be colonizable someday.

But none of that would matter if Sera didn't make it back with me.

Hurry, said Sera's voice in my head as I carried the panel toward the door.

I resisted the urge to kick the cryotube on the way out. "Don't worry," I grumbled. "I'll get you back home soon. Back to your research, your internships, your awards, your stupid publications."

Before we left for this ill-fated mission, Sera had gotten her first research paper into a big-name scientific journal. At age sixteen, she would be the planet's youngest scientist to see her name in print. Kind of made my root implant look lame in comparison. No wonder my parents hadn't paid much attention to my pilot's test—they were too busy bragging to the neighbors about Sera's publication and asking me why I hadn't read it yet.

And if I failed now, they would know it was my fault she died. My fault our planet had lost one of its most brilliant minds.

"You shouldn't have been there," I said quietly as the door hissed open.

I couldn't let you go alone.

I stepped into the desert. "You didn't trust me?"

Bixby's door slid shut, but Sera's voice followed me outside. *I trusted you. But what if something happened? Who would put you in a cryotube?*

Sera was mature like that. Grown-up. Self-sacrificing. Just another way in which she was the better daughter.

I clambered onto Bixby's back and began installing the second panel.

If you cross-network them, Sera whispered in my head, *you can boost their power an additional six percent.*

I gritted my teeth. "I was going to do that." Eventually.

It took hours to get all the panels connected to Bixby, especially when the wind kept blowing clods of red sand at my plexibubble. Finally, I had all eight panels glowing a vivid green.

"Bixby," I said, "do you have enough juice to get us out of here?"

His computer whirred and clicked. "I have enough power for liftoff, yes. But I don't know how long it will take to arrive at our destination."

That didn't matter, as long as we could keep Sera cold the whole time. "What about life support?"

"At my lowest cruise speed, thirty-six percent. Enough for air filtering and radiation shielding. No sustenance production, I'm afraid."

"I don't need you to make food for me." I could go hungry until we got home, but I couldn't live without air, and once we got off the moon's surface, the cosmic radiation of space would fry me and Sera in minutes without Bixby's shielding. "How much more do we need to power the cryotube's coolers?"

More clicks. "Approximately five percent more energy."

The cross-networking! That would give us six percent. Then we'd be off this moon and on our way home.

I found plenty of network conductors, a roll of solder, and a solar-powered soldering iron in my tool belt. The iron's panels were fully intact, and there was enough sun in this desert to melt all the metal in Bixby. Soldering was an easy task.

Don't forget to align the magnetic fields, Sera whispered in my ear. *Positive, negative, positive—*

"I know," I snapped as I heated up a blob of solder. "I can do it myself."

That was exactly what I'd said before the asteroid flew by, clipping Bixby's rear thruster and sending us spinning into the moon's gravitational field. We'd seen the asteroid on our radar, and Sera had rushed to help me adjust our course. But I wanted to do it myself. I thought I had time, because the asteroid wasn't moving very fast at first. But Sera's brilliant mind calculated—correctly—that the wormhole's magnetic field would cause the asteroid to suddenly speed up.

Sera had been standing up, racing to the controls, while I was safely buckled into the pilot's seat. The impact had sent her flying across the room.

"*You* should've been wearing your seatbelt," I muttered.

I was trying to help you. If you hadn't been so stubborn—

"Quiet," I growled. "If you want to get out of that tube, you need to let me do this."

Don't you feel anything? her voice asked in my head. *I'm your only sister.*

I groaned. "Don't be so dramat—ouch!"

I pulled my hand back. I'd stopped concentrating on the soldering iron and burned a hole in the glove of my exosuit.

"Life support systems at forty-two percent," said Bixby's robotic voice.

I smiled. That was all we needed.

The cryotube's blue light glowed steadily as I crossed the room and buckled myself into the pilot's seat. The nav files were still offline, but it was easy enough to recover an auto-saved copy of our last course. I selected our original starting point—home—and punched in the coordinates.

"Destination confirmed," Bixby said.

I grabbed the joysticks and initiated the takeoff sequence. Bixby shuddered as his thrusters fired, and my stomach did a familiar tumble as we lurched off the ground. I grinned. This was why, even if I could afford one of the newfangled H-class hovercrafts, I would never abandon Bixby. Nothing compared to that feeling.

"Estimated time to arrival: seven days, four hours, twenty-two minutes."

"Hear that, Sera? We're on our way—"

Bixby shook and rattled violently. An ominous scraping noise echoed inside the shuttle.

"Bixby!" I gripped the joysticks until my knuckles turned white. "What's happening?"

As Bixby's computer hummed in thought, a leathery brown wing flapped over the windshield.

"Holy cosmos!" There were animals here after all.

"We have taken on an additional one hundred and twenty kilograms, approximately," said Bixby, his voice as calm as ever.

From the look of the wing, the added weight was from a single large animal—something similar to the flying pterosaurs of Mesozoic Earth. I had to shake it off, or we'd never make it back to Silar Three.

My brain switched into pilot mode. "Initiating evasive maneuvers," I announced, punching our velocity up and zigzagging the joysticks. Bixby may have been a dinosaur, but I'd refurbished his engine six months ago, so he had the horsepower of a brand-new shuttle. Even with our reduced power, this animal was in for a wild ride.

We zigzagged through the air, still moving up toward the clouds. The animal screeched and scratched Bixby's back. It must have lost its grip partially, because Bixby rolled sideways. I leaned forward against my safety harness and saw, through the windshield, the bizarre reptilian life-form dangling from Bixby by one claw.

I gritted my teeth, punching more buttons and twisting the joysticks. Bixby rolled a full 180, until he was upside-down and I was staring at the red desert far below.

"Get—off!" I grunted.

More scraping; the animal was climbing onto Bixby's underside. Flaming asteroids, this thing was persistent. What did it want, anyway? Bixby was too big to make a meal of. Maybe the animal was looking for a mate.

"Okay, Bix. Hang on."

I cut the engine, sending us into free fall. I jerked the joysticks to one side in an attempt to roll us out from under the creature. My stomach lurched, in a good way. This move was my trademark, though I rarely got to use it. If Sera hadn't been in cryostasis, she would have freaked out—this went against all the rules in all the protocol manuals. Sure, she could calculate the time until an asteroid strike. But she couldn't tell where an animal was by the feel of the shuttle's weight distribution, couldn't judge how long to free fall by the purr of the engine. This was my arena. Too bad the judges for my pilot's test couldn't see this.

Bixby rolled over in midair with a creak, and I saw the animal fall away, flapping its vast wings.

"Halfway there," I muttered, bringing the engine back to life

with a roar. I started a steep climb at maximum speed, still
zigzagging. Clouds broke over the windshield. On the radar
screen, the little green blip of the animal moved away from us.
"Ha! It gave up." I looked over my shoulder at the cryotube.
"You should've seen that, Ser—"
I did a double-take. The cryotube's blue light was blinking
again. I reduced us to cruise speed as we broke the moon's
atmosphere, then unbuckled and checked the cryotube.
The battery image flashed at me.
"Bixby, why isn't your life support charging the cryotube?"
"Life support systems at thirty-nine percent," he repeated duti-
fully. "Some functions may be unavailable."
"Oh, no," I breathed. We needed at least forty-one percent for
air filtering, radiation shielding, and the cryotube. I stamped
my dusty boot on the floor. "That animal must have damaged
one of the solar panels."
I looked over at the cryotube's screen. *TIME LEFT: 4 days, 12
hours.*
"Bixby, how long until we reach Silar Three?"
He calculated. "At my current speed, seven days and four
hours."
"Can you go any faster? While maintaining life support systems?"
More calculations. "Yes, but I would not advise it. It would
pose a serious risk to my engine's—"
"I'll fix your engine later! How fast?"
"The shortest possible time to destination is five days, sixteen
hours."
I chewed on a fingernail. We needed to shave our travel time
down by another day. I scoured our supply compartments, in
case there was another backup solar panel lying around. Nope.
I cursed loudly, glad Sera wasn't awake to hear *that*.
"Captain Max," said Bixby, "would you like me to return to

the moon for additional repairs?"

I thought about this. If Bixby landed again, I could look over the broken solar panels. Maybe one of them could be repaired—or maybe not. And every moment wasted brought Sera closer to melting.

I checked the cryotube's screen again. Four days and twelve hours from now, my big sister would thaw and bleed to death. Or not. Not if, after four days and eleven hours, I ordered Bixby to turn off the air filter and redirect that power to the cryotube. Sera didn't need air in cryostasis. Bixby would only be a day away from home; he could remain on course for the launch pad and deliver Sera safely. Meanwhile, without air, I would slip into unconsciousness and die a painless death.

"Captain Max?" Bixby repeated. "Would you like me to return to the moo—"

"No." I pressed my lips together and took a deep breath. "Stay on course for Silar Three. Maximum speed."

"Very well."

Suddenly, I missed Sera desperately. I wanted to talk to her, to hear her voice talking back. To apologize for being so mad at her the last couple years. I would never get the chance—I'd be gone long before she woke up.

But maybe... Maybe I could leave her a message.

I walked across the shuttle to the luggage compartment. I rarely used it—it was only necessary for long trips—but maybe Sera had. I snapped open the heavy metal buckles and peered inside. Sure enough, Sera had packed some emergency supplies. Two therma-vests. A few tubes of protein gel. Her holotablet, naturally—she was so busy and important, she couldn't go anywhere without having access to her work.

I grabbed the tablet. It sensed the warmth of my fingertips, and the screen lit up: a picture of the cover of *Galactic Innovations*, the journal her research paper was in. Of course.

I sighed. When she came out of cryostasis, she would barely

notice I was gone. I tossed the tablet back into the compartment. As it landed on the therma-vests, the picture changed. A familiar face smiled out.

"Is that...?" I scrambled to pick up the tablet again. There it was, a photo of *me*. My grin was so big it covered half my face. I held a trophy shaped like an atom with electrons whizzing around it.

The science fair, said Sera's voice in my head.

I nodded. "First place."

Yeah. I was so proud of you.

I stared at the picture until it changed back to the journal cover. I sniffed. "Sorry, Sera. Sorry I haven't read your article."

You can read it now.

Of course—the article must be on her tablet. I pressed a finger to the holoscreen, and the journal cover dissolved. *Passcode?* appeared on the screen, followed by a keypad with letters and numbers.

I looked over my shoulder at Sera's cryotube. "What's your password?"

Silence. I didn't know her passcode, so my brain couldn't pretend she was telling it to me. I rapped my fingers on the tablet, thinking.

I typed in *Galactic Innovations*.

The screen lit up. *Passcode incorrect.*

What was her article about? Something related to power transport in space travel. I tried several variations of this, but none worked.

The screen lit up again. *Attempts remaining: 1.*

The tablet would automatically lock if I entered the wrong password again. I sighed and leaned back against the wall. "Sorry, Sera," I said to the cryotube. "Guess I'll have to wait till we get home." Even when she was in cryostasis, I couldn't bear to tell her what was going to happen.

The tablet went into screensaver mode again, and my photo appeared. I got one more idea. I punched the screen again until the passcode prompt came up.

I typed in *Maxine.*

The login screen slid away, revealing a sea of apps and files. I found the one titled *Galactic Innovations*, then scrolled through the pages until I found the article with Sera's name.

"Huh," I said, reading the title. "*Using Magnetic Fields for Wireless Power Transfer in Space Travel.* Sounds fascinating."

And it was. No wonder everyone thought Sera was such a genius. Piloting a shuttlecraft was nothing compared to this. Sera had figured out how to transfer energy from a solar cell to a hover-craft engine a hundred meters away—no wires, no connectors, no conductive materials at all. Just air. At the end of the article, she hypothesized that it could work in space as well. If it did, this would revolutionize space travel. Shipwrecked travelers like me wouldn't have to replace our broken solar panels—we could recharge our batteries from any nearby power source.

A light bulb flashed on in my brain. "Wireless power transfer. Of course!" I wrapped my arms around Sera's cryotube and kissed the glass over her face. "You're a genius!"

All I needed was Sera's article and a power source. I snatched my tool belt from the supply compartment and pulled out the solar-powered soldering iron. I taped it to the windshield, where its solar cells could draw power indefinitely as we approached Silar Three and its sun. Then, copying what Sera had done in her experiment, I used the magnetic fields of Bixby's cross-networked solar panels to transfer the soldering iron's power to the engine.

"Bixby," I said when I was finished, "you should be getting a power surge. Is it enough?"

As Bixby thought about this, I watched the cryotube anxiously. "Power has increased. Life support at 43 percent."

The blue light blinked on.

"Yes!" I shouted. "It's charging!" I smiled at the cryotube. "We're going home, Sera. Both of us."

I settled back into the pilot's chair, feeling the familiar hum of Bixby's thrusters beneath me. I would probably fail my pilot's test—the judges would take off major points for the asteroid thing and for not having the first-aid kit secured. But I could take it again next year. I couldn't wait to see the look on Sera's face when I told her that I had proved her hypothesis and that we had discovered a new moon together.

We make a good team, don't we? That's what she would say.

I nodded. "We make a good team." That's what I would tell her when she came out of cryostasis.

Woomie Saves the Day

by Holly Schofield

Holly Schofield travels through time at the rate of one second per second, oscillating between the alternate realities of city and country life. Her short stories have appeared in *Analog*, *Lightspeed*, *Escape Pod*, and many other publications throughout the world. She hopes to save the world through science fiction and homegrown heritage tomatoes. Find her at hollyschofield.wordpress.com.

Kayla Ng ran along the spaceship's corridor, her bare feet stomping on the metal decking. Her little brother, Travis, staggered behind, a fourteen-month-old miniature monster wearing nothing but a huge diaper. Kayla sped up, even though outpacing him was pointless. There was nowhere to go on Deck One of the research ship that he couldn't follow.

She entered the bridge and skidded to a stop. Her mother sat in the captain's seat as usual. Her hands, clad in data-gloves, waved madly like she was conducting a symphony. On the big screen at the front, a chart of mining data scrolled alongside the image of a gray asteroid hanging in the blackness of space. Her mother glanced over her shoulder and gave a quick, distracted smile. "How's Travis?"

"What's that element?" Kayla pointed at the chart. "I know 'Fe' is iron, but what's 'Ce'?" If she was reading the numbers right, this asteroid had an awful lot more of that than most of them in the Belt.

"Did you wake up Travis and give him his milk for—" Her mom broke off as Travis waddled past Kayla, wailing. She stopped signalling instructions to the console and stripped off her gloves before scooping him up. "Kayla, why is his diaper so big?"

"Um, I changed the dimensions on the template. I might have made them...a little thick." Kayla shrugged. She'd 3D-printed a whole bunch of them before she'd realized her mistake.

"Kayla..." Her mom's eyebrows lowered.

"Mommm, I didn't want to have to change him so often." She knew her voice was whiny, but toddlers could have such giant poops.

"I just asked you to watch him for a minute."

"It's been four hours! I had to change him twice! And there weren't any more diapers on the shelf!"

Her mom frowned. "It's really been that long?"

"Mommm!"

Travis hiccupped, his lower lip trembled, and he hid his face in Mom's shirt.

"Quit shouting, you're scaring Travvie."

Kayla crossed her arms. Travis always got the snuggles. She'd never asked for a little brother. No one had consulted *her*.

Since turning eleven, she'd expected she could finally do more things with Mom, like analyzing data. Or hanging out with the cute alien animals on Deck Three, tending to the whole bunch of woomarrins. Or other grownup things at the big research station with Dad. But no, she was stuck here on this deck with crabby, overworked Mom and the brat. "It's not fair!"

Mom's eyebrows gathered even tighter, but then all of a sudden her mouth drooped. "I'm sorry," she said, "Without your dad here to help, I've been so—" The console *beep-booped* and Mom's eyes flicked up to the big screen as more results appeared. "Just carry on, Trav'll be fine," she said and nuzzled Travis' snub nose before setting him back on the floor.

He clung to her leg, his lower lip still jutting out.

Mom caught Kayla's eye. "Remember, hon, we'll be at the station with Dad in just two weeks. Just get zen, and you'll be fine." The phrase "get zen" was Mom's favorite. It meant telling yourself to chill, to calm down, to relax. It seemed impossible to do—your feelings were your feelings, and just thinking about being calm didn't mean you *got* calm.

Mom put her gloves back on and began to wave her hands like there was an entire orchestra on the main screen. Kayla couldn't even begin to follow the commands to the geology program, but it seemed like as much fun as the best video game ever.

She sighed. Two weeks was forever. And Travis was such a pain. He'd been jumping on her bed for the past half hour after playing with her stuff all morning. Right now, his chubby fingers even clutched her best miniature spaceship model— one that had taken her days to build—instead of his favorite woomarrin stuffy or one of his other stupid baby toys.

"Come on," she said, with another long sigh. "Let's go find Woomie." She peeled Travis off Mom's leg and hauled him away, ignoring his sniffles.

Mom called after her, "If he fusses too much at his diaper, just take it off and let him go naked."

Kayla rolled her eyes as she led Travis down the corridor. Nobody wore much clothing in space, but still, if Travis went naked, he'd probably pee on the decking, and then guess who'd be cleaning it up?

Back in the tiny bedroom they shared, Travis started flinging her stuff around again. She managed to distract him for a few minutes by dressing him up in her shoes, bracelets, and the seashells she'd gotten for her last birthday from Auntie Gemma who lived back on Earth. She even put a ribbon in his thin strands of baby hair. But then he started pounding her spaceship model into the metal bulkhead until she thought her head would explode.

"Here, don't you want to play with Woomie?" she said in a false, bright voice, holding up Travis' stuffy.

He'd loved the lumpy blue stuffy since he was a tiny baby. It had been hand-sewn by one of Dad's friends and really looked like one of the round, fluffy aliens. When Dad had first laid it in Travis' crib last year, the toy had actually seemed pretty cool.

But during the past year, Travis had spilled every food imaginable on it along with dripping enough drool on it to fill a moon crater.

He hadn't noticed her, intent on the model. She dangled the stuffy right in his face by one smelly blue ear. "It's a woomarrin! Play with it!"

Travis' face lit up and he grabbed Woomie for a quick hug. "Woo!" he said, using one of his few words. Then he laid it gently on her bed pillow and pulled up her sheet to tuck it in.

"Ew!" She used one of her art markers to push the disgusting thing onto the floor. Mom said the stuffy's unique fake-fur material couldn't be cleaned. Kayla felt like putting on an evacuation suit whenever she went near it—the helmet and air tanks would make it impossible to smell Woomie's strong odor.

The toy's big round eyes looked up at her from its place on the floor.

The woomarrin aliens *were* pretty awesome, even if the stuffy wasn't. They'd been discovered on an Earth-like planet in another star system ten years ago. Now they were now being brought to the Belt for even more studies. Kayla's mom had been specially selected to transport the woomarrins from the Hub to the big research station deeper in the Belt. Kayla's dad had rushed ahead on a passenger ship last week to make a place for them to live, a sort of giant terrarium. They breathed air full of oxygen and nitrogen just like people, but Dad said they would be much happier with special nutrients and shrubby forests to make tree-homes in. That was Dad's new job: humanity's only woomarrin habitat expert.

Kayla hugged herself. It was so awesome that dozens of actual live woomarrins were in the cargo hold just two decks below her bare feet! She loved the way the popular science videos showed their bumpy bodies snuggled together like puppies, their large brown-and-white eyes swirling like the cream in Mom's coffee. Mom said Kayla could hold one when they got to the research station.

But, until then, they were off-limits. And she was stuck with the brat.

"Travis!" While she'd been lost in thought, Travis had taken the marker and scribbled all over her best slippers and was working on the wall. She stuck the black marker up on her highest shelf. Sure, she could recycle and reprint the slippers, but they wouldn't be the same. Stupid brat! He started slamming her spaceship model again.

"Any harder and you'll breach the hull, and we'll lose all our air," she told him, and his face crinkled up at her tone.

"Aihhh," he repeated after her, worriedly.

"You want to lose it all? So you can't breathe?" She blew at his face, and his lower lip stuck out. "Look!" She lifted him up, staggering under his weight, and pressed his face against the porthole. She loved watching the distant sparkle of stars and the velvet nothingness in between, even though it hardly ever appeared to change. It was so fascinating to think that tiny rocks, meteoroids, were whizzing all around them faster than bullets. The bigger rocks scooted past too—the asteroids that Mom was learning about—even though you couldn't exactly see them move.

"Aihhh?" Travis stared out the porthole window, puzzled.

"No, silly, not air. Stars!" He was such a baby. She had to explain *everything*. She set him down. This was the most boring day ever.

Dad had told her stories about how he had taken care of Auntie Gemma a long time ago when she'd been a toddler and all the trouble she'd gotten into. Now she understood what that really meant. Babies were so annoying!

"If only you were older, Trav, we could play better games."

Games like hide-and-seek. Before Travis had been born, Mom and Dad had played hide-and-seek on the ship with Kayla all the time. Back then, things hadn't been so busy. Once, Dad had even shown her how to override the computer so the trackers that they all had imbedded in their wrists didn't record where they were on the ship. That had made Mom really mad, but it had made for the best hide-and-seek ever.

Mom never understood stuff like that.

Mom never understood Kayla.

Not ever.

And now, thanks to Mom, Kayla was stuck babysitting the world's most awful baby.

She could feel her stress and irritation. Maybe Mom's idea was good, and she should "get zen."

Yeah, right.

Mom and Dad both said that getting zen was a lifelong journey without a destination—whatever *that* meant—and that the phrase *getting zen* was just a short way of saying a whole bunch of things that took forever to understand.

Well, she could try. It wasn't like she had anything else fun to do.

She drew in a breath, trying to listen to her breathing like Mom had taught her.

She concentrated.

In. Out.

In. Out.

Travis farted loudly.

She giggled. So much for that.

Now what? Her stomach gurgled. "All right, Travis, time for lunch!"

Travis nodded, eager, and dragged Woomie behind him to the tiny galley where he managed to splatter spaghetti sauce onto the stuffy and all over the table and the wall. Kayla ate her own spaghetti neatly, using her favorite pair of chopsticks—the ones with the peacocks printed on them—not getting any on her coveralls at all.

After she was full, she realized she'd forgotten something. She intercommed the bridge with a sauce-tinted finger. "Want anything to eat, Mom?"

"Later, hon, I've got to finish..." Mom's voice drifted away, and Kayla took her finger off the intercom button. Then she wiped up only the table, pretending she didn't see the rest of the mess. Mom could scrub the wall later, in the evening or whenever—parents didn't need as much sleep as kids.

The afternoon dragged on. Travis wandered around, dragging Woomie by one smelly bump, Kayla's model clutched in the other hand. Twice he fell when his diaper dragged him down. He'd tried to take it off several times, but she'd added extra stickiness to the sticky tape when she'd printed it, and his fingers plucked at it uselessly. She'd probably have to take it off with scissors when it got full enough.

By two o'clock, he was whining and impossible. He'd been refusing to take naps this past month. Mom said it was a stage he was going through, the same as his teething.

"Trav, watch your woomarrin vid. Please." She displayed his favorite cartoon show on her bed screen and turned the annoying music up really loud.

He watched for three minutes and then yelled, "Want woo!" and threw her model. The tiny spaceship broke apart into a dozen pieces, and the antenna cracked.

"Trav!"

"Want woo!"

All the stuffy and vid had done was to make him want the real thing. Somehow his baby brain understood that the live

woomarrins were on the ship with them. He'd probably over-
heard Kayla and Mom talking.

"Here, have Woomie." She kicked the stinky thing over.

"Woomie *is* a woomarrin."

Travis threw it across the room. "No! Want woo!" Drool cas-
caded down his chin. He threw a piece of broken plastic and it
hit her in the face.

"You stupid brat!"

"Want woo!"

"No kidding! Who doesn't?" She could be cuddling a silky-
haired alien right now.

"Want woo!" Travis was turning red, and tears threatened. Kayla couldn't take much more of this. And the answer was just
two decks below.

"Fine! Let's go!" If he wanted real woomarrins, she'd *give* him
real woomarrins.

There were good reasons her parents had forbidden her to go
below Deck One—and all of them concerned safety. The sharp
edges of the crates and other cargo, the tricky lower artificial
gravity nearer the outer edges of the ship, the chance of space
debris or meteoroids hitting the hull...yeah, a whole bunch of
reasons.

First, Kayla pulled Travis along to the bridge and peeked in.
Should she ask permission to go below decks? Mom's hands
still swooped and soared. It wouldn't be fair to interrupt her—
that would be like interrupting Kayla in the middle of a new
SuperSpaceKidz novel.

Going to Deck Three would be okay. She'd been doing safety
drills since she was four years old. Nothing would go wrong,
and they'd only stay a minute.

Kayla edged away, dragging Travis, but then she stopped at the
corridor control panel. Mom didn't need to know what they
were up to. That would just add to her stress. Kayla tapped in

the coding Dad had shown her and turned off both her and Travis' trackers.

The trip took a while. Slowly down the ladder, clutching wiggly Travis who clutched stinky Woomie. Then along a corridor, through a hatch, down another ladder, then along Deck Three's corridor to the cargo hold's thick door.

She set the brat down with a sigh of relief and tapped the door panel. The hatch clicked open with the soft chime that meant the cargo hold was pressurized and had air. It *better* have air. The woomarrins wouldn't last long without it. Kayla had wanted to keep the big clutch of aliens on the upper decks, but Mom said they needed the pen and heat lamps and some room to explore so that they'd develop right.

Suddenly unsure, she stuck her head in. Maybe this wasn't a good idea.

The cargo hold was about the size of a school classroom back on Earth. Just inside the hatch, evac suits hung in a neat row. On both sides, boxed supplies lay on shelves, next to stacks of crates full of goods for the research station. In the center of the room, fenced in by temporary netting that Mom had rigged up, a whole lot of baby woomarrins cuddled together like kittens, dozens and dozens of them. They were about as smart as a turtle or a hamster, the scientists thought, and just as friendly.

Should she go in? She'd be in big trouble if Mom found out.

Travis whined and pulled her forward, banging stinky Woomie against her leg. "Woo!"

Maybe seeing the woomarrins would entertain him for a while. And they sure were cute.

"Come on, then, stupid."

They stepped inside.

One of the woomarrins shuffled over to the side of the pen to meet them. Travis went "Oh!" and put his hand over his mouth, giggling.

They were so very many shades of blue. The warmth from the heat lamps felt like sunshine.

"Woo!" said Travis happily, smiling for the first time that day.

The intercom squawked with Mom's voice: "Kayla! Where are you? And where's Travis?"

"Ummm..." Kayla couldn't think of a good answer. She was in for it now.

Then several things happened at once.

Travis squatted down and poked a finger through the netting.

Kayla bent over to help him pet the nearest woomarrin, a short-haired blue-gray one.

Bang! A loud noise, as if a firecracker had exploded next to her ear.

Instinctively, she grabbed Travis and dived between two crates. Alarm bells rang faintly. Shouldn't they be louder?

Travis' face screwed up and he began to cry, almost noiselessly.

Suddenly, Kayla realized she was pretty much deaf.

There was only one thing that would cause a noise loud enough to deafen her and also set off alarms. A meteoroid must have shot through the hull!

Where there was one, there might be more.

She hugged Travis to her. Now what? Maybe if she could slide one crate on top of two others and get herself and Travis under them, they'd be better protected.

"Sit beside me and don't move! I'll make you a little bear cave, okay?" Her voice sounded muffled and odd.

She half-stood and pulled the nearest crate, heavy with some kind of equipment, over the top of the one to her left. One jerk, two. Almost there! Just a bit more before it would also be on top of the other crate on her right.

She braced herself, extending one leg and gave one more big heave.

The crate teetered, and she pushed Travis out of the way before it crashed down on her outstretched leg.

Sharp pain, worse than anything she'd ever felt, followed by a moment of total blackness, and then, slowly, her vision cleared.

Her heart was thundering. And, along with the distant alarm and Travis' hiccups, she could hear a high-pitched whistle, like Auntie Gemma's old-fashioned tea kettle.

The cargo hold's air was escaping out the meteoroid's hole into space!

What was the safety rule? For a moment, her mind was blank. Then she remembered: for a hull breach, you were either supposed to put on the evac suits or else run out of the room, sealing the hatch behind you.

If they didn't do either of those things soon, they'd both die.

She swallowed past her tight throat.

Her leg was trapped under the crate, and Travis was too little to help.

They were doomed.

"Kayla? Kayla! Answer me!" Mom's tinny voice over the intercom held worry. "The hold had a breach a minute ago, and your trackers don't seem to be working. Where *are* you?"

"Mommm, Mommy," Kayla cried out. The intercom was an endless distance across the floor, right near the evac suits. If she didn't press the button next to the speaker, Mom couldn't hear her.

She pushed again and again at the crate on her leg, but it wouldn't budge.

Travis cuddled next to her and pushed his wet face into her neck. She wrapped an arm around him.

Several meters away, beyond the abandoned Woomie toy, the living woomarrins stared at her with frightened eyes. They couldn't get out of their pen, and they weren't bright enough to help, but they sure knew something was wrong.

And, like Travis, they were depending on her to fix things. Mom's voice again. "Kayla, I'm outside the cargo hold door. I'm guessing you and Trav are inside. The computer didn't know you were in there, so it's sealed off the hold due to the hull breach. I can't override it. I'll have to cut a few wires and maybe hack a subroutine. It'll take me a few minutes."

"Okay," Kayla whispered even though Mom couldn't hear her.

"Listen carefully. If the meteoroid has made a hole of under ten millimeters, then you've got about ten minutes before...well, I should be able to open the door in six or seven minutes."

"Okay, Mommy."

"But if it's bigger than ten millimeters, then we've got real trouble. Put on your evac suit, then put Travis' on him, then see if you can stick something in the meteoroid hole or against the wall, like a sheet of rubber or something so the air won't rush out so fast."

How big was ten millimeters? Kayla couldn't remember.

"That's a centimeter, approximately the width of your index finger." It was like Mom could read her mind. "Kayla, you can do this. Get zen."

Kayla held her breath, trying for a zen-like state. No go. And no *time*! How big *was* the hole? She let go of Travis and twisted around, trying to locate it. Her injured leg shot pain up to her stomach, and she fought the blackness that threatened to engulf her again. "Trav, can you see a hole? Find the hole, Travvie."

Beside her, Travis cried steadily. A stream of snot ran down to the corner of his mouth, and he clapped his hands over his ears. The awful whine was giving her an earache too. Or probably, the pain was due to a pressure change. It didn't matter. What mattered was stopping the leak.

Her coveralls pulled at her butt as she managed to get up on one elbow. She craned her neck forward but still couldn't see any damage to the walls.

In the middle of the room, the woomarrins shifted uneasily.

Their long, fine guard hairs were being gently pulled toward the far wall. There! A ragged opening with sharp edges about knee-high up the wall. Blackness filled it, the terrible blackness of outer space itself. Worst of all, the hole was about the size of the Canadian two-dollar "twoonie" in Kayla's coin collection–at least two centimeters across!

That math wasn't difficult: They had *way* less than ten minutes before all the air would leak out.

"Oh no. Oh no. Oh no." If only she could get free, she could stuff something in it. There weren't any rubber sheets or anything, but maybe she could use a sock.

Except she was barefoot.

Or one of Mom's data-gloves, if Mom had been there.

If Mom were there, she'd have a tissue, and she could wipe Travis' nose and then shove that mess in the hole to block the air leaking out. Some of that didn't quite make sense, and Kayla knew her leg—maybe it was broken?—meant she wasn't thinking straight. Another wrench to get free made her hips hurt like crazy but didn't shift her trapped leg at all. And her ears really ached.

The problem was, there was no time to think. Every breath might be her last!

Maybe, just maybe, it was time to *get zen*. Mom always said, "Make your last breath a deep one," but Kayla hadn't understood what that meant.

Until now.

The chi gong breathing exercise that Mom kept trying to teach her was really about visualization. You pretended to suck in a little glowing dot of power. That was called your chi. Then you pictured it sliding down your front, along a line that ended just below your belly-button. With each breath you drew, your chi would grow stronger and stronger, giving you steadiness and strength.

She closed her eyes tightly and drew in a really long breath. If it was going to be her last one, she'd make it count.

At first, she concentrated fiercely. Then she realized that was all wrong.

Relax, she told herself, just relaaax.

Ahhh, there it was! A tiny golden orb of chi, slipping along the meridian that ran from her nose to her mouth to her chin, and down, down, down. She guided the orb home to her dan tian, the energy center that lay in her lower belly.

And now she was calm enough to know what to do.

"Travis? Trav, stop snuffling." She kept her voice steady. "Get up, there's a good little buddy."

Travis kept howling. His ears must ache as much as hers did. And the room was growing colder.

She shouted as loud as she could, as nicely as she could, "Stand up. I'll take off your diaper, and you carry it over there and stuff it in the hole, okay, Travvie?"

Travis obediently got to his feet and shoved his giant butt in Kayla's face, and she snorted back a laugh, knowing it wasn't really laughter that wanted to bubble out. She scrabbled at the sticky tapes for what seemed like a long time until her fingernails hurt. The tapes weren't budging.

"Kayla? Honey? It's been another two minutes. I've cut the override, but I haven't been able to fix the systems to let me in. A hull breach is very..." Mom's voice dropped to a mutter as she focused on her hack.

Kayla took a few more steadying breaths and waited until her chi had stabilized. What else could Travis use to block the leak? She stared around, willing an answer, and her eyes lit on the grubby stuffed toy abandoned on the floor.

"Trav, listen to me. Go get Woomie. Go on, quick! Good buddy." Travis looked puzzled—why would his big sister want something he knew she despised? But he staggered off in his toddler way and grabbed Woomie by an ear.

"Now, go over to the far wall, there." She gestured at the awful hole with her cold, goose-bumpy arm.

Travis wailed and stamped a foot, not wanting to get too far away from her. His other hand clutched the side of his head, and he trembled in fear and the growing chill.

Niceness wasn't going to work.

"Go, stupid!" This time the phrase felt nasty and wrong.

He shambled away toward the hole, no longer a miniature monster but her own baby brother.

Her heart clenched as he got closer to the danger. Twice, he looked back at her for reassurance.

She yelled, "Stick Woomie on the wall over that nasty hole. Now!"

Travis pressed a hand against the hull to brace himself, right next to the ragged metal edges of the hole. He looked back at her again, clutching his toy, his thin hair lifting.

"Do it, stupid!"

Slowly, he covered the hole with the stuffy, then plopped down on the floor silently, probably too scared and cold to cry.

Kayla's heart lurched again.

Would using Woomie as a plug work to seal the hole?

For long seconds she stared at the toy. It stuck to the wall like it was held by a magnet.

Finally, she noticed the woomarrins' guard hairs were not moving at all, and their eyes were a lighter brown. She relaxed against the warmth of the decking and held back sobs. "Come here, Trav, come on over here and have a hug."

It was another two whole minutes before Mom burst into the room, looking so large and scary and un-Mom-like in her evac suit that Travis started to wail again.

"I'll never ever override the trackers again." Kayla rubbed a finger on the cast Mom had put on her leg.

"I know you won't, hon."

"And I won't ever go see the woomarrins, even when we're at the research station. Or anywhere. Never ever."

Mom stroked her hair. "Well, I don't think you need to promise all that, but I'm glad you're sorry about what you did."

Kayla *did* need to promise that, to make herself feel better. Mom didn't understand, as usual.

A sudden rush of tears threatened. Kayla tried to get zen, but her little globe of chi stayed dim and wobbly. "The worst thing of all is that Travis thinks I made him kill Woomie. Do you think he'll ever forgive me?" From her propped-up position in her bunk, she looked over her rumpled bedsheets to where Travis was pointedly ignoring her and slamming her second-best spaceship model into the bulkhead.

Mom smiled. "Sure, he'll forget. Over time." She squeezed Kayla's arm. "I'll print him another Woomie tonight, and I'll throw the smelly old damaged one in the recycle chute when he's asleep. He'll probably never know."

But Kayla knew that he would. "Can't we fix the original Woomie?"

"It's full of rips and tears. And it's pretty gross." Mom smiled down at her. "I thought you'd *want* to get rid of it."

Mom didn't understand Travis, either, not like Kayla did. He wouldn't want a new stuffy. And he was going to hate her *forever*. "If you get me some thread and a needle, I'd like to try."

"Okay, hon." Mom smiled and shook her head. Then she got serious. "Kayla, I know I've been asking a lot of you lately. And I know you're interested in the asteroid work. How about we build Travis a blanket fort, and then I'll teach you how to read the charts, here on your bedroom screen, okay?"

"Deal!" She high-fived Mom.

Maybe Mom *did* understand her, after all. Just a little. But that still didn't make Kayla feel better. She'd treated Travis so badly so many times.

"Why the big sigh, hon?"

"Before you teach me about the asteroid, can Travis draw on my cast?"

Mom raised her eyebrows but handed Travis the black marker from the high shelf. His face lit up, and Kayla immediately felt her chi grow warmer and bigger.

Then she giggled and giggled as Travis drew dozens of squiggles on the cast, the bedsheets, and all the way up her arm.

The Magnificent Matter of the Mischievous Monkey

by Dawn Vogel

Dawn Vogel writes and edits both fiction and non-fiction. Her academic background is in history, so it's not surprising that much of her fiction is set in earlier times. By day, she edits reports for historians and archaeologists. In her alleged spare time, she runs a craft business, co-edits *Mad Scientist Journal*, and tries to find time for writing. She is a member of Broad Universe and an associate member of SFWA. Her steampunk series, *Brass and Glass*, is being published by Razorgirl Press. She lives in Seattle with her awesome husband (and fellow author), Jeremy Zimmerman, and their herd of cats. Visit her at historythatneverwas.com.

Chrysanthemum stood on tiptoe outside the dining room window. Nearby, her sister Marigold dusted artificial pollen across the petals of a patch of mechanical daisies.

"I can't tell what they're doing," Chrysanthemum said with a sigh, landing hard on her heels.

"Father said they would be meeting with an architect. I suspect they're discussing architectural things."

"But what sort of architectural things would they be discussing?"

Marigold laughed. "If you're so keen on finding out, then go inside. I'm certain they'll tell you what they're doing." She glanced at Chrysanthemum's neglected oil can. "And then perhaps you can finish your part of the chores."

Chrysanthemum chewed at her lip, her mind warring over sating her curiosity or doing her chores around the mechanical garden. In the end, her sense of duty won out. "I'm sure Father will tell us after they've finished their meeting. But I do hate not knowing."

The two girls went about their chores. As the older sister, Marigold, age twelve, had recently taken on more responsibilities in the garden, including Grandfather Brecht's experimental pollination project. Not only was she the one to introduce the artificial pollen to the mechanical flowers, but she also recorded the results of the experiment.

Meanwhile, Chrysanthemum, who was eight, had taken over some of Marigold's previous duties, like oiling the delicate clockwork inside the mechanical flowers. It was a duty she took very seriously, but she also found it monotonous, particularly when anything interesting was occurring at Marsh Gardens.

Chrysanthemum worked her way around the Marsh family's small cottage at the center of the garden, edging ever closer to the open front door. Only snippets of conversation made their way to her listening ears.

"—propose over here?" That was Father's voice.

The architect's voice was soft, and Chrysanthemum had to nudge the front door open farther to hear any of the woman's words. "—enclosed walkway at ground level might be best."

"What about—" Mother's voice was drowned out by a mechanical scuffling sound nearby.

Chrysanthemum turned away from the door and saw a mechanical monkey swinging from a tree in the front yard of the cottage. Its head and body were made from hammered copper plates that had been shaped into the approximation of a real monkey, while its limbs consisted of a series of smaller and smaller piston-driven articulated rods. Its tail was piston-driven, as well, but made of a linked chain that curled and straightened as the monkey desired and even allowed the monkey to hang by his tail, as he was doing now.

"Hello, Dickie," Chrysanthemum said, smiling at the monkey.

The monkey responded with a shrill cooing sound dimly reminiscent of the monkeys Chrysanthemum had seen at the Dover Zoo, but not quite right.

"Go back to Grandfather Brecht and tell him he needs to adjust your vocal box again, Dickie."

Dickie swung up and sat atop the branch he had been dangling from. He made another noise at Chrysanthemum, this one sounding even further from the sort of noise he ought to make.

Marigold walked around the corner of the house. "Oh, hello, Dickie. Here I thought Chryssie was just talking to herself."

Chrysanthemum spun and stuck her tongue out at Marigold, in full view of the cottage's front door, which opened completely at that exact moment.

The architect, a dark-haired woman who looked younger than Mother and Father, dressed in an elegant purple walking dress, looked startled by Chrysanthemum's appearance.

Chrysanthemum blushed and stammered, "Oh, I'm...pardon me...it's a pleasure...umm, hello, I'm Chrysanthemum Marsh. I'm terribly sorry to have stuck my tongue out...in your direction. It's quite rude." She looked down at her boots, ashamed of her behavior.

The architect chuckled as she stepped outside. "No need to apologize, Miss Marsh." She shifted her glance toward Marigold and gave her a kind smile. "I, too, had an older sister growing up, and three younger brothers. I understand teasing all too well."

Now it was Marigold's turn to feel ashamed. She murmured, "I'm sorry, Chryssie."

Chrysanthemum looked sidelong at her sister, but her face spread into a smile. "I forgive you. And thank you, ma'am, for your understanding."

"Oh, please don't call me ma'am. I'm not nearly old enough

for that. My name is Eileen Davenport. And your parents told me about all three of their darling children." She paused to glance at the small cottage. "I suspect you may need my assistance again to expand your living space, Mr. Marsh."

Father stepped outside and joined Miss Davenport on the porch. "Yes, I am certain we will call on you again." He looked at his two daughters. "Mother is putting Sprout down for a nap, and she's asked me to sing to him. Will the two of you walk with Miss Davenport to the main entrance?"

"Of course, Father," Marigold said. "Right this way, Miss Davenport."

Miss Davenport paused beneath the tree where Dickie was again dangling by his tail. "Such interesting creatures your family has created. Are there many animals like this one?"

"Mostly smaller ones," Chrysanthemum said. "Dickie is new, and Grandfather is still working on his design. He doesn't sound very much like a monkey."

In a flash, Dickie leapt down from the tree and grabbed Miss Davenport's valise out of her hand. The Marsh sisters and the lady architect stood in stunned silence as the mechanical monkey scrambled back up the tree and bounded away.

"Oh my goodness!" Miss Davenport cried. "After him!"

"He can't go far," Marigold replied. "The animals are trained not to leave the garden."

Chrysanthemum ran after Dickie, watching the monkey swing from branch to branch with only one arm, while he held Miss Davenport's valise with the other. Even encumbered, he moved through the trees faster than Chrysanthemum could move across the ground, especially as she weaved around the flower beds, sticking to the paths between them.

As she rounded a bend in the path, she lost sight of the mechanical monkey, and she craned her neck to look for where he might have gone. With her gaze away from the path, she stumbled over the edge of one of the beds and fell to her knees.

Bits of gravel dug into her skin, and she cried out in pain.

"Chryssie, what's wrong?" Marigold called.

"I've lost him, and I fell down."

Marigold ran up and crouched beside her younger sister. She scanned the trees above and caught a glimpse of Miss Davenport's valise as it vanished out the main entrance to Marsh Gardens. "Oh no! The monkey escaped!"

"You'd said it couldn't do that, I thought," Miss Davenport said as she joined the girls.

"It shouldn't be able to," Chrysanthemum said, wincing as she rose. "We should go and talk to Grandfather Brecht. Perhaps he'll know what happened."

Marigold helped Chrysanthemum brush the gravel from her knees. Fortunately, none of the small bits of rock had broken the skin, and Chrysanthemum was able to walk with Miss Davenport and Marigold to Grandfather Brecht's small workshop.

The filtered sunlight glistened off Grandfather Brecht's white hair and gold-rimmed spectacles as he regarded his two granddaughters and the lady architect. "Have any of you seen Dickie?"

"That's exactly why we're here," Marigold said. "He took Miss Davenport's valise and left the garden!"

"Oh my, that's no good!" Grandfather Brecht exclaimed. "I had been making some adjustments to his voice, but it seems perhaps I altered some of his other programming at the same time. May I ask what was in your valise, Miss Davenport?"

"Mostly blueprints I need to do my work." She paused. "And my lunch. Oh dear, I think the monkey must have been interested in the banana I packed with my lunch today."

Grandfather Brecht nodded. "That seems likely. I've tried to make my mechanical animals as realistic as possible."

"Do they eat?" Miss Davenport asked, her brow furrowing. "I thought they were just mechanical constructs."

"They are, but I've developed a mechanism by which some of the animals can convert the food they consume into energy to power them. Dickie shouldn't be hungry, as I fed him this morning. But perhaps he was curious about your banana anyway."

"Grandfather, where would Dickie have gone?" Chrysanthemum asked. "He's never been out in Dover before. Where should we begin looking for him?"

"I'm not certain, but with you and Marigold on the case, he'll soon be found. The two of you will be able to find any clues he's left. In the meantime, I'll keep an eye on the entrance to see if he returns on his own. If he does, I'll send one of the pigeons out with a message. They're quite good at finding their way back home when they leave the garden."

Chrysanthemum nodded. "Thank you, Grandfather." She looked at Marigold and Miss Davenport. "I suppose we'd better get started, then!"

Chrysanthemum and Marigold looked around at the bustling street outside of the mechanical garden. Marsh Gardens was on the outskirts of Dover, but in an area near a major thoroughfare that led out of town. All around them, carriages rumbled down the street, and pedestrians walked between the shops that lined its sides.

"I don't see any signs of Dickie causing trouble," Marigold said. "But perhaps someone noticed him going past."

"That seems probable," Chrysanthemum said. "He's not very sneaky." She crossed the street to where a young girl, seated on a barrel, was selling newspapers. She was dressed in a blouse and trousers, wearing a flat newsie's cap over her cascading auburn curls.

"Morning! How'd you like a paper?" the girl asked.

"Not today, thank you," Chrysanthemum replied. "You didn't happen to see a monkey come through here not too long ago, did you?"

The girl smiled. "Oh yeah, the most curious monkey I ever seen. It was made of metal and had a valise. Suppose it was off to work."

Marigold joined her sister beside the newsgirl. "Did you happen to see which way it went?"

"Of course!" The girl pointed down the street. "Straight toward the money bags—er, the financial district, that is!"

"Thank you!" Chrysanthemum and Marigold said in unison.

Miss Davenport joined them and presented a coin to the newsgirl. "I would like a newspaper, if it isn't too much trouble."

"No trouble at all, ma'am!" the newsgirl said, handing Miss Davenport a newspaper.

Chrysanthemum frowned as they walked away. "Haven't you already read the newspaper, Miss Davenport? I thought I saw you bring one in when you came to talk to Father and Mother."

"Well, I did buy a newspaper this morning, but I hadn't had a chance to read it yet. And now Dickie has it in my valise." She smiled. "And I also wanted to thank that girl for taking the time away from her sales to talk to us."

"Oh, yes! I'm certain she'll remember us now," Marigold said. A thought struck her, and she hurried back to the newsgirl. "Excuse me, I didn't catch your name."

"Therese."

"Pleased to meet you, Therese. I'm Marigold Marsh, and the other girl you spoke to was my sister, Chrysanthemum. Miss Davenport bought the paper from you." Marigold handed the girl another coin. "If it isn't too much trouble, if you do happen to see that monkey again, would you be so kind as to run into Marsh Gardens and let someone there know that the monkey has been spotted?"

Therese nodded. "I will! Thank you, Marigold!" She tipped her flat cap toward Chrysanthemum and Miss Davenport. "And thank you too!"

Miss Davenport smiled as Marigold rejoined her and Chrysanthemum. "Well done, Marigold. She will be a valuable acquaintance to have made today."

Marigold smiled at the architect's praise. "So, if Dickie was headed toward the financial district, we should go that way as well. And perhaps we can see if anyone else has seen our naughty monkey."

"Very well, then I shall accompany you," Miss Davenport said. "I know a few bankers, and though I doubt they themselves would have noticed a monkey making his way down the street, their staff might have seen something."

"But what would a monkey want to do with your valise in the financial district?" Chrysanthemum asked as they walked down the street.

"I don't know, Chrysanthemum," Miss Davenport replied.

"Perhaps the monkey was headed somewhere else, and that was simply the fastest route," Marigold suggested.

"Ah, yes, that makes sense!" Chrysanthemum said. "Let's see now." She paused at the intersection. "If he turned here, he might be going to the market."

Marigold looked down the street that led to the market. "I think if the monkey had passed this way, there might be more interest in his journey. There are a great many things he might have disrupted, with all of the vendors preparing their wares."

Chrysanthemum nodded. "Yes, of course." She peered at a sign halfway down the next block. "Oh, look there! A bit of copper on that sign! I don't think it's always been there.

The girls and Miss Davenport hurried across the intersection and stood beneath the sign, peering up and the wooden sign.

"Hmmm," Marigold said. "It's almost as though Dickie left a layer of his skin behind, like a sort of fingerprint!"

"Then we should be able to track him much more easily if we can find more fingerprints!" Chrysanthemum exclaimed, taking a step forward while keeping her gaze on the signs along the street. With her next step, she collided with a tall gentleman in a suit and top hat.

"My goodness," the gentleman said. "Pardon me, miss!"

"No, I must beg your pardon, sir," Chrysanthemum said. "I wasn't paying attention to where I was walking." She sighed. "We are looking for our monkey."

"Monkey, you say? This wouldn't happen to be a monkey made of metal, would it?"

Marigold nodded. "Yes, sir! That is the monkey we're looking for."

"A-ha! Then not only do I accept your apology, young lady, but also I give you this information. Your monkey swung across to the other side of the street and turned left at the end of this block, as though he were heading toward the docks."

"Thank you, sir!" Chrysanthemum said. "By the way, I'm Chrysanthemum Marsh, and this is my sister Marigold. And Miss Davenport. She's an architect."

"A pleasure! I am Mister Franklin. And, strangely enough, I am soon to be in need of an architect's services."

"What a pleasure to make your acquaintance, Mister Franklin," Miss Davenport said. "I would offer you my card, but I fear the monkey has taken my valise, which contains all of my calling cards."

"Not a worry, Miss Davenport," Mister Franklin replied. He handed her his calling card. "You might call on me instead, once you have retrieved your valise. And your monkey." He tipped his hat to Miss Davenport and each of the Marsh girls in turn. "Now please do excuse me."

"Well, I hope he will have plenty of work for you, Miss Davenport," Chrysanthemum said. "Then perhaps this excursion won't have been a complete loss for you."

"Indeed, this is proving to be a rather enriching search," Miss Davenport said. "Let us see what we can learn at the docks, then."

The girls looked both ways and crossed the street at Miss Davenport's side and soon passed the last of the storefronts before they gave way to warehouses near the small bay where the docks sat.

"Well, I don't see Dickie," Chrysanthemum said.

"What's this?" Marigold asked, stepping ahead of the group and picking up a discarded banana peel.

"You there!" a loud voice called out from somewhere on the docks. "What'd you do with that banana?"

Marigold's eyes grew wide. "Nothing at all," she called back, unsure who had called out to her. "We were wondering if perhaps our monkey might have been here, and I believe this is a clue!"

"Your monkey?" One of the dockhands approached the girls and Miss Davenport. His once white shirt was grimy to the point that it matched the color of his gray trousers and hair. Only a dark red bandana tied about his neck lent his appearance any color at all. "That was your monkey?"

"Our grandfather's creation," Chrysanthemum said. "He escaped from Marsh Gardens with Miss Davenport's valise."

"I see," the dockhand said. He turned back toward the ship and called out, "We found who took the bananas, Constable!

A short woman dressed in a constable's uniform came into view at the top of the gangplank. She wasn't a constable whom either of the Marsh sisters was familiar with, and she frowned deeply as she regarded them. "These little girls?"

"No, ma'am," Marigold said, shaking her head. "It was our monkey. Our grandfather's mechanical monkey."

The constable frowned. "Mechanical monkey? What's a mechanical monkey want with bananas?"

"We're not sure," Chrysanthemum said. "Dickie—that is, the monkey—can gain energy by eating food, just like a real monkey would."

"He filled up a valise with bananas," the dockhand said.

Marigold gasped. "Oh, goodness. What could he have wanted that many bananas for?"

The dockhand shrugged. "All I know is that's what he took."

"Well, we've found the culprit, then?" the constable asked.

"Not yet," Chrysanthemum said. "But we are trying to find him."

The constable nodded. "Well that's fine and well, but we can't arrest a clockwork monkey."

"Arrest him?" Chrysanthemum said with a gasp.

"You said the monkey belongs to your grandfather?" the dockhand asked. "Can your grandfather pay for the lost bananas?"

"Of course," Marigold said. "Just tell us how much they cost!"

The dockhand looked back and forth between the constable and Miss Davenport. "I don't know, but it's a pretty penny. I'll have to find out."

"Do that," the constable said. "And when you've brought us the payment, we'll return the papers the monkey dumped out on the deck."

"Papers?" Miss Davenport asked.

"From the valise," the constable said. "Looks like they belong to a Miss Eileen Davenport."

"Yes, that's me," the lady architect replied.

"Well, we thought they might be evidence in the case, but I suppose they aren't." The constable frowned. "But for now, I think I have to hold them here as a surety that you'll bring payment for the bananas. Then the case will be closed."

Marigold looked at Miss Davenport. "Oh, Miss Davenport, I'm terribly sorry that we're causing you all this difficulty."

"It will be all right, Marigold," Miss Davenport replied. "I think the constable has the right of it. We'll find the monkey and my valise, return the monkey to your grandfather, and then return here with payment for the bananas. Then everything will be settled, correct, Constable?"

"Right as rain," the constable said.

"Then let's find our monkey!" Chrysanthemum exclaimed.

The trail of banana peels wound across the streets and sidewalks of Dover like a long yellow snake, finally terminating at the gates to the Dover Zoo.

"How peculiar," Miss Davenport said. "Your monkey has gone to the zoo?"

Chrysanthemum grinned. "Of course! Dickie wanted to see the other animals like him! I know just where to look now!"

Marigold took out her coin purse and paid for their admission to the zoo, a shilling apiece, before she and Chrysanthemum made a beeline through the paths of the zoo that led to the enclosure for the captive monkeys.

The monkeys lived within a wrought-iron enclosure, decorated with all sorts of foliage. Bananas littered the bare earth of their cage, as though they had been thrown through the narrowly spaced bars. And to the outside of their cage clung Dickie, making his shrill monkey sounds at the monkeys within. The living monkeys had clustered to the corner of the cage farthest away from Dickie and regarded him with suspicion.

"Oh, Dickie," Marigold said. "We'll have to ask Grandfather Brecht to adjust your vocal cords again. You don't sound at all like a real monkey."

"I'm certain they can't understand a word you're saying, Dickie," Chrysanthemum added. "Now come down here and bring Miss Davenport her valise at once!"

Dickie looked down at the Marsh sisters, his head cocked to one side, as if he were considering his options. Finally, he leapt down and looked up at the girls and Miss Davenport.

Miss Davenport held out one shaking hand toward Dickie. "Might I have my valise, Dickie? I will need it to carry my papers, when we've retrieved them."

Slowly, Dickie raised the valise toward Miss Davenport, releasing it as soon as she had hold of the handles. Then he leapt up to Marigold's shoulder and held out his two small hands.

"Oh no, Dickie," Marigold said with a laugh. "You won't be getting a treat for good behavior after you've caused so much trouble. Wave to your monkey friends. It's time for you to come along home."

Dickie waved at the monkeys, who had begun creeping away from the corner. A few bolted back to the security of the larger monkey still seated there, but others waved back.

"There, you've made some friends," Chrysanthemum said. "Perhaps if you don't run away again, we can ask Mother and Father for a leash to bring you back to the zoo."

"But no more taking valises," Marigold said, patting the mechanical monkey's head. "Or bananas!"

Mr Pock-Pock!

by Sheila Crosby

Sheila Crosby is a British writer who came to La Palma in Spain with a six-month contract, where she fell in love with the island and a local man, whom she met under the stars in the Isaac Newton Telescope.

She's published 50 short stories and three books. There's a nonfiction guide to the European Northern astronomical observatory (A Breathtaking Window on the Universe), an anthology of children's stories inspired by La Palma's starry skies (*The Seer's Stone*, which includes *Mr Pock-Pock*), and a science fiction anthology (The *Dodo Dragon and Other Stories*). She's currently working on a whodunnit set in the observatory. Her blog is http://sheilacrosby.com

Friday, 2 Oct 1959, Gallegos

The commotion in the henhouse woke Daida up. Had a neighbour's dog got in?

She jumped out of bed and ran outside in her nightgown. They couldn't afford to lose any hens—things were bad enough already.

As she ran through the kitchen, Daida grabbed the frying pan. It was heavy enough to knock a big dog dizzy, if she could swing it hard enough.

And if she couldn't swing it hard enough—

Daida refused to think about that as she tore down the garden, past the cabbages and the pig. She flung open the gate to the hens' enclosure and stopped dead with her mouth open.

It wasn't a dog.

It didn't look like any animal she'd ever seen, even in a schoolbook.

It looked even less like a person.

The creature was lilac-coloured and stood a little taller than her mother. But most of it wasn't solid. The three legs—if they were legs—seemed to be hollow tubes of wire mesh. The body was the same colour but solid. And the head—she supposed it was a head because there was a nose with greeny tentacles in the middle and a mouth below it—looked like a wide triangle, with enormous ears stuck on at each end.

It had no clothes, either, just a thick hexagon hanging on a chain around its neck a medallion, which was clucking like a chicken. And something on or near it was making pock-pock-pock noises.

The creature turned to Daida and stared. Or rather, she got the feeling that it was staring, but it had no eyes. It seemed to stare with its ears—they "looked" her up and down while it pock-pock-pocked up and down the musical scale. How did it find its way around without eyes?

Daida stared back. It didn't look dangerous, but she hung onto her frying pan. Eventually she said, "Er, good morning."

The creature pock-pock-pocked, and the hexagon said, "Good morning. Can you tell me where I might find some food? I've been asking these people"—the creature waved tentacles at the chickens—"but they just argue about who's the most important among them."

"Er, they're not very clever."

"Aren't they? They've made themselves a shelter."

Daida tried to picture chickens hammering wire onto posts and thatching the roof, and grinned. "My father made it for them. Haven't you met chickens before?"

"I'm not from here. I'm visiting Las Palmas to see the eclipse."

Oh yes. She was looking forward to the eclipse. Don Carlos said they were going to have a special lesson today because this morning the moon would pass almost exactly in front of the sun. It would go dark just before noon. They were very lucky because most people never saw this in their whole lives.

But this wasn't the best place to see the eclipse. "Did you say Las Palmas? Because this is La Palma."

"Pardon?"

"Las Palmas is a different place. A city. On a different island. I don't think the eclipse is quite as good here."

"Oh. How far is it to Las Palmas?"

Daida frowned. "I don't know."

"Oh. Excuse me."

And the creature picked up the hexagon with its nose tentacles and fiddled with it. A map of the Canary Islands appeared floating in mid-air.

Daida gasped. She'd never seen anything like this!

The map had a blue dot in the north of La Palma and a green dot on Gran Canaria—that must be where Las Palmas was.

The creature sagged. "It's too far. I've come all this way, and I'm going to miss the eclipse."

Which reminded Daida of a question. "Where are you from? I beg your pardon, my name's Daida."

"Pleased to meet you. My name's Kzztx, and I'm from Xy-zzzikk. It's a planet near the star you call Canopus. We don't have eclipses on my planet."

Oh.

My.

Goodness.

From a star. This—person—was a very long way from home indeed.

Even farther than Papa, who was only in Venezuela. And he had been asking for food. Where were her manners?

"Would you like to have breakfast with us? What do you eat?"

"Why thank you. I eat almost anything."

"Well, follow me then." And she led the alien back to the house. On the way, she said, "I'm sorry, I don't think I can pronounce your name. May I call you Mr Pock-Pock?"

"Certainly, Daida."

As they reached the house, Mr Pock-Pock said, "And did your father build this, or did the chickens return the favour?"

Daida found it hard not to laugh. "My grandfather built this bit, and my father added those two rooms there."

Daida opened the door and went in. "Mama, we have a visitor for breakfast. He's called Mr Pock-Pock, and he's from a star."

Mama was warming fresh goats' milk in a pan. Her mouth and eyes opened wide, but she said, "Good morning, sir. You're a long way from home."

Mr Pock-Pock explained about the eclipse and about mixing up La Palma and Las Palmas. "I'm sorry to be a bother," he said. "I do seem to make a lot of mistakes." And he drooped.

Mama's eyes were still wide, but she said, "Don't mention it, sir. I believe quite a few travellers confuse the two places because the names are so similar. And it's quite natural to have misunderstandings in a strange country. My husband had lots to begin with."

Mr Pock-Pock stood a little straighter. "Very kind of you to say so, madam."

Daida lifted down the gofio. She said, "Is gofio all right, sir?"

They ate a lot of gofio because it was cheap. Mama had made this batch with barley and the last of the corn, and it was rather good. You toasted the grains before you ground them into flour, and then you mixed it with milk if you had some and water if you didn't have milk.

"Gofio?" said Mr Pock-Pock. He came over and inspected it. He still seemed unsure, so Daida mixed a little with milk and gave it to him on a spoon.

The tentacles reached out and took it into the strange mouth. "The brown bit's very nice," he said. "I don't think I can eat the metal bit though."

"The metal part is just an eating tool," said Daida, and took down four bowls and spoons.

Then she went into the bedroom and fetched one-year-old Julio, who was still half asleep. When she came back, she saw that Mama was frying the last of the cheese as a treat for their guest, so she put out three plates too. Julio was still too young for cheese.

They ate breakfast together, with everybody trying to not stare at Mr Pock-Pock. Then Daida said, "Excuse me, sir, I have to feed the hens before school."

"And I should get ready for the eclipse," said Mr Pock-Pock. "Would you like to see my ship?"

What a silly question, thought Daida, although she only said, "Yes please!"

Mama said, "I should very much like to see a star ship, and I don't suppose that I'll ever get another chance."

Daida collected a little grain, and they all went off towards the chicken pen together. Then they followed Mr Pock-Pock past it, into the potato field.

Then Daida stopped in surprise. She'd been expecting a shiny flying saucer. This wasn't shiny. It looked as though it was made of clear glass. You could hardly see it at all, just the things on the other side looking slightly out of shape. But it seemed to be about the shape of a broad bean, and about the size of a very big bull. It floated about halfway to Daida's knees. The potato plants underneath looked completely un-squashed and unburnt.

It didn't seem to touch the ground at all.

Mama and Daida looked at each other in astonishment.

Baby Julio chuckled and pointed at it.

Mr Pock-Pock disappeared as he went inside. Then his legs reappeared, followed by the rest of him carrying a normal-looking tripod and a pink box. He said, "Is it all right if I set it up outside the house?"

"Certainly," said Mama.

They went on ahead, leaving Daida to feed the hens.

Daida scattered the grain, and while the hens were busy eating, she looked under all the bushes. Three eggs—good. That was lunch sorted.

She went back to the house to find Mr Pock-Pock fiddling with his equipment on the patio. Obviously Mama was inside.

Mama was sitting in the kitchen, white and as still as a statue. She was taking fast, shallow little breaths as though a deep breath would hurt too much. When she saw Daida, she smiled—a horribly twisted smile that didn't reach her eyes.

Daida's guts went cold and squeezed. "Mama, you've got the pain again?"

Mama spoke in little gasps. "It'll go soon. I'm sure it'll go soon."

"Of course," said Daida. "It always has before." But secretly she was terrified that one day—perhaps even today—the pain would get worse and worse until Mama died. And then what would happen to her and little Julio? She—Daida— couldn't look after Julio on her own. She couldn't cook much, she couldn't make clothes, she didn't know when to plant things, and she certainly couldn't manage the money...

She blinked back tears. All she could do was look after things now. She said, "I'd better stay home and look after Julio." She'd miss the eclipse (Don Carlos had warned them that you could go blind looking straight at the sun) but there was nothing to be done about that. And at least Don Carlos would understand. She'd told him about Mama's pains, and the next time he'd gone to Santa Cruz he'd kindly spent some time in the library, but he hadn't been at all sure what Mama's problem was.

"I think perhaps she should try to eat less fat."

Daida had thanked him kindly, wondering how on earth they were supposed to manage that. They had enough to eat—usually—as long as they ate everything they grew or picked from the forest. Being fussy wasn't an option.

This morning Mama had eaten fried cheese , and now she was sick again.

Little Julio tugged at Mama's skirt. "Mama! Mama!"

Daida wanted to smack him. But he was a baby—what did he understand? So she picked him up and started playing peek-a-boo with him.

It didn't work for long. Julio seemed to catch on that he didn't have Daida's full attention, and he went back to pestering Mama.

Daida was beginning to panic when Mr Pock-Pock came in. "I have everything ready," he said. Then he looked at Mama. "Are you ill, madam?"

"I have a pain, yes," gasped Mama.

Mr Pock-Pock stared at Mama with his ears and made pock-pocks and trills. Then he said, "Are humans supposed to have a little stone there? The young ones don't have one."

"Where? What stone?" Daida didn't like the sound of that at all.

"Your mother has a little stone, about this big—" he held his tentacles in a circle a few millimetres apart "—inside, behind here—" and his tentacles pointed to Mama's breastbone, "which seems to be blocking a tube. There's some liquid trapped behind it."

"That's where it hurts," gasped Mama. "Someone wise said it might be a gallstone."

"You've got several little stones in the little bag that seems to produce the liquid. And one that's blocking the tube, as I say."

"So I just have to wait for it to shift," said Mama.

Mr Pock-Pock drooped. "It's bigger than the tube just there. It might not move. You need a doctor."

Mama gave a bitter little laugh, then her face twisted with pain. "We're simple folk. We can't afford a doctor."

Daida's eyes opened wide with horror. "I'll go and beg him!"

"He wouldn't come for your brother, my love, so he won't come all the way from Barlovento for me."

Daida tried to force the sobs down, but they escaped anyway.

"Perhaps it'll move," said Mama. "It always has before."

So they waited. And waited. And waited.

It started to get dark. Mr Pock-Pock said, "I think the eclipse has started. Excuse me." And he went out.

Julio kept pestering Mama, so Daida picked him up and went outside too.

It seemed a little dark for half-past ten in the morning. Daida sneaked a peek at the sun. She was dazzled, of course, but the after-image that danced around in front of her eyes definitely had a bite out of the sun.

Mr Pock-Pock had a square *thingamabob* on top of the tripod. He said, "You shouldn't look at the sun. It will hurt your eyes. Here." And he touched something on his *thingamabob*.

It turned into a picture of the sun. Daida squinted past the dancing after-images and saw that yes, a bit of sun was missing. She showed Julio, but he only wailed and wriggled to be put down.

"I wonder if he'll sleep," she said and took him back into the bedroom.

She had to sing almost every song she knew, but eventually he slept.

Daida went back into the living room and sat beside Mama, holding her hand. Mr Pock-Pock came in and stood on the other side of Mama. After a while he started stroking her cheek with his tentacles.

And all the while it slowly got darker.

Mr Pock-Pock said, "You have no one who can help? Really, no one?"

Mama shook her head slightly. "Lots of kind neighbours, but no doctors."

Mr Pock-Pock said, "I think... But then..." He wiggled his head from side to side. "If there is really nothing else, then I can try to break it with sound."

"Sound?"

He picked up an egg with his tentacles. "May I break this?"

Daida put a saucer on the table. "If you put it on this first."

Mr Pock-Pock put the egg gently on the saucer. "I break it like this—POCK!"

"OW!" Daida and Mama put their hands over their ears.

"POCK! POCK! POCK!"

The eggshell shattered, and the yolk and white plopped out onto the saucer. Daida stared with her mouth open. Then she looked at Mama, who had her mouth open too.

Mama said, "And you can break my stone like that?"

"Oh yes. That's easy. The difficult bit is not squashing the soft bits around it."

There was a short silence. Daida wondered what soft bits were next to Mama's stone and how badly they'd get hurt.

Mama said, "Daida, fetch me the stone with a carved eye on it from the gourd up there."

Daida obeyed. It was the first time that she'd seen this stone that Mama had put away so carefully.

Mama stroked the stone and closed her eyes for a while. Then she opened her eyes and said, "Daida, come and give me a hug first."

Daida ran to her mother and buried her face in Mama's neck.

"Mama, don't! I can't bear it if you die."

Mama stroked Daida's hair. "Shhh. If this stone doesn't kill me, the next one probably will. And I want to see you grow up and get married. But if it goes wrong, Papa's address in Venezuela is in the blue tin, and Don Carlos will help you write the letter. I want you to know that I love you, and I've loved being your mother." She kissed Daida's cheek. "And I want to get this over with, because it'll hurt. And well, I'm scared too. It's okay to feel scared, my love, but sometimes you have to act brave anyway."

Daida felt tiny and frozen as Mama gently pushed her away. The room seemed huge, with Mama sitting on her chair in the middle.

"Are you sure?" asked Mr Pock-Pock.

"Yes," said Mama.

"Cover your ears." He lowered his head until it was below Mama's breast.

"POCK! POCK! POCK!"

Mama went white, and she twitched with each blow of sound.

"POCK! POCK! POCK!"

Mama bit her lip hard.

"POCK! POCK! POCK!"

A wail came from the bedroom. The noise had woken Julio. Just as Daida thought she was going to cry, the noise stopped. Mr Pock-Pock stood up, and Mama said, "I'm going to be sick."

Daida got the bowl there just in time.

When Mama finished, she heaved a big sigh. "The pain's gone." She stood up cautiously. "You didn't break anything, sir. I'm just a little bruised. And so very, very grateful to you."

Daida wanted to kiss Mr Pock-Pock, but she was still holding the bowl, so she took it outside and dealt with it. Then she looked up and saw the stars. "Mama, Mr Pock-Pock, come and see!"

Mr Pock-Pock came out, followed by Mama, who was carrying Julio. They all stopped and stared.

The moon covered almost the whole sun, so the uncovered bit shone like a diamond ring. Away from the sun, towards Barlovento, the sky was so dark that a few stars twinkled.

Then it got so dark that all the stars came out—hundreds and hundreds of them.

"Oh, how beautiful," said Mama. "How sweet to be alive!"

The sun turned back to a diamond ring. As they watched, the diamond on the ring grew brighter, and the ring grew broader. "Stop looking at the sun," said Mama.

Daida looked at Mr Pock-Pock's thingamabob and saw the crescent of the sun grow and grow.

The sky paled.

The cockerel crowed.

Mama laughed. "He thinks it's morning."

The birds came down from the trees where they'd been roosting.

"Look," cried Daida pointing. The dapples of sunlight under the avocado tree were crescent- shaped like the sun, which grew fatter by the minute.

And little by little, the sun came back into Daida's life.

Blue Blood Bleeders

by Deborah Walker

Deborah Walker grew up in the most English town in the country, but she soon high-tailed it down to London, where she now lives with her partner, Chris, and her two teenage children. Her stories have appeared in *Young Explorers' Adventure Guide* 2015-18, *Nature's Futures*, *Lady Churchill's Rosebud Wristlet* and *The Year's Best SF 18* and have been translated into over a dozen languages. 2017 saw the publication of her first novel: *As Good as Bad Can Get*.

I should be at school. But I'd rather be here, in the market, watching all the commotion. For the last week, the teachers have been obsessed with the Winter Prince's visit. I'm not in the choir with the other girls. I'm not in the mini play. I am audience. After you've heard the Welcome Great Saviour song a dozen times, you get a bit bored. I'd rather be getting on with my work and learning stuff, but then nobody asks me what I think about it.

Besides, everybody is mad with me at school, because I said I didn't think we should make so much fuss about the visit. Season is our world too. The people of Winter should give us our fair share. I don't even know if I believe that. I just say things sometimes.

But everyone looked shocked. And I had to write an essay about gratitude. I was spoiling the party, I could see that.

Everyone is ready to be happy. Everyone wants to be grateful to the Winter Prince.

So I'm in the market. Playing hooky.

The market looks good. Everything has to look good for the Winter Prince. It might be better if everything looked bad. If we looked poor and needy, he might give us some more charity.

There's fresh straw on the mud floor. The stalls are hung with banners. I pause in front of a stall where the fruit looks polished and oddly the same size. I don't mean apples and dogberries are the same size. Although that raises an interesting question. Why aren't dogberries as big as apples? Maybe they are in the Winter lands.

People are going about their business with big happy grins on their faces. It seems as if everyone in Summer is excited about the Winter Prince's visit...except me.

I *suppose* he's a good man. He was the first to sell Summer people precious energy at a reasonable price. During the coughing plague, he donated medicines. He staved off the black starvation with his endless bounty. He's a great hero. Hoorah. Someone should write a song about him.

Because of his charity, we finally got around to recognising the Winter folk as human.

It wasn't always like that. I know. I've read the stories.

There's a pair of grises guarding the gate between Summer and Winter. Beyond the gate I can glimpse the misty transitions lands, where the air grows colder and darker until the cold and the dark become complete. What's it like to live in the unforgiving lands of Winter? They might be rich with their energy mines, but it must be a harsh place to live. No wonder there are so few Winter folk.

Trying to look as inconspicuous as possible, I wander past the grises. They ignore me, continuing to stare at nothing with serious, official looks on their faces. Then I see Beauty.

She leans up against an old beaker tree opposite the gate, and she's asleep. Beauty is my friend. I have plenty of friends my own age, (although not many of them are talking to me at the moment, but they'll come around—they always do).

But Beauty's special. She is *old,* perhaps the oldest person on Season planet. And she looks it. Her skin is like an old, wrinkled apple. Her skin is all wrinkles. And quite yellow. Her hair has grown in strange ways: heavy on the eyebrows and chin and weak on her head, which she covers with a scarf of Earth silk. Old and worn as it is, that scarf is still very valuable, and it's a contrast to the rest of her clothes, which you could buy for the price of a wrinkled apple. She wears what looks to be an ancient spacer's jumpsuit covered by what smells to be a pig farmer's cloak.

Beauty is, she tells me, three hundred and nine years old. I like to talk to Beauty and see where her life has led. It must feel good to have your life rolled out behind you so you can look back at it. And Beauty's life is longer than anyone I've ever met. Sometimes I imagine the path of my life stretching out before me. It worries me a bit, because I don't know where it will lead.

I call her Beauty because she's a sleeping beauty. Not a beauty so much, but there aren't any stories about sleeping old women. Perhaps I shall write one when I'm older.

An éminence grise emerges from the gate office, elegantly dressed in Summer yellows. He stares at Beauty. After a few words hurried words with the grises on guard duty, he crosses the street, making his way towards my sleeping friend.

When he reaches her he shouts, "Wake up, woman."

Beauty lies there, as insensible as a rock. It takes a lot to wake this sleeping beauty. I feel uneasy. Attracting the attention of a grise isn't good news.

And bad news travels fast. A group of stall owners and customers wander over to watch the commotion.

"It's no good trying to wake her," shouts one woman.

The grise is angry. The people in the crowd are smiling and looking at each other, and that makes him angrier.

"I said, wake up, woman." The grise leans down and shouts in her ear. He shouts loud enough to wake the dead. But not loud enough, alas, to wake Beauty.

"Try shouting a bit louder, that might do the trick," says Constance. She sells tomatoes from her stall. Good 'uns. And sometimes she'll give me a bag of them that are nice and squishly ripened.

When the crowd laughs, the grise's face reddens with fury.

"What are you doing sleeping here? Who are you?" His voice squawks, tight with anger and lost authority. He's not going to last long in this job, I can see that. He pulls out his truncheon and holds it in trembling hands towards my friend.

Hey. I step forward. There's no need to be poking her. She's an old woman.

But before I say anything, Beauty's hand shoots out and grabs the stick. She opens her eyes. "Who am I, Mr Grise? I am just me. Myself. None other than a lowly human woman with her animal soul in ascendant."

"She's got a tight hold of your stick," cries Constance, not so helpfully. "Is that allowed?"

"Ah, so I have," says Beauty. She releases the stick, and the grise staggers backwards.

He scowls. "This is no place for beggars."

Beauty shakes her head. "You're wrong about that. I've sat for many years in this place on and off, watching the gate between Winter and Summer."

"Move along now."

"I don't think I will."

I'd like to say that to my teachers one day, just lazy like that and not caring. "I don't think I will." I taste the words in my mind, relishing them.

Beauty has drawn a bit of crowd as she's wont to do. Though nowadays for innocent reasons, not like in the long time go.

"What's are you doing here?" asks the grise.

"She's very holy, monsieur," replies a man in the crowd.

"She can't be here when the Great Prince arrives," says the grise.

"She's been coming to this place as long as anyone can remember, on and off," I tell him. I know I need to be inconspicuous, but I also have to stick up for Beauty.

"Hello, Jessie." A great big grin falls over her face as she notices me for the first time—her eyes aren't what they used to be. "I remember you telling me. Is the blue blood coming today, then?"

The grise eyes widen in shock. "Woman, we don't call them that."

Beauty winks at me. "No. Not anymore. Neither do we call them bleeders, sub bloods, animals, or abominations. But we used to."

I stifle a giggle.

"Just make sure you've gone before the Prince arrives."

Beauty's annoyed. "She doesn't like being ordered about. Especially by anyone who is too young. And *everyone* is too young to Beauty. She sits up a little straighter. She clears her throat, and she says, "I am old, and I am old, and I am not remembering what I should. I can't be bothered to call them anything else. They have blue blood, don't they?"

"Their blood is rich in hamecyanin. It's colourless," says the grise.

"Tsk. They bleed blue, don't they?"

The grise nods reluctantly. "Their blood is blue when it's exposed to air. That's a biological fact. But we don't call them *that* name. It's an offensive term."

"I don't think its offensive."

"That's for them to decide, not you."

"I don't mind people calling me a Methuselah."

"That's your choice, madam." The grise doesn't bother to hide his disdain. "I think you should move on now."

"I am old, and I am old. I am dirty and I smell bad. I am perhaps the oldest Methuselah on the planet. I am old. A Methuselah. That's my sin, passed on from my parents, written into my genes. I am old beyond my natural span. Many times I have sat on this corner, here between Winter and Summer, in sight of the barrier gate, slipping into sleep as I watch the Summer folk. Gene gave me great age, and he took away my waking hours. Gene has a taste for balance, giving with one hand and taking with the other."

The market people look impressed with this speech. As I am. Beauty often has good words to say. And her words have a type of power. And I like that power. I think if you can find words like that, you can touch people in their minds and their hearts. You see why I like Beauty, so much, now, don't you?

But after that wonderful speech, Beauty's eyelids start to close.

"You can't sleep here," hisses the grise. "This is an important visit. The first from the Great Prince."

"Why don't you just leave her alone?" says a man.

"Yes," says another. "She's not doing any harm."

"I am tired," murmurs Beauty. "I think that sleep is stealing me away and will consume more and more of me until it eats me in entirety. It is not a bad way to go. Better than I could have expected."

The mood of the crowd has turned. Even the grise has noticed. The crowd could turn ugly in the blink of an eye. "Please go," says the grise. "Please, just go."

Beauty's eyes open. She does look tired, but she shakes her head. "You're right, your eminence, your griselyness. I'll be off then, begging your pardons. But I implore a favour."

"What is it?" asks the grise.

"Will you give the Great Prince Blue Blood a kiss from me and tell him that I say hello?"

The grise is speechless at that. The crowd laughs. The tension drains away.

I run forward and pull Beauty to her feet. She allows me to lead her away. "Where should we go, Beauty?" I ask her.

"There and back to see how far it is."

We walk away. When I look behind me, I see that the crowd has wandered off, but the eminence grise is staring after us. I think there's a faint smile on his face.

"We will come back to see Great Prince, won't we, Beauty?"

"I can't. The grise told me to clear off."

"I think it will be all right," I say. The grise was smiling after all. "Anyway, he can't stop you. You're full human, after all. You have rights."

"Well, rights are a tricky thing. I'm still getting used to them."

"You've been full human for ten years," I remind her. "Surely you're used to them by now?"

"You would have thought so, wouldn't you?" Beauty stops by the market fountain. She sits down on the stone steps. She trails her hand in the water and splashes a little water on her face.

"If we stay here, we'll miss the Winter Prince. And he's a great man. Or so they say."

"So they say, indeed."

Beauty is my friend. She's good company. But it must be admitted that she isn't as interesting as the Prince. I don't want to leave her, but I don't want to miss seeing the Prince. "Don't you want to see him?"

"I've already seen him."

"You have not. He's never been to Summer." I was ticked off. It was one thing, lying to the market people and to the grise, but quite another thing to lie to me.

"Ah. But he has, a long time go."

"Have you got a story, Beauty?"

"I might have."

"It's not a holy story is it?

"No."

"Good," I say, with a nod.

"Don't you like the holies?" she asks me. "I've always been entranced by the holies. In all my years when I could have left this dreadful, cruel Summer, it was the stories of the holies that held me here. If Summer folk could write such beauties, there must be good here."

I shrug. "I like them well enough. But I've heard them all. I like your stories because they're new."

Beauty nodded. "That is the way of the young. They like the new. It's a peculiarity that you like me, Jessie. I am not new."

I look at Beauty with all the marvellosity of her wrinkles, and all her stories written into her memories. "But your words are new, Beauty. They're more important than looks."

She smiles, and her eyes all but disappear into her wrinkles. "Well, this story is about the first time I saw the blue blood prince."

"We don't call them that."

"In the time of my story we called them that. We called them many bad things."

I nod. "I know all about that. They tell us about it all the time. Long time go, people thought the Winter people were subs, and it is only in the last decade that we have recognized them as full human."

"Yes." Her eyelids begin to close.

I nudge her. She'd woke my appetite for this story, true or not. "You said that you saw the Great Prince, Beauty?"

"I did. And I kissed him."

I laugh. It's hard to think of her kissing anyone.

She stretches her thin arms in front of her. It seems like her bones are clicking into place. She says in her story-telling voice, "So, let me set the scene for you. You know at that time what we thought of the blue bloods."

"Winter people," I remind her. I swear she does it on purpose.

"Yes. Sorry, you're right. We thought of the Winter folk as different. In fact, we thought bad of any people whose parents had allowed Gene to alter them. Methuselahs and Slowpokes and Catch-it-alls, all hid what they was. But worst of all was the Winter folk. Because their blood had been changed, and the holies say that in the blood is our second soul. The soul, which can understand the animal pleasure and the pleasures of the holy. The soul, which resides in the left ventricle and is carried around the body in the blood."

I nod. "And it is only because humans have their heads higher than their hearts that their second, thinking soul is above this animal soul."

"Could be. And the other reason that Summers hated the Winters was that the Winters didn't seem ashamed of not being human. The Winters just carried on mining the energy from the cold, dark side and selling it to the Fed planets and growing richer and richer. And it was rumoured that not only did the Winters consider themselves human, they considered themselves superior human, Gene giving them the power to breathe the natural Summer air and the cold, thin stuff that passed for air in Winter."

"Do they really believe that, Beauty?"

"I don't know. I've only ever been close enough to speak to one of them, and he was not in a position to be discussing much. But as I was saying, that day I was sitting by the gate. And my animal soul was in ascendant, as I was not reading the words of the holies, but watching the goings and fro of the youngsters, which I sometimes watched like a grand opera played on a mundane stage. I knew all their ins and outs, and they never minded me, being like an old rock, still and pretend reading.

Just part of the staging.

"There was a rebellious fashion then for the young Summers to dress up like the Winter folk. It was a fashion that the elders found outrageous. And of course that made the young ones do it all the more. As you know, Gene gives and he takes. Those who had the blue blood might be able to breathe the normal and the thin air, but they were afflicted with the bleeding disease. The Summer youngsters in their disrespectful way had used makeup to simulate the Winters' bruises and hematomas. They padded out their trousers and jackets to look like swollen joints.

"That was when I saw the youngster. To the common eye, he looked no different from the others. Bruises up his arms, his jacket transparent to showcase the bruising of his ribs, all painted on.

"Except it wasn't painted on for him, but the other youngsters didn't know that.

"But *I* could see him. I knew him as Winter. A blue blood bleeder, gene-modded, a non-human prince, and rich as sin."

"Why did he come to Summer?"

"Because he was curious, I imagine. He wanted to see how the other half lived." Beauty laughs. "It didn't take long for him to find out. A scuffle broke out. A minor thing, a lot of shouting, some shoving. A minor thing until he fell.

"Fell against a jagged rock, knocked himself senseless and ripped his arm. Not bad, but bad enough for a Winter man."

A ripple of shock went through the teens when they saw him bleed. They stood and stared and saw him bleeding out bright blue onto the cobbles.

"It was easy to see that he was not human. But worse than that, he was a thing pretending to be human. An animal what doesn't know it was an animal. And an animal who was able to fool those boys. Oh yes, I knew all the arguments."

I reach out and pat Beauty's knee.

"That Winter boy shouldn't have been here on his own. Truth is, I'd seen them here before. But always two or three or four of them: safety in numbers. And I didn't know what to do. I was younger, but not young as you'd call it. Truth is I was a-feared. It was a bad time for us non-humans in Summer. If they caught us, they'd send us somewhere. To the Fed worlds they said. But maybe it wasn't there they sent us."

"Why did you stay in Summer, Beauty? If you was a-feared?" I ask.

"I'm not sure. Many times I thought about leaving. Many did. But always I thought someone would do something to make things better." She sighs and looks wistful. "And there was the non-human boy, bleeding out. And there was everyone else just standing around doing nothing.

"What shall we do, Rustique?' asked the boys. Rustique being the name of the gang leader at the time.

"'Let him bleed out,' he said. His mouth curled into a look of such hatred.

"The grise who had been in the gate house finally noticed the commotion. He walked towards the bleeding boy. *Good,* thinks I. *At last someone will do something.*

"But that fine grise, all dressed in his Summer yellows, never said a word. He strolled on by, as if that bleeding boy was nothing. And one by one the boys turned and left him, bleeding out on the cobbles.

"It was risky to stand out, to draw attention to yourself, that's what my mum and dad had always taught me. That's the way it was then.

"Subhuman, automatons, golems, glue bloods, blue blood bleeders.

"They said the blue bloods were the worst. I might have even believed it at the time. Blood is the life and blood isn't blue." Her story falls into silence, as she remembers.

After a time, I ask her gently, "What did you do, Beauty?"

"I went over. I having a modicum of training, having worked as a battlefield orderly on the war fields. Great prince he might be now, but he was a big fool then. He'd got nothing medical on him, no clotting factor, probably a-feared of giving himself away.

"He was going into shock. I snapped a tourniquet around the artery in his arm. Then I hauled his carcass through the gate over to Winter side. In his hat I found an electronic beacon and set it peeping and scurried back to my spot. But before I went, I gave him the lightest kiss in the manner of a blessing.

"'Where's he gone?' they asked me when they returned.

"'Gene Devils took him,' I told them.

"They nodded, believing in such in those days. It is a sin to lie, but it is a sin that I gladly took upon me."

"You saved him, Beauty?"

"Yep, that's my story."

"You saved the man who grew up to save Summer?"

"Reckon I did," she says, not so modestly. "It wouldn't have been human to do otherwise."

"I will write a story of it."

"Will you, indeed?"

"I know that my stories ain't very good yet. But just think—if I am a famous writer one day, then everyone will know your story."

"I like your stories just fine, Jessie. I would like you to write up this story, indeed." Then sleeps steals upon her. Her chin falls heavy to rest on her chest. She begins to snore.

I kiss my friend lightly on her brow in the manner of a blessing.

I leave her and go back to the gate, thinking about the Prince and his wild days. I wonder what they would think of that at school. I won't tell them, though. I don't want to spoil their fun.

And I am glad that I did not go to school, for I know that I have learnt something today that they could not have taught me.

Relief: A Tale of the Jitney

by J. L. Bell

J. L. Bell spends most of his time these days writing about the American Revolution in New England. He's the author of *The Road to Concord: How Four Stolen Cannon Ignited the Revolutionary War*, a government report on Gen. Washington's Cambridge headquarters, many articles, and the Boston 1775 blog. But he's also published ersatz folk tales, latter-day adventures in Oz, a study of the first thirty years of the character Dick Grayson, and a collection of science experiments for kids. He first created the characters of Jex and Ticca in two stories published by the WonderFunders comics collective.

My father said he'd fly home a month ago. "I'll be back before the moons switch places, Eeshal," he told me. "I'll miss working here with my best girl, but right now people need my help."

"I understand, Daddy," I told him. Flyers had been landing at our resupply base with reports of how the planet Wengu had suddenly flown through an asteroid cloud. "Dozens of meteorites!" "Two cities just *devastated*." "I heard there were tsunamis!" A Confederation patrol ship had come with a call for volunteers to repair Wengu's infrastructure.

"You have to go help those people," I told Daddy. We were standing out beside the landing field, looking up at Wengu's star. "You're the best mechanic in this solar system. And I'm old enough to run Gadder's Landing while you're gone."

"I guess you are now, Eeshal," my father said. He gave me a bristly mustache kiss on the forehead and went inside to pack his tools.

So I'd been running the base for two months. Whenever a ship landed from outside our system, I asked if there was news from Wengu.

"At least the meteorites have stopped," said one four-armed lady. "Top off my radon tanks, would you, dearie?"

"Confederation's still advertising for relief ships," growled a furry yellow hauler. "Sure you can't tune my ion jets?"

I can repair computers, but my father hasn't let me work on engines yet. So pilots who needed that sort of tune-up flew off to other bases. I watched our landing field empty out and our creds account drop. One fuel tank ran low, and the delivery droids stopped letting me sign for new shipments.

I still thought I was doing fine, but then I had a dream about missing my momma. I was only a baby when she died, and here I was waking up crying. Really I was missing Daddy, I knew. I had to do something to bring him back.

Then this little jitney flew in—half the size of most cargo ships, none of the comforts of passenger liners. The registration code on the tail was too scratched to read, but I recognized the ship right away. No other flyer had those refurbed engines and mismatched landing legs. "Held together by wire and epoxy," Daddy had muttered when he first saw it. "But at least it's thick wire."

"So you inspected it?" I said.

"Not officially," Daddy said. "Jex never asked."

Jex was the little jitney's pilot. I don't know how his species ages, but Jex looks about as old as I am. Sometimes he acts younger.

"Is his ship safe to ride in?" I asked.

Daddy hadn't answered. But now I was desperate.

Thinking about inspections gave me an idea. I rooted around

in Daddy's desk and went to have a talk with Jex.

The door of the jitney's rear loading hatch was swung all the way up to air out the hold. I walked up the ramp and called, "Anybody here?"

Up front two legs were sticking off the side of the big pilot's chair. One rubber sandal dangled off a tan foot, another lay on the floor. Slowly the chair twirled around to face me. Jex was wearing a blue short-sleeved shirt over a white long-sleeved one. The frayed ends of his pants legs flopped around his ankles the same way his cornsilk hair hung over his eyes. He slurped a spoonful of noodles out of a plastic bowl. "Hey, Eesh."

"iteekitch'k, Eekzut†." I spotted Ticca bowing from its perch on the ceiling. Ticca is an Ixtuqan—about a meter long, thin, green, and six-limbed. On some planets Ticca would look like a big stick-bug. But it's the jitney's engineer.

I bowed and answered, "Iteekitch, Ticcatee¡ac¡ac."

Jex snickered. "You're still not pronouncing that right."

"But Ticca appreciates the effort. Don't you?"

"chuq," Ticca agreed.

Jex rolled his eyes. "It's just being polite."

I knew Ticca never cared about being polite. Most days I would have told Jex that, but today I needed a favor. "Are you open for a job?" I asked him.

Jex sat up. "Someone needs a ride? A shipment?"

"One passenger to Wengu and two back."

"Hm. That planet's in bad shape."

"You're not scared, are you?" I said.

"No! We can definitely fly there. The fare would be—"

"I don't have any creds." I held up an inspection certificate with Daddy's stamp in one corner. "But when we're done, I can give you this. A certificate that this...spacecraft passed class-1 inspection."

"gik!" said Ticca in surprise. Jex's blond eyebrows rose a few millimeters. They hadn't seen a stamped class-1 certificate in a long time. Maybe never.

"As required for all vehicles carrying official passengers or freight through subspace bypasses," I said. Though the authorities in most systems rarely checked.

Jex's eyes narrowed. "One cert isn't much for an interstellar trip. How about three?"

I should have known he'd bargain. "Um, I can bring along two blanks, and once we find Daddy, he can stamp those for you as well."

"Gadder's stuck on Wengu?" Jex tossed his soup bowl into a refuse vac. "Get the two blank certs, pack a bag, and be back here in half an hour."

Gravity woke me up. I felt my body being pushed down into my bunk in the jitney, and there wasn't much padding. Even worse, my stomach felt like it was being pushed down harder than the rest of my body. "Ergh."

"Feeling heavy, Eesh?" Jex leaned back from the controls and glanced into my cabin.

"I'm fine," I insisted, sitting up slowly. It had been six years since I was off planet, but I wasn't going to tell him that.

"Just don't throw up on Ticca's instruments."

"I'm not going to throw up!"

Jex smirked. Ticca laughed: "tee tee tee."

Just because I don't fly around all the time! I have responsibilities, I told myself. But I still needed Jex's help, so I kept quiet as he landed his jitney on the edge of wide orange desert, a Confederation logo scratched into the dirt.

Ticca flipped a lever, and the rear hatch swung open. I went back to breathe the fresh air. A silver cart was rolling out from a hangar to meet us, a big lady with four arms inside. She called, "Welcome to Dorlei!"

"Dorlei?" I turned to Jex. "I said I wanted to go to Weng—"

"Shh." He brushed past me and trotted down the ramp to meet the lady. "Ahoy! We heard you need ships to fly relief supplies."

"We do! We haven't had volunteers for a month," said the lady, thirty of her fingercles wiggling over a keyboard. "Of course, I have to see your paperwork—Confederation law for all relief ships."

Jex handed over a card. "Class-1."

"Fine, fine." The lady slid the certificate into the slot on her clipboard and ticked off some buttons to register the mission. A line of robo-carts rolled out of the hangar. "We'll load you up and get you on your way. I just wish all chillun were as responsible as you."

I turned to Ticca. "Where did he get that—"

"tzzh," Ticca hissed, working the controls for the loading crane.

Jex came back inside. "We're going to Wengu next," he muttered as he passed me. "If we bring supplies, they'll owe us a favor."

I had to admit that made sense. Jex knew how to make his way on different worlds. And of course it was also nice to help the poor people there. But still— "You shouldn't go into a person's bag and take their inspection certificate."

"I needed it," Jex said.

"You never even asked me!"

He scowled. "And you never asked Gadder before you used his inspection stamp, did you?"

I turned and stomped into my cabin. I *had* to use Daddy's stamp—that was the only way to make a deal with Jex! Just because he was right about one little thing didn't mean he was right.

We had to go through two more subspace bypasses to reach Wengu's system. Then Jex made a wide loop to stay clear of the asteroid cloud. Wengu was the fourth planet from its star, its atmosphere swirling with white and gray over a blue and tan surface.

"Dust clouds," Jex muttered. He aimed for the south pole and made entry in the crisp air there. Gravity came back again. After the minute of plasma burn we could see through the viewscreens how the ice continent below was scarred with a big, sooty crater.

Jex turned the jitney toward the equator, crossing an azure ocean. The lady on Dorlei said the Confederation had sent Daddy's relief ship to a country in Wengu's southern hemisphere called Meelok. Jex followed the nav instructions, parked in orbit over the capital city, and radioed down. "Bringing supplies."

"Good news."

I took the microphone and added: "And we're tracking another ship that arrived about two months ago. It brought pipeline engineers."

There was a pause on the other end. "Please hold," another voice said.

"kitz ge¡xiq tzaði†," said Ticca.

"Yeah, they know *something*," Jex agreed. "Gadder got this far."

"Pilot, you're cleared to dock on top of the royal palace," said the voice. Then came exact coordinates that Ticca pecked into the guidance system.

The palace was a tall, modern tower of stone and steel. We landed on a pad that was still shiny from being hosed down. All around the edge was a neat hedge. Behind that were statues in blue marble. Two men in uniforms slowly began to unroll a light blue carpet toward the ship.

"They're happy to see us," I said.

Jex grunted and ducked into his cabin. He came out wearing

pants without holes in the knees and his leather pilot's jacket with patches from three dozen landing sites stuck onto the shoulders and back. He was proud of that jacket.

We slid out the bottom hatch onto the strip—me first, then Jex, then Ticca, landing on Jex's shoulder. The two servants said, "Welcome to Meelok" in unison.

"Thank you," I answered for all of us.

We walked along the carpet toward an archway leading into the marble tower. A young man in a white coat with gold piping stepped into the light. Behind us the servants announced, "His Highness and First Minister, Prince Hylinouk!"

What was Wengu etiquette? Should we bow—and how? I looked at Jex, but it was obvious from his face (which, the sunlight showed, wasn't exactly clean) that he hadn't met a lot of First Ministers.

The prince solved our problem, striding forward and declaring, "So good of you to come." He seemed only a few years older than Jex and me, though no one would call him a kid. He had orange hair cut close to his rippled scalp, a deep olive complexion, and a pearly smile. A small cape hung off the left shoulder of his coat. "

"At this time of calamity, we are—is this right to say?—utmost grateful to the Confederation."

"Oh. Um, 'most grateful,' probably," I said. "And...you're welcome?"

"Please come with me, generous friends." The prince stuck his elbow out at me. I put my hand in the crook of his arm. "What may I call you, miss?"

"Eeshal," I said. "Your Highness."

The prince glanced back at Jex. "And you are...?"

"The pilot."

"gikka'cµtapuh," Ticca added proudly.

"Chief engineer," the prince murmured. "A spacecraft that

size with an entire engineering department. How fortunate
for you."

"tzek iɬz," Ticca snarled. It crawled down Jex's back and headed back to the jitney.

Prince Hylinouk took no notice. "Please indulge me as we
document how much we appreciate the Confederation." He led
me out onto a blue marble balcony, stopping on a small silver
marker. A couple of cameras were trained on that spot. The
prince smiled and waved at the distance. In a clear voice he
announced, "People of Meelok, today we welcome Miss Eeshal
and her crew. We are *most* grateful for the relief supplies."

I waited for applause or cheers to sound from the crowd below,
but nothing happened. I leaned forward and peered over the
rail. Down on the ground there were only a few gardeners at
work.

"We will insert the applause before we send our message to
Dorlei," Hylinouk explained. "I do not enjoy these appearanc-
es—to be frank, the height makes me dizzy, but I feel obliged."

"So you're scared of heights?" asked Jex, leaning way over the
rail with a smirk.

I glared at him to stop teasing and took the prince's elbow to
go inside the palace. "We brought supplies because we really
need your help," I said. "We're searching for people who came
on an earlier relief mission. One of them's my father—his name
is Gadder."

"Miss Eeshal, I would be happy to assist your search," the prince
assured me, "regardless of whether you brought supplies."

I raised my eyebrows at Jex. He pretended not to see. We all got
into a shiny elevator.

"They were pipeline engineers," I said. "Their flight left Dorlei
forty-two of your days ago."

"And arrived in this city forty-one days ago," Hylinouk confirmed. We entered a large silver-trimmed office full of tables,
each piled high with notebooks and letters. The prince led me

to a big relief map hanging on one wall. "The squad of your father flew east to repair a vital fuel line to our coast, landing near the shore *here*. And that, I'm sorry to say, was the last report we received."

My heart chambers fluttered. I peered at that gray spot on the map. Next to it was a large, irregular shape outlined in blue wax pencil. "What's this?"

"A refugee camp. Waves destroyed half the villages along that coast."

Jex reached between us and poked a swath of dark green hills labeled with three Meeloky letters drawn in black. "And this?"

"That is—how might you say it?" Prince Hylinouk pulled a small device trimmed in white and gold from his back pocket and spoke a Meeloky word into it.

"No-go zone," said a mechanical voice from the device.

"Precisely. A thick forest," the prince added. "The people living inside are bandits and separatists. Sometimes they emerge to rob villages or take hostages."

"Hostages?" I gasped.

"I am sorry to say, Miss Eeshal. That is why we advised your father's squad to await a military escort and to follow this route to the pipeline damage." The prince arced his finger around the dark green. "But when our transport copters arrived, the squad had already departed."

"Do you think the bandits...?"

The prince sighed. "Some seacoast villagers are in league with the separatists. Such people could have promised your father's squad safe passage through the forest and, once they were inside, taken them prisoner."

"I've got to go there!" I said. Jex took out a marker and started writing the coordinates of that spot on the inside of his wrist.

Prince Hylinouk pursed his lips. "Your plan might work, Miss Eeshal. A personal plea, from an appealing young miss seeking her father—that is more likely to stimulate sympathy than a military search party. Please take this translator to aid your efforts." He held out the white device.

"But that's yours." It was so fancy, matching his uniform.

"You will put it to much better use," he insisted. He showed me the microphone hole and the buttons for recording and translating.

"Well, thank you, Your Highness," I said into the device. It translated my words into Meeloky. The prince smiled.

Jex flew southeast and landed the jitney on a swath of lavender sand dividing thick green woods from the azure ocean. A large, dark gray spaceship sat nearby, casting a long twilight shadow. Farther up the beach stretched a matrix of tents and huts assembled from five different colors of plastic sheeting. As soon as our engines stopped, people began to stream out of that camp.

While Jex and Ticca got ready to unload, I slipped out the bottom hatch and ran over to the bigger ship. Its landing gear was already half-covered with lavender sand. The cargo hatch hung open, revealing an empty hold.

I looked around. A tall older man was standing nearby. I ran over and pointed Prince Hylinouk's translator at him. "Excuse me, please! Did anyone see the squad from the big ship?"

The man just stared.

I restarted the translator and tried again. "I'm looking for my father! He was on that ship! Can you help?"

A young woman touched my shoulder. She said something. The translator sounded at last: "Miss, your machine is programmed for the dialect they use in the royal provinces. Here many people speak only the *classical* form of Meeloky."

I jumped, but happily. "Great—thank you! My name's Eeshal, and I'm looking for my father! He arrived forty days ago on this big ship."

"My name is Mahand," said the young woman. "And we never saw your father."

"What?"

Mahand pointed to the gray spaceship. "The big ship arrived in the night. We didn't leave the camp because it came with a military copter. In the morning, the copter was gone. We waited for people to come out. No one ever did."

"But someone must have unloaded the supplies."

"The supplies." Mahand rolled her eyes. "Fur clothing. Snow shoes. Shovels. After ten days, traders took them away to sell to people who could use them. That is all we saw. I'm sorry."

I walked slowly back to the jitney. Jex was at the top of the loading ramp, sweeping out the empty hold. I relayed what Mahand had told me.

Jex rolled his eyes. "And you believed her."

"Why would she lie?"

"Maybe people wanted to take the supplies. Your friend Hylinouk said there were bandits here."

I frowned. "I guess you run into lots of liars, traveling around the galaxies. I like to start by believing people."

Jex shrugged. "Too late to do anything tonight anyway."

A scarlet sunset was already spreading over the ocean horizon. I went into my cabin to eat dinner. Then I came out and asked Ticca if it could open the prince's translator.

"chuq." It quickly levered off the back with one claw.

"Thanks." My first step, I'd decided, was to fix that device so it worked for both classical and modern Meeloky. All the memory slots were full, but one of those chips was a locator, and we already had nav equipment on the jitney. I popped that out and slid in an extra memory chip from my repair kit. Then I used the ship's radio to search Wengu's datanet and download a file on classical Meeloky.

This was the sort of work I liked. It relaxed me. As I worked, I tried to imagine what Daddy might have done when he arrived at this beach. Hylinouk had said the broken pipeline was up in

the woods. Daddy and his squad could have been so eager to
fix it that they went right out, not waiting for an escort. Maybe
they were lost, maybe they were captured. Either way, I knew
where I had to look.

I went to bed as the viewscreens all showed thick, dusty clouds
blotting out the stars.

In the morning I took all the things that wouldn't be useful in
the woods out of my backpack and shut them inside my cabin
locker. Over breakfast I told Jex about my plan to go talk to
the forest people.

"gik," said Ticca.

"That's not a plan," said Jex. "What makes you think Gadder's
in the forest?"

"He's not here. I have to go ask. Prince Hylinouk said a 'personal plea' might 'stimulate sympathy.'"

"Prince Hylinouk said a lot of things," Jex grumbled. "If bandits grabbed Gadder, they might grab you too."

"Then Daddy and I would be back together."

"That's just stupid."

My veins sizzled. "You think you know everything just because
you've been to so many planets! But I'll tell you something
new, Jex—you don't know how families work."

He blinked.

"Families don't just leave people behind! They don't just give
up looking for each other! If they have to be in trouble, they'd
rather do it together."

Jex tossed his breakfast wrapper into the refuse vac. He went into
his cabin and came out wearing scuffed brown leather boots. He
stomped around the cabin, dumping food canisters and equipment into his own backpack. Ticca skittered along the walls after
him, talking so fast I couldn't understand. Finally Jex answered,
"*You* can stay with the ship. *I'm* going to look after Eeshal."

I didn't *need* looking after, but I felt glad to have it. As we climbed down the bottom hatch, I called, "Bye, Ticca!" All I heard back was angry chittering.

At the camp, I asked for Mahand. She came out. I held up the translator and asked, "Do you know the people in the forest?" Mahand looked nervous. "I know some of them."

"Would you please take me to meet them?"

Mahand took a deep breath. "I will lead you over the first set of hills."

For two hours we hiked alongside a thinning river, moving uphill. The tree trunks got thicker and grayer, the spots of sunlight hitting the ground smaller until there were none left. Finally, Mahand stopped and pointed out a narrow path leading northwest. I looked past her finger. The ground sloped down and then up more steeply in a bank of green. The translator spoke her words as: "His Honor makes his home past that hill. You're in his territory now."

"Thank you for bringing us this far," I answered.

Jex and I continued for another hour. He was crashing through the underbrush, breaking twigs underfoot.

"Are you *trying* to make noise?" I asked.

"Yeah," he answered, entering a clearing covered with broad leaves. "The faster we get 'His Honor's' attention, the faster we get out of here."

"At least we're getting closer," I said—and everything blurred. My head was spinning, my backpack was pulling at my armpits. The tree trunks looked strange. The light shafts were coming from the wrong direction. Finally I realized I was hanging upside-down ten meters over the clearing. There was a rope around my right ankle. It was tied above to a fork on a thin tree trunk that had snapped back upright when I stepped in the wrong spot. "Ergh."

Jex was hanging beside me, grumbling: "Doggit, doggit, doggit."

"This is bad," I agreed. "Sorry."

"Doggit."

"But I'm not giving up."

I curled and grabbed the cuff of my right pants leg. I pulled myself up and with my other hand grabbed my right ankle. I got one hand on the knot of the rope, and then the next on the rope just above the knot, and then the next on top of that. Jex had stopped cursing. He saw what I was doing and grabbed for his rope too. Hand over hand we pulled ourselves up until we were upright, swinging slowly under the bent tree trunks. We caught our breath.

"You found the forest people," Jex told me. "They'll come check these traps sooner or later. You still want to meet them?"

"Yes," I said. "But I'd prefer to be on the ground."

We shinnied up our ropes and pulled ourselves onto the swaying tree trunks. Then we tugged the knots off our ankles and started climbing down. Of course Jex had to make sure he reached the ground first. He was still blowing on his palms when I hit the bottom.

I looked around. "Which way now?"

"Nowhere. We wait for them." He set his pack down on the leafy ground and sat on it.

Now that we weren't moving, I could hear birds calling, bugs buzzing, even a low growl. I kept scanning the spaces between the trees, seeing nothing but more trees. And then suddenly there were a dozen people around us, their clothes in black patterns that disappeared in the shadows. Most carried laser rifles. A woman with a gray streak in her short hair said something.

I reached for the translator in my pocket. Jex's hand clamped onto my wrist. "Slowly," he whispered. "Don't let them think you have a weapon."

I slipped two fingers inside my pocket and slid out the white and gold device. Everybody watched. I held it up to my mouth.

"We came from other planets with relief supplies for Wengu. We are looking for my father, who came to this forest two months ago."

The translator sounded. At first the mechanical voice surprised the people, but by the end I could see them relaxing slightly.

The woman put a metal tube to her lips and blew, making what sounded like a bird call. Another call came from nearby.

A minute later, five more soldiers came through the trees. At their center was an old man with a round, low stomach and a tuft of white hair. The woman went to talk to him.

The old man nodded and walked toward me. I started talking: "Your Honor, I'm looking—"

He waved his hand no and spoke. The translator told me: "Let an old man sit, little niece. I've walked a long way to meet you."

One of His Honor's soldiers brought out a wicker folding stool. He lowered himself onto it. "I'm sorry I wasn't faster, but at least you weren't hanging upside-down this whole time." He chuckled.

I didn't laugh, not even politely.

"Tell me why you came to our territory."

So I told His Honor the story of looking for my father, from the time Daddy decided to fly to Wengu to the moment the ropes caught us.

The old man nodded again. With a sigh he pushed himself to his feet. He stepped over to me, put his big hands on my shoulders, and slowly bowed until his forehead rested on my head. I just stood still, hoping that was the right thing to do.

His Honor sat down again. "Here is how I can help you: Your father is not in our territory."

"But their ship is at the camp."

The old man shrugged. "I would have no honor if I told you a lie."

By now I knew I could be as stubborn as he was. "I won't leave without my father!"

"I permit you to travel anywhere in our territory, little niece." He spread his arms wide.

"Eesh," said Jex quietly. "We can't search the whole forest."

"Little nephew understands," His Honor said. "And I must warn you that these trees hold more snares for soldiers."

I glared at His Honor. Jex came over and put his thumb across the translator's microphone. "We can go back to the ship and start over. We'll try something else. We're not giving up on Gadder."

I was still trying to think and still coming up with nothing.

His Honor stood up happily. "Captain, escort these young travelers safely back down to the shore. After all, they're only looking for their fathers."

Technically, only *I* was looking for my father, but Jex didn't object.

The hike back down to the coast went faster than the trek up. We were going downhill, and the captain knew the trails through the trees. Before two hours passed, we reached the last line of trees before the breach. Jex squinted into the distance at his ship. "Doggit."

Three copters were sitting on the landing field beside the little jitney. People in gray uniforms were massed around it. Almost all those people carried laser rifles. A crowd of refugees stood near the camp, keeping their distance from those soldiers. Everyone was watching one man in a stark white uniform with gleaming trim, cape arranged over one shoulder—Prince Hylinouk.

I looked around for the captain and her squad. They were gone. But I knew they were just a few steps back in the woods, crouching with their guns.

"Come on." Jex strode down toward his ship. "He likes you."

When we got close, the prince asked me, "Did you go into the forest?"

I thought he might be mad at how I took that risk, so I said, "Yes, but we came back fine. I—"

"I gave you the translator so you could speak to the people here. Why did you leave it here in your rattly little ship?"

"I didn't!" I pulled the device out of my pocket and held it up to his face. "I had to reprogram it—Say! Why did you think it was in the jitney?"

Because of the locator chip, I realized. Hylinouk had tracked the translator because...because he wanted to know where I was...and he expected me to go into the woods and meet His Honor. That's why he had brought all these soldiers—to capture the separatists!

But how would that help me find my father?

Jex cleared his throat. He had edged around the prince's left side. I thought at first that he was objecting to me calling his ship a "jitney." But he was holding up his right hand, fingers spread, and counting down 3, 2, 1...

At zero the jitney's two big engines tilted down, pointing their exhausts at us. The soldiers murmured. The engines started to rumble back. The soldiers broke ranks and scattered out of range.

"Now!" Jex yanked the prince's cape to one side and sprinted for the jitney. The ship's back legs bent, lowering its rear end to the ground. "Run!"

I had an instant before Hylinouk regained his balance. I ducked around his other side and ran for the jitney as well.

"Stop, you little fool!" the prince shouted. I could hear his shiny boots pound the sand behind me. Jex was scrambling up the footholds on the rear hatch and onto the jitney's roof. I jumped for those holds and got halfway up before the prince grabbed my backpack.

"Launch, Ticca!" Jex yelled. "Hang on, Eesh!"

The rocket engines whooshed. The whole ship rose straight up. I could feel Hylinouk's weight on my back as his feet left the ground, and then he let go of me to clutch at the metal hatch. He also screamed like a baby.

The beach and the camp shrank below us, all the soldiers and refugees staring up, mouths open.

"Keep it steady!" Jex yelled from the top of the jitney. We hovered at forty meters, slowly moving over the ocean. I looked down at the empty gray ship that had brought Daddy to the beach—or had it? I held on. The prince did too, plus more screaming. He really was scared of heights.

"Swing up the rear hatch!" Jex ordered. The hatch, hinged at the top, started to open. That meant the wall I was clinging to turned into a solid floor beneath me. Hylinouk's legs dangled over the edge. He was still screaming.

The hatch door rose to the level of the jitney roof. I could see Jex crouching beside the top hatch. "Eesh, come this way! Soon as you're inside, we'll tip him off into the water!"

"I have a better idea!" I rolled over so I was facing the prince. I pointed the translator at him. "No pretending you don't understand! Did you send me to find His Honor?" The device spat out my words.

"That man is a threat to the nation!" the prince yelled.

I took that as a yes. "My father's squad never came out here, right? You had your soldiers land their ship on this beach in the night and fly away! So where's my father?"

"He is safe, little miss! Set this ship down!"

I shouted over my shoulder, "Higher, Jex!"

The jitney didn't even move before we were back to the screaming.

"Where is my father?" I repeated.

More screaming.

"Where?"

"At my winter palace!"

So after everyone climbed down into the hold, and Ticca attached itself to the prince's neck so he wouldn't do anything dangerous, we flew to the winter palace. It was secluded in the dry hills of a northern province. Jex wouldn't land the ship until Hylinouk ordered his guards to bring out the pipeline squad and march away.

Soon eight mechanics and a pilot were walking toward our rear hatch. I spotted Daddy right away, even under his new beard. I ran outside. "Eeshal?" Daddy gasped. He ran and gave me an extra bristly hug for a whole minute.

I explained things to the squad as they boarded the jitney. "After Hylinouk locked you up," I said, refusing to call the young man a prince any longer, "he waited for someone to come looking for you so he could use that person to find the separatists."

"And the first person in the whole galaxy to come looking was my girl," said Daddy.

"Well, me and Jex." I hugged him again.

Ticca crawled off Hylinouk as he walked down the rear ramp. At the bottom he cleared his throat and said in his carrying voice, "Such is what the young miss believes. She would find it difficult to convince the people of Meelok that such an outlandish story is true."

I held up his translator. "Actually, while we were talking in the air, I pushed the RECORD button on this device. Thanks again for giving it to me."

Jex insisted on flying to Gadder's Landing first. "I made a deal," he told the rest of the pipeline squad. "I'll fly you all to Dorlei next—the Confederation can pay your fares there."

Daddy promised Jex all sorts of tune-ups the next time he came to our base. All that talk about deals made me so nervous I couldn't follow Daddy's and Ticca's conversation about what the jitney needed. As we entered our home system, I took my father to the back of the hold and whispered, "I, um, kind of promised Jex three class-1 inspection certificates for bringing you home."

"Oh, honey!" Daddy said quietly. "There's no way this ship could be class-1. I mean, I'll make sure the systems are as solid as they can be, but..." He looked around at the exposed wires, the jury-rigged filters.

"But I told him—"

"There are a lot of liars in this universe, Eeshal, and I don't want to be one more. I don't want you to be one either."

I gulped. "I understand, Daddy."

Finally we touched back down at Gadder's Landing. As my father hurried down the hatch to be on home ground again, I told Jex, "Thanks for flying us to Wengu and, um, everything else."

Jex shrugged. "Sure."

"Um, Daddy says he won't stamp the last two inspection certificates."

"I figured that's not Gadder's style."

"But I did make a promise," I whispered, rooting in my bag. "I can leave you the blanks—"

"You don't have to do that."

"Really? Thanks!" Feeling so much relief, I started down the hatch, too. Just as my head reached floor level I stopped. "Ticca already broke into the locker in my cabin and took them out, right?"

From the bowels of the jitney I could hear, "tee tee tee."

Jex smirked. "We'll see you later, Eesh."

The Last Flower on Earth

by Aubrey Campbell

Aubrey Campbell enjoys writing about witches, creepy mansions in the mountains, sometimes vampires, sometimes sci-fi gunslingers, and always with a twist of the macabre.

To learn more about her writing, visit her website, www.aubreycampbellauthor.weebly.com or follow on Twitter for updates: @ACampbellAuthor

Misaki saw the robot fall from the sky like a shooting star. A trail of red-hot sparks glowed in its wake, blazing against the velvet blue of midnight.

It wasn't unusual for things to fall from the sky. With so many planets and moons in the galaxy, fewer and fewer people had remained on Earth as its resources dwindled, the trees died, and the lakes and ponds and oceans dried up to nothing but dust. Passing ships began floating their garbage near Earth, and it got sucked into the planet's atmosphere. Most of the garbage burned up before it ever touched the ground, but occasionally pieces made it through, pieces Misaki hoped she could use.

She started moving, scrambling through the debris that littered Earth's surface. Her gaze never wavered from the spot where the robot had landed, half a mile in the distance. A mushroom cloud of orange dust plumed into the air then settled and faded to gray soot.

"Please, please, please," Misaki whispered under her breath. Finally, the robot came into view, tangled metal arms and legs. Its head was tipped back, wires ruptured like veins at its throat. Thin fingers of smoke curled out of the robot's chest where most of its main sensors would be tucked away.

It was an older, outdated model, judging by the LEO-12043 stamped on its right shoulder in black, chipped letters. Well before Misaki was born, the LEO line of robots had been discontinued because of faulty parts and lagging power. But she didn't need it to be perfect. All she needed was the robot to be functional for more than a minute or two so she could send a signal into space.

Misaki dropped to her knees beside the robot, tugged her backpack off, jangling and clanking with tools, and she set to work.

It was well after dark by the time the sensor pad embedded in the robot's chest flickered to life. Misaki gave a small sound of triumph around the flashlight she held clamped between her teeth. She fished a rusty microchip she had found last week from her backpack and wiggled it into the slot just beneath the robot's chin. Its fingers twitched. She sat back on her heels and waited.

Gears whirred and shifted. Circuits sparked and snapped.

The robot blinked. Its heavy metal eyelids scraped over the synthetic eyeballs, creating a scratchy, raspy sound in the stillness. A blue scanner beam stuttered from one eye and traced over Misaki before it flashed green and vanished.

"Hi," she said with a smile.

"Hello," the robot replied in a voice rough and grainy with static. "I am LEO-12043, former captain's aide aboard the SS Athena. But you may call me Leo. Who are you?"

"Misaki."

Leo's eyelids ratcheted up and down and his head angled to the side. "A name originating from Japan. Definition: blossom or flower."

She nodded. "My mother is a botanist. She studies flowers all over the galaxy."

Then Misaki's smile faded, and she glanced down at her hands.

Leo said, "My sensors are detecting sadness."

Misaki sniffed as she dashed the back of her hand across her eyes and picked up her screwdriver again. She crouched in front of Leo's sensor panel and started prying wires out of place in order to change Leo from a captain's aide and turn him into a giant signal tower.

"I beg your pardon," Leo said, pulling back as much as he could when his body wasn't quite warmed up yet. "May I ask what you are doing?"

"Getting a signal into space."

Leo paused. "Your eyes are red. That is an indication of distress."

"I'm fine," Misaki insisted as she reached for his sensor panel again.

Leo put up a large metal hand and placed it on top of her head, pushing her back and keeping her at a safe distance. She swiped at him, stretched one arm all the way out in the hopes of poking him with the screwdriver. But she couldn't even touch Leo let alone reach his sensor panel. She plopped into the dust, arms crossed with a scowl.

Leo removed his hand and the flickering blue scanner of his left eye roamed the surrounding landscape for a full minute.

"I can detect no other sources of human life," he said. "You are the only one here."

Misaki doodled with her screwdriver in the dirt, not meeting Leo's scanning eye.

"I am a captain's aide," Leo added. "The purpose of my existence is to help the captain guide the ship through the galaxy. But I do have some programming for the meaning of human emotions and customs. A human comes from a family. Where is yours?"

"They left," Misaki whispered.

"I do not understand."

"My family bought land on Shenyin Moon in the Izara system. Last year, they stopped on Earth to make some repairs and I..."

"You got lost," Leo finished for her.

Misaki swiped her sleeve across her wet face, leaving two trails of dirt on her cheek where her tears had been.

"They didn't mean to leave me behind. They'll come back for me."

Leo just looked at her, eyelids ratcheting, head tilted to the side, sensors on his chest beeping and chattering like birds at sunrise.

"What is it?" Misaki said. "Quit staring at me like that."

"By my calculations, one year on Earth is not quite two minutes in hyperspace travel. Your family may not yet realize you are missing and when they do—"

"I get it, okay? I know."

"On Earth, it could be many years before they return. In hyperspace, it could be only minutes."

Misaki gritted her teeth. "I said stop talking, you stupid robot." She jabbed her screwdriver at Leo's sensor panel, but he caught her wrist easily.

"Even though I am not fully operating yet," he said, "I would appreciate it if you did not try to take me apart."

"I need to get a signal into space. That's the only reason I fixed you."

"Your family is too far away to receive it."

"But if another ship hears it, maybe I can ride with them. Catch up to my family."

Leo was quiet for a moment. "That's a brave plan."

She squinted at him, suspicious. "You don't agree."

His fingers tapped out a metallic rhythm on the rocky ground. "I am a LEO unit. My captain threw me overboard for my inadequate service. I'm afraid that if you were to use my sensors to build a signal, it would not last very long before I short-circuited, and you could not repair me. The signal would not break Earth's atmosphere."

"Meaning there's no chance of reaching any ships at all."

"Unless they land on Earth," Leo said. "Which is unlikely when Earth has very little interest for humans now."

Misaki slouched beside him, discouraged. She tossed her screwdriver aside, and it skittered across the ground.

"I'm sorry I could not be of more use," Leo said, head bowed.

"Not your fault," she muttered.

Leo's hand crept towards his sensor panel, metal fingers plucking at the precious microchip Misaki had given him. If he pulled it out without properly shutting down, she wouldn't be able to restore him again.

"Don't do that!" she said, swatting at his hand.

"I have no purpose now," Leo said. "You can take me apart and use the pieces in other ways to get a signal into space."

Misaki pulled her knees up to her chest. "But it's been so long since I've had someone to talk to."

"I was never built for conversation. I assisted the captain with shipping route information, wind speeds, fuel and resource calculations—"

Misaki blinked at him, her eyes glazed with confusion. Leo stopped.

"I don't know what that means," she said.

Leo stared at the ground for a moment. Misaki could hear the fizz and crackle of the converter in his head getting overheated as he searched his memory for a simpler explanation.

"I gave the captain advice on how to fly his ship safely," he said.

Misaki shot to her feet, heart galloping against her ribs, and she looked out across Earth's surface. Thousands of spaceships lay like the enormous hollow skeletons of beached whales, bellies up.

"Do you think you could get a dead spaceship to fly again?" she said.

"I...don't know. But I believe I might have enough knowledge needed to make a passable attempt at—"

Before Leo could finish, Misaki flung her arms around his neck and hugged him so tight that his circuits threatened to pop.

For weeks, Misaki and Leo searched through the graveyard of spaceships for one that wasn't damaged. Most of them were too torn up from the fall through Earth's atmosphere to be of any use.

Misaki wormed her way into another ship's engine, smelling like ashes and dirt, in the hopes that she could still use it. But once she was inside, she found wires, circuits, and converters brittle as bird bones, crumbling in her hands. If she managed to piece this ship back together again, it would never get off the ground, let alone survive the pressure of space.

"Misaki?" Leo said from outside the ship.

"What?" she called back, her voice echoing in the cavern of the engine.

"I believe I am stuck."

She sighed and bowed her head. Leo was right. He hadn't been much help. His memory cache might be stocked full of information on flying but he got distracted by every shiny trinket that he came across.

Misaki squirmed out of the engine, streaks of grease and ash across her face. She found Leo had crammed his gigantic metal body into what was left of a circus ride. It was a tiny rocket ship with red and yellow flames blazing down the side with blocky letters that read, THE BERSERK BIG TOP.

"What are you doing in there?" Misaki said. "That's not a real ship."

"It was bright and colorful, and I thought it might cheer you up."

"I don't need cheering up, Leo. I need a ship. One that works. Not a circus ride."

She tugged at his arm in an effort to loosen him from the rocket ship, but he didn't budge.

"You are frustrated," Leo said.

"Of course I am. Look at all those ships." She pointed to the landscape around them, pieces of spaceships gleaming pink and gold in the fading sunlight. "How come none of them work? How come we still don't have anything?"

Leo poked at a cracked red button on the console of the circus ride. "I warned you that I can't help much."

Misaki shoved him in the shoulder. "Stop talking like that. Like you don't have a purpose anymore just because you're old."

"My program was created for flying spaceships. I have no ship, and I have no captain."

"You have me, okay?" Misaki shoved him again, harder this time, and it felt good to hit something, to release the anger that had been boiling inside her for so long, even though she felt a little guilty about it too. "What if my parents don't come back for me? What if I'm stuck here, and you're all I've got? I don't care if you're a clumsy robot. I just don't want to be alone out here anymore."

With the scrape of metal against metal, Leo wrapped his arms around Misaki and picked her up. He settled her in the tiny rocket ship beside him, squished between the door that had rusted shut and his own bulky frame.

"I'm not scrapping you for parts," Misaki mumbled. "We'll figure something out. But I'm not giving up on you."

Leo brushed the back of one cold metal finger over her cheek. Misaki flinched, surprised. He held up his hand, and a drop of water trembled on the smooth surface of his fingertip.

"There was moisture on your face," he said. "It's not raining." He paused, head tilted to the side, eyelids ticking as he searched his database for information. "My temperature reading says it is not humid enough to sweat. The only reasonable answer left is that this is a tear, and you are crying. Definition—"

"I know what it means, you big bag of bolts."

She burrowed under his elbow until he raised his arm, and she wiggled in closer. It wasn't comfortable when she kept getting poked and prodded by wires and sharp metal corners, but she didn't really mind. Slowly, Leo lowered his arm and patted her head in an awkward attempt at reassurance.

Misaki shifted to watch the sun dip below the horizon, and the stars winked themselves awake one by one. She always watched the sky, night and day, hoping to see the white streaming tail of cloud that would signal the return of her family's ship.

But tonight, there were only stars, thousands of them, millions of them, freckles of planets across the face of the galaxy.

"Why do you do that?" Leo said.

"Do what?"

"Stare at the sky so much."

"I'm looking for my parents' ship. *The Stargazer*."

Leo swiveled his head to look up at the sky as well, his metal body screeching from the movement. She'd have to find some oil to loosen his joints soon, or he would rust stiff.

"It's getting late," he said after a while. "You need sleep. I will watch the sky for you in case your family returns."

"Thank you, Leo."

He picked her up again, lifting her clear of the circus ride, and set her on the ground. Then he pulled himself free, crumpling the tiny rocket ship in the process. As he pried his foot out, his elbow knocked over a can, and red paint oozed over the ground. Misaki smiled and swiped her hand through the paint. Before Leo could stop her, she climbed up his arm and streaked it across his chest.

Leo looked down at himself, touching the outline she had left there with two fingers. "It appears to be a heart but it is not an accurate rendering. There are no ventricles, aortas—"

"Leo," Misaki said with a laugh. "It doesn't have to be perfect. It's a gift."

Slowly, Leo placed his palm flat against his chest. "Gift. Definition: an item given from one person to another. Exchanged between friends." He glanced up at her. "I've never had one of those."

"A gift?"

He shook his head. "A friend."

Then Leo swung Misaki up onto his shoulders, and she wrapped her arms around his giant round metal head, leaving small red fingerprints on his ears as she held on. Whenever she was on the ground, she had to push aside all sorts of trash. It made movement slow and difficult, even impossible in some areas. But from her perch on Leo's shoulders, it was easy to get where she wanted to. He was so tall that he simply stepped over almost anything that was in his path.

During the past year Misaki had spent on Earth alone, she needed somewhere to sleep, to call "home" even though it wasn't really one. There were plenty of spaceships to choose from, but it burned a hole in her stomach to sleep in a ship that could never fly her away from this awful planet she was trapped on.

So she had found an old truck instead, tipped onto its roof, windows cracked or chipped but still intact, keeping the dust from getting in her face as she slept.

By the time Leo reached the truck, Misaki was already dozing off, draped over his shoulder. He curled his fingers around her, cradling her in one hand as he tucked her into the bed she had built for herself out of mouse-eaten blankets and pillows in the truck's cab.

Careful not to jostle or bump anything in Misaki's little room,

Leo backed out and sat down next to the truck's door. His long legs sprawled out in front of him, one finger idly tracing the heart Misaki had given to him as a gift. And he watched the sky all night long.

Three months later, Leo disappeared.

It had become their routine for Leo to keep watch at night while Misaki slept in case her parents came back and she missed them. Every morning, she would wake to see Leo's back to her, his face tilted skyward, his enormous metal body coated in a thin layer of dew.

And every morning, without turning around, Leo would say, "I'm afraid there is no good news to report."

Misaki would reach out and pat Leo's shoulder to reassure him that he was still being useful and to reassure herself she wasn't alone.

This morning was different. When she opened her eyes, Leo's bulky frame wasn't there where he usually sat. Instead, the sun flared its blinding light straight into her eyes and she grimaced.

"Leo?" she called.

Silence.

Had her parents returned, and Leo went to get them? Misaki shook her head. No, he would have woken her if that happened.

But then...where was he?

A gust of wind sent dirt swirling into Misaki's face and she coughed, choking on the grit in her mouth. She shielded her eyes with one hand, looking out over the junkyard of Earth. That familiar sinking feeling was blooming in her stomach again.

Had Leo left her behind too?

"Leo!" Misaki yelled, and her voice cracked with panic.

Nothing.

Misaki inhaled a trembling breath and searched the ground until she found Leo's footprints—big craters where his feet sank into the dirt. She followed his footprints until the sun towered high in the sky and burned the back of her neck raw. At times, she lost the trail when the garbage was too thick, Leo's trail impossible to see in piles of spaceship parts.

Misaki scrambled up onto a bent and twisted wing of a spaceship. From the top, she could see in every direction.

Mountains of garbage.

Spinning clouds of dust.

No trees. No grass. No streaming white tail of a spaceship belonging to her family.

And no Leo.

Had he malfunctioned somewhere? Broken down? He could have wandered off. He did get distracted too easily. One of his parts might have failed, and he could be lying out there, sensors dying, circuits cooked in the sun, unable to make his way back to her.

Then Misaki remembered when she found Leo, how he had nearly taken out his microchip to shut himself down before she had stopped him.

What was it Leo had said before?

My program was created for flying spaceships. I have no ship, and I have no captain.

Leo was always supposed to help a captain aboard a spaceship. Not a lost little girl in the middle of a garbage dump.

Misaki stood there, unsure what to do. Should she search for Leo? It might take time away from getting a signal into space to contact her family. But it would be lonely without him...

Before she could decide, a horrible sound screeched in the silence. Misaki's head snapped up, her gaze searching the horizon. There. To the north was the white glare of sunlight on a round metal head she knew well. Leo was still functioning!

But...was he dragging something behind him?

Misaki's eyes widened. He was. He'd found a spaceship, and it looked like it was in practically perfect working condition!

Misaki took off running, tripping and stumbling in her excitement. She barreled into Leo, her arms around his waist. Leo started and patted the top of her head.

"I didn't want to wake you," he said. "I thought I would try looking for a spaceship a little farther than we have gone before."

Misaki peered around him at the ship. It stood tall and proud, with a dull, dusty silver exterior like a star that had been buried only to be unearthed to shine again.

"Do you think it will work?" she said.

"That's why I brought it to you."

Misaki hurried up the ramp and into the pilot's seat. A panel of controls spread out in front of her, a little dirty, but nothing appeared broken or beyond repair. The ship was so large that Leo could fit inside with her, and he pried a panel aside so she could see into the engine.

"Misaki?" Leo said.

"Are you stuck again?" she replied, her voice muffled as she ran her hands over the engine parts, taking inventory of each piece that might be cracked or broken.

"No, I was simply wondering how you know so much about fixing ships."

Misaki crawled backwards out of the engine, three charred burner coils in her fist. "I always helped my papa on my family's ship, pulling things apart and putting them back together. It's fun to make things work again. Like you," she added with a smile.

Leo studied her face for a moment, eyelids twitching, searching his database. "My sensors recognize your smile, but your posture says you are unhappy."

Misaki held up the burner coils. "No, it's just...I mean, the engine only needs three replacement coils to get it started. We'll have to check a few more things first, but you found us a good ship, Leo." She poked him in the arm. "Don't run off like that without warning me next time, okay? You scared me."

Leo wrapped his fingers around Misaki, and as he picked her up, she held onto his thumb.

"I would never give up on you," he said.

It took two weeks to get the ship running. Then Misaki was finally strapped into the pilot's seat, and Leo had crammed himself in behind her. He was too big for the co-pilot's seat, but he could get his head and shoulders into the cockpit to help her navigate, and that was all she really needed.

Misaki let out a long, slow breath and flipped the switch to get the engine started. The ship rumbled and growled, then shuddered beneath her.

"Power is at seventy percent," Leo said.

"Will that be enough to make it through Earth's atmosphere?" Misaki replied

Leo nodded. "Yes, Captain."

Misaki raised her eyebrows. "Captain?"

"You are the one flying the ship, correct?"

She spread her fingers over the controls with a smile. "Yes. I am."

"Flux generators are primed and ready for takeoff, Captain," Leo said. He pointed at a lever to her right. "Push that forward. All the way."

Misaki curled her hand over it and shoved. The ship bucked, surging upward, steadily climbing higher and higher into the sky.

"All systems are holding steady," Leo reported.

Misaki didn't look down, didn't take one last glance at the

Earth. She kept her gaze trained on the stars above, the white arc of Earth's atmosphere just waiting for her to challenge it. The controls trembled beneath her palm, and a curl of fear squeezed her heart.

"Leo," she said, her voice shaking. "What if we can't do it?"

"We will." His hand settled at her back for comfort as he nudged a few levers with one giant fingertip. "The repairs you made were good. Your father taught you well."

The ship lurched, and flames burst across the window, whiting out the sky as they soared through the Earth's atmosphere. Misaki felt as if she had been locked in an oven. The metal arms of her chair burned under her fingers, but she didn't let go.

She could see scraps of dark sky through the fire. Deep space. It was so close. Just a little longer. Even if the ship's system failed, as long as her food and oxygen didn't run out, she had a better chance of being seen floating outside of Earth instead of stuck on the surface in all that garbage.

Then a high-pitched beeping started somewhere on the control panel.

"What's that?" Misaki said, concerned.

Leo stabbed at buttons, tapped a sensor screen. "It's a warning."

"Warning? For what?"

"One of our generator batteries has failed."

Misaki closed her eyes and pressed herself into her seat. A dead generator battery meant more strain on the other six to keep the ship going. If those other batteries stopped working as well before they broke the atmosphere, they would crash back to Earth.

"I'm sure I've got a replacement battery in my backpack," Misaki said, already unstrapping herself from her chair and jumping to the floor. "I'll change it out."

"No," Leo said even as his fingers darted over the controls. "Other parts of the ship are shutting down as well."

"You mean..."

"We're going to crash."

Misaki curled her fingers around Leo's wrist, shifting closer to him as fear shivered through her. They weren't going to break Earth's atmosphere. They weren't going to make it into space to send a signal to her family after all.

"I can fix it," Leo added.

"How?" Misaki croaked.

He tapped his chest beneath his chin where the microchip was. Misaki shoved his hand away.

"No," she said. "You'll fry yourself."

Leo put his hand back to the same spot, determined in his decision.

"My microchip is old," he said, "but it works. If I enter it into the ship's control panel, it will take over and replace the systems that are failing."

"What about you?" Misaki sniffed.

"I will serve my captain as I was programmed to do."

Before Misaki could protest further, Leo ripped his microchip out. He twitched and buzzed, but his large fingers managed to jam the chip into the control panel slot. The ship sighed and went level again. No beeping, no warnings, just the quiet rumbling purr of the engine in the background.

Leo slumped over the control panel, his eyes still, the usual whirl and blink of his sensor lights gone dark. Misaki crawled under his arm and curled up in the crook of his elbow. The emptiness of space stretched out across the windshield, black as ink frosted with silver stars like snowflakes. No floating garbage to get in the way. No haze of Earth's atmosphere.

They'd made it into space. They were flying, and Misaki could send a signal now, as far as she needed to.

Thanks to Leo.

"Signal received," a voice said, crackling with static. *"Stargazer* responding to Misaki-12034. Come in."

Misaki blinked awake. For the past few hours, she had tried her best to repair Leo. She didn't have another microchip, though, and without one, she knew Leo would never work again. But she had tried anyway. She had made a promise.

I won't give up on you. We'll figure something out.

Misaki had fallen asleep at some point, pieces of Leo's sensors and circuits scattered on the floor around her in an orbit of debris. Until that voice echoed in the cockpit, a voice she had ached to hear again.

"Mom?" she said.

"Misaki, sweetie, is that you?" Her mother's voice was clear now, laughing with relief. "We couldn't find you. We've been worried sick. Are you okay?"

"I'm fine." Misaki cast a sad glance at Leo. "Can we dock? I've got so much to tell you."

"Of course. I'm looking forward to the part where you explain how you're flying your own ship."

The crunch and grind of metal thundered all around her. Misaki's ship rattled as it locked airtight with the loading bay of the *Stargazer* and docked. Then the door opened, and Misaki's parents stepped in.

For a moment, they stopped, shocked at the sight of Leo's massive body stuffed into the ship. But then Misaki flung herself at them, her arms around their necks, and they forgot about the robot, hugging Misaki so tight that she wheezed.

Misaki's father released her first and studied Leo's unmoving form.

"Is this...a Land and Efficiency Observer unit?" he said as he picked up one of the sensors from the floor where Misaki had left it. "I thought these didn't exist anymore."

"He used to belong to a ship, but he was dumped on Earth," Misaki replied as she patted Leo's shoulder. "I got a new microchip for him, and we flew the ship together."

Misaki's father shook his head. "But that's...not possible. LEO units were only programmed to give suggestions and advice. They're not meant to be co-pilots."

Misaki crossed to the control panel and pulled the microchip out, handing it to her father. Now that she was docked with the *Stargazer*, she didn't need the engine running anymore, but it was too late to put the microchip back into Leo's body and wake him up. His system had become too hot and burned out when he didn't shut down before taking out his microchip.

"This certainly looks like it belonged to a LEO unit," her father said, shaking his head in amazement. "To get one of those units working again after it was scrapped, that's an impressive accomplishment. I always knew you'd be a better engineer than I am. Just didn't realize it would happen by the time you were ten years old."

He wrapped an arm around her shoulder and guided her towards the *Stargazer*.

"Are you hungry?" her mother said. "We can make some fresh mochi if you like."

Misaki nodded, eager to eat something besides dried rations she had been living off of on Earth for the past year. As she stepped out of her ship and onto the *Stargazer* with its ruby-red interior, warm and clean, she wished Leo could have seen it.

Her father shut the door, and as his hand moved to the release button, Misaki's heart hiccupped in panic.

"What are you doing?" she demanded.

"We can't keep the ship, you know that," he said. "It's dead weight. We'll lose too much fuel dragging it along with us."

"But Leo's still inside. If you release the ship, he'll go too. Then he'll be lost, just floating out there."

Her father's hand left the release button as he crouched in front of her to look her in the eye.

"I'll get you another robot, Misaki," he said. "One that works.

A new model."

"I don't want a new model. Leo is my friend. He stayed with me on Earth. He watched the sky for me when I was asleep so if you came back, I wouldn't miss you. He gave up his microchip so we didn't crash."

"But sweetie," her mother said, taking her hand. "He's not working anymore. It looks like he's been short-circuited. No one can bring him back from that."

"I'm not giving up on him," Misaki insisted. "I promised I wouldn't."

Her father sighed and bowed his head. "There might be something we can do for him."

Misaki perked up, but before she could say anything, her father raised a hand for silence.

"His old body will have to go," her father added. "And his program will need some updates."

"But I can keep him?"

"Maybe. It might not work. You'll have to help me put in some long hours with the ship's communication system. Are you ready for that?"

Misaki nodded. "I'll do anything."

Four months later, Misaki came skidding into the cockpit of the *Stargazer*. Through the massive windshield, she took in the sight of Shenyin Moon, golden clouds swirling across its surface. They were finally here. They were home.

"Command is yours," her father said as he rose from the captain's chair.

Misaki scrambled into the chair, her legs swinging in the air, too short to touch the floor.

"Good morning, Captain," Leo said from the ship's overhead speaker.

"Hi, Leo," Misaki replied with a smile.

It had taken weeks and weeks of hard work but enough of Leo's data had survived from his system to be placed in the Stargazer's mainframe. Leo wasn't a robot anymore, he was part of the ship, and Misaki could talk to him anytime she liked.

"Zoom in," she said.

On a smaller screen to her left, next to the captain's chair, Shenyin Moon grew and grew until she could see the silver rivers like liquid moonlight and forests of red trees like roses in bloom.

"How long until we land?" she said.

"Estimated at twelve minutes, fourteen seconds." Leo paused. "I have a question."

"Yes?"

"When you land, you won't need a captain's aide any longer. What will happen to me?"

Misaki tapped the screen and the image of Shenyin Moon vanished, replaced with an image of Leo's face.

"We've talked about this, Leo. You're part of the family, not just the ship. No matter where we go, your home is with us."

"You won't scrap me?"

Misaki glanced at her father still standing off to one side.

"Papa said that after we've moved in, I could take the ship and explore the planet. Do you know what that means?"

"Explore. Definition—"

"It means I'll need someone to show me around. A guide to keep the ship going. I can fix things, but I'm still learning how to fly. I'll need a captain's aide for that."

"I am a captain's aide."

"I know," Misaki replied, grinning. "Unless you *want* to be scrapped..."

"I would prefer to fly with you, Captain, for as long as you need me."

Nine Minus One

by Bruce Golden

Bruce Golden was a youth baseball coach for 17 years, and his love of the game led to this story's "sports theme." His book *Tales of My Ancestors* combines the historical with the fantastic, and has been described as "The Twilight Zone" meets Ancestry.com. His latest book, *Monster Town*, is a satirical send-up of old hard-boiled detective stories featuring movie monsters of the black & white era. It's currently in development for a possible TV series. http://goldentales.tripod.com

Bats slammed into lockers, cleats scraped the floor, and frothy spittle stained the walls. An influx of uniformed combatants filed into the room, some mumbling, others grumbling—the sure sign of another loss. In moments, the place smelled of dirty socks and planetary jocks.

As if to alter the mood, one of them began revolving around the post-game spread, waving his arms.

"I say we put this one behind us," called out Saturn in an upbeat tone. "I say we go out and find some local satellites and check out the hot spots. What do you say?"

His idea was greeted by a colorful array of eruptions. No one was in the mood to party. By the time little Mercury showed up with the *really* bad news, the room was already subdued. Most had changed out of their uniforms and were already in and out of the showers. Mars noticed that the normally peppy infielder appeared unusually glum.

"What's wrong? You look like you've seen a black hole."

"Did you hear what happened to Pluto?" the speedster asked the room in general. "They cut him."

"What?" Mars slammed his fist against the wall. "I knew something was up."

"Are you sure?" asked Jupiter, scratching his oversized head with sausage-like fingers.

"Yeah," replied Mercury. "He's in with management right now. I hear they're sending him down to the dwarf league."

"I bet it was Terra's fault," groused Mars. "He's always stirring up trouble. No telling what he told management behind Pluto's back."

"Well, Pluto's always been a little erratic," said Saturn, fresh out of the shower and adorning himself with his usual bling. "He's not the fastest guy in the galaxy either."

"Maybe," said Mars, "but he's a scrappy little player, and he was always there for us, eon after eon."

Jupiter stood, stretched his massive arms, and yawned. "I'm going to miss the little guy."

"What's this going to do to team chemistry?" wondered Venus.

"Management doesn't care about chemistry," carped Mars. "All they care about is astronomy."

"We should tell the others before he gets here," suggested Venus.

Saturn volunteered, "I'll get Neptune, he's still in the shower."

"That figures," responded Mars. "Hey, while you're in there, get Uranus out of the head."

Before Saturn returned, Terra walked in and said excitedly, "Did you guys hear what happened to Pluto?"

That was all Mars needed. He grabbed Terra by his jersey and slammed him up against a spate of lockers.

"What did you do, you prissy, waterlogged, rodent-infested little—"

Jupiter and Mercury moved quickly to intervene, separating the pair.

"What did you tell them?" Mars ranted as Jupiter held him back.

"What are you talking about?" Terra seemed stunned by the attack.

"Mars thinks it's your fault they're sending Pluto down," explained Venus.

"What? I didn't have anything to do with that. How could I? Why would I?"

Before Mars could continue his diatribe, Pluto walked in. He was already in street clothes but went straight to his locker. The room hushed noticeably and, for a moment, everyone acted as if nothing were amiss. But when Pluto began emptying out his locker, Mercury put an arm on his shoulder.

"Sorry, my man. We all heard. It's a bum deal."

Pluto shrugged. "It's part of the business. I didn't get the job done." Then, mustering a bit of bravado, he turned to face the room and added, "I'll be back. Don't you worry about that. I'll go down, I'll get my game together and then I'll be back. It's just a slump. You'll see, I'll be back up here in no time."

Jupiter nodded his big head and his bassoon-like voice bellowed, "That's right. You'll be back in no time at all. You go down there and give them a good showing, Pluto old bud."

"Yeah," called out a couple of other voices with less than genuine enthusiasm.

Unable to hold back the tears, Venus turned away. Mars looked like he wanted to break something.

Searching his rather voluminous cranium for something else to say—something inspirational—Jupiter came up with, "Just remember, you can't steal first base."

"Yeah . . . right. Thanks, Jupe," responded Pluto. He knew the big guy well enough not to waste time puzzling over anything he said.

But Jupiter wasn't finished.

"Did I ever tell you how I could have been a star?"

Venus waved him silent.

"Not now, Jupiter."

Pluto finished bagging up his stuff and started out. Terra stepped up and shook his hand.

"Good luck, Pluto."

"Yeah," said Mercury, "knock 'em dead down there."

Pluto looked like he wanted to say something else but couldn't get the words out. Instead he glanced away and walked out.

Mercury stared at Jupiter. "You're a real gasbag, you know that? *You can't steal first base?* What kind of idiotic thing is that to say?"

Jupiter shrugged his mammoth shoulders. The gravitational effect of the movement pulled Saturn back in from the showers with Neptune and Uranus in tow.

"What happened?" asked Neptune, still dripping.

"They cut Pluto. He's gone."

"Cut him? Why?"

"Why do you think?" Mars replied sarcastically. "He wasn't orbiting up to expectations."

"It's not *why* that matters," offered Mercury. "It's *who*—who will they cut next?"

Interplanetary Ghost Rushers

by Kate Sheeran Swed

Kate Sheeran Swed loves hot chocolate, plastic dinosaurs, and airplane tickets. She has trekked along the Inca Trail to Macchu Picchu, hiked on the Mýrdalsjökull glacier in Iceland, and climbed the ruins of Masada to watch the sunrise over the Dead Sea. She holds degrees in music from the University of Maine and Ithaca College, as well as an MFA in Fiction from Pacific University. You can find her on Twitter and Instagram @katesheeranswed.

I'm sorry to say that by the time my parents joined the Interplanetary Ghost Rush and yanked us off to Planet 14, the only spirits left there were rumors.

At least there's still a tourist industry.

Well. I should clarify that.

Say you're on your way to ski on Planet 16, or to meet Astro Mickey Mouse on Planet 21. So you stop on the way to refuel your space porter, maybe stock the snack bin with fresh moon fries. And where do you get those moon fries?

That would be Planet 14. The pit stop of planets.

Best bathrooms in the galaxy.

But on the way to the surface, your porter might hit a block of ice, because flying ice loves P-14 more than a black hole loves matter. So you might end up with a ruptured solar panel or leaky fuel tank. And if *that* happens, you *might* decide to kill time with a visit to the Planet 14 Ghost Mining Museum (P14GMM) to kill time while your porter gets repaired.

Or you might stick around the mechanic's waiting room all day drinking bad coffee and watching reruns of *Who Wants to be a Cosmic Millionaire*. The entertainment value is about equal.

Luckily, someone's gotta hawk key fobs to the five visitors who wander in every week. So while my parents dig fruitlessly for ghost energy, I've got a job in the P14GMM gift shop.

My boss, Mr. Difrizplfkjdmnophodole, isn't human. It's not an insult. It's a fact. He's one of the aliens that've shared P-14 with humans since the alliance of 3800.

We humans don't have enough throats to pronounce the aliens' proper name, so we call them Rocklings because they hail from the asteroid belt between Planets 4 and 5.

I'm thinking Mr. D's museum-slash-keychain-stand is probably some kind of a front. Slot machines in the basement, maybe. But I basically get paid to sit behind a counter playing games on my handheld and talking to my friends back on P-1 (when I've got enough credits for inter-planet communication, which at the moment, I don't).

I'm not about to ask any questions.

This morning, I'm so occupied with plans for obliterating space noodles with my thumbs until my paycheck comes in, I don't see the new girl until I'm almost sitting on her.

"Excuse me," she says in this prim little voice—like my very breathing might upset her stomach. "This area is for employees only."

"I *am* an employee," I say. "I'm Maddie."

"Oh," she says, dismissive. She's a Rockling like Mr. D, her arms willowy and elbow-less, which I can see because she's wearing a purple tube top. Just looking at her makes me shiver; I'm wearing three sweatshirts, a scarf, and a knitted cap. The Rockling girl's ears are like giant saucers, giving her this kitten level of cuteness that's immediately annoying.

"Uncle D didn't say there'd be another girl," she says.

For a second, I wonder if Mr. D found the words I spelled with the personalized key chains last week.

Maybe I'm fired.

But then she says, "I'm Rose. I was bored, so I asked to work here today."

I laugh. It sounds loud and rude next to her musical voice. "You think working here will make you less bored?"

She folds her hands in her lap. "I'm all for new experiences."

"Yeah, OK. Well, I'm all for a paycheck. So let me behind the counter, please."

"You don't look old enough to work here."

"I'm going into seventh grade," I say, indignant. Of course, everyone else on this planet is chasing ghosts, selling fuel, or fixing porters, so I'm pretty much Mr. D's only option.

She doesn't need to know that.

Rose glances at the ceiling. It's not an "I'm-considering-your-request" glance. It's an "I-hid-my-poker-winnings-up-there" glance, which I've seen any number of times after my older brother comes back from a spin on lucky Planet 7.

But Rose seems to decide she doesn't want me asking questions. She relents.

There's only one stool, though, and she's perched on it with her knees curled beneath her, her skirt puffing out like a colorful mushroom.

Rocklings do better in the P-14 cold than humans do.

I prop my handheld on the counter and get to work blasting space noodles. Usually, I try to make my communication credits stretch the full two weeks between paychecks. But Aly's cat died last week, so I spent everything in the first three days, cheering her up in conference chats with our other friend, Tina.

I miss them so much it aches.

They're going to start seventh grade without me.

"Excuse me," Rose says, as I blast rotini out of orbit with my meatball lasers.

I look at her, confused.

She points at the handheld. Her hands are too clean. Because the A-belt is sooo much more civilized than P-14.

"Your sound effects," she says. "They're interfering."

"With what?" I ask. "Your staring?"

"No. My listening."

I listen.

Silence.

I raise my eyebrows—I've been working on that one-at-a-time thing, which would come in really useful at moments like this—and cup my ears, exaggerating.

I'm not expecting to hear a thing.

Above us, something crashes to the floor, shaking the whole ceiling. "Oh, right," I say. "Don't worry. Gus knocks over the Phantoms of Pluto display every day around this time. He's right on schedule."

Always denies it too. Like I care that he's clumsy.

Rose's eyes are on the ceiling, like those poker winnings are in danger.

"I'll go check," I say.

I wish I could tell you I'm offering because I'm nice and want to comfort her. But I just kind of want to know what her deal is.

Rose slips down from the stool and brushes past me. "I'll check."

I shrug. Fine.

My astro-cats have fettuccini to destroy.

In addition to walls and warmth and people to talk to, what I really miss about P-1 is my gerbil, Ginger. I hope Aly's taking good care of her and letting her run in her ball.

I just got paid. I can ask Aly myself. Maybe even splurge on a few minutes of video. I always transfer most of my credits to Mom, to help out with the household budget (or tent-hold budget, since the home my parents snagged us here is literally a canvas dome). But she's firm about me keeping a few credits for myself.

Ginger would not have loved P-14, or the not-so-super dome where we live. It's not a whole lot warmer than the outside—where I swear there are ice crystals collecting between my fingers. And there's not much privacy. Which, I guess, is not such a big deal for a gerbil. But before I even open the door, I can hear Mom and Dad talking about how many ghosts they snagged this week.

None. It's always none.

Ghosts are residual energy. That's it. They wander around, looking all human, but the souls that inhabited them are gone. They don't talk. They don't avenge wrongs. They don't try to finish any business. They're just energy, trapped in old patterns.

When you suck up that energy with kinetically modified fiberglass tubing, you can sell the capsule for a couple thousand credits.

Which is why Mom and Dad dragged me out to the boonies of the solar system after my brother pulled his own energy miracle and ghosted with their life savings. He's probably tossed it onto a roulette wheel by now.

"We can scrape by this week if we skip coffee," Mom says. They're calculating numbers on Dad's handheld. The screen busted last week when it took a tumble from his bunk to the floor, which is basically a tarp laid over ice. The poor thing never had a chance.

He doesn't say anything. I know without looking that he's scanning the numbers, trying to figure out how Mom can have coffee while we all still consume actual calories.

"It was supposed to be easier here," Mom says.

We were never supposed to be here at all.

When I finally get the guts to open the door, I take dinner to my bunk in the corner, and I transfer my entire paycheck, measly as it is, from my account to Mom's.

At the very least, she should get her coffee.

Mom doesn't say anything about the credits over breakfast, but she gives my arm an extra squeeze as I head out the door-slash-tent-flap.

In all the excitement of not being like my jerk of a brother, I forget about Rose until my hand's on the museum door.

Maybe she won't be here today. Maybe it'll just be me and the space noodles. My goal is to have them all completely Bolognese-d by the time I can talk to Aly again.

I pass the Early Ghost-Catching display—as if the discovery of Martian spirit energy a thousand years ago is anything more than a boring history lesson—as quickly as I can. This place couldn't possibly have been enough to satisfy her boredom.

But she's back on my stool, wearing an orange headband to hold back her metallic silver locks and a matching tank top. There's no way it's so cold in the A-belt that she's comfortable in that.

She's got her eyes rolled toward the ceiling in a move my brother would call "giving away your hand." I let the door clatter to a close, making Rose jump. Which is how I know she's not faking.

I'm forming a plan to propose a museum exploration, just so I can figure out what she's up to, when Mr. D himself lopes in. I'm pretty sure he bought this old fort for the high ceilings, even though his ears come close to brushing them.

He clears his throats. "Business isn't booming," he says and pauses. Like we need a few moments to digest that news flash. "I need more postcards delivered to mechanic's row and the fueling stations. And anywhere else you can think of."

"Mr. D," I say, trying to be gentle, "the last time I brought cards around, I got yelled at for talking over a Space Jeopardy answer."

It was 'What is Astronaut Ice Cream,' which they should have known anyway.

"Wait for a commercial break." He snaps his fingers, his ears quivering. "*You* be the commercial, Maddie."

It'll be a real shame if it turns out Mr. D doesn't actually have slot machines in the back. If I lose this job, I'm not sure my family will eat at all. But the way he's looking at me, he really wants this place to work out.

He's a historian. Not a criminal.

We're in trouble.

Mr. D's shaking the cards at me. "Come on, Maddie. I got a tip about a deal on antique energy lasers on Moon 7. If that won't bring in some curious customers, well, I don't know what will."

Something interesting, maybe. Like holos depicting real ghosts, or interactive enhanced-reality displays, or a range where visitors can try out actual Ecto-hoses.

OK, that last one is unlikely. But you get the idea.

"I'm heading out there for a day or two," he adds. "I need these postcards distributed in the meantime."

"I'll do it, Uncle D," Rose says before I can agree. I shouldn't be surprised that she's sweet as her name when a grownup's around.

Mr. D grins and hands her the cards.

I can't believe she's willing to leave the museum, and her secret. In fact, I don't believe it. So as soon as Mr. D's gone, I follow his niece out of the gift shop.

It feels so good to be right.

Rose doesn't leave the museum. Instead, she loops around and skips up the narrow staircase in back.

This place used to be a fort. Fifty years ago, humans and Rocklings thought there might be a fight over P-14, until they all sat down together and figured they could share.

Before that, though, the humans used this spot as a military base. And before *that*, it was the site of the first P-14 colony.

This is the kind of useless knowledge you acquire when you work in a museum.

Rose takes the staircase from the courtyard where the soldiers used to do their exercises and goes all the way up to the old barracks. I follow at a distance, careful to mind the creaky screws on the step between the third and fourth floors.

When I hear her voice, I stop.

"...left Chewy in the A-belt with Mom and Dad," she's saying. "They said it's too cold here for a dog, but they're wrong. The A-belt is way colder."

Rose is missing a pet she left in the A-belt? Is she hiding a stray dog up here?

I'd hide a stray gerbil, if I could.

I peer around the corner.

When I see who Rose is talking to, I can barely retrain a squeak of surprise. In the middle of the floor is a boy about our age, maybe twelve or thirteen, and he's tossing something to the end of the hall in an eight-second loop.

The boy is a ghost.

And my family's problems are solved.

It's not hard to nick Mom's Ecto-hose for a night of ghost hunting. The not-so-super dome has no closets or hooks, so she coils the hose into a careful heap by the door when she comes home. Sneaking out is a little more nerve-wracking. But Mom and

Dad work so hard all day, picking up odd jobs where ghosts are scarce—which they always are—so once they're asleep, they're dead to the planet. I manage not to knock over any chairs and make it outside without waking them.

P-14 is weird at night. Frost crunches under my boots, and the whole dome-village where we live is silent. There are a few spots of glowing lamps, people and Rocklings awake here and there, but they're easy enough to avoid.

The Planet 14 Ghost Mining Museum isn't as weird. Here, I'm used to the silence.

I sneak in the back, heading up the stairs.

The boy with the invisible dog probably doesn't come out at night. The ghosts all have their cycles, their times. But if the boy is still here, I'm sure the Planet 14 Ghost Mining Museum hasn't been swept for ghosts at all.

Ironic.

It's not the kind of thing Mr. D would think to have done. He spends most of his time staring at books about ghosts. I can definitely see him missing real ones. I should have thought of it, though. Gus knocking over that display every day at the same time and denying it? That reaks of ghost activity.

I don't have to wait long before I find more.

Or rather, it finds me: the sound of marching, invading my stairwell in a sudden wash of rhythm.

I peek onto the second floor.

It's three pairs of feet, attached to three human ghost soldiers. They look young. They look scared.

If anything makes sense to me, it's that. They're soldiers reviewing their exercises in the dead of night, on a planet where they might be obliterated. They repeated this action so much, and with such intensity, that a bit of their energy returned here after their deaths.

They must have been terrified.

Well, so am I. I tug the Ecto-hose loose from my backpack and creep forward.

As soon as the ghosts march back to my end of the room, they'll be porter fuel, and Mom can have all the coffee she wants.

I make my move.

Someone tackles me from behind, arms latching behind my knees. I scream as my attacker falls with me, shoving my cheek against the cold linoleum.

When I scramble around, it's Rose who's trying to avoid getting kicked in the face.

"What the Jupiter?!" I say as the ghosts march over us, sending thrills of static electricity through my limbs. It's eerie and invigorating, and super creepy.

"They're my friends," Rose sobs. "You can't."

"It's just energy. The people are long gone."

I really want to move out of their way, though. They're tingly.

She's too busy crying to answer. I think of her dog back in the A-belt, and I realize I don't know anything about her. Why she's here. Where her parents might be, if Mr. D is her uncle. How she developed killer tackling skills.

My hands are smushed behind me, and Rose is gripping my knees like she's got her own gravity. Tears track down her face, and her silver hair is wild around her head.

"OK," I say. "OK. Let's talk."

The soldiers and the boy are only a beginning. There's a woman in an empty room upstairs, opening invisible drawers as she searches for something she's lost. There's a captain talking into his comm and writing notes, late into the P-14 night.

We go back to the soldiers when I've seen the rest, to watch them pace. They screw up their formation, try again. March out of step, try again. Endlessly.

"You talk to them?" I ask. It doesn't seem likely; they ignore us, like holos in an enhanced reality program. If we could ask them, they'd be afraid of Rose; they'd think she and the Rocklings want to kill them.

Rose passes through the middle soldier to plop cross-legged in the corner, saucer ears drooping.

I wait for them to march by before joining her.

"All my friends are on A-7471," she says.

"And your dog."

She's not surprised I know about him. "And Chewy. Yeah. We don't...there aren't any ghosts in the A-belt. I've never heard of a non-human ghost at all. I really wanted to see one. So I came here and explored the museum, and I found a bunch."

Enough to feed a family of three until I'm old enough to get a real job.

Rose seems to know what I'm thinking. "You can't mine them, Maddie. They're safe here."

I want to repeat that it's just energy. There've been a gazillion tests to prove it. Atmospheric pressure readings and radar screenings and pass after pass with the best séance technology on the market.

But right now, I see three nervous ghosts running drills, again and again. Afraid.

They don't know the Rocklings will turn out to be our friends.

They don't know it's the other humans that might not be, that we'll show up to wrench the last shreds of them into capsules for space porters.

I sit back against the wall and bounce my head against my ponytail bump.

And I tell Rose everything. My brother's gambling and my parents' attempts to help, their debt, his disappearance. Our last house on P-1 and the ball course we made for Ginger.

"They brought us here for a fresh start," I finish.

Quick money. Quick fix. It never works that way.

The end of the story is hanging. Rose knows how few ghosts there are left to mine out here.

"Uncle D came for the same reasons, I guess," she sighs. "My parents sent me here to 'help' during the school break. While they 'figure out' their relationship."

Translation: while they decide whether to stay together. I get it.

"Seems no one can make money on P-14," she adds.

That makes me sit up. I look at her. "I hadn't seen ghosts before I came to P-14, either."

"They haven't figured out how to find them on P-1 yet."

It's kind of the whole point. Why their energy was never mined before. Some atmospheres won't show them, or won't hold them. No one knows.

"This place has a built-in audience," I continue. "We just need the right hook."

No one wants to look at glorified posters or stand and read Mr. D's dry stories about pre-ghost energy or the eighty-eight parts of an Ecto-hose (and how to clean it).

But they might want to see *real* ghosts.

I think I know how to save both our families.

Getting the word out is easy. I borrow a couple credits from Rose so I can ping the details to Aly, and I ask her to pass it on.

Which she does. Because the idea is so cool it'd thrive on P-14 like a polar bear, that's why.

Rose sends it to her friends, too, and by the time Mr. D gets back from Moon 7, our ad's gone viral. He's just standing there, jaw ajar, as he stares at the crowd in front of his museum. He can't even take a step without someone telling him to wait his turn.

Rose and I are selling admission tickets as fast as we can, and she's announcing, "The lonely wanderer emerges from the attic in approximately five minutes. If you have tickets, please make your way to the stairs."

"This viewing is sold out," I add, as people and Rocklings jostle closer. P-14's economy just got the boost of a lifetime. "But a game of tag will knock over the Pluto display upstairs in half a spin, and we've got a chicken crossing the coop in ten. Those are included in general admission."

We don't know why the chicken shows up and the dog doesn't. Ghost energy still has its mysteries.

"What is going on here?" Mr. D calls when he gets his vocal cords working. He's still stuck in the doorway.

"We added a few exhibits," Rose says. "You don't mind, Uncle D, do you?"

I can practically see credit tokens flashing in his eyes. Imagine how many history books he can buy with them. Bricks and bricks. "I think I'm going to need a bigger staff," he says.

We'd counted on that.

Mom and Dad are already clipping tickets in the courtyard.

"Maybe Planet 14 is more than just a pit stop, after all," Rose says.

Maybe she's right. Maybe I've got a new friend.

Next mission: convincing Mr. D to add sweatshirts to the gift shop.

The Most Important Job on the Ship

by Emily Martha Sorensen

Emily Martha Sorensen writes clean young adult, middle grade, and adult fantasy and science fiction. She's kind of an oddball, too! She has hair long enough to sit on (which she has no intention of cutting; why do people keep asking her that?), she has a rather loud laugh, she strikes up conversations with complete strangers, and she licks her plate at mealtimes — why wouldn't you, when the food is good?

She's published more than thirty books and more short stories. She draws two comics: *A Magical Roommate* and *To Prevent World Peace*. You can read more about her at www.emilymarthasorensen.com.

"So, what are you going to do for your Test Day?" Dad asked, prodding the spout in the middle of the table. A large bubble of water floated up, and he caught it in his cup. It splashed a little as he placed it on the table beside him.

"It's a secret," I said, taking a bite of my noodles. They were made from textured algae, like most of our food on this ship. We mostly carried things like meat and spices only for the alien passengers. It was a drag.

"Come on," Dad prodded, twirling his noodles around his fork to keep the sauce from dripping. It, at least, was not made from algae. It was made from powdered cream mixed with water when needed. On most noodles, it tasted pretty good.

"Nope," I said. "I wouldn't tell you even if you were the captain."

"I'm sure the secrecy doesn't apply to parents," he wheedled.

I snorted. "I'm sure it does."

Dad pouted while he shoveled a mouthful of noodles into his mouth. I scratched my left foot, which itched. Sometimes I wished both my feet were prosthetics. I never had to worry about my right foot itching, for one thing.

The door to our quarters opened, and Mom walked in. She looked haggard, pulling off both of her gloves of office without saying a word.

"Would you tell the *actual* captain?" Dad asked hopefully.

"Nope," I said. "Hey, Mom, you're late for dinner."

"Status reports," she said shortly. "So many status reports. Tomorrow I'm going to talk to the chief engineer about the meaning of *urgent*. Also, *delegating*."

Dad hid a smirk. The chief engineer was his boss, and he loved it when Mom griped about him. He and his boss had never gotten along. Then an exaggerated pout showed up on his face. "Astrid won't tell me what she's doing for her Test Day!"

"Good," Mom said. "She's not supposed to. If rumors went around before the requestee had a chance to say yes or no, it would pressure them to agree."

Dad scowled.

I stared at Mom, my heart hammering. Did that mean she hadn't read the message I had sent this morning? She might have mistaken it for a personal message and put it off till later . . .

Mom rolled up her captain's gloves. She unzipped the top of her shirt and tucked them into a hidden pocket, then zipped it back up again and clicked the top closed with a miniature fingerprint lock. She tapped the deflated ball by her place at the table with her foot, and it immediately inflated so that she could sit on it.

Mom ripped open the insulated cube sitting at her place on the table, and she pulled out her plateful of food and accompanying silverware. The cubes were edible and flavorless and were fortified with vitamins and nutrients just in case, but they had a woolly, off-putting texture, so most people just sent them back to the kitchens to be recycled into new cubes. Basically, they were meant to serve as a backup source of food to stave off hunger in case of emergencies.

We sat there in silence, eating.

I was starting to feel antsy. I surreptitiously used my free hand to pull out one of the gloves from my pocket, and summoned the display under the table. I tapped to pull up my messages and re-sent the one from this morning, now marking it "urgent."

"Astrid, are you checking something?" Mom asked suspiciously. "I've told you, no gloves at the table. Dinnertime is for conversation, not texting with your friends —"

A terribly annoying beep came from her interior breast pocket. Mom put a hand to her forehead then unzipped the front of her shirt to retrieve the gloves.

"Hypocrite," Dad teased.

"There's no choice," Mom sighed. "Someone sent me a message marked as urgent."

I held my breath as Mom pulled up her gloves and tapped her finger in midair to pull up her message display. It was invisible to everybody but her. Generally you could see other people's displays, just reversed as if the whole thing were shown in a mirror, but the captain's messages were always privacy-protected.

"WHAT?!" Mom shouted.

She'd gotten my message.

Mom looked up sharply. "Astrid, you must be kidding."

I straightened. "I'm not kidding. I have the right to request any job on the ship."

"And *I* have the right to refuse it."

"Hang on," Dad said, looking from one of us to the other. "Am I to understand you requested the *captain's* job for your Test Day?"

"Yes," I said.

"No," Mom shot back. "You didn't. We'll pretend this never happened, and you can ask somebody else instead."

"That's not how it works," I said, tightening my fist under the table. "I only get one request, and I've made it. If I pass, I'll be assigned your job once I've finished the minimum training."

"And if you *fail*," Mom said sharply, "you'll be assigned a generalist!"

I knew that. Did she think I didn't know that? On a ship of specialists, a generalist was considered the bottom of the heap.

In theory, a generalist could be the equal of any given specialist, and possibly several. But in practice, that wasn't how it worked. The only people who worked as generalists were failures. Nobody requested that job on purpose.

Generalists were necessary because they could substitute for any job they had completed the minimum training for. If somebody got sick or needed a vacation and they had no trainee, a generalist would fill in. But most generalists never bothered to complete the minimum training for the more prestigious jobs, since the training requirements for any of those would take years, and there was almost always a trainee to take over anyway.

So yes, I was taking a terrible risk.

"Why wouldn't you ask me before making an official request?" Mom exploded. "That's the usual protocol! What were you *thinking?*"

"I was thinking that you wouldn't give me a chance unless I backed you into it!" I shot back.

"Hey, hey!" Dad held up his hands. "No need to fight. Just refuse the request. Then she won't have a chance to fail, and she'll be assigned to some other job."

Mom eyed me. "*Why* do you want my job?"

That really ought to be obvious. I was the most qualified preteen on our cityship, and I knew it. "Because it's the most important job on the ship."

There was silence that stretched between us.

"I don't think you'll pass it," Mom said. "It would be better if I deny your request. You're good enough at most fields that you'll definitely be assigned a good job."

"I don't want you to deny the request," I said, setting my jaw. "I want the chance to prove myself."

"Even knowing the risks?" she asked.

"Even knowing the risks."

"Even though I'm almost certain it'll end in you being assigned a generalist?"

That hurt. Why did she have so little faith in me?

"Even knowing the risks," I repeated firmly.

Mom drummed the table with her fingertips. The table was inflatable, like all furniture on the ship, so it made dull thumping noises as she tapped the thick rubbery surface.

I looked her in the eyes. The waiting was driving me crazy, but I didn't want to look away, so I shifted my leg with the prosthetic up onto my lap and started squeezing the sides to eject it and then slip it back on again. Over and over again.

"Fine," she said at last, breaking eye contact and swiping her finger through her invisible display. "On your own head be it."

I burst out a loud cheer. I had my Test Day!

"But," Mom said sharply, "if you fail, I never want to hear you whine one second about being a generalist."

That was an easy condition to agree to. I had no intention of failing.

"No problem," I said confidently.

⊰🚀⊱

On the morning of my Test Day, I was awakened by a sharp

series of knocks on my door.

I rubbed my eyes blearily. I'd been so keyed up last night, I'd had an impossible time falling asleep. Apparently I'd managed it eventually, though.

Then I noticed the time display on my ceiling.

Holy heck! I slept through my alarm!

I scrambled out of bed and hopped the two steps to the doorway, not even bothering to shove on my prosthetic or turn the lights on or deflate the bed. I slammed my hand on the panel beside the door.

The door slid open smoothly, vanishing into the wall.

"Good morning," Mom said, holding her pair of captain's gloves out to me. "These will be yours for the next twelve hours. I assume you've studied all the relevant features and necessities."

"Y-yes," I stammered, grabbing them.

She made no comment about my still-inflated bed or sleepwear. "You can, at any time, cancel the test and ask me to take over again. Doing so will constitute an automatic failure. That would be wise to do if you feel the ship is in danger, however. Do you understand?"

"Y-yes." I squeezed the gloves in my hands. I had no intention of failing and giving up halfway through. If the ship wound up being in danger, I would handle it on my own.

"Good," Mom said. "I'll leave you to it."

She turned and walked the five steps from my bedroom door to the entrance of our quarters, tapping the panel lightly to open the door and step out through it. It closed behind her.

Cursing myself for sleeping through the alarm today of all days, I slammed the panel to shut my door and hopped the two steps across the room. I put on my prosthetic, careful to avoid the spots where squeezing would cause it to automatically eject, and used my real foot to stomp on the button to deflate the bed.

Once the bed was shrunk down and the room had more space,

I stuffed it into the corner it belonged in and turned to my closet.

"Closet" was probably too generous a word, given that it was a wall covered in flexible loops that had an article of clothing stuffed through each one. But it was the closest thing to a closet anybody on the ship had.

I yanked down half a red shirt, half a grey shirt, and three sections of pants — red, black, and grey. Everybody on the ship wore modular clothes; it was the best way to have variety when your maximum weight capacity for personal items was so small. Most people wore a lot more than three colors in a given outfit, but I was in a hurry, and I didn't have time to mix and match much smaller pieces. Besides, I figured particolor would look less authoritative than just a few colors, anyway.

I unhooked the sealant from its spot in the corner and laid out the pieces of clothing in the pattern I wanted. I gave them a quick spray, and the sealant hardened quickly, gluing them together in a seamless, flexible design. One of the seams over the bottom third of my pant legs wound up slightly lopsided, and I was tempted to grab the seal-remover from the hook beside the sealant so I could try again, but that would take precious minutes, and I couldn't afford any unnecessary delays.

Your pants always look lopsided on the right side anyway, I reminded myself, pulling the pants on. *Thanks to the prosthetic.*

The reason I wore a prosthetic was that my right leg ended at the knee. It wasn't an injury; it was a birth defect. Warp jumps had a one-in-one-thousand chance of causing birth defects in first trimester fetuses. I was one of the lucky few.

Dirtside passengers were required to do a routine pregnancy scan before they could board a starship, and by law they weren't allowed to board if pregnant unless they signed a dozen liability waivers. When you belonged to a cityship, though, there was little else you could do but accept the risks. That was why most prosthetic limbs belonged to cityship citizens.

I didn't mind. There were a hundred other people on board with similar problems, and at least I wasn't missing an arm. Really, the only reason it mattered was that I thought I looked weird in skirts, so I avoided them.

I pulled on my clothes and glanced at the ceiling again. Nearly five minutes had passed. I was going to have to run to reach the ship's core in time.

"Hi, Astrid!" Dad called as I ran down the hallway past him. He was unsealing a panel in the hallway that looked like somebody had knocked it askew. "Are you heading off to start your —?"

"No time!" I shouted. His job as a maintenance engineer started two hours earlier than Mom's job as captain, which was presumably why he hadn't been home to wake me up. Mom had no doubt been happy to let me sleep in, wanting to see me fail. "I'll see you later!"

"See you!" he called back, waving.

I glanced at the ceiling in the corridor and saw that I had only two minutes left to reach the core. I panicked and sprinted desperately.

The morning of my Test Day was off to a roaring start.

When I got to the core of the ship and held up my captain's gloves in front of the glowing red panel, I thought for a moment that the locked door wouldn't accept me. But then the panel turned green, and the door opened.

I stepped in, panting heavily. I felt a thrill of pride that I had been the one the door had let in, not Mom.

An unfriendly-looking Gotharn stood in the middle of the room with his arms folded. Since Gotharns looked kind of like *Tyrannosaurus rex*, down to the white feathers, the gesture looked absurd with his spindly little arms. It was a mannerism he had no doubt picked up from the other citizens, who were mostly human.

A rumbling growl came from his mouth. "You're late," the

translation box at his throat informed me.

I shook my head and doubled over, panting. "Not late. Ran all the way here. I —"

Rigel was already growling again.

"The captain is supposed to arrive ten minutes early," the box at his throat said in its usual monotone.

I stood up, indignant. "Well, that's not in the manual!"

The Gotharn rumbled. The box said, "It should be obvious."

I clenched my fists. I *had* planned to arrive early—and I was pretty mad at myself for sleeping in—but the fact of the matter was, I hadn't been late, and I refused to let him accuse me of it when I had, in fact, met the minimum.

Of course, fighting with your assistant had to be a definite no, even though that wasn't in the manual. So I kept from retorting, barely.

"Let's get started," I said briskly. I unbunched the gloves and tucked my hands into them. They had been molded after Mom's hands, and so they were slightly larger than mine. The fit wasn't so bad that I couldn't get used to it, though.

I pulled up the new display I had as captain, which presumably was what Mom looked at every single day. I stood there, savoring the moment.

The settings were turned to being contacted only in emergencies for everything, but I presumed that was because Mom hadn't been on duty before. I quickly changed the settings to maximum authorizations required for everything.

Then I tapped my prosthetic foot down on the switch near the center of the room, and the ball for sitting on inflated.

I took a seat and settled down to go to work.

Every time I got rid of one item on my to-do list, another five popped up to replace it. The proliferation of messages was even worse.

"Is it like this *every* day?" I asked in exasperation.

Rigel rumbled, "You might be requiring too many authorizations."

"No," I said, setting my jaw. "I'm the captain. I need to know everything that's going on in the ship."

The Gotharn growled. "No, you don't," his translation box said.

Ignoring his unhelpful advice, I opted to pick up the pace. A lot of the messages I was getting were duplicates, so I only needed to skim them, tap, skim, tap, skim, tap—oops, that one hadn't been a duplicate. What had I just approved?

"Can I take back an approval if I did it accidentally?" I asked nervously, finger hovering in midair.

"No," Rigel said.

"Who designed this system?" I exploded.

"People who didn't expect captains to turn on 'all approvals required,'" Rigel said unsubtly.

I was starting to hate these messages. It was amazing just how many were being generated. It seemed like there were two or three more every second.

Maybe Rigel was right. I hated to admit it, but this was too many for anyone to get through, even me.

"Fine," I said and I went back to my settings. I turned down the approval requirements by one notch in all categories. Now they were at nine, instead of ten. "Is that better?"

He growled. His translation box said, in its usual monotone, "If by 'better' you mean 'I just turned the settings to no authorizations required except for emergencies,' then yes."

"Mom only had it that way because she was off duty," I said huffily.

He rumbled. "No, she always keeps it that way."

I was annoyed, but I followed his advice with poor grace. I turned off all authorization requirements except for emergencies. By the time I finished, the number of messages that had proliferated thanks to the previous settings had more than doubled, but at least that stemmed the tide for now.

"Why is that setting even there if the captain never uses it?" I complained.

"Because, every so often, there's a good reason to use it in select places," Rigel growled, folding his puny arms again. He somehow managed to convey incredulity at my idiocy, despite the fact that his growls were unintelligible and the translation box spoke in a monotone. "In extreme emergencies, or in the case of someone who's brand new to the job, the captain might need to approve every little thing."

Fine, fine. It made logical sense. Mom was always talking about the importance of delegating. And of course, that was because the captain had more important things to do than approving things. I'd known that. The captain saved the ship on a regular basis.

I flicked my way through the pile of messages, approving everything, even the ones I didn't understand. By the time I got through all the hundreds of them, I was getting a headache. I stood up, stretched, tapped my non-prosthetic foot against the floor because it had fallen asleep, and then sat down again. I checked my to-do list, which should have populated automatically, but it was empty.

"Hey, Rigel?" I asked.

"Hmm?" He was fully absorbed in his own display and ignoring me.

"Why is my to-do list empty?"

"Mmm."

Neither he nor his translation box was being very helpful.

"Wanna hear a joke?" I asked.

He rumbled something so quiet that the box at his throat didn't even bother to translate it. No doubt because the Gotharn had no sense of humor whatsoever. The cityship had a betting pool on who could make him laugh first. It had been going for ten years, ever since he'd moved on board, and nobody had won yet.

"Two Gotharns boarded a cityship," I said. "The first one said, 'I think the temperature control is broken.' The second one said, 'Why is that?' The first one said, 'Because it's so cold.' The second one said, 'It isn't cold—you're molting, stupid!'"

I waited. Rigel made no response.

"Hello?" I hinted. "Molting?"

No reaction.

"Wanna pay some modicum of attention to me?" I asked.

He growled something soft that the box translated as, "Nnnn." He still didn't look up from his display.

So I hopped off the ball and stepped on his tail.

He let out a loud roar of fury, looking up from his display with fully bared teeth and glowing eyes. The translation box helpfully translated this: "Don't do that again."

"You're my assistant," I said. "Do your job. Assist me. What am I supposed to be doing?"

He growled, swishing his tail across the floor away from my reach. He went on growling and letting out quiet-but-threatening roars for a while. The translation box waited patiently until he was finished, and then repeated what he'd said in an intelligible language for me.

"You are supposed to do what captains are always supposed to do. You are supposed to wait for emergencies. A good captain is not needed for day-to-day operations. A good captain trains everyone so well that the captain is superfluous ninety-nine percent of the time. That is what good leadership means."

I stared at him in horror. "You can't mean that I'm supposed to sit here and do *nothing!*"

He growled and waved his flimsy little arms, the ones that looked so weak, they were almost vestigial. "You can entertain yourself, if you wish. I'm in the middle of a novel."

I was absolutely appalled. Here were two of the most capable, educated people on the entire ship, qualified to do almost any job, and their jobs were to do *nothing?*

I'd seen Rigel personally attack space pirates. I'd seen Mom stay awake for four days straight to argue for the lives of two of our citizens who'd been accused of murder while they were on vacation on a hostile dirtside world. I'd seen both of them yell (or in Rigel's case, roar) at high-ranking people who had failed to do their jobs properly.

That was what they'd done when I could see them. I had assumed that was what their jobs were like all the time. But the times when I didn't see them, it was . . . *this?*

It was this *boring?*

I sat there, feeling increasingly twitchy as I flipped through training manuals. I checked the ship's systems every few minutes, reread every status report and authorization message I'd gotten while I'd required them and carefully researched each one I hadn't understood. Nothing had gone awry. Nothing was amiss. I desperately wished something had, so that that I could fix it.

By the end of the day, I realized in horror, *I'll end up with nothing at all to prove that I can be a captain. I'm going to fail unless there's an emergency.*

This explained what Mom had meant when she'd thought I would fail. She'd figured this would happen. My blood boiled to think of it. She'd risked me being assigned a generalist just because she wanted her job security!

Well, I wasn't going to let her win. If an emergency wasn't forthcoming, I would *make* an emergency.

I summoned up one of the miniature repair robots, the kind that were meant to crawl through ducts to replace small parts or reweld microfractures, and I ordered it to drill through the outer hull in a place right near the second storage bay. The safety precautions came up, of course, but that was the nice thing about being the captain—I could override everything. I sent it to that spot, I rechecked the emergency protocols for that kind of problem, and then sat back to wait for the messages to pour in for emergency instructions.

They weren't long in coming.

Eight hours later, two hull breaches repaired, the rogue robot that had begun drilling a third hole captured, and the robot destroyed, my shift ended. I had been pacing and furiously barking orders for hours, and my throat was raw, and I was exhausted. In a good way, as I had accomplished something terribly important. I felt exhausted and satisfied.

I was concluding the last of my debriefs. An engineer was praising me for all my decisiveness and leadership, which was impressive given that it was my first day—

My display vanished.

"Hey!" I complained. "What happened?"

Rigel glanced over at me. He hadn't budged from his position all day. He had, apparently, been so engrossed in his novel that he had not considered it worth his time to offer his expertise. Or perhaps he'd just been waiting for me to ask for his aid.

Well, it was just as well. I'd been enjoying the glory too much to want to share it.

"I was being complimented," I snapped. "By the chief engineer! He said I handled the situation admirably, with decisiveness and aplomb, especially given that it was my first day. Why did the display disappear?"

Rigel said nothing, but he made his display visible and had it show the time in large numbers.

Oh. My Test Day was over. The gloves were no longer responding to me.

"I guess my shift is done," I said with disappointment.

Rigel growled softly. "So it is," his box said.

"Are you going to leave, too?" I asked.

He rumbled for a while. His box said, "No, I'm usually on duty during the hours your mother sleeps. I took a booster shot to stay awake through the hours I usually sleep so that I could be here to advise you on your Test Day."

Ouch. I almost felt bad that I'd ignored him so much. Still, his advice had been valuable near the beginning.

"Thank you," I said.

He growled softly. "You're welcome," the translation box said.

"Hey," I said brightly, "what do you get when you cross a Gotharn with a lightning bolt? Give up? It's fried chicken!"

Nothing.

"Fried chicken?" I said. "Get it? Because you kind of look like giant plucked chickens?"

He said nothing.

I sighed. It had been worth a try. I headed toward the door, and it opened to show Mom's angry face glaring at me.

Uh oh.

I moved to step out of the core, but instead, Mom stepped into it and held out her hand. I placed the gloves in it. The door swished shut behind her.

"Um, so how did I do?" I asked.

Mom glared at me.

My heart raced. "How did I do?" I repeated, in a rather higher pitch.

She said nothing. She pulled on the gloves and pulled up her invisible display. She tapped through several things and nodded sharply, then twisted her wrists to make it disappear.

"I was on the team that caught the robot," she said. "I told them to hold off the investigation until tomorrow. Thankfully, they listened to me. What were you *thinking?*"

I swallowed. "I was just thinking that—"

"Oh, I know what you were thinking," Mom broke in. "You

were thinking that you wanted to play the hero. Is that it?"
Feeling a little ashamed, I nodded.

Mom let out a long, explosive sigh. "Astrid, what were you *thinking?* You put every citizen on board in danger! You punched a hole in the helm!"

"Only a little one," I said.

"Two and a half," she snarled.

"The second and third weren't my idea!" I defended. "Those were the robot's! It must have gone off the rails after I altered its programming—"

"Which makes what you did even *worse!*" Mom shouted.

I gulped. Okay, yeah, she had a point.

"The funny thing is," Mom said in a tight voice, "if you had been willing to just sit there and wait patiently in case anyone needed you, you probably would have passed. You have the educational qualifications to handle emergencies, and goodness knows you have no problem giving orders. But I knew you didn't have the patience, the humility, or the discipline to wait until needed. You said the captain is the most important job on the ship, right?"

I nodded, feeling a huge lump in my throat. Was she saying I'd . . . failed?

"Well, that's exactly the wrong attitude," Mom said. "A good captain trains everyone else so well that their job is the *least* important one on the ship."

The least important job on the ship . . . I felt faint.

"Not only that," Mom said in a clipped voice, "a captain's job is not just to save the ship from emergencies. It's also to prevent emergencies from happening in the first place."

Which . . . I can now see is a thing I may have slightly misunderstood. I swallowed.

Rigel rumbled and growled for a while.

His box translated, "Overall, her temperament seems unsuitable to being a captain, and I agree that her manufacturing of an emergency was unwise in the extreme. Still, her potential is so high in most fields. It would be a shame to waste her as a generalist."

So Rigel knew all along that I'd manufactured that emergency? I wanted to die. No wonder he hadn't bothered to step in and help. He'd been politely allowing me to play the hero.

"I agree," Mom said in a clipped voice, "but this was the path she chose. I warned her of the risks. She chose to take them anyway. I'm not going to bend the rules for her. I don't believe in nepotism."

Tears stung at my eyes. So I'd failed. I had failed, hadn't I? Come to think of it, Mom hadn't actually said it.

"Did I . . . pass?" I ventured in a small voice.

"*No,* you didn't pass!" Mom roared. "I can't believe you even asked that! You failed!"

I shrank down into myself.

I'd failed. Me. I'd be a generalist. *Me!*

Suddenly, I was angry. I was so angry that I wanted to hurt somebody. I needed something to throw, but there was nothing on hand, so I reached down to squeeze the spots on my prosthetic and wrenched it off. I launched it through the air, and it thudded really loudly into the wall.

"Honestly —" Mom began indignantly.

Then it bounced and konked Rigel hard on the head.

Rigel let out blood-curdling roar unlike anything else I'd ever heard before. It went on forever and ever and ever, each scream more terrifying than the last.

"HA HA HA HA HA," the translation box at his throat informed us.

Wait.

"Were you *laughing?*" I burst out.

Rigel's tail swished back and forth. He growled with great dignity.

"Of course not. Don't be silly," his translation box said.

"You *were!*" I accused. "You were laughing!"

Rigel rumbled quickly. "I would never do any such thing."

Mom's lips trembled. She was looking amused.

Rigel growled. "I fail to see what's so funny," the translation box said.

I hopped over and held out my hand, mimicking his great dignity. "May I have my half-leg back, please?"

Mom burst out in a long snort of laughter.

With an air of feeling very put-upon, the Gotharn kicked my prosthetic half-leg over to me. I scooped it up from the floor and reattached it to my knee.

Mom and I caught each other's eye, and we burst out laughing, doubled over. It had been a long time since we'd laughed together. It felt like years.

"Go home," Mom said at last, sobering. "You'll start as a generalist tomorrow."

I nodded. There was no point in arguing. I had said I wouldn't complain, so now I had to live up to it.

I adjusted my prosthetic to fit comfortably, went to the door, walked out, and headed down the hallway.

The worst thing possible had happened. I was a generalist.

And yet, it didn't seem like a complete and total defeat. After all, I'd made a Gotharn laugh. A person who could do that could do anything.

Maybe they could even make an overqualified generalist the most important job on the ship.

Asmodeus Flight

by Siobhan Carroll

Siobhan Carroll is an English professor who lives in Philadelphia. Before she was twelve, she had discovered a tomb, ridden in an air balloon over the desert, and almost been eaten by lions and crocodiles. Now she reads books for a living. For more of Siobhan Carroll's fiction, see http://voncarr-siobhan-carroll.blogspot.com/

The day she turned eleven, Effie's father showed her how to die. "Even the best aeronaut can be taken down by a spark," he said, his hand tracing the air between the Asmodeus engine and the oil-varnished paper over their heads. Effie swallowed. The ground below the air balloon looked unreal now, falling away into a picture of farmland and houses. But the hot flame that licked and danced before her—that threat seemed real.

Effie's father hesitated, studying the engine's blue glow. Carefully, very carefully, he reached out as if to take the brass globe off its resting place. Effie braced herself but relaxed when she saw her father was not actually going to touch the engine's surface.

"Mr. Sadler, when he was going down, kept his wits about him." Her father mimed pulling at the two rolling hitches that tied the globe to the brass circle. "He undid the fastenings, and . . ." He pressed an invisible globe to his face and mimed blowing his last breath into the smallest of the three valves on the engine.

Effie watched, amazed. She had glimpsed her father making this gesture before, through doorways, when he thought he was alone. She had not realized he was rehearsing his death. If she hadn't been so captivated by his performance, the realization might have chilled her.

"And that's it," her father said, returning his hands to the sides of the globe, framing the flickering blue grate. "That's him in there. Mr. Sadler's ghost. Still flying after all these years."

At a thousand feet, the air around them was clear and cool. The sun glowed red and blue through the paper of the *Dover*, and below them, the world was spreading out like a map in green and gold. But what Effie noticed was the reverence on her father's face as he watched his old friend dance in the air balloon's hot engine.

Four years later when the news of the accident reached them, the memory of that moment made it easier for Effie to compose herself. She walked through the white glare of shock, past her sobbing mother, and approached the gentleman standing awkwardly in the entrance hall.

"Thank you for retrieving it," Effie heard herself say. She watched her hands pluck the globe from the stranger's hands. The engine's surface was cool to the touch, and for a moment, it felt unfamiliar. But peering down through the grate, she saw two blue undulations. The ghosts of Mr. Sadler and her father. "Thank you," Effie said again. "It's what he would have wanted." And she hugged the globe as though she herself were already falling from the heavens, as though it were her own death and not her father's that she had been called to witness.

"It's no' for sale."

Effie didn't bother looking up from her knots. The redoubtable Mrs. Brown was as adept at dispatching gentleman buyers as she was in dealing with local tradesmen. Despite her limited height—Effie's assistant measured only four feet three inches to the objective gaze—Mrs. Brown somehow still managed to loom at people. Effie could practically hear her looming now.

"It's no' for sale young man—and don't you go shaking that puss a' me. D'ye think we're country faffle you can swindle with your sing-time songs? Off wi' ye."

"But Mr. Baxter—"

"Mr. Baxter'll be hearing his man's portuning puir wimmin like a common ragart!"

Effie straightened up in time to see the young servant cower away from Mrs. Brown, his face displaying the confusion that typically attended her barrages of (partly invented) dialect. He obviously wasn't sure what he had been accused of but suspected it was deeply improper.

Taking pity, Effie wiped her hands with the stain-rag. "Is that Mr. Stanley Baxter of Endsgate?"

"The same!" The young man's eager-to-please face dissolved in alarm when he realized he might have committed another faux pas. "Er, Madam—"

"You're new to service, I take it? I am to be addressed as Miss Mitchell. And you are?"

"Fielding, Ma-Miss Mitchell. Samuel Fielding."

"Well, Mr. Fielding," Effie said, "Please, tell your master that we are not entertaining offers for the engine, now or in the future."

"Miss Mitchell," Fielding shifted uncomfortably. "Mr. Baxter said you'd say that. He said to say . . ." (The young man closed his eyes, evidently trying to recall the message exactly.) "I cannot imagine my fleet without a high balloon like the *Dover.* Therefore, I am proposing to hire the services of Miss Mitchell, her assistant, the balloon, and the *Dover*'s Asmodeus engine, for £2,000."

Mrs. Brown sucked in a sharp breath. Effie tried to keep her face still while her mind raced. Two thousand pounds! The balloon itself was only worth a hundred. The engine, true, was worth more—how much more was unclear these days, given

Parliament's ban on West Indies aether and the old aeronautical families' reluctance to part with their engines. But £2,000!
With that money, she could secure a land lease for her mother
and still have years' worth of income set aside.

"Tell your master I will consider his generous offer." Feeling a flare
of pride, Effie added, "Though my answer will probably still be
the same." She flushed, wondering if she sounded childish.

Fielding appeared not to notice. "Thank you! Miss. Uh. Mrs."
He slid out a rolled piece of paper—evidently a contract—and
dropped it on the counter. He managed an awkward bow to
her and a hesitating bob in the direction of Mrs. Brown before
fleeing down the street.

"What's that about?" Mrs. Brown's dialect was sheathed now
that combat was over.

Effie gazed after the servant, her mind racing. "It's the Exhibition," she decided finally. "Mr. Baxter has his aerial display
planned for the solstice. To truly outdo Mr. Green, he needs to
put a ship close to the Crystal Palace."

Mrs. Brown sniffed. "He wilna do it wi' those lumbrin'
creechurs."

"Not the dirigibles," Effie agreed. The new inventions might be
cheaper to fly than Asmodeus balloons, but they were clumsy.

"If he hadn'e wrecked his own, he wouldn'e be looking," Mrs.
Brown observed.

Effie nodded. Mr. Baxter had lost his *Witch of Atlas* some years
ago after launching his balloon in a brewing storm. Since then,
he had gained a reputation as a man who had gambled much
of his family's money away at card tables but then won it back
with some clever investments in the colonies. A dubious sort of
man.

"It would be a lot of money for Mother." Effie was suddenly aware that she had been toying with the rag in her hand,
smearing her fingers with oil in the process. She re-wiped
them, but it was too late: the telltale stains had crept into the

cracks of her knuckles. "I'll have to consult with her."

As she turned away, two things flickered at the edge of Effie's perception that, in retrospect, she would wish she'd paid attention to. The first was the blue smudge the contract's seal left on the counter. The second was a figure in the crowd whose posture strongly reminded Effie of Mr. Baxter. But why would Mr. Baxter watch his own servant's delivery? Effie looked back. The man had vanished into the churn of the London street.

That night, Effie lay awake fretting over Mr. Baxter's offer. Her father's marriage bond guaranteed Effie's mother a small stipend, and Effie's aeronautical demonstrations brought in occasional tides of money. But a reliable source of income would be useful. Unlike the marriage proposals Effie had fielded in recent years, Baxter's offer would also enable her to keep flying. What then was the source of her unease?

Something kept turning at the back of her mind—a smudge of blue as though from a hex seal. Though that was impossible.

Around three in the morning, Effie realized her decision was already made. The Asmodeus engine was her family's legacy. She would not sell it for a million pounds.

Thankful for an excuse to close her eyes, she rolled onto her side.

She was woken by a clamor outside.

Lurching up, Effie saw the orange glow at her window and knew.

She plummeted down the stairs in a rush of dark. Figures clustered uselessly in front of the workshop, lit by orange and yellow.

"Fire!" someone hollered, but Effie was already running past them, her bare feet bruising the ground, her nightdress—*improper*, part of her noted—a frustrating drag on the night air. Sparks floated up from the workshop—*Even the best aeronaut can be taken down by one*, she thought—and she struggled with the massive padlock, forcing in her necklace key while some faint voice behind her cried "Miss! Please don't!"

The workshop was a blaze of heat, its walls moving fire. Eyes stinging, Effie dropped to her knees, where the pure air was thickest. She crawled toward the safe. No good saving the *Dover's* paper now. That and the galley she'd stained were gone, but neither of these things were the heart of an Asmodeus balloon.

Something crashed beside her, letting in a gust of air. *I might die here, on the ground of all places*—but Effie set that thought aside. The entire world came down to this: feeling her way to the mercifully cool metal of the safe.

It was empty.

Effie groped inside the space the Asmodeus engine should be. It couldn't not be here.

Suddenly, hard arms yanked her away. She struggled, trying to protest, but her burning lungs lacked air. She was dragged backward through the flaring dark. She was on cold ground, rolling and coughing while ice water drenched her body. Pushing herself up on a numb arm, Effie saw her father's workshop collapse in a shower of sparks.

"Today," Effie said grimly.

Mrs. Brown glanced sideways. Since the fire, she'd treated her young mistress cautiously, as though Effie were one of her mother's fine Wedgwood cups. "There's no proof Mr. Baxter had owt to do with the fire—"

Effie shook her head, unwilling to replay her frustrating conversations with Scotland Yard. "He offered that contract to cover himself," she muttered. "Nobody will suspect a 'gentleman' of stealing an item he was about to purchase. He knew I'd refuse. The contract seal was hexed. It silenced our alarms—"

"Oh aye," Mrs. Brown agreed, "but coppers want proof if they're to lay hands on a gen'l'man." For a moment, Mrs. Brown looked abstracted, perhaps reflecting on some episode

from her mysterious past. Then she said, "If you're caught
filching, it'll be a hard sing. They won't drop you, miss, but—"
"I'll sell my confession to the newspapers," Effie said, her chin
jutting defiance. "It'll be a scandal."
"He'll shirk about for a day or two," Mrs. Brown agreed.
"They'll clap you in Bedlam a mite longer."
Effie had visited Bedlam once, and her recollection of that
tour—which had, after all, only shown the Ladies' Botanical
Club the respectable cells—brought her up cold. "You think
they'd do that?"
Mrs. Brown gazed at her with flat, hard eyes. "If you weren't
respectable, miss," she said, "you'd already be there."
Effie swallowed, taking in Mrs. Brown's meaningful glance at
her unusual dress with its flexible stays and higher petticoats.
The sideways glances of the shuffling crowd suddenly struck
her as menacing. It was one thing to attract such glances as a
female aeronaut with a balloon—an outré figure to be sure, but
one protected by the aura of British science. But as an oddly
dressed woman without a balloon, she suddenly felt her vulner-
ability keenly.
"Still," Effie said, hearing the stubbornness in her voice and
half hating herself for it. "We're going to find it. Today."
She turned, craning her neck to catch sight of the aerial fleet
bobbing behind the Crystal Palace. There was Mr. Green's
Nassau, the largest Asmodeus balloon ever built, turning in
the breeze like a glorious red-and-blue planet. There was an
old-fashioned Montgolfier. There were passenger vessels, taking
paying customers up in cautious trips to view the top of the
palace. And then there were the detestable Mr. Baxter's dirigibles, hovering at a distance from the rest.
Effie and Mrs. Brown dutifully filed in with the shilling crowd.
The Great Exhibition had attracted a seething mixture of
nationalities—scar-faced Americans, queue-sporting Chinese,
green-scaled Inner Earthers—even an odd Frenchman, the latter

drawing suspicious glances from John Bull and continental exiles alike. But nominally, at least, the *Pax Francia* treaty still held. The Frenchman wafted through the crowd, an unhappy-looking security agent plodding in his wake.

Under different circumstances, Effie might have joined the crowd in gaping at the Crystal Palace's dazzle of fabrics, its pink diamonds and arching dinosaur bones. As it was, she and Mrs. Brown had one destination in mind: the great aerial docks, futuristically imagined.

The crowd entered the observation platform for the docks. Upturned faces gawped at the shadows of dirigibles and at the statues commemorating aeronautical luminaries: Joseph Priestly, whose quest for pure air had led to the isolation of the aetherial element; the Montgolfier brothers, who had first demonstrated humanity's capacity for flight; and lastly, Sir Humphry Davy, who had successfully driven Napoleon from England's skies only to expire from his wounds in the Battle of Britain's final hour. A bouquet of flowers lay at Davy's feet. Two guards stood on either side of the display case for the *Veritas's* engine, scanning the crowd. No doubt they were looking for the usual dangers: foreign agitators and religious enthusiasts who mistakenly identified aether "ghosts" with immortal souls.

Forgetting herself, Effie pressed forward with the rest of the crowd for a glimpse of Davy's ghost circling its brass confines. "Miss," Mrs. Brown whispered. Reluctantly, Effie pulled back. Now that they had actually arrived, she could feel an anxious pit forming in her stomach. She *ahemed* some distracted laborers out of her way. Behind her, she heard a series of surprised wheezes as Mrs. Brown, unconstrained by social niceties, elbowed her way to the front of the platform.

"'Ere you!" Mrs. Brown thundered. "What's this!"

Effie ducked under the guard rope as the crowd behind her exploded into shrieks of alarm. "Grenado!" someone shouted. "He's workin' for Boney!" Mrs. Brown declared.

As Effie swung herself over the raised platform, she glimpsed a Vril'ya splayed to the floor by one of the guards, its yellow eyes wide with astonishment. Effie found herself hoping the guards would figure out quickly that the "grenado" Mrs. Brown had planted on the Inner Earther was a dummy.

In the shadow of the now-chaotic platform Effie whipped off her skirt, revealing the aeronaut's trousers underneath. She pinned the forged performer's ribbon to her collar, tucked in her pocket, and started forward, trying to look as though she had somewhere to be.

Nobody challenged her as she walked into the aeronauts' workshop. She strode between the benches, trying to glance surreptitiously at each station she passed. In her pocket, the Hobbs pick-lock chafed uncomfortably against her leg. "It'll open all but cold iron, miss," Mrs. Brown had promised. Under different circumstances, Effie would have been taken aback by her servant's familiarity with such devices, but now was not the time to ask questions.

Then she saw the gold-and-purple colors of the *Donna Julia*. Effie slowed to an amble, smiling vaguely at the young men sanding the tackle blocks. They did a double take when they saw her, eyes wide at the sight of a female aeronaut. Effie let her gaze float over the workstation. She saw no safe.

"I'm the new pilot," she said pleasantly. "Mr. Baxter's new engine wants airing. Where am I to get it from?"

It was a gamble, of course. But if Baxter had stolen her engine— *and he did*, Effie thought furiously—it had to be somewhere nearby.

The two men looked both amazed and blank. Then the first one waved his hand at someone behind her. "Oi! Fielding! The miss is looking for a new engine."

Effie turned to see Baxter's mop-haired servant bounding toward them. The air seemed to freeze around her. Fielding's pleasant face changed expressions in slow motion, first taking on a look of surprise and then one of happy recognition.

"Miss Mitchell! What a—I'm glad to see you're back on the field! That is," he said, remembering himself, "Mr. Baxter will be glad. He was terribly disappointed to hear you wouldn't be joining us. What a horrible thing! That fire! Did you lose much of the workshop?"

Effie stared. If Fielding was a liar, he was the best she'd ever encountered.

"The *Dover* won't fly this season, I'm afraid." She smiled, delivering the line she and Mrs. Brown had practiced. "One of my father's friends invited me to assist today. Alongside my chaperone, of course," she added, remembering balloons' dubious reputation as French inventions.

She blushed, and Mr. Fielding blushed. No progress whatsoever occurred until one of the sanders said, "The miss wants a look at the new engine?"

Fielding practically bounced with joy. "He told you about the engine!" Catching himself, he lowered his voice. "It's a remarkable innovation, Miss Mitchell. You have to see it!"

Smiling tensely, Effie followed Fielding out of the workshop and toward the looming dirigibles. They looked like something out of an antediluvian nightmare, huge and iron grey. It was hard not to believe the Nonconformists were right when they said the burning of fossilized aether—the very innovation that had permitted the elimination of the West Indies trade—infected their crafts with the souls of ancient beasts. Effie shivered in the bright sunlight, feeling as though she were indeed coming into the territory of massive predators.

"Mr. Baxter!" Fielding waved his hands toward one of the figures examining the strain on an almost filled dirigible. Baxter—a slender man clad in impractical ruffles—froze. His expression told Effie all she needed to know.

Certainty exploded into rage. She pointed at him. "Thief!" she yelled. "Arsonist!"

This was not part of the plan. Neither, however, was Mr. Baxter's reaction: to lean over the galley and order one of his men to cast off the bowlines.

Effie took off at a run. The bowline had just left its mooring post when Effie caught hold of it. Forgetting any pretense of propriety, she launched herself up the rope, hand over hand.

Below, she saw the shadow of the balloon drift away from the ground and a bewildered Fielding being pulled into the air by the bowline's loop. She hoped the man had the sense to let go before they were too high. Effie, having abandoned all sense, hauled herself up into the galley, almost at the feet of a frightened-looking Baxter.

"You!" she puffed. "Stole! My! Engine!"

Baxter raised his hands as if in protest. "I needed to show it could be done!" He gestured toward the dirigible's glowing engine. Following his gesture, Effie saw, to her horror, a familiar brass globe burning blue within the green flame of an Owen engine. He'd stacked the two devices, a combination of power that ought to be impossible and that would—she saw now—grant this dirigible more maneuverability than it had ever had before.

She realized her mistake a second later when a blow to the side of her head blackened her vision. Effie crashed onto the galley deck. Above her, Baxter wielded a heavy pole. "I didn't mean to kill you," he apologized. "If you only understood! I've seen the future, you see. In the emperor's telescope. Napoleon's got a new alliance. The men from Mars and their mechanical ships. They'll invade from the sky and turn England red."

A well-placed kick cut short the madman's rant. Effie scrambled away, her head throbbing. Somehow, in all her scheming, she had never envisioned the possibility of dying. *If only I can get my engine back*, she thought wildly, *it'll be worth it.*

Her hair was yanked backward. Effie had to clutch a cleat to keep from falling. In the corner of her eye, she saw the dark shape of the pole coming for her and turned away. But before it hit, there was a crash behind her, and the grip on her hair loosened.

Mr. Fielding, having pulled himself on board the airship, was apparently terminating his employment with his fists. "Working for Boney, is it?" he yelled. "You Frenchified villain!"

Effie hauled herself up. It wasn't just her head wound, she realized. The dirigible was listing. With a mind of its own, the monstrous airship was heading straight for the Crystal Palace. The sharp point of a British flagpole sailed into view.

"Brace!" she yelled, her training leaping to the fore. Effie pulled into four-point contact with the galley as the shatter of glass announced the worst. Glancing down, she saw Baxter push the overbalanced Fielding overboard—and was relieved to see the servant tumble onto one of the Palace's iron ribs, just missing a fall through its glass ceiling. The dirigible leapt free.

"No, no, no!" Baxter, his face bleeding, launched himself at the helm. "Why aren't you working?" Buckets of tools skidded down the deck as the dirigible's tilt increased.

Effie, hearing the hiss of air above, knew. Wasn't this the moment she'd practiced since she was eleven years old? Carefully, she reached for a loose line, found its tension, and slid down toward the engines.

All the fight seemed to have gone out of Baxter. He stared up at the dirigible's sagging envelope like a blind man. "It can't be."

Effie landed on the engine's frame. The heat from the fire was excruciating, but she had no time. Even as Baxter turned, she was already snatching the blistering Asmodeus engine from the flames, already raising it—

"No!" Baxter grabbed at her.

And suddenly he was falling, and she was following, the green ground rushing up to meet them both.

The wind was loud around Effie. Screechingly loud. She tried to drag the engine toward her face. *This is how you die*, her father had said.

The engine pulled away from her. It twisted underneath her, crunching into her abdomen, forcing her upward. The wind died. Below her, a tiny figure—Baxter—hit the ground. Effie turned her face away. Her own fall had slowed to a crawl. The hard fist of the engine pushed her up, the fierce heat of her family's ghosts lowering her gently to Earth.

The engine deposited Effie, burned and bleeding, in the middle of Hyde Park. Energy expended, it settled in the grass beside her. She stared at it as the running people approached. *Something new has been discovered today*, she thought dazedly. The Asmodeus ghosts were still conscious. And they could move independently, without flame. Shapes were aligning different-ly in her head: the famous dexterity of Asmodeus craft, the hideous accidents attending West Indies "slave" balloons, the alien ponderousness of the dirigibles. And somewhere, too, she was remembering what Baxter had said about the Continental Emperor and Mars and an invasion. She wasn't sure how it all fit together yet.

In later years, Effie would say she'd felt the shadow of destiny in that moment. That for a brief second, the Asmodeus engine had shown her the shape of things to come.

But the moment passed. A crowd raced across the green. The determined shape of Mrs. Brown led them, and, behind her, a limping Fielding looked confused.

Effie glanced down at the gleaming engine sitting on the grass, its familiar ghosts circling contentedly.

"Thank you," the next aerial admiral said. And she clambered up to greet the future.

The Lighthouse

by Alyssa N. Vaughn

Alyssa N. Vaughn is a writer and teacher from Dallas, Texas, where she lives with her husband, son, and two dogs. The Lighthouse is dedicated to her Grandad. You can follow Alyssa on Twitter @msalyssaenvy or visit her website at blog.anvaughn.com

People say manning the lighthouse must be lonely work.

"Not at all," my grandfather will tell them, smiling at his own terrible joke. "It's work, and then it's lonely."

While my father was deployed on a deep-space vessel, and my mother was busy preparing for a conference on advances in the field of teleportation, I was packed up and sent off to stay at my grandfather's lighthouse.

It was a longer journey than I'd ever been on before, and the ship had to be specially chartered. The pilot asked me how it felt to be going all the way to the edge of the galaxy; I shrugged. I was only ten, and I had already been to over thirty colonies and space stations with my parents. The edge of the galaxy didn't seem like a big deal. Besides, I hated talking to grown-ups.

I didn't start feeling suspicious until we landed. The spaceport docks were enormous, big enough to hold a colony ship, maybe even two. But, except for our ship and one battered-looking passenger pod, it was completely empty. The pilot walked me through the port and out onto the planet. We were on a sort of boardwalk, looking down over a beach. The sun was setting, and the brilliant blaze flashed off the gentle, crashing waves. Farther down the beach, the boardwalk branched off, leading to a tall, striped tower. I had never seen an old Earth-style lighthouse, but I wasn't particularly impressed with it. The pilot, however, got a little misty-eyed, though he tried to hide it by complaining of the glare of the sun off the sea.

The door stood open, waiting for us. It looked cozy with warm light spilling from inside, lighting up the windows with their boxes of flowers.

My grandfather met us at the door; he was a tall, thin man with snow-white hair and a significant bald spot. His leather-brown skin seemed to hang off him in places, like a piece of clothing he was expected to grow into. He reminded me of a particular tool my father kept in his work belt—outdated, worn, and unfashionable, but sturdy and nearly unbreakable.

He cried out a welcome and ushered us into his kitchen, seating the both of us at a wooden table and bustling about, getting coffee for the pilot and a mug of hot chocolate for me. My grandfather spoke easily to both of us, and the pilot eagerly conversed with him in return. Every so often the pilot would stammer and blush as though he had said something foolish, and my grandfather would pat his hand kindly, although I never understood what there was to be embarrassed about. Normally in the company of two grown-ups, I would have felt overlooked and left out, but Grandfather had a way of bringing all of us into conversation together, with his bright smile and easy ways.

Still, as the evening wore on and I watched the way the pilot listened wide-eyed to my grandfather's stories, I came to realize how different this man was to the grandfather I knew from visits away from the lighthouse. He was always kind, easy-going, and what my mother called a bit of a talker, but when he visited us wherever we were currently making berth, he had a way of compacting himself, folding himself up. It was as if he was trying to make more room for us, for our lives and our stories. In that tiny kitchen, his long legs stretched out underneath the table, his feet poking out from the other side. His voice filled the room like a cozy haze of tobacco smoke, thick and sweet and familiar.

That night, after we saw the pilot off, Grandfather tucked me into a little bunk in the room behind the kitchen. Like most of the lighthouse, the room was small and a bit crowded with furniture but undeniably comfortable. I went to sleep feeling contented and significantly less apprehensive about my stay.

In the morning, Grandfather put me to work.

Everything in the living quarters needed to be cleaned and tidied; corners swept, baseboards brushed, furniture polished, and shelves dusted. He did it all by hand, explaining that the furniture was actually antique old-Earth furniture that had been shipped all the way to the lighthouse, and that using any kind of robotic cleaner would certainly have meant some damage.

I probably could have understood that, but he also hand-polished the lenses of the telescopic viewers in the observatory and washed the windows by hand as well! The observatory was the only room in the whole lighthouse that didn't look as though it had been copied from an old-Earth photograph. It reminded me of the launch bay of the space station my father had been stationed at the year before, empty except for a few benches and a couple of monitors. It was like walking into an entirely different building, so bare and austere compared with the comfort of the other rooms. The one redeeming quality was its wall of huge windows that looked over the sea and up toward the enormous expanse of sky.

I don't think I ever worked so hard my entire life, but through it all my grandfather whistled and sang, told jokes and stories, and made the whole lighthouse echo with our voices. When

I collapsed into a kitchen chair at lunchtime, he set a bowl of steaming tomato soup and a grilled cheese sandwich in front of me, beaming with pride.

"I'm so glad you're here," he said, resting his hand on my shoulder. There was such sincerity in his voice as he said it, and warmth in his eyes. "You know our family has manned this lighthouse for over a hundred years. It's very important work, and now you're a part of it." He gave my shoulder a squeeze and turned back to make his own lunch.

I hunched down over my soup, the satisfaction of my work tainted by something akin to shame. I had now been up and down and all over every square inch of the lighthouse, and I still didn't understand why my grandfather lived there or what kind of work he did.

My mother was a physicist, and I'd seen the laboratories where she did her experiments and the long reports where she explained the results of her experiments and what they meant. My father was a mechanical engineer, and he specialized in understanding how interplanetary transports worked and how to keep them running. I knew where Grandfather worked, and I could understand that it took a lot of time and dedication to keep the lighthouse clean and running. I just didn't understand why it was important.

For the first few weeks, we cleaned and cleaned then sat at the kitchen table and ate Grandfather's delicious cooking while I did my lessons and Grandfather fiddled with old-Earth machines like radios and record players. He always had one eye on the view screen in the corner of the kitchen, although he pretended he wasn't paying much attention to it. Every once in a while, I would do some research. On old Earth, lighthouses showed boats that they were getting close to rocky shores at night or in bad weather.

That only confused me more. There were no boats on this planet. There weren't even any other buildings or people—just

Grandfather and me. As time passed, I thought if I had just asked on that first day, it wouldn't have been so bad. The longer I stayed at the lighthouse, the worse it would be if I didn't figure it out for myself. I imagined myself all grown up and my grandfather asking me if I wanted to take over the lighthouse, and having to admit that I didn't understand the job. I resigned myself to an embarrassing conversation but one that I hoped to be able to have with my mother much, much later and far, far away.

Then one day, they came.

A group of deep-space explorers, back from a mission. They hailed Grandfather and were soon docking and practically running up to Grandfather's door. They looked haggard and sickly to me; they had dark circles around their eyes, and they all had gray-green tinges to their skin. They moved strangely, as though their bodies had been still for too long, and when they held onto things, their knuckles turned white from their tight grips.

Still, Grandfather greeted them just as warmly as he'd welcomed me, fed them, and listened to the story of their travels; he even walked them into their rooms and told them good night, although he didn't go as far as to actually tuck them in.

I waited until they had all gone to sleep, and then I hurried to my grandfather, who was making bread in the kitchen for the next day's meals.

"What's wrong with them?" I whispered. "Do they have some kind of virus? Can infectious bacteria exist in deep space?"

Grandfather shook his head slowly as he finished kneading the dough.

"Nothing medically wrong with them. They just need rest," he said, setting the dough aside to rise. "Come help me in the greenhouse. We'll need more potatoes for tomorrow."

They rested at the lighthouse for almost a week, talking with Grandfather, eating his cooking, and walking along the beach, staring out at the waves. I tried to avoid them at first, but whichever room Grandfather sent me to clean (except for the perpetually empty observatory) seemed to have one or two of them sitting in it, talking quietly or staring out the window. They smiled at me when they saw me, but they didn't try to make me talk to them.

I decided that whatever was wrong with them, it must not be *terribly* wrong.

After a couple of days of good, warm food, nights of comfortable sleep, and listening to Grandfather's stories, most of the crew started looking and acting more like normal people. They stretched out their legs under the kitchen table, they borrowed Grandfather's fishing rods and sat out on the boardwalk in the sun, they persuaded the first officer to let them bury him in the sand.

One of the crew, a botanist named Waceera, wouldn't leave the lighthouse. She sat by a window, wrapped in a thick quilt, and stared into a mug of tea or out at the waves. Grandfather would sit with her, and they would talk quietly. He sent me up to keep her company one afternoon. I just read a book next to her and never said a single thing, but when Grandfather called us down for dinner, she said "Thank you."

I knew that the crew didn't just have *something* to do with Grandfather's work in the lighthouse. The crew was the *reason* for Grandfather's work in the lighthouse. But I still didn't understand. My own father had been on missions like the one this crew had just returned from—he was on one at that very moment—but he had always been completely normal when he came back to my mother and me.

The day they were preparing to leave, some of the crew went back to their ship to get ready, and some of them went and sat on the beach before packing their things, "just for a bit longer," they said. I found Grandfather in the observatory with their captain. They were cleaning the big window together. It was strange to see anyone other than Grandfather in the observatory; all the crew seemed to avoid it completely. It reminded me of the way my mother's dog refused to go near the bathroom after its last bath. It was as if an unsavory memory was waiting for them, or an unpleasant task would be forced on them as soon as they entered the observatory.

Grandfather and the captain were working steadily and speaking quietly without looking at each other. They seemed equally intent on their work as on their conversation, and they didn't notice me as I came in behind them.

"She's not ready, you can see it on her face, but she won't speak for herself." The captain sounded frustrated.

"That's the way with many of the ones I've seen. They see the deepness and the emptiness out there, and they can't do anything but shut down." My grandfather's voice was gentle. "She won't say anything because she can't—especially when she thinks she's the only one that can't cope."

"She's only twenty." The captain's shoulders drooped, and my grandfather reached out and placed a hand on his back, reassuring and warm in that cold room.

I turned and hurried out before they could see me. I knew I wasn't meant to hear what they were talking about. I thought I had better go sit with Waceera for a bit, though. She was the only crew member other than the captain still in the lighthouse.

I clumsily made up the kind of tray Grandfather usually prepared—masala tea, thick slices of bread with butter—although there were more drips and crumbs than there would have been if Grandfather had done it himself. She was still sitting by her usual window with a quilt across her lap, watching the others stand on the shore, playing and laughing as if they were my age.

I set the tray on her lap and climbed up next to her.

"Here," I said awkwardly and mostly out of breath after climbing the stairs. "I know you didn't eat much at breakfast."

She looked startled but managed something like a smile.

"Thank you." Her voice was quiet, and it still had that strained sound that so many of the crew had when they arrived, like they'd been silent for such a long time that their voice boxes had rusted shut.

"The tea will be good for your throat," I said without thinking, and then I blushed a bit, thinking of how Grandfather had insisted that none of the crew were ill. But Waceera didn't seem to mind and dutifully sipped from the mug.

"It's very nice."

"Oh, good," I said. "I put a little honey in there. Grandfather always puts honey in mine."

Her smile seemed more genuine now, and her eyes a little clearer. "Do you learn a lot from your grandfather?"

"Loads!" I said, stealing a piece of bread from the tray. "Like how to make bread, and how to tend the seedlings in the greenhouse, and how to polish all the furniture."

Waceera took a piece of bread, too, and began to eat it but had a look on her face as though she was thinking about something else.

"It must be so peaceful to live here in the lighthouse... here at the end of everything," she said. It was like she was looking at something else, talking to someone else.

"It's really hard work!" I interjected, crumbs falling down my chin. "We do everything by hand, you know. No robotic cleaners, no automated systems at all!"

Waceera looked startled again.

"Oh, of course! I know that the work your family does here is very important, absolutely. We couldn't do our work without the lighthouses."

I stopped chewing, my mouth hanging open.

"There are more lighthouses!?" I nearly shouted.

Then I handed Waceera my handkerchief and apologized for

spraying her with bits of bread.

I'll be forever grateful to Waceera for explaining to me the network of lighthouses at planets along the edge of the galaxy, with no trace of surprise or reproach that I didn't already know.

We sat for hours as she described to me the vast undertaking of deep-space voyages, the planning and the months of solitude. She told me what it was like for her, on her first mission, to venture to the edge and beyond. She tried to describe the experience as their ship entered the blackness of space, as they gazed at the surfaces of empty, unfamiliar worlds and the infinite spray of curious new constellations. How small she felt, and how easy it was to believe that it was only her and the handful of people on the crew in the whole, enormous universe.

"Do you know what lighthouses were for on old Earth?" she asked me.

"They were supposed to keep sea vessels from crashing into the rocks by shining a light out on the water so they'd keep away. But this lighthouse doesn't have anything to do with the sea, and it doesn't even have a light, just the observatory at the top, and no one even goes up there."

"No, you're right," she said. "The lighthouses are not here to warn anyone of danger. The ships' systems are much better equipped to detect debris and potential collisions than any stationary observer now."

"Then why do we keep the lighthouses, if they aren't meant to keep people safe?"

"You're here to remind us, as we travel farther and farther away from the light of our people, that we are not alone."

Waceera did not leave with her crew but waited another two weeks until Grandfather's regular supply delivery, and she left with that transport. When she left, her voice was full, strong, and clear—like the first notes of the clarinet on Grandfather's favorite jazz record.

I remember standing on the beach watching Waceera's rocket's chem-trails fade as the waves lapped on our bare feet.

"I wish reminding them that they weren't alone didn't make me so lonely," I said, holding Grandfather's hand.

He squeezed my hand in return.

"That's the lighthouse for you. It's work, and then it's lonely."

It was just Grandfather and I for three more weeks until my mother came to get me. When it was time to go, I cried my eyes out, promising that I would come again as soon as I could. My heart ached as I watched the lighthouse grow smaller and smaller... until I saw another vessel docking and imagined Grandfather putting a pot of coffee on and getting ready for the new arrivals.

SEP 0 3 2019